RISING CROW

K. L. Byles

Sarah,
Thank you for saving
the crow. Enjoy!
&
K. L. Byles

BARREL
PROOF
PRESS

Rising Crow

ISBN 978-0-9966016-0-3
Library of Congress Control No. 2015911424

Printed in the United States of America

Barrel Proof Press, LLC

Cover and Interior design by Still Point Press Design Studio.

Cover concept by Dom Murphy of Vendetta Comics LLC.

CONTENTS

ACKNOWLEDGEMENTS

It's been a long and sometimes difficult and discouraging journey, but all of you have amazed me with your generosity of time and spirit. Thank you for helping *Rising Crow* take flight.

Let's watch him soar!

Reading and encouragement: Tom Stone, Jackie Rhodes, Leigh Blount, Dr. Jeffrey Luckett, Ph.D., Lynne Victorine, Mary Walker, Krista Mays, Bernadette Ellis, Mildred Beni, Rebekah Murphy, Dom Murphy, Chris Byles and so many others simply by expressing interest.

Technical assistance: John Byles weapons and anything else needed, Lori Greer horse expert and encouragement.

Editing: Dave Alluisi.

ABOUT THE AUTHOR

K. L. Byles has worked in bookkeeping, real estate, and broadcasting, and managed a healthcare office, a restaurant, and a grocery department. The author is currently considering the next career but is hoping writing and coaching will pay enough on their own. If you think the characters are lucky to keep living, the author is on the twelfth life by now.

1

DECISION

If he'd gone the other way, it might have made all the difference in the world. It's funny how a simple change of direction can determine the fate of a nation, a battle, a life, or, in one special instance, the opportunity for dispensation for all our souls.

He entered from the east, so he didn't see the hanging platform built as a permanent structure at the west end of town. His first stop was the livery stable to get his horse settled for the night. As he dismounted and entered the tack room, hoping to find the owner, he thought it odd no one was around, not even a stable boy. The room was dim, lit only by the last few rays of the red, glowing sun as it reluctantly surrendered and fell below the horizon.

The young man sniffed and shook his head at an odd smell, one that was familiar but out of place. He found a lantern at the near end of the work counter that enclosed a back corner of the room. He struck a match, lit the lamp, and looked down. He then saw the source of the smell encircling his boots. In his surprise, he let the match fall. It floated in the dark liquid, momentarily heating the substance, accentuating its almost metallic scent. Then the match died with a hiss. He was standing in a pool of blood.

It had seeped from under the counter. Before he could look across to see the cause, he heard footsteps above him. They were heading toward some stairs at the back of the room. Recognizing the tread of a woman, he realized the stairs must lead to the living quarters.

The woman called down and began to descend. As she emerged from the darkness, she froze for a brief moment and then screamed.

The stranger, following her gaze, leaned over the counter. He saw a man's body lying face up with a gash in his neck.

"I'll get help," offered the young man. He turned to go out the door, but some men were already running in, summoned by the woman's cry.

"What happened?" asked the first one to enter. He was wearing a leather apron, and the young man knew he must be the blacksmith.

"I don't know," answered the stranger. "I came in to see about my horse, lit the light, and she came down and started screaming. Then I saw the man on the floor."

The smith looked behind the counter. He shook his head as he motioned to a couple of the men to help the sobbing woman down the steps and out of the room.

The drifter started to leave as well, but the smith stopped him. "You'd better stay here."

"Why? I didn't do anything," he protested.

"That'll be for the sheriff to decide," stated the smith.

Before the young man could object any further, a man wearing a star on his chest entered, followed by two other, younger men, also wearing badges. The smith told them what had happened.

"Who are you?" asked the sheriff, turning to the young stranger.

"Jim Morgan."

"So you just happened to come in here and find old man Watson dead, huh?"

"Yes, sir."

"Search him!" ordered the sheriff to his deputies.

They grabbed the boy roughly by the arms and turned him around. He allowed them to restrain him by pinning his hands to the counter. They removed his gun from his right hip and the knife he wore from his left and then patted him down. When they started to pull up his shirt to make sure he didn't have other weapons hidden in his clothes, Jim tore away from them with a remarkable show of strength. He turned quickly, but it was too late. The sheriff had seen something. He ordered his deputies to turn the stranger again and lift his shirt. Jim refused to budge until the sheriff drew his gun. Then the deputies jerked the boy around and raised his shirt. The men caught their breath and exchanged glances. The drifter had scars criss-crossing his back. Jim endured their stares, but his measured breathing and the tension in his jaw showed his emotion.

The sheriff nodded and the deputies turned the boy around to face him. "Where'd you get those?" the sheriff asked.

Jim didn't answer. He just glared at the man, his blue eyes blazing with an intensity that made the sheriff and the other men uncomfortable.

"Well, maybe a night in jail will loosen your tongue," growled the sheriff, his weapon still levelled at the young man.

As they tried to move his hands behind his back, Jim resisted. To their surprise, the deputies found it impossible to pull their prisoner's hands close enough to bind them. The older of the two deputies hit the young man in the ribs. The blow had little effect, but the sound of the sheriff pulling back the hammer on his revolver caused Jim to reconsider any further resistance. The deputy knotted the rope tightly around the young stranger's wrists. Jim instinctively tensed and put his thumbs together, but the older deputy yanked the rope up between the young man's hands and knotted it again so their prisoner couldn't work his way loose. Then they forced him outside.

As he passed his horse, Jim ordered the animal to cooperate. Then he nearly tripped as one of the deputies shoved him forward. Though he didn't struggle, the men pushed him along.

The townspeople stared as he passed. Jim thought they were enjoying the spectacle of a prisoner being taken to jail. He didn't realize what most caught their attention were his eyes, flickering like blue flame in the gray twilight.

Jim stumbled once, falling to his knees.

"Need some help?" the younger deputy asked, smiling along with the sheriff and the older deputy.

"I'd crawl first!" Jim growled, getting to his feet, nearly falling again in the process.

They came to a small building on the other end of town. Even in the near darkness, Jim could see the structure of the hanging platform next to the jail. He realized then he probably didn't have a chance.

The men shoved him into a cell the size of a closet. The older deputy cut him loose. Then the sheriff slammed shut the door. Jim steeled himself against a shudder at the clang and loud clink as the key turned in the lock. The cell had solid walls on three sides and bars on the front. In it was a bed consisting of a piece of wood resting on a wooden frame with a sack of straw thrown on it. There was also a stool, a bucket of water, a cup, and a chamber pot. *I've slept in worse,* he thought, and settled in after lifting the mattress to look for bedbugs.

He was glad there was a small window in the opposite wall on the other side of the bars. Though he couldn't see much through it, he appreciated the fresh air, even if it was cold. He gazed at the window and took a deep breath to convince himself he wasn't going to suffocate. *It's not like it's the first time you've been behind bars,* he thought to himself.

A little while later, when the older deputy came in to check on him, Jim asked if they had taken care of his horse. The man nodded and looked surprised when Jim thanked him. After a long while, the young man realized they weren't going to give him anything to eat, so he let himself fall asleep. He'd gone hungry before. He just regretted not having an apple in his pocket.

The next morning he awoke early because of the cold and wished he had a blanket. He got up, shook himself, and walked back and forth to keep warm. He stopped once, grabbed the bars, and yanked on them, hoping they were loose. They weren't. He pulled on the bars again, but, even with his full strength, they didn't budge. He continued to pace. He could only take three steps in any direction.

After a while, he heard men in the sheriff's office. He could catch some of what they were saying through the shut door between the outer room and the cells.

The sheriff was fussing because one of his deputies was missing. "He's probably off with some girl," he guessed. "I knew I shouldn't have hired some newcomer."

The others laughed and made rude comments and dirty jokes.

A little while later, Jim heard the door open to the cells. The younger deputy brought him a breakfast of bread and cheese, along with a cup of the worst coffee he'd ever tasted.

"You're lucky it's Sunday," quipped the man as he pushed the plate through a slot in the bars at the bottom of the door. "You'll get to live another day."

"I didn't do anything," Jim insisted. "Don't I get a lawyer, a trial, or something?"

The man just laughed and left.

Jim spent the day sitting on the bed, thinking. He was only fifteen, but he decided if he lived through this he was going to do more with his life than travel around working as a farrier or for a blacksmith or doing whatever else he could find. He wanted meaning to his life. There had to be more to living than just existing. He wanted a reason to keep breathing. He thought briefly about God, but it was only a passing consideration. He'd given up on God long ago, in a mineshaft deep underground.

The deputy didn't bring him another meal until after dark. At least it was a little better this time, consisting of boiled chicken and potatoes, a piece of bread, and some coffee he could actually drink. Then he lay down, thinking briefly that it might be his last night amongst the living. He pushed that thought aside with a sigh and slept.

The next morning he awoke early again because of the cold and began pacing to keep warm. He shook the bars another time as well. Then he sat on the bed, hoping the cold air would help cool the anger and frustration burning within him because of his helplessness. It didn't. He continued to seethe.

The deputy brought him some bread and cheese again, and the coffee was even worse than it had been the previous morning.

A little while later, the sheriff came in along with his two deputies and unlocked the door. "Time for your trial," the sheriff announced with a grin.

Jim stood and thought about putting up a fight, but the sheriff was holding a double-barreled shotgun, and the younger deputy had his pistol drawn. The older deputy grabbed Jim's wrists and started to pull them behind him. The young man tensed his muscles, keeping his hands at his side.

Finding he couldn't overpower the prisoner, the deputy kidney punched him. To the deputy's surprise, even after he had hit the young man three times, it wasn't until the sheriff cocked one barrel of the shotgun that the boy finally relented. As he tied the boy's hands behind his back, the deputy found himself wondering how hard he would have to hit the boy to convince him to cooperate. The blows hardly seemed to hurt him. They barely caused him to grunt.

The two deputies grabbed Jim's arms and pushed him roughly out of the cell. The men took him outside and down the street to the church.

Jim realized he hadn't been in a church in years and appreciated the irony. When they entered, it looked as though the whole town was there.

The men took Jim up to the front, shoved him into a chair set near the altar, and stood behind him holding their weapons.

A man entered from a side door and ascended the four steps to the pulpit. "Thank you all for being here," the man said, addressing the people. "I also want to thank Pastor Johnson, who is with a failing parishioner right now, for letting us use the church again. As mayor, I'll be presiding over these proceedings, and my decisions will be final, as always." He paused. "I'm sure all of you have heard about what happened Saturday night," continued the mayor. "Mr. Watson, our beloved livery stable owner, was brutally murdered by that man right there." He pointed at Jim.

Jim started to stand, but the sheriff grabbed his shoulder and forcefully pushed him back down.

"I didn't kill him," Jim stated evenly, controlling his anger.

"Quiet!" ordered the mayor and makeshift judge. "We'll hear from you later. Now, I want to speak to the first person who entered the room."

"That would be me, sir," Jim replied with an edge to his voice.

"Not you! Sheriff, who was the first *townsperson* in the room?" inquired the judge.

"Other than Mrs. Watson?" asked the sheriff in return.

"Yes," answered the judge with a condescending nod.

"That would be Len here," said the sheriff, motioning to the smith, who was sitting in the first row.

"What did you see?" asked the judge.

"Well, when I ran in, I saw that man there," replied the smith, rising and motioning to Jim. "Standing at the counter over Mr. Watson."

"Then what happened?"

"Well, a whole bunch of us were in there in just a second, and Mrs. Watson was standing on the stairs crying."

"When did the sheriff get there?"

The smith glanced at the sheriff. "Oh, just a minute after I did."

"Sheriff, was the man armed?" asked the judge.

"He sure was!" answered the sheriff. "He was wearing a gun and had a knife, too. He also had a rifle and a shotgun outside on his horse. Then he resisted when we searched him."

"No I didn't!" Jim growled, jumping to his feet. "If I'd killed that man I *would* have resisted! And all these men would be dead, too!" he added, nodding toward the sheriff and his deputies.

"Didn't I tell you to be quiet?" asked the judge harshly.

The sheriff hit Jim in the back with the butt of his shotgun. In response, Jim spun to face him, but the other two had their weapons trained on him, so he just glared at the sheriff and sat down.

The judge then asked, "Was any money taken from the livery office, Sheriff?"

"Well, we didn't find any, so we have to suppose that there was. I haven't asked Mrs. Watson because she's still upset."

"That's understandable, Sheriff. Did you find any money on *him*?" asked the judge, pointing at the prisoner.

"Yes, we found fifty dollars and some change on him."

"Was there anything else unusual about this man, Sheriff?"

Jim had been listening, quietly seething, but at this question he stiffened.

"Yes, there was, Judge. He has whip scars, probably from prison, on his back."

"Why do you think they're from prison, Sheriff?" asked the judge.

"Because he's white, so he wasn't a slave. So where else would he get them?"

The judge thought for a moment and then nodded. "Could we see them, Sheriff?"

Jim resisted as the two deputies pulled him to his feet. He managed to throw one of them off and would have freed himself from the other if it weren't for the sheriff hitting him in the side of the head with the butt of his shotgun. The blow bloodied and stunned him, but Jim remained conscious. The deputies held his arms and supported his weight as the sheriff lifted Jim's shirt. The young man recovered and struggled again, but it was too late. He heard the gasps of the people and dropped his head. Then the men turned him so the judge could see. After he nodded, they sat their prisoner heavily back in the chair.

Jim glared at the judge.

The man caught his breath at the intensity of the stare, but collected himself. "Where did you get those, young man?"

Jim just continued gazing at him, his eyes lit by an inner fire.

"Well, I think the sheriff is right," the judge continued. "This man must have gotten those marks in prison, and he's definitely not someone we want running around loose. Even if by some chance he didn't kill Mr. Watson, he's probably killed someone else. So, as mayor of our town, and thereby given the power of judge by the town charter, I pronounce this man guilty and sentence him to hang tomorrow, on the fifteenth day of March, in the Year of Our Lord 1870, at three pm. May God have mercy on his soul."

After the verdict, the sheriff and the deputies led Jim out of the church amid snickers and nods from the crowd and returned him to his cell with a shove. The sheriff locked the door. Then he let the older deputy free the prisoner's hands by cutting the rope through the bars.

Jim sat on the bed with his back to the wall and bled. He knew if he lay down his head would throb and bleed longer. He contemplated what the so-called judge had said, that if he hadn't killed that man he'd probably killed another. He remembered the man he had shot in self-defense a few weeks earlier. If only his chair hadn't caught on the floor, it would have been a clean kill. Instead, he'd gut-shot the poor bastard, and the man had taken three days to die. Jim couldn't help but think his situation now was some sort of justice, and he would have laughed if he could. His mind wandered, and he mused about all the things he'd lived through: hunger, pain, abandonment.

He shook his head and muttered. "Just to die in some dusty little town, for something I didn't even do."

He thought about Paul, the teacher he'd lived with for the past four years. He wondered if Paul would be surprised or even saddened to learn about his current situation. They hadn't parted on the best of terms. Paul had taken a job back east. He had wanted Jim to go with him and attend a university, but the prospect of more school and a grimy city hadn't appealed to him.

Jim recalled the look on Paul's face when he bought his first gun with the money he'd earned working for the blacksmith. Paul couldn't understand why he would practice with the weapon for hours every day, and tried to warn him about the dangers and loneliness of the life of a gunfighter. Jim recollected trying to explain that he had no intention of becoming a hired gun but that a man needed to be able to protect himself. Paul's comment had been that a peaceable man doesn't need protection. Violence begets violence. Jim could have cited numerous examples of peaceable men murdered for no good reason, but he knew the futility of arguing with the man.

Jim also remembered the prediction made by one of the townswomen that he'd hang for sure before his twenty-first birthday and shook his head.

Then he found himself pondering about the day he'd left. Paul had said nothing as he gathered his belongings. The man must have known arguing with him was just as useless. Paul hadn't said goodbye or stepped outside to see him off, even though he had waited for a minute before urging his horse forward. He'd even looked back once just to see if Paul had stepped outside, but the front door stayed shut.

He sighed. He suddenly realized he really hadn't wanted to leave. There was comfort in the familiarity of routine, even in the worst circumstances, but Paul hadn't given him a choice. The teacher couldn't expect him to stay in that town alone. He'd heard the things people said about him and seen the looks in their eyes. He'd seen it again that day in the church. As soon as people found out about his scars, they despised him.

Even Paul had treated him differently than he had his other students, and not just because they lived together. The teacher seemed to think something might be wrong with him, and didn't trust him. If he hadn't gotten into a fight in the schoolyard and had his shirt pulled off, no one would have seen his back. After they did, the looks and whispers started. He'd tolerated it all for years, but after the shooting, people didn't try to hide their dislike or disgust. They blamed him for the man's death, even though it was the man's own fault for drawing on him. *If that man had been faster*, Jim thought, *they'd have probably given him some sort of medal for shooting me.* He rested his head against the wall behind him and sighed.

He had just managed to doze off when he heard the door between the outer room and the cells open and what sounded like two men approaching. He didn't move, but looked toward the door to his cell. The older deputy opened it and let in a man Jim hadn't seen before.

"I'll be all right," the man assured the deputy, motioning for him to leave.

The deputy shrugged, locked the door behind the man, and left.

"I'm Dr. Jackson. I heard you'd been hurt."

Jim still didn't move, just eyed the man suspiciously.

"Well, let me take a look," said the doctor, setting his bag on the stool and sitting on the edge of the bed facing Jim. The doctor saw a young man of average but strong build, with jet-black hair and strikingly blue eyes. The physician thought women would probably consider the young man good-looking. With his trained eye, he realized his patient was still only a boy. He set to work cleaning the wound and noticed the young man didn't even wince. "You'll need a few stitches, but it won't hurt too much."

"You always bother stitching up a dead man?" Jim asked dryly.

The remark surprised the doctor, and he took a moment to answer. "I'm just doing my job. I don't necessarily agree with everything that goes on."

"Were you there this morning?"

"No. I was with a patient, but I heard about it."

"If you think I killed that man, why are you in here alone with me?"

"Like I said, I don't always agree with all that happens around here."

Jim thought for a moment before he replied. "I guess that means I'm not the first innocent man to be hanged in this town."

The doctor didn't say anything. He glanced at the young man and let his silence speak for him.

Jim sighed and gritted his teeth in suppressed anger.

"I'm sorry, son. If there was anything I could do, I would."

Jim didn't reply, just stared straight ahead, his eyes smoldering.

"You don't know what it was like before," added the doctor softly.

"Before what?" Jim asked, his voice almost a growl.

"Before the Charter of 1869 was approved last year. If a man committed a crime here and was arrested, it could be months before he was tried. The lawyers and judges don't like to leave their nice cities and come out here just to try a man for murder. And the US Marshals have more important things to do than come out here to pick up prisoners."

The doctor sighed. Then he continued. "One time, there was a man in here because he had killed a good friend of mine. His friends wanted him out of jail, so they staged a fight on the other side of town. While the sheriff and his men were handling that, some other of his friends came and broke him out. They shot two more people on their way out of town. One of them was my wife. After that, we got together and wrote up the town charter. It seemed a good idea at the time, though I'll admit, things have gotten a little out of hand. Like I said—" He paused as he completed the last stitch.

"If there was something you could do, you would," Jim stated for him, not trying to hide his contempt. "Yeah, I know."

The doctor finished, packed up his bag, and stood. He didn't bother with a bandage or instructions about caring for the wound, since he knew they wouldn't be necessary. "I'm sorry, son. Is there anyone you want me to contact?"

"No thanks."

The doctor picked up the cup from the floor and hit the bars with it three times to signal the deputy.

"Thanks for fixing me up, Doc," Jim said as the deputy opened the door to let out the doctor. "And I'm sorry about your wife."

The doctor nodded and left. The young man's calm assurance and manners struck him. He remembered his Hippocratic Oath and hoped it didn't apply to a situation like this.

Later, the deputy brought Jim some potato soup, bread, and coffee. The young man ate, not allowing himself to consider it his last meal. Then Jim lay on the bed and dozed. He thought little about his life or his impending death. Since the situation seemed hopeless, he decided not to fret about it. He had a remarkable ability to compartmentalize his thoughts and emotions. Years of mistreatment, neglect, and torture had taught him that.

Late that night, he recognized the voices of the deputies as they talked loudly and laughed in the office. Then he heard the older deputy clearly. "She's drunk, but let's give him the chance anyway."

He heard the two men laughing as they stumbled to his cell. They appeared at his door holding a nearly unconscious woman between them, and the younger one was carrying a lantern turned low.

"This is Merilee," announced the older deputy to Jim, indicating the girl. "We thought you might want a screw, it being your last night and all."

Both of them laughed again.

Jim didn't even bother to sit up. He just glared at them in the dim light.

"I know she doesn't look too lovely," commented the older one, "but get your cock out and she'll perk up."

"What?" mumbled the girl, and both deputies laughed again.

"Only thing is," explained the older one, "you'll have to do it through the bars."

This caused the younger man to laugh so hard he nearly dropped the girl.

"One fellow actually did that," the older one continued.

"You're joking!" snorted the younger one, laughing even harder.

"No, it's the truth. He stood at the bars and pulled out the longest cock I've ever seen. Hell, even the whore was impressed. She bent over and he screwed her through the door, and she loved it."

"Too bad you had to hang him the next day," mumbled the girl.

"We didn't," laughed the deputy. "When I told the sheriff, he thought it was so funny he let him go."

"What did you tell everybody?" asked the younger one.

"The man had been convicted of horse stealing, so the sheriff just gave the owner of the horse some money and they called it even."

"Too bad for you," sneered the younger man at Jim.

The deputies laughed as they turned and dragged the girl away.

Then Jim heard the door to the outside close. He realized at least one of them must have left with her, because the night grew quiet again, and he was able to go back to sleep.

The next morning, they didn't give him anything to eat. He figured the sheriff probably thought it a waste of food. Then, when three pm neared, the sheriff and the deputies came to escort him to the hanging platform. The older deputy grabbed Jim's wrists to tie them behind his back. Jim instinctively made the man work for it, in spite of the two weapons trained on him, but he didn't put up as much of a fight as he had before. He thought about trying to escape and forcing them to shoot him, that way robbing them of their fun, but he didn't want to die a coward. The sheriff was fussing about his missing deputy again as they made their way outside. When they arrived at the platform the sheriff ascended first, followed by Jim and the two deputies.

"Any last words?" asked the sheriff.

"Would it make any difference?" Jim replied evenly.

"You've got pluck, I'll give you that," remarked the sheriff with a cruel smile. "Want a blindfold?"

"No!" Jim growled, glaring at the man.

The sheriff put the noose around Jim's neck. It was rough and the knot heavy.

Jim swallowed for what he was sure was his last time.

"The preacher is here and can say a few words if you want," offered the sheriff, motioning to a man who had been on the platform when they arrived.

"Just get it over with," Jim replied coolly.

The sheriff had never before seen a condemned man remain so calm. He shook his head as he checked his watch.

Jim remembered when he was younger fearing he would die alone, unnoticed, and unremembered. He gazed out over the crowd and wondered if anyone would give him a thought afterwards, or even a tombstone. He saw a bird flying in the distance, its body black against the clear, blue sky. What he didn't know was that his eyes shone with a bluer intensity than the sky itself. The bird called once. To Jim, it sounded like a crow. He felt his soul lift and soar with the creature. For just a moment, whether through the power of imagination or something supernatural, he and the bird became one.

The sheriff glanced up at Jim, enjoying the tension. Then he motioned to the older deputy. The man grabbed the handle, about to lower it and end the life of the condemned, when everyone heard a cry as a rider galloped up.

"No!" the rider shouted. "Stop! Don't do that!"

The deputy took his hand off the handle.

"Harris!" cried the sheriff. "Where have you been?"

"Take the noose off him, boys," insisted Harris. "The murderer is in jail in Tipton."

"What?" asked the sheriff as the crowd gasped.

"I went in the livery right after Watson was murdered," Harris explained, eyeing the older deputy until he stepped away from the lever. Then Harris turned his attention to the sheriff. "I heard someone riding out of town in a real hurry. Since my horse was already saddled, I followed him. I caught up with him in Tipton and had the sheriff there arrest him. I wouldn't have known about this hanging, except Mrs. Watson has a sister there. Someone sent her a message on yesterday's stage about the murder and arrest. So I rode all night hoping to get here in time."

The sheriff gazed at his deputy in disbelief for a moment. Then he looked to the mayor, who was in the crowd.

"My verdict still—" the mayor started to say, but the doctor stopped him by whispering something in his ear. The mayor looked at the doctor in surprise.

The physician nodded to show his determination.

The mayor then looked at the sheriff, threw up his hands, turned, and walked away angrily.

"Take the noose off him," the sheriff ordered. He turned to the crowd. "Sorry, ladies and gentlemen, there won't be a hanging today."

Some people actually groaned as the older deputy removed the noose from Jim's neck.

"See?" said the sheriff to Harris as he motioned toward the crowd. "If you'd just gone ahead and stayed the night there, we wouldn't have to disappoint all these people."

Harris looked at him in disbelief. "And let you hang an innocent man?"

"Look at his back and tell me he's innocent," the sheriff replied. Then, trying to ignore the glare Jim gave him, he roughly turned the young man around and cut him loose as he spoke to him. "Come with me to the office and I'll give you your weapons. I trust since you just escaped the noose you won't try to use them."

Jim shook his head, anger still burning in his eyes.

"Get his horse!" the sheriff ordered the younger deputy.

Harris dismounted and followed them. "I'm glad I got here in time," he remarked to Jim.

"Yeah, thanks," Jim replied, shaking the man's hand but still glowering.

"You don't seem too happy for someone who's just escaped the gallows," commented Harris.

"No offense, but I just want the hell out of this town."

"Sounds like a good idea," Harris muttered under his breath.

When they reached the office, Jim gathered his weapons, money, and saddlebags. Then he stepped outside and started walking toward the livery stable, followed by the sheriff and the older deputy, whom he supposed wanted to escort him out of town.

The younger deputy had run to the stable and quickly saddled their former prisoner's horse. The animal had been grudgingly cooperative, but the man ignored the horse's attitude and decided it would be quicker to ride him back than lead him. As soon as he wrapped the reins around the saddle horn, but before he had a foot in the stirrup, the animal tossed his head, jerked his body to the right, and tore off. The deputy would have been dragged if he hadn't had enough sense to let go. Then he ran after the animal, afraid of what the sheriff or the stranger might do to him if the animal wasn't caught.

Jim had only taken a few steps when he saw his horse jogging toward him, fully saddled. He stepped into the street and waited for the animal, which obediently stopped right in front of him.

When he saw the horse had returned to his owner, the younger deputy stopped running, too. Then, seeing the dark look the former prisoner shot at him, and the sheriff shaking his head in annoyance, he turned and walked the other way.

Jim loaded his saddlebags, slipped his shotgun and rifle into their holsters, and tugged on the saddle to make sure it was secure. Then he handed the older deputy some money for his horse's keep, nodded to Harris and, without a word, rode off.

As soon as the town was out of sight, Jim dismounted and sat on the ground. He was shaking, and it didn't stop for some time. He wondered if he would ever find acceptance or would remain castoff, like dust from someone's shoes.

2

REALIZATION

Jim continued to travel west. He wanted to go where there were few people, where he wouldn't feel trapped. Familiar faces didn't hold any comfort for him, since everyone he'd known had looked on him with contempt. He often travelled at night, not because he didn't want to be seen, but because it was cooler and easier on his horse's black coat. Under a full- to half-moon, he had plenty of light, and, from observing their behavior, he knew horses could see perfectly well in the dark. His horse, Ness, knew to follow the road, so all he had to do was urge him on every now and then if the animal got bored. Ness was gaited, and though the saying "hundred-mile-a-day horse" was usually an exaggeration, Ness, at seventeen hands, had a long stride and could amble all day if necessary. Ness had an unusual desire to please Jim, and if Jim told him a destination the animal knew, he didn't even have to guide him. Ness would just take him there.

This talent came in handy one night. Jim had continued after the moon had set. The homesteads were getting closer together, so he knew they were nearing a town, and wanted to be within sight of it by morning. The thought of sleeping in a real bed and refreshing his supplies appealed to him, and it would give Ness a chance to rest as well. As he continued, he realized how road-weary they both were. He had about decided the town was too far to reach that night when he saw an odd glow above the trees a little way ahead. He continued toward it, but the road dipped then followed the side of a hill, which obscured his view of the unusual light for a few minutes.

The road rose as it rounded the hill. From the higher elevation, Jim looked toward the glow and caught his breath. *Fire!* he screamed in his mind. The malevolent flames sharply revealed a house even as they consumed it, devouring the chimney and roof. Jim felt ill, as though he was watching death gleefully destroy its victim.

He urged Ness forward at a run, ordering the animal to take him to the fire. He wrapped the reins around the saddle horn, freeing his hands so he could remove his gun belt. He looped the belt over the saddle horn too as Ness tore through the darkness. They followed the road as it wound back down around the hill, and Jim lost sight of the flames again, but Ness followed his nose and didn't slow. A few moments later, the animal turned onto a narrow lane that cut through the trees. Jim was unable to see the path until they were on it. He still couldn't see the fire but trusted Ness would find the way. The track eventually opened up to a yard, and Jim saw a sight he would never forget: a house engulfed in flames.

The fire had started in what appeared to be a storage area at the back of the house, and the flames had already begun to lick at the roof of the rooms where the occupants would be sleeping. Jim jumped off Ness and ran in the front door. The heat and smoke were already almost overpowering, but just as Jim stepped into the house, a woman ran to him.

"My children!" she shrieked, heading for a ladder leading to a sleeping loft.

Jim reached it first and climbed the ladder, hardly touching the rungs in his haste. At the top, he found five children snuggled together on a bed of straw. He ran to the older children at the back of the loft. The mother woke the little ones closest to the ladder, and they immediately started crying from fright. She quickly comforted them and lifted the youngest, a little girl. She started back down the ladder intending for her next child, a boy, to follow her. The child stepped to the ladder but froze from fear, staring at the ceiling as the flames stretched like fingers over his head.

"Paul!" the woman screamed at the child as her feet touched the floor.

Jim ran to the child and scooped him up, grabbing the next oldest on the way, who was also a boy. Jim threw the older one over a shoulder, and the boy clung to him. Then Jim slid down the ladder by placing his feet on its sides, steadying himself with one hand while holding the younger child with the other. He called to the two remaining children to follow him. When he reached the outside, Jim looked back but didn't see the other two children. He dropped the two he had on the ground next to the mother and little girl. Then he turned and flew back inside, pulling his bandana over his mouth to filter the smoke as he ran.

He found the other children, a boy and a girl, cowering behind the base of the ladder. They were too frightened to run to the door, now obscured by smoke. Jim grabbed the boy and pushed him toward the door, but the child balked, so Jim threw him over his shoulder. Then he took the girl by the arm. She dug in her heels and fought, so Jim pulled her to him, held her around the waist, and headed for the door. Luckily, both children stopped struggling as he began to move, or all of them would have died. The smoke was now so thick Jim could no longer see the way out, and all of them were coughing and choking.

He turned, hoping for another exit. He saw an open door and headed to it, still carrying both children, who were almost as big as he was. When he entered the room, the only light was from the fire. He saw a window on the far wall, over what he realized must be the mother's bed. He set the children on the bed and tried to open the window. It was stuck. He wrapped one of the bed covers around his arm and swung with all his might, shattering the glass and tearing out the wood between the panes. He threw off the fabric, shards of glass peppering his clothes and cutting into him. Then he lifted the girl, dropped her out the window, and did the same with the boy.

He was about to crawl out himself when he heard something whimpering under the bed. The fire was in the room with him now, but he dropped to the floor, reached under the bed, and touched a box. The whimpering changed to a low growl. Ignoring the warning, he grabbed the box, dragged it out, and, without even looking inside, dropped it out the window and launched himself out after it. He got to his feet, picked up the box, and led the children to their mother.

They heard the animals in the barn shrieking in fear.

"Our horse!" the mother gasped.

"I'll get him," Jim assured her.

He ran toward the barn, which was behind the woman's room, attached to the house. This arrangement kept everyone warmer in winter and made tending the animals easier in cold weather. It was on the opposite side from where the fire began but was already burning.

As he threw open the door, the heat and smoke nearly knocked Jim to his knees. He tore toward the back of the structure first, where the horse was screaming and stomping. He fell against a wagon on his way but continued. He found an empty sack and had to jump to throw it over the huge draft horse's face. Then he led the animal out, stumbling into the wagon again and nearly losing his grip on the horse.

Jim ran back in. He untied a goat and a cow, both of which scampered out of the barn, the goat leading the way. Then he heard bleating and opened the door to a small stall housing a ewe and her lamb. He took her by the wool on her head and led her out, with the lamb following his mother. As he turned back, he noticed a cage against the opposite wall from the stall and saw a good-sized rabbit cowering in a corner. He gathered the animal up and tucked it into his shirt so it wouldn't run away.

He turned again to make sure he had released all the animals and then realized the wagon he had been falling into was fully loaded. Not wanting the family to lose everything, he decided to roll it out. He made sure the brake was off, stepped between the shafts, and began to push. The wagon didn't want to budge. The smoke was so thick by now he could hardly see the door, the raging of the fire so loud he couldn't hear the mother calling for him to get out.

The barn was beginning to fall apart around him, but still Jim continued to push. He hurled his weight against the wagon. He was so intent on his task he didn't notice the glass he had gotten in his hands cutting even further into his flesh or his clothes as they started to smoke. He focused his entire strength, both mind and body, into compelling the wagon to move.

He threw his body against the wagon so fiercely he repeatedly forced what little air he had out of his lungs with a grunt. At last, the wheels began to turn, but Jim didn't let up. Like a good draft horse himself, he continued to push as the wagon began to inch its way toward the door. The ground was level, so Jim had to continue the effort even after the wagon began to move. A burning board fell at his feet. He kicked it away. Another fell across his shoulders bent against the weight of the wagon. He shook it off and still kept up the strain. His lungs filled with burning gases and his feet began to slip in the embers and ash, but he could see the door now. He refused to give up and run to fresh air and safety. He heard the mother calling to him and saw that she was holding back her oldest son, who wanted to run in to help.

The boy realized they'd need the harness and tack, so he tore away from his mother and ran around the side of the barn to the tack room. It had its own door to the outside, and, luckily, the flames hadn't reached it yet. The boy grabbed the things he needed and dragged them back to where his mother stood.

Jim was still in the barn. He felt something fill his lungs with each gasp. Then he felt it forced out of him as he heaved himself against the wagon. Since he was suffocating, he knew it wasn't air. He gave one more mighty shove and finally broke through the heat and smoke. He pushed the wagon a few more yards, out of the reach of the flames, before he collapsed.

The mother ran to him, turned him over, and pulled down the bandana to reveal his face.

"Who is he?" her oldest daughter asked between coughs as she and the other children gathered around him.

"I don't know. But he saved us," the mother answered.

Jim stirred and opened his eyes.

"Thank you," said the mother.

Jim was almost too weak to nod.

"Where's Welly? Where's Mr. Wellington?" asked the youngest daughter with a sob.

"Who?" Jim coughed.

"Her pet rabbit," answered the mother. "Honey, he couldn't—"
She stopped as Jim, still lying on the ground, removed something from his shirt. Luckily, he'd fallen to one side, sparing the creature.

The little girl snatched up the rabbit and began kissing

and petting it.

"Unbelievable!" breathed the mother. Then she noticed the blood on Jim's hands, the dark patches on his clothes from burns, and that he was almost too weak to cough. "Bobby," she said to her oldest son, "get the horse. We need to get this man to a doctor."

"Yes, ma'am!" replied the boy as he ran off. He too was still coughing.

She turned to her oldest daughter. "Help me with this, so we don't kill our horse on the trip to town." Between the two of them they were able to push two sacks of feed off the wagon, lightening the load by two hundred pounds.

Jim managed to crawl over one of the shafts so he'd be out of the horse's way but then collapsed again.

"You should have let us help you," said the mother to him as she climbed down from the wagon.

Jim managed to shake his head in reply and noticed the youngest girl watching him, her brow wrinkled in concern. He nodded to her and started coughing again weakly.

A few moments later, they had the horse hitched, and the woman and children were helping the young man off the ground.

"Ouch!" cried the oldest daughter, shaking a finger and then sucking on it. "He has glass stuck in him!"

"Sorry," Jim coughed. "I can do it. Thanks," he said, as he slowly pulled himself to his feet, grabbing onto one of the wheels, hoping the brake was set and the horse wouldn't move. Gripping the side of the wagon, he made his way hand over hand to the back. Then he tried to climb in, but his limbs refused to support his weight. "Ness!" he called.

The horse came jogging up, surprising the mother and children, who hadn't noticed the large black animal standing in the shadows.

"Push!" Jim commanded.

Ness put his head under him and pushed with so much force he lifted the young man into the air.

Jim landed with a thud, his head only inches from the wooden frame at the far end of the wagon. He stifled a groan as he turned over. "Thanks, Ness."

"I'll tie him to the back of the wagon," offered Bobby.

"No!" Jim gasped, now acutely aware of the pain. "Don't

touch him. He'll hurt you." Jim gritted his teeth against another groan. Then he choked and started coughing as he rolled and threw an arm over the side of the wagon. "Ness!" he called.

The horse walked to where Jim could reach him and nuzzled his arm.

"Follow," Jim whispered, before sinking back, still coughing.

The children piled into the wagon, with the littlest girl still clutching the rabbit. Bobby ran back for the box with the mother dog and her pups and set it on his lap. The mother and oldest daughter took the seat.

"What about the rest of the animals?" asked Bobby.

"They'll be fine," stated the mother as she took the reins. "They won't wander far."

Jim tried not to groan as the wagon lurched forward. Though the town was only a few miles away, and the trip not long, to Jim it seemed interminable. The wagon finally stopped, and the mother jumped to the ground and knocked on a door. Jim heard a man's voice, some shouting, and the mother's voice cautioning someone to be careful because of the glass. Then he felt numerous pairs of strong hands lift him as carefully as they could and lower him from the wagon.

As the hands laid him on a stretcher, he heard Ness snort. "It's OK, boy. Let them take care of you," he managed to gasp before he felt himself lifted.

The men carrying him laid him gently on a table covered with a white sheet. Jim heard a man telling the mother that she should see to her children and come back in the morning. He also heard what sounded like him giving her some instructions, but they were outside the door, or in another room, and he couldn't hear what the man said.

Then the man returned and spoke to him. "I'm Dr. Samuel Thorne, and this is my wife, Martha. She's also my nurse."

"Jim Morgan," Jim replied, trying to lift his head to see them, though his body didn't want to cooperate. "Are the children OK?"

"Lie still, young man," ordered the doctor gently. "They're fine, but you're pretty banged up. Brave thing you did, though. Mrs. Petersen also said that you pushed her wagon out of the barn by yourself."

"Yes, sir," Jim coughed.

"Amazing!" breathed the doctor. "But not too good for your health. I can see that you're cut up, burned, and bruised. Is there anything else that I should know about?"

"It hurts to breathe. And I can't move when I want to," Jim replied between coughs.

"Your lungs are probably singed." The doctor touched Jim's arms. "Can you feel my hands?"

The young man nodded.

"Now?" asked the doctor, as he touched Jim's legs.

Jim nodded again.

"Your body is exhausted. That's why you're having trouble moving. That wagon was loaded with almost 2,000 pounds of goods. It's going to take you a while to get your strength back. Right now, I'm going to concentrate on removing the glass, stopping the bleeding, and tending to the burns." He turned to Martha. "Have you got the syringe ready?"

"Yes," she replied, handing the needle to her husband.

"What's that?" Jim asked.

"Morphine," replied Sam, "for the pain."

"No!" Jim growled, trying to pull his arm away. "I don't want to need it!" He started coughing again.

"OK," replied the doctor handing the syringe back to his wife. "I have laudanum. Neither it nor the morphine can cause addiction after only one use."

"No, thank you," Jim replied, trying not to cough. "I've never had either, and I never want to."

"I can't give you chloroform because of your lungs, but I have some strong whiskey if you want it."

"No thanks. It doesn't help. Just water, please."

Sam nodded, so Martha hurried to the kitchen. Since her husband insisted water should always be boiled before drinking, she returned with a glass filled with water she'd boiled earlier that night, so it would be cool and ready to drink in the morning.

"Just sips," advised the doctor as he lifted Jim's head. Martha held the glass so the young man could drink.

Jim grimaced as he swallowed and coughed some more before taking a few more sips.

"I know your throat hurts," the doctor said sympathetically. "But unfortunately, there's really nothing I can do for it, or your lungs. You're young, you'll heal, but it'll take time. I'll work as fast as I can, and screaming is always allowed."

Jim steeled himself and hardly winced as the doctor set to work. Sam was amazed at the young man's tolerance for pain, but the reason became clear when he removed his patient's shirt. Jim tensed, accustomed to the usual gasps and rejection, but the doctor and his wife ignored the scars and continued working without even exchanging a glance that he could see. Even through the haze of pain and exhaustion, Jim noticed their lack of reaction.

The doctor removed the large pieces of glass and debris first. The cuts were to the bone on the undersides of the young man's upper arms, and there were numerous gashes in his legs, along with serious burns. He had burns on the back of his shoulders, as well as on his hands from pushing the wagon. The doctor worked for hours treating all of the large wounds, with Jim conscious or semi-conscious the entire time, but not once did the young man cry out or even complain. The most he ever did was groan softly, clenching his jaw tighter to stifle himself.

Then the doctor started on the meticulous work of removing the glass from Jim's hands. They had started to swell from the burns, making the procedure more difficult. The doctor winced as he opened Jim's left hand. These cuts were worse than the ones on the right, because he had used his left hand to support his body as he climbed through the window. The pain caused Jim to shift on the table and inhale audibly through his nose.

"I'm sorry, son," the doctor said. "Changed your mind about the whiskey?"

Jim shook his head.

"I hate to keep hurting you, but I need to get your hands taken care of."

Jim nodded weakly, and the doctor continued. After he removed the largest pieces of glass, Jim dozed off. Then he woke up again when the doctor washed the wounds and had to use a brush to remove all the soot and dirt. Sam had seen grown men scream and cry from this treatment, over burns much less extensive and severe, but Jim just gritted his teeth and looked away. Martha put her hand on the young man's arm to comfort him. She felt him tense at first, then relax under her touch. She wiped the sweat from Jim's brow as well as her husband's during the lengthy procedure. Finally, the doctor bandaged Jim's hands and patted him on the arm.

"Thanks, Doc," Jim whispered hoarsely.

Sam simply nodded. He and his wife were exhausted, but they got their patient settled into one of their spare rooms before the doctor headed off to bed, just as the night sky began to lighten in the east. Martha settled onto a daybed in Jim's room in case he needed anything.

The young man slept soundly until early afternoon, when the pain woke him. No one was in the room with him, and it took him a few minutes to remember where he was and why.

Martha was first to enter, as she had been checking on him every few minutes. "Is there anything I can get you?" she asked. "Are you hungry?"

"Just thirsty," Jim managed to whisper through his ravaged throat. It hurt more than it had the night before.

"Slowly," Martha reminded him as she held his head and raised the glass to his lips.

Jim took a sip and then drew away slightly at the pain of the cool liquid hitting his throat. He took another sip, and the coolness eased the pain slightly. After a few more sips his stomach felt ill, so he stopped. Martha laid his head gently back on the pillow.

"Are you hungry?" she asked.

Jim shook his head.

"In a little while, after you've had some more water, I want you to try and drink some cool chicken broth," she said, expertly arranging the pillow and bed covers to make him more comfortable. Then she opened the curtains.

"Thanks," Jim replied hoarsely.

"You're welcome. But you need to talk as little as possible. Your throat needs to rest and heal, so you don't have to thank me. OK?" she asked with a smile, noticing that he was gazing out the window.

Jim nodded but didn't smile. He was unused to kind words and a gentle touch.

Later that afternoon, the doctor returned from seeing another patient and checked on Jim as soon as he entered the house. "Are you having any pain from injuries I might have missed last night?"

Jim motioned to his back. With Martha's help, Sam rolled Jim slightly to one side, and could see a good-sized bruise developing just below Jim's waist on his right side.

"Tell me if the pain increases markedly," said the doctor as he began to touch Jim near and on the bruise.

Jim motioned to him only when he actually touched the injury.

"I'll keep an eye on it, but you probably fell or something hit you. Anything else? You have some swelling a little further up near the spine." Sam lightly touched the area. "Any pain here?"

Jim shook his head.

The doctor noticed the young man tensed as he touched the scars but sensed it wasn't from pain. "Martha must've told you not to talk," Sam said, forcing a smile. "That's good, because you shouldn't."

"Well he's going to have to talk to me," replied a man, standing in the doorway.

"Sheriff Bryant!" announced the doctor cordially. "I didn't hear you."

"Well, the front door was open, and I heard you in here, so I hope you don't mind that I let myself in," explained the sheriff, who was considerably older than the young doctor and his wife.

"Not at all," replied Sam.

Jim eyed the sheriff and wondered how effectual he could be at his age.

"So this must be the young man who saved the Petersens last night," said the sheriff, sizing Jim up in return. The quiet confidence in the young man's eyes struck the sheriff, and, because of it, he thought Jim much older than his fifteen years. "Can he answer a few questions?" asked the sheriff of the doctor.

"A few. He should talk as little as possible. His throat and lungs are burned."

"Is that serious?" asked the sheriff.

"Yes, but at his age I'm sure he'll fully recover," Sam answered.

"Well, young man, as you heard, I'm Sheriff Bryant. What's his name?" the sheriff asked Sam. "Mrs. Petersen didn't even know."

"Jim Morgan," the doctor replied for Jim, motioning to him to be silent.

"Well, Jim, it's a pleasure to meet you. Mighty impressive thing you did, though I can't figure out how you ended up there.

Did you see anyone else hanging around the Petersen house last night?"

"Just nod or shake your head," Sam advised his patient.

Jim shook his head.

"Were you coming from the east?"

The young man nodded.

"So did you see the fire from the road?"

Jim nodded again.

"The Petersen place is pretty far off the road. How did you find it, just follow the flames?"

The young man shook his head.

The sheriff looked puzzled. "Did you smell the smoke?"

Jim shook his head again.

The sheriff looked at the doctor and his wife to see if they had any suggestions.

"Did something else lead you there?" asked Martha.

Jim nodded, not wanting to anger the doctor by speaking against orders.

They all looked at each other.

"What?" asked the sheriff, at a loss. He turned his gaze back to the young man. "All that was with you was your horse."

Jim nodded again.

The sheriff looked at Sam, who shrugged. "You'll have to speak on this one," said the doctor to Jim.

"He led me," Jim answered quietly, to spare his throat.

"Smart horse," remarked the sheriff.

Jim gave another nod.

"So your horse led you to the fire and then you got the Petersens out?" asked the sheriff, to be sure he understood.

The young man nodded.

"You were alone?" asked the sheriff.

Jim nodded again.

"Did you use your horse to get the wagon out of the barn?" inquired the sheriff.

The young man shook his head.

"It's our understanding that he pushed it out himself," said Sam.

"Sam, how could he?" asked the sheriff. Then he turned to Jim. "Is that how you got it out?"

Jim nodded.

The sheriff whistled in disbelief. "That's what Mrs. Petersen said, but I thought she might be shaken up a bit. I took a look at that wagon this morning, and it has 1,850 pounds of supplies in it. And you got it out of the barn by yourself?"

Jim nodded again, wondering if the sheriff was taking into account the two hundred pounds the woman and her daughter had pushed off before they left.

"If you don't believe him, I can show you his hands," offered the doctor.

"That's OK. I saw the bloody handprints on the wagon. I just couldn't believe it, that's all. You take care of yourself young man, and get well. We need more like you in these parts. I'll let myself out," said the sheriff, and he nodded to Martha as he left the room.

The sheriff had just walked out the front door when Mrs. Petersen and her children arrived. He stepped aside and descended the steps to the street as they entered the house. A moment later, they were in Jim's room. Mrs. Petersen and Martha had their hands full at first, getting the children to understand that they shouldn't sit on or bump the bed. Even though the children hurt him a couple of times, Jim didn't get cross or fuss at them. The youngest daughter was very concerned about the bandages on Jim's arms and couldn't resist touching one of them gently as she looked up at him questioningly.

"I'll be all right," he reassured her softly and coughed.

The little girl smiled and kissed his arm.

Sam noticed that Jim seemed strangely struck by the gesture. The doctor saw an odd expression cross the young man's face, and the meaning of it gave him a chill. He realized the boy was completely unaccustomed to affection.

"I'm sorry to just barge in here like this," said Mrs. Petersen, "but we all wanted to thank you."

The doctor told her Jim's name, and she introduced herself as Uma, and the children, starting with the oldest, as Mary, Bobby, Richard, Paul, and Lilly. Then she asked Jim how he was doing.

Dr. Thorne explained Jim's silence and reminded her that he couldn't discuss anything else without Jim's approval. The doctor looked to Jim for an answer, and the young man raised one hand slightly and shook his head, indicating he didn't want the doctor to bore her or the children.

"I just hope it's not as bad as it looks," Uma commented.

Little Lilly looked worried again and put her hand on Jim's arm.

"Well?" asked the doctor.

Jim nodded and shrugged slightly.

Uma and the children listened intently as the doctor listed Jim's injuries. At the mention of each one, little Lilly gently touched Jim at each place she could reach, even his legs through the bedcovers.

Jim watched her, and his glance softened when he looked at her.

At first, Uma tried to stop her, but when she looked at Jim in embarrassment, he nodded to show he didn't mind and understood the child's gesture.

When the doctor was finished, Bobby whispered, "Wow!"

Lilly asked Jim, "Did you cry?"

"No, he didn't," answered Dr. Thorne for him. "In fact, he didn't make a sound through the entire procedure."

"Wow!" breathed Bobby again.

"Is there anything I can do?" asked Uma. "Do you need someone to stay with him at night?"

Martha looked at her husband. "We'll be all right. You have the children to take care of and need your rest."

"We're staying with Mrs. Canady," Uma explained, "so I can rest some during the day. Mrs. Canady really surprised me by offering to share her house with us."

"Well, some help would be appreciated," acknowledged Martha.

"I'll come back around nine, then," Uma promised. Then she looked at Jim. "Take care, and thank you again," she said, touching his bandaged hand.

As they were about to leave, Bobby turned back. "Oh yeah, I checked on your horse. He's fine, and I told the livery men not to put a lead on him or anything."

Jim nodded his thanks.

"And if you want," Bobby continued, "they offered to bring your weapons and saddlebags here."

Jim looked to Sam.

"That would be fine," answered the doctor.

"Leave the apples for Ness," Jim whispered.

"Apples?" asked Bobby.

"In the saddlebags," Jim explained, still whispering.

Bobby smiled and nodded.

After Uma and the children left, Martha smiled at her husband and, indicating Jim, asked, "How old would you say he is?"

"Around fifteen or sixteen," Dr. Thorne answered.

"I say he's closer to twenty-five," said Martha. Then, turning to Jim, she asked, "Am I right?"

Jim shook his head.

"Seventeen?" guessed Dr. Thorne.

Jim shook his head again. "What you said before," he whispered.

"Fifteen?" the doctor asked.

Jim nodded.

Martha looked genuinely surprised.

"I could tell he wasn't through puberty yet," Sam stated. "You'll probably grow a few more inches in height," he added to Jim. Then he smiled. "And you'll soon need to shave every day, too."

"I bet I wasn't the only one who thought he was older," remarked Martha. "I'll have to be sure to let Uma know. I haven't seen her look at a man like that since her husband died two years ago."

Jim shifted in the bed.

"I'm sorry," smiled Martha, patting his arm. "I was just teasing. You're only a year older than her daughter. I'm sure she would approve if you wanted to settle down."

Jim shook his head slowly.

Martha and Sam laughed and gave each other a squeeze.

Jim wasn't angry, but he didn't smile. He just looked at them more in confusion than anything else. He had never seen people so open and so obviously in love.

Martha left to get Jim some broth from the kitchen, and the doctor checked him for bleeding, still chuckling. "Everything looks OK. Eat something and get some rest."

"When will I be able to ride?" Jim asked softly.

"Well, walking will come first, and I don't want you out of bed for at least a week. You'll probably be able to sit up in a couple of days. We'll just have to see."

Jim looked away in frustration, trying not to cough.

"If you're worried about the bill, don't. You didn't ask for this, and my only concern is to get you well."

"No one does something for nothing," Jim stated.

"Did you expect anything in return when you rescued the Petersens?" asked the doctor.

Jim gazed at the man, then his eyes softened. He shook his head as his body forced him to cough.

"An exception to your own rule?" Sam asked with a smile, though worry showed in his eyes.

Jim noticed the expression and realized with surprise that the doctor's concern was genuine.

Later that evening, Uma arrived carrying a tray loaded with baked goods given to her by townswomen and a large container of soup she had made. Since her family and Mrs. Canady had received more food than they could eat in a week, she knew that if Dr. Thorne, Martha, and Jim didn't need all of it, Dr. Thorne would be sure to take the extra to someone who did.

Martha led her to the kitchen and couldn't resist lifting the towel over the soup. "This smells delicious!"

"It's a family recipe," Uma replied. "It has herbs that are supposed to help with healing."

"I'm sure Jim will enjoy it. Just make sure it's cool when you give it to him."

Then she showed Uma where things were and explained what she might have to do in the course of the night. Martha made a point of mentioning, seemingly in passing, how old Jim was. Uma was also surprised, and remarked that he was only a little older than her daughter in age but seemed so much older in behavior.

"I don't think he's had a very easy life," replied Martha. Because she knew Uma would see them, Martha informed the other woman about the scars on Jim's back and told her not to ask any questions about them or tell anyone.

Martha showed Uma into Jim's room and, quietly, because he was sleeping, showed her where things were. Jim stirred, groaned, opened his eyes, saw it was Martha, and shut them again. Uma looked worried, but Martha explained he always woke up when someone entered. Then Martha gently lifted the sheet, which caused Jim to stir again. He pulled the bed-clothes back over himself.

"I have to show Uma how to care for you," Martha explained

softly, and Jim released the covers.

Martha showed Uma what to look for as far as bleeding and other things that would require her to fetch the doctor. Uma seemed taken aback because Jim was naked. Martha apologized and explained that she didn't even think about it.

"It's like taking care of a child," Martha whispered. Then she smiled when she noticed Jim frowning at her. "If he was your son you wouldn't care. It's the same thing."

Uma nodded and patted Jim's arm.

Martha took her out into the hall and made sure she didn't have any questions, then encouraged Uma to wake her and Sam if she had any problems at all. Uma nodded so Martha thanked her and retired.

Uma returned to Jim's room, closed the door quietly, and settled into a large, comfortable armchair. Martha had told her it was OK to sleep on the daybed, that she was only there if Jim needed anything, but Uma had decided to try and stay awake. It was the least she could do, she thought. She had brought a book and some knitting, but there wasn't enough light for reading, and she worried that the clicking of the needles might disturb the young man, so she simply sat and composed a letter to her sister in her mind. Uma didn't realize how tired she was and dozed off.

She awoke a couple hours later when Jim became restless and mumbled in his sleep. She saw he was perspiring and suspected he had a fever. Martha had assured her this was normal. Uma wetted a towel at the basin on the bureau and placed it on Jim's brow, holding it so it wouldn't fall off.

Jim pushed her hand away without opening his eyes.

Uma patted his arm and replaced the cloth.

This time, Jim grabbed her wrist, and his eyes fluttered open for an instant. "No!" he groaned, writhing in pain.

"I'm just trying to help you," explained Uma.

Jim shook his head slightly but didn't release her.

"Jim, look at me," she said.

When he didn't move, Uma thought he had fallen back asleep and tried to pull herself free.

Jim stirred and mumbled. "No."

She tugged against him again.

Jim writhed, groaned. His grip tightened on her arm.

She yelped in pain. It felt as though he was crushing her bones. She continued to struggle and call out.

Awakened by her cries, Sam and Martha ran in, wearing their nightclothes. Dr. Thorne immediately tried to pry Jim's hand loose. The boy grabbed the doctor's wrists, freeing Uma. The young man's eyes burned with fever, and Sam knew Jim didn't know what he was doing. The doctor tried to wrestle himself free, but Jim was too strong for him.

"Get the sheriff!" Sam yelled to his wife. "Tell him to bring two sets of handcuffs!"

Martha tore out, leaving her husband still grappling with Jim. She returned a few moments later with the sheriff, who had his nightshirt tucked into his pants, the manacles clinking in his hand.

"Lock one end of each to the bed first!" grunted the doctor, still trying to free himself.

The sheriff ran to the other side of the bed and obeyed, attaching the cuffs to the bars running vertically on the metal headboard directly over Jim's head.

"There's a different key for each set," the sheriff stated, holding a key up to the doctor's mouth.

Sam shook his head. The sheriff put both keys in his mouth and held them with his teeth so they'd be ready when they got the boy into the handcuffs.

"OK, we'll have to do this together or we'll never get him restrained," ordered the doctor. "You're on his right, so be prepared. He's incredibly strong."

The sheriff nodded.

"One! Two! Three!" counted Sam.

The sheriff seized Jim's right arm, causing him to release the doctor and turn his attention to the new threat. Sam grabbed Jim's left arm. The young man continued to fight. Though it was two to one, they still couldn't subdue the boy. The sheriff saw Jim nearly throw Sam off, so he hit the young man in the side of the head with his elbow. The blow stunned Jim long enough for them to slide his wrists into the metal rings. The sheriff dropped both keys into his left hand while holding the cuff closed with his right and held the keys out to Sam. "Yours is the one with the red paint on it," he said.

Sam took the key, and both men quickly secured the locks.

"Thanks," said Sam, breathing heavily as he handed the key back to the sheriff. "But I don't approve of you striking my patient."

"What else was I supposed to do?" asked the sheriff, also out of breath. He glanced at the young man's weapons in the corner, relieved to see his pistol still in its holster and his knife in its sheath. "Let him kill us both? Is he really that strong or is it the delirium?"

"The delirium contributes, but he did manage to push that wagon," Sam reminded him.

A moment later, Jim recovered and started struggling against the manacles.

"No!" he shouted through clenched teeth as he tore against the restraints. "Not again!"

Jim grabbed the bars and tried to shake them loose. He wrenched at them, lifting his back off the bed in his effort. Then he let go of the bars and began pulling at the cuffs, jerking against them so violently his wrists began to bleed.

"Jim, stop!" pleaded the doctor, but the young man couldn't hear him through the delirium.

Jim flipped over onto his stomach, necessarily crossing his arms. Then he pulled himself up onto his knees and threw his body back, desperately hurling his weight against the irons.

The doctor saw spots of blood begin to appear on Jim's bandages as his stitches started to loosen and his burns to open and ooze.

The sheriff and Uma gasped. They hadn't seen Jim's scars.

Every muscle in Jim's body strained at the effort. Sweat and blood glistened and dripped from his skin. He thrashed and twisted, pitting flesh against metal.

"Jim! Please stop!" begged Sam. "Jim! Please!" he nearly shouted.

Jim glared at him, his eyes flashing like blue flame. Then he paused for a second, and the doctor saw a glimmer of recognition.

"Jim, do you know who I am?" asked Sam.

Jim gazed at him for a moment before he replied. "Dr. Thorne." He dropped his eyes to the cuffs and yanked against them again.

"Then for the love of God, stop!" Sam cried. "You were delirious, and hurt Mrs. Petersen, then you grabbed me. This is for your own good."

Jim quieted, still unaware of his nakedness, and looked around the room. His eyes shone with anger and pain, and the intensity of his glare made them all catch their breath.

"If you'll calm down, we'll take them off," offered Sam gently. Jim sat still, breathing heavily.

Sam nodded to the sheriff, who stepped forward and unlocked the handcuffs, with Jim watching his every move.

Then Dr. Thorne held up the sheet so Jim could lie back down without further exposure. Martha stepped forward and took the sheet so Sam could help Jim. The young man turned and, unable to support his own weight any longer, collapsed. Sam caught him. Jim tensed, but Sam laid him down gently.

"I'm so sorry," whispered Sam, tears filling his eyes. "I shouldn't—I mean with your scars—" he knelt by the bed with his hand on Jim's arm.

Jim looked at him with a mixture of confusion and incredulity.

Sam rested his head on his hand and tried to fight back the tears as they fell to his cheeks. Then he looked up into Jim's eyes. "I hope you can forgive me. I didn't know what else to do. You've suffered enough cruelty. Please believe me when I say we meant you no harm."

Jim nodded.

"Where did you get those scars?" asked the sheriff.

Jim looked at him evenly and replied bitterly, "None of your business!"

"I only asked because I'd like to see the son of a bitch who did that to you behind bars," explained the sheriff quietly, forgetting there were women in the room.

Jim gazed at him for a moment, then dropped his eyes. "It was nowhere around here," he replied.

Dr. Thorne returned to his feet and began examining Jim's wrists. He shook his head and whispered. "What you must've gone through." The remark was more to himself than Jim.

The doctor began repairing the physical damage Jim's anger and delirium had caused. Sam wished in his heart that he could soothe the young man's spirit as well.

"Damn!" whispered the sheriff as he removed the cuffs from the bed.

Sam and the women glanced up.

"The metal's bent," the sheriff explained. "And it's a wrought iron headboard."

"Sorry," Jim said softly. "I'll make you another one."

"You'd have to be a smith to do that," Sam stated, smiling at the young man's innocence.

"I am," Jim replied.

They all gazed at the boy in surprise.

"No wonder you're so strong," the sheriff remarked.

Dr. Thorne thanked the sheriff as he took his leave and then continued his work, with Martha and Uma assisting him. Jim was exhausted but still tense. The doctor feared he had lost the young man's trust.

After treating all the wounds, Sam asked Jim, "So, what should I do if you get delirious and violent again?"

Jim thought for a moment. "I don't know. What started this?"

"I tried to hold a damp cloth on your head," explained Uma.

"Did I hurt you?" Jim asked, genuinely concerned.

"I'll be all right," Uma replied, showing him her arm. The imprint of his fingers was still visible on her skin.

"I'm sorry. I'm not used to—before, I was always left alone," Jim said softly, his eyes lowered.

The doctor nodded. Then he patted Jim on the arm. "Rest now, son," he said.

He left the room, with Uma and Martha following. Martha turned down the light before shutting the door.

Sam trudged into the kitchen and sank heavily into a chair at the table.

"Coffee?" asked Martha.

Sam just sat for a moment, deep in thought. Then he looked up at her and shook his head. "Let me see your arm," he said to Uma. "It's not broken," he announced after examining it. "You're lucky. He's as strong as an ox. I've seen a lot of men delirious before, but I've never seen such violence. I really think if we had let him, he would have torn off one of his hands to get free. What could have done that to one so young?" he whispered, fighting back tears again. "Who could have treated him with such cruelty?"

Martha sat next to him, caressing his shoulder. All three of them shook their heads. Martha wiped a tear from her eyes, and they all cried a little.

Jim lay in darkness broken only by the low light of the lantern. He shook his head at his behavior. His reaction to the handcuffs surprised even himself, but he realized that, in his mind, he had been back in the hell he'd known as a child. Still, he was embarrassed. He wanted to leave and never see these people again, and he felt trapped because he couldn't. He tried to get up, but his body wouldn't cooperate. He hit the mattress with a fist and cursed under his breath.

A few minutes later, Sam peeked in Jim's room. He could see the young man's eyes shining in the dim light, so he entered and closed the door quietly behind him. He noticed that Jim didn't look at him as he approached the bed. "The pain too bad to sleep?"

Jim shook his head. "I need to leave tomorrow," he said, still without meeting the doctor's gaze.

"You can't. You'll be dead within the week."

Jim turned away.

"Do you know anything about coyotes?" the doctor asked.

"A little. Why?"

"I have a patient who's a trapper. I don't approve of the practice, but it's his livelihood. He told me that sometimes a coyote will chew its own leg off to get out of a trap. If an animal will do that, doesn't it stand to reason that a man might have a similar reaction? Especially if that man wasn't thinking clearly, was in great pain and had been ill-treated earlier in his life?"

Jim looked at him, and, even in the near darkness, the doctor could see the hurt in the young man's eyes. Jim gave a slight nod, and Sam patted him on the arm.

"Still have that whiskey?" Jim asked.

"Yes, but I thought you said it didn't help the pain?"

"It doesn't. It deadens the mind."

Sam left the room to find Martha and Uma in the hall. He passed them and the operating room where he always kept a bottle and continued to his study. He returned carrying a full bottle of bourbon. The women followed him as he entered Jim's room. Sam opened the bottle and lifted Jim's head. The young man took a couple of sips before pausing because of the pain in his throat. Sam started to lower the bottle, but Jim raised it back to his lips. He drank it like it was water, consuming two-thirds of the amber liquid, ignoring the burning in his throat. None of them had ever seen anyone, especially one so young, drink like that before.

"Do you want any water?" asked Sam as he lowered Jim's head back onto the pillow.

"Yes, please," Jim replied softly.

Sam filled a glass from the pitcher on the bureau, and Jim drank almost all of it. Then he relaxed with a sigh as he felt the soothing effect of the alcohol flow over him.

Sam gently patted Jim's shoulder. Then he and Martha returned to their room, and Uma stayed with Jim the rest of the night.

For the next couple of weeks, Uma returned often to stay with the boy overnight. He became delirious again during this time, but she didn't touch him, and he calmed.

When Uma wasn't available, Martha stayed with Jim, often sleeping on the daybed. One night, Jim awoke to find her kneeling in prayer before going to sleep, and he watched her.

"You shouldn't waste your time," Jim commented as she got to her feet.

"It's not a waste of time. Have you ever tried it?"

Jim looked away. There were things in his past he chose not to remember.

The next morning at breakfast, Martha voiced her concern for Jim's spiritual wellbeing to Sam.

The doctor thought for a moment, then replied, "How can someone who has known only the cruelty of man have any concept of a loving God?"

All Martha could do was nod.

Then Sam muttered, "Even the least of these—"

"What?" she asked.

Sam looked up. "Nothing, my dear."

Usually, Dr. Thorne would treat Jim's burns in the morning. Uma would often stay, and she and Martha would assist him. This was a painful process for Jim and difficult for anyone with a heart to watch. Each time, Uma thought how lucky she and her children had been that Jim came along that night. Otherwise, even if they had lived, they would be going through this. Jim maintained his composure throughout. Other than a groan, he never made a sound. Dr. Thorne had worked in a hospital and knew the typical reaction to pain of this magnitude. Privately, in his journal, he marveled at the young man's fortitude, but he added that this type of self-control is learned, not natural. He shuddered to think what Jim must have gone through in the past.

3

SOCIALIZATION

Jim continued to recover over the next few weeks, and eventually he was able to go out on short walks to get his strength back. Martha would accompany him, and they usually headed to the stable first to check on Ness. The horse had become a subject of conversation in town due to his intelligence and devotion to Jim.

Martha noticed that the young women of the town seemed infatuated with the nice-looking young man now that everyone knew he was much younger than he appeared. Jim, on the other hand, didn't seem to notice their attention. Then one evening, while they were taking one of their usual strolls, Jim and Martha passed two of these young women. They just happened to be sitting on a bench looking at a newspaper as Jim and Martha walked by. They could see the girls peeking over the paper as Jim approached, but they ducked back behind it as he passed, giggling.

Martha noticed Jim tense, and his right hand slid to his side where his weapon would be hanging if he were carrying it. She shuddered. "Why didn't you say hello?" she asked, hoping to determine what had caused his reaction.

"Why would I do that?"

"They were trying to get your attention."

"They were laughing," Jim replied evenly.

"They weren't laughing at you," Martha assured him, now certain what had caused his discomfort. "They were just nervous."

"Nervous about what?"

"That you might notice them or look at them or something."

"So they wanted my attention, but they were nervous that I might give it to them?" Jim asked.

Martha nodded with a smile.

"That doesn't make any sense," Jim replied.

"They're girls. You'll soon learn that we women often don't make sense to men."

Jim shook his head in confusion.

"You should speak to them when we go back by," suggested Martha when they reached the end of the boardwalk and turned around. "A smile wouldn't hurt, either."

Jim just shook his head.

Martha realized that, in the weeks he had stayed with them, she had never seen him smile. He had a sense of humor, but a softening to his gaze was the closest he ever came to smiling.

As they passed the girls, Jim touched his hat and spoke. "Ladies," he said.

The girls quickly put down the paper, hopped up, and said hello to Jim and Martha.

Martha stopped and introduced them. "Jim, this is Margaret and Ann Bowers. Their parents own the clothing shop," she said, motioning to the store window behind the girls.

The girls whispered conspiratorially to each other for a moment. Then one of them ran into the shop, only to be followed out a minute later by another, older woman.

"Why Martha, how are you?" the woman asked.

"I'm well, thank you," Martha replied. "Julietta, I would like you to meet Jim. Jim, this is Julietta Bowers. Jim's staying with us until he recovers," Martha added, turning back to Julietta.

"I'm very pleased to meet you!" Julietta smiled, offering her hand.

"Thank you, ma'am," Jim replied, shaking her hand firmly but gently. He didn't want to hurt her as he had Mrs. Petersen, and his hands were still sore.

"Mrs. Petersen is one of my closest friends. Thank you for helping them in their time of need," said Julietta.

"My pleasure, ma'am," Jim responded modestly.

"Martha, I would like to invite you, Sam, and young Jim here to dinner tomorrow night. It's been ages since we have had the opportunity to entertain. That is, if you're feeling up to it?" Julietta asked Jim.

Jim turned to Martha to gauge her response, as well as to say *Thanks for getting me into this.*

"We'd love to," replied Martha, ignoring the displeasure in Jim's eyes.

"Around seven, then? I hope that's not too late, but Albert— that's my husband, Jim—and I must close the shop."

"We don't want to put you to any trouble," said Martha in an effort not only to be polite but to appease Jim.

"Oh, it's no trouble. The girls do most of the cooking. They're both very accomplished," Julietta commented, looking at Jim.

"We'll see you at seven, then," agreed Martha, turning to leave. "Thank you."

"It was nice meeting you, Jim," said Julietta.

"Nice to meet you," added each of the girls.

"And you," Jim responded, touching his hat again. Then he turned and was greatly relieved to be heading back to Sam and Martha's.

Martha eyed him for a few minutes as they walked. "What's wrong? You have fine table manners, there's nothing for you to feel uncomfortable about."

"I've never—" Jim made a motion with his hand back toward the shop.

"You'll be fine. You've been eating with us, haven't you?"

Jim nodded and considered escaping on Ness later in the night but realized that would be disrespectful to Sam and Martha.

The next morning, Jim awoke to find his clothes missing from the chair where he had laid them. Rather than walk around naked, he resigned himself to staying in bed a while longer. He had rarely had the opportunity to enjoy a morning lazing on a comfortable bed, except recently when he was hurt. He wondered why he felt guilty as he dozed off again. A little while later, Martha peeked into his room to check on him. She was always amazed at how young he looked when he slept. She would often shudder to think about the horrors he must have suffered already in his young life for him to have the appearance and bearing of someone much older. Jim sensed her presence, stirred, and opened his eyes. An expression of pain crossed his face for a moment before he was able to make a conscious effort to mask it.

"I'm sorry if I woke you," Martha said, opening his door and bringing in a tray. "I brought you breakfast in bed because your clothes are still damp. They should be ready in a little while, or you can save them for this evening and wear some of Sam's."

"Why are they wet?" Jim asked, sitting up painfully.

"I washed them for you. I didn't think you would want to wear dirty clothes to dinner tonight."

"Thank you," Jim muttered without enthusiasm.

"What's wrong?" asked Martha as she settled the tray on the bed.

Jim thought for a moment, and without looking up replied, "I'm not what you think—or want me to be." Then he remembered something that had been said to him in the past, and he repeated it almost unconsciously, his voice soft, low, and distant. "You can take a rat out of the mine, but it's still a rat."

"What?" asked Martha, not sure whether to laugh or cry.

"What?" Jim asked in return, almost like he'd just awakened from a dream.

"Who told you that?"

Jim looked down and began eating pensively.

"You're just nervous. Don't worry, everything will be fine," Martha assured him. Then she opened the curtains before leaving the room and glanced back at Jim as she shut the door. She had learned he liked them open because he always gazed out the window with a faint expression of relief while he took a few deep breaths.

When she got back to the kitchen, she sat down and thought about what Jim had said, as well as how he had said it. She wondered if Jim had been quoting whoever had mistreated him. She cringed as she recalled Sam noting to her in private that all of the scars were at least four or five years old, some of them even older. She shuddered as she remembered Sam speculating that Jim may have been as young as eight when the abuse began.

Later that afternoon, she mentioned Jim's comment to Sam as they were getting ready for the dinner party. "His voice was different, distant somehow," she explained. Then she told her husband about Jim's reaction to the girls' laughter the evening before.

Sam shook his head. "Well, let's see how things go this evening and try not to remind him of his past. That's about all I know to do."

Martha nodded.

That evening, Martha, Sam, and Jim gathered in the front room as they prepared to leave. Martha remarked how handsome Jim looked and mentioned to her husband that he hadn't protested at all when she insisted he take a bath that afternoon. Sam laughed and gently patted Jim on the shoulder. Jim followed them as Sam and Martha walked hand in hand.

When they arrived, Julietta met them at the door.

"I hope we're not too early?" asked Martha.

"Not at all. The girls are just finishing up, and I managed to get Albert out of the shop," she replied, turning to her husband, who had come up behind her. "Jim, I'd like you to meet my husband, Albert Bowers. Albert, I'd like you to meet the young man who saved the Petersens, Jim Morgan."

Jim and Albert shook hands and exchanged greetings. Albert's grip was firm, as was Jim's. Then Albert remembered hearing Jim's hands were burned. "I hope I didn't hurt you, son."

"No, sir," Jim replied, surprised by the man's concern.

Julietta led them into the dining room where the girls were placing the last dishes on the table. There was a smaller table off to the side where two younger children, a boy and a girl, were sitting. The children eyed Jim curiously.

"You've met Margaret and Ann," said Julietta, "and these are Ryan and Lydia." She then introduced Jim to them, and the children mumbled a "Pleased to meet you," under the obvious influence of their mother.

Then everyone sat down to a meal the likes of which Jim had never seen. The girls had cooked four chickens, along with baked potatoes, green beans, and stewed apples, and Julietta promised pie for dessert.

"You two must have been busy all day," remarked Sam with a smile at the girls, who giggled and blushed.

They said grace and then Julietta began serving the plates. She started with Jim since he was their special guest, which made Jim even more uncomfortable. Then she asked him for his preference concerning white meat or dark meat. Jim replied that either would be fine. He was glad Martha had told him not to eat until after the hostess took her first bite. When everyone had a plate, and after the first hush as they started eating, Julietta remarked that she hadn't seen Jim's horse recently. She was just trying to make conversation, but the statement took Jim by surprise. He drank some water, not sure how to respond. In the interim, Albert, sensing Jim's discomfiture, asked his wife why she would have seen the animal in the first place.

Julietta laughed and replied, "If you ever ventured to the front of the shop, you'd know why. For a couple of weeks there, every day or so we'd see him run by towards Sam and Martha's, followed by one of the stable boys trying to catch him. It was quite amusing, especially since he'd always stop at the general store to take an apple from the barrel out front."

"You're kidding," replied Albert with a laugh. "He must be a smart horse," he said to Jim.

"Too smart for his own good," commented Jim half-seriously, but without smiling.

"What was the cause of this?" asked Albert.

"He wanted to see me," Jim answered.

"Amazing!" breathed Albert.

Julietta continued. "Then, Mr. Whithers moved the apple barrel inside the store."

"I guess your horse was disappointed then," smiled Albert.

Jim shook his head, but didn't say anything, so Julietta explained.

"The next day, we heard a horrible commotion outside. When the girls and I ran out, we saw the horse standing with his front feet on the boardwalk in front of the store, snorting and making all sorts of noise. Mr. Whithers was standing at the door of the shop telling the horse to go away, but when he stepped outside to shoo him, the horse tossed his head and knocked Mr. Whithers down. Then the horse stepped into the store, stuck his head into the apple barrel, took one, and ran off, and Mr. Whithers was left sitting on the boardwalk, very surprised indeed!"

Everyone laughed, including the little children, but Jim just shook his head again.

"The next day the apple barrel was back outside," Julietta concluded.

"That was probably wise," remarked Albert, still laughing.

"I've paid him for the apples," Jim added seriously, which just caused everyone to laugh all the more.

"What's your horse's name?" asked Albert.

"Ness," Jim replied.

"That's an unusual name," said Julietta.

"It's short for Necesito," Jim explained.

"From the verb 'to need,'" said Albert, showing that he knew Spanish. "Literally, 'I need.' In this context, it would mean 'the needed one.'" His wife looked at him in wonder. "Did you forget that I apprenticed with a Spanish tailor before we were married?" he asked her.

She nodded and touched his arm.

"Do you speak Spanish?" inquired Albert, turning back to Jim.

"No, sir."

"Does your horse always behave like this?" the tailor asked.

"He's always been difficult," answered Jim. "I got him for nothing. The Mexican who owned him was going to put him down because he couldn't train him. I was able to work with him, but he's never let anyone else lead or ride him unless I tell him it's OK first. When the Mexican saw that, he suggested the name."

"Amazing!" exclaimed Albert again. "At least you don't have to worry about anyone stealing him."

Jim nodded. "But it makes people think he isn't well trained."

"I don't know," replied Albert. "One might conclude he's been quite well trained, indeed."

The others laughed, but Jim just nodded and shrugged.

Suddenly, the littlest girl started crying, and the little boy started fussing at her.

Albert stood up and stepped to their table.

Jim tensed and turned slightly, eyeing the man.

Albert dropped to one knee and put his hand on the little girl's shoulder. "What's wrong, Lydia?"

"Ryan touched my potato. Got it dirty," she pouted through her tears.

"Is that true, Ryan?"

"Yes, sir," replied the boy. "But it's her own fault. She was kicking my chair, and I told her I'd do it if she didn't stop."

"Lydia?" asked Albert.

Lydia nodded.

"Well, stop kicking his chair," Albert said patiently to the little girl. "And you, young man," he turned to the boy, "next time, tell me or your mother, and leave other people's food alone."

Both children nodded.

Then Albert assured the girl her potato was still good to eat and returned to his chair. He noticed Jim staring at him with a mixture of amazement and confusion on his face. Albert looked away and asked his wife about dessert. When he turned back, Jim had dropped his gaze to his plate and seemed lost in thought.

The girls cleared the table and served the pie. It was a custard pie. Jim had never had anything like it, and wanted a second slice when offered, but he refused, not wanting to be rude.

After the girls cleared the dessert dishes away, Julietta took the two youngest children up to bed, and the adults strolled into the parlor. Albert suggested Jim follow Margaret and Ann out onto the back porch.

Jim found the girls sitting in a swing. One was on each side, leaving room in the middle. Jim chose to stand, leaning against one of the posts supporting the porch roof, and gazed out into the gathering darkness.

"Are you feeling better now?" asked Margaret, the older of the two, summoning her courage to speak.

"Yes, thank you," Jim replied without turning.

"We saw the wagon at the sale," said Margaret.

"Sale?" Jim asked.

"Since Mrs. Petersen is living with Mrs. Canady now," the girl replied, "she sold everything. Mama said it should be a good dowry for Mary, but Mary said it's for the boys to go to university later." Then she unconsciously looked Jim up and down as she added, "I can't believe you were able to push it."

"Wasn't easy."

"How are your hands? Are they all better now?"

"Almost," he replied.

"Do they still hurt?" asked Ann, speaking for the first time.

"Some."

"Can we see?" Ann asked.

Jim turned so the light from the kitchen window shone across him and extended his hands. The girls stood. Each took one hand and examined it. The skin was still tender, and some of the burns hadn't finished healing, but that wasn't why the young man tensed at their touch. Already, the girls could see scars from the cuts and burns.

"Does it hurt to move your fingers?" asked Margaret.

"Not anymore."

The girls sat back down on the swing and exchanged a glance. They couldn't believe Jim was the same age as Margaret, who was only a year older than Ann.

"We're glad you could come to dinner," said Margaret.

"Thank you. It was very good."

They heard a coyote howl in the distance, and the girls shivered.

"That always scares me," whispered Ann.

"The coyote isn't interested in people," Jim explained. "Unless it's rabid."

"I've never seen one except after it was killed," remarked Margaret.

"I've had them nose around while I was trying to sleep," Jim commented.

"Weren't you scared?" asked Margaret.

"No. I had my gun. It made Ness nervous."

"What was it looking for?" asked Ann.

"Leftovers. Luckily, I didn't have any. It didn't hang around very long, otherwise I'd have had to shoot it," Jim stated.

The girls exchanged a glance, not sure whether the boy was serious or just trying to impress them.

Then they heard Julietta calling them, so they stepped back inside. Sam and Martha were ready to leave. Everyone exchanged goodbyes. Albert put his hand on Jim's shoulder and instructed him to come to his shop, promising to make the young man a couple changes of clothes. Jim thanked him and they left.

Sam and Martha chatted lightly on the way home, but Jim followed in silence. Albert's patience and gentleness with his children had struck him. He still thought Sam, Martha, and the Bowers were only nice to him because he'd saved the lives of the Petersens. He let his mind wander as they walked. Suddenly, a mental image of clinging to a tree as ravening wolves circled underneath dropped into his mind, causing him to shudder and shake his head. He heard Martha laugh and was brought back to the present. He realized the only way to assure his place in polite society was through his own personal sacrifice.

4

DEFENSE

It was a few days later. Jim, still recovering, was getting restless, but Sam ordered him to continue to stay quiet. He was worried because Jim was still coughing, especially at night. Sam wanted to be sure the young man's lungs had healed before he started riding and working again. The doctor insisted Jim rest often throughout the day, so it was late morning and Jim was still in bed, per doctor's orders, when the sheriff arrived. Martha let him in and told him Sam was in Jim's room. He found Jim dozing and Sam sitting near the bed reading, or pretending to. The sheriff realized from Sam's posture that he was listening to Jim's breathing.

Sam looked up and started to rise, but Jim opened his eyes. "I'm not sleeping. You don't have to leave."

The doctor looked at the sheriff, who shrugged. "I just wanted to let you know, Sam, that there might be some trouble tonight," stated the sheriff.

"What kind of trouble?" asked the doctor.

Jim sat up with his back to the headboard to listen.

"Some of Carlos's men rode into town last night."

"How do you know?" Sam asked.

"One of them told one of the girls," explained the sheriff, referring to the prostitutes. Since they were usually a man's first stop, the sheriff let the ladies carry on their business as long as they let him know if there was someone in town he should keep an eye on.

"Who's Carlos?" Jim asked.

A sudden ruction rent the air as a murder of crows immediately started cawing raucously outside the open window, forcing the sheriff to pause. Both he and Sam jumped involuntarily at the racket, but Jim was unfazed and continued gazing evenly at the sheriff, ignoring the birds and the warning they may have been trying to give.

When the clamor subsided, the sheriff replied, "He heads a bunch of men that make their living mainly by robbing stages, but they've also been known to attack homesteads or steal anything else they can get their hands on."

"What are you going to do?" Jim asked.

"There's not much I can do except hope that they're just passing through. Frank, who works for me sometimes, is a family man. I can't expect him to go up against these men. Hell, it'd be suicide for me, and I'm a better shot than him."

"I'll help," Jim offered calmly.

"What?" asked Sam. "You'll do no such thing!"

"Thanks," said the sheriff to Jim, "but I'm afraid you'd be no match for them. No offense, but you're still a boy."

"Not to mention that you still aren't well," added Sam.

"I'm good with a gun, and I don't have a family to worry about," Jim replied dispassionately.

The sheriff thought for a moment. "How good are you?"

Sam turned on him. "You can't be considering sending Jim up against them?"

"No, not directly," answered the sheriff. "But he could help me keep an eye on them. So how good are you?"

Jim got out of bed, put on a pair of pants and his gun belt. "Stand over there," he said, pointing to the other side of the room.

"What? Are you going to shoot me?" asked the sheriff, half-jokingly.

Jim emptied his revolver. The sheriff did the same. Then both men exchanged weapons for the other to examine, before handing them back, holstering them, and taking their positions.

"We'll let Sam be the judge," Jim suggested.

"Judge of what?" asked Sam.

"We're going to draw on each other," explained the sheriff, "and you're going to decide who's fastest."

Sam looked at Jim, who nodded. "You're both crazy," muttered the doctor.

"Not at all," replied the sheriff. "You saw us empty our guns."

"I still won't aim right at you," Jim assured the sheriff, who nodded in return.

"OK," agreed Sam reluctantly. "Do I need to count or anything?"

"No," answered the sheriff.

He and Jim stood facing each other. Jim waited for the sheriff to make his move. Then, faster than lightning, Jim had his gun drawn and cocked before the sheriff had gotten his out of his holster.

"Wow," whispered Sam.

"Yeah," agreed the sheriff. "But let's try it one more time."

Again, they faced each other, and again, Jim had his weapon out and ready before the sheriff had his drawn.

"I guess you're pretty accurate, too," remarked the sheriff.

"Yes. I can show you if you'd like," Jim offered.

"No," the sheriff responded. "Someone would see, and then you might get the wrong kind of attention, if you know what I mean." Jim nodded in reply, and both men reloaded their weapons as the sheriff continued. "I'm not going to deputize you, and I don't want you to speak to any of these men. All I need you to do is find them tonight and keep an eye on them. Then let me know if it looks like they're going to cause trouble. I don't want you to even think about using your gun. If you got hurt, Sam here would skin me alive, and he's a doctor, so he knows how."

Sam nodded, then said to Jim, "You better rest now. It sounds like you're going to have a late night. Though I want you both to know, I don't like this, and the only reason I'm allowing it at all is to avoid anyone getting hurt."

"Don't worry," Jim replied. "These men don't know me. They'll probably be in a saloon and just think I'm there to get a drink."

"All I want you to do is watch them," the sheriff repeated firmly. "They're sleeping it off now, but they'll probably be up and about by afternoon. Later on, just wander around until you find them. More than likely they're not planning anything here in town or they would have done it before anyone knew they were here, so just be careful."

"How will I recognize them?" Jim asked.

"From what I was told, one of them is a big man with messy black hair, one of them is an average-sized fellow with pockmarks on his face, and another one has red hair and his skin is almost as red as his hair."

"Is one of them Carlos?" Jim inquired.

"I doubt it, but no one knows what he looks like," replied the sheriff. "Remember, you're just supposed to keep an eye on them. That's *all.*"

"Yes, sir."

Later that day, Jim ate an early supper and then cleaned his rifle, pistol, and shotgun. "Just in case," he explained to Sam and Martha. Then he put on his gun belt.

He left the doctor's house just as it was getting dark. Though the night was warm, Martha insisted Jim wear his coat. He didn't protest, not only because it would do no good, but also because the coat hid his gun and he wanted to be inconspicuous. The drinking establishments were already busy when he arrived on Saloon Row, as some called it, or Tiger Alley, depending on whether one put the emphasis on whiskey and whores, or gambling. Jim wandered back and forth across the street, spending little time in any one saloon, and kept his hat pulled low to avoid recognition. He realized it wouldn't really make any difference if someone saw him, but he didn't want to draw attention.

Every now and then, he saw someone he recognized. A couple of times, he saw someone whom he knew had a wife and children take one of the girls upstairs. He'd seen this kind of behavior before so it didn't surprise him, but he always wondered how a man who was lucky enough to have a good wife could treat her that way. Sometimes, the men were married to shrews and he understood their behavior, but some of them had a kind and beautiful woman at home, and he couldn't understand why they would betray her.

He was beginning to wonder if the sheriff had been mistaken when he heard music and, out of curiosity, followed the sound into one of the larger saloons. Music was something he had rarely experienced until he lived with the teacher, and it still fascinated him. The piano was on a small stage. Jim stood off to the side watching the man play for a few minutes, before turning and taking in his surroundings. The women were better here, too. They were finely dressed in costumes that left little to the imagination. To Jim's surprise, they looked clean, and their perfume smelled good, not sickeningly sweet or sour like that worn by the women of his childhood. The place was full, so Jim had to shoulder his way to the bar to order a beer. He looked around as he sipped it, and thought he spied one of the men the sheriff had described sitting at a table at the back of the room.

The globes of the lights were sooty, and cigarette smoke curled in the air, so even though there were plenty of lamps the room was dim. Jim casually made his way along the bar toward the man he'd seen. Because of the crowd and the haze, Jim had to leave the bar and get very near the man's table to see who was sitting with him. Luckily, there was an empty chair against a nearby wall, and from it, Jim had a clear view of the man and his companions.

All three of the men the sheriff had described were sitting around the table, and two others had apparently joined them. One of the newcomers was dressed all in black, and the other had noticeably bad teeth. Jim couldn't hear what they were saying, but from their behavior he could tell they all knew each other. He sat in the shadows and watched as the men drank and pawed at the women. Every table had at least one woman either sitting on a man's lap or going from man to man dancing or moving provocatively.

After a while, the bartender called one of the girls over from the men's table and spoke to her. He apparently gave her instructions, because when she returned to the men, her attitude had changed, and she seemed to be negotiating something with them. She pointed to the other women at the table and, using her fingers, listed something off. The men looked disappointed, and Jim heard one of them raise his voice above the din.

"That's outrageous!" he shouted.

The girl shrugged and gestured toward the bartender, as though telling the man to talk to him if he didn't like her terms. The man seemed to consider taking his complaint to the management, but it looked like one of the others reminded him of something, so he just shook his head. Then the girl and the other women minced away prowling for more suitable companions.

One of them saw Jim, slinked up to him, and sat on his lap. Though this type of woman disgusted him, Jim tolerated her attentions so as not to draw notice, and he enjoyed looking down her extremely low-cut dress. She had just started negotiations when the men got up and left. Jim named a price, which she apparently found insulting, because she hopped off his lap and flounced away, allowing him to leave unnoticed.

The night was dark. The moon had not yet risen. Jim was able to follow the men relatively closely as they headed to the outskirts of town where the women were cheaper.

"Maybe we can get the same one tonight," the dark-haired one said.

"Oh, I hope so!" smiled the pockmarked one.

"Was she good?" asked the newcomer with bad teeth.

"Oh, yeah!" replied the redhead.

"Yeah," added the dark-haired one, laughing. "I just wish her teeth weren't so sharp."

The others laughed.

"Is that all you got?" asked the other newcomer, who was dressed all in black.

"Oh, no!" answered the dark-haired one. "I got my share. She's young and desperate for money. For a few extra cents, she'll do anything, and I mean anything," he said, poking the red-haired one in the butt and causing him to jump with a laugh.

"You're kidding?" the one with bad teeth asked.

"Would I kid about something like that?" the dark-haired one replied.

The others laughed.

"It's the closest thing to a virgin *you'll* ever get," the dark-haired one continued, causing more laughter. "One that's willing at least."

They stopped at a small hut. A dim light shone through the cracks in the door. They could hear a man grunting inside, so they waited patiently.

"I hope he leaves something for us," the one dressed in black muttered.

The one with bad teeth nudged him to keep quiet as he rubbed his hands nervously on his pants.

The dark-haired one watched him for a moment, then smiled

and asked, "Nervous, or just rearing to go?"

"Can't help it," replied the one with bad teeth. "It's been so long my balls are hurting."

"We'll let you go first," offered the dark-haired one.

"Are you sure that little girl can handle him?" asked the redhead. "His cock's as big as my arm."

The man with bad teeth looked worried. "You don't think she'll say no, do you? That's what happened the last time."

"You can always take her by force," suggested the one in black.

"But that's no fun when it's a whore," the one with bad teeth replied.

A few minutes later, the man they'd heard inside opened the door to leave and seemed surprised to see anyone waiting outside. Jim stood in the shadow of a neighboring hut. As the light from the door fell on the man's face, Jim understood why he immediately looked down and appeared embarrassed. He was the preacher at the church Sam and Martha attended and had visited Jim while he was recovering. Jim felt at the time there was something strange and disturbing about the man, but now he knew why. The preacher didn't see him but still ducked his head to hide his face from the others and hurried back toward the respectable side of town.

A moment later, a young, scantily clad girl appeared at the door. She looked no older than twelve or thirteen, but when she spoke to the men waiting, her voice was low and gruff, and Jim realized she had to be older than she appeared. All of the men entered the hut together, and Jim heard her order them to wait on the other side of a curtain, that she'd take them one at a time. Then, for the next hour or so, Jim heard sounds that brought back bad memories.

He felt the ground under a small table behind the girl's shack. It was dry, so he sat and settled in to wait. The sounds and activities in the hut held no curiosity or excitement for him. He had seen it all before when he was a child, and it disgusted him. He'd never known a woman and found sex only for its own sake repulsive. He knew Sam and Martha enjoyed each other—he'd heard them, too—but they were married and loved each other. He thought about the woman in the saloon. He'd liked looking at her, but the thought of touching her made him feel ill. He wondered if he would ever find a nice woman and, if he did, if he would be able to put aside the memories of the filthy, vile creatures he'd known as women when he was a child.

Finally, the dark-haired man exited out the back door. From the sound a moment later, Jim realized he was relieving himself. The redhead soon joined him. Jim leaned down and was able to see them by the light of the doorway, from where he hid in the shadow of the table.

"She's the only decent thing in this stinking town," remarked the dark-haired one.

"At least this is our last night."

"I don't understand why we couldn't just wait up in the hills. What if someone figures out why we're here?"

"How are they going to do that?" asked the redhead in return.

"I don't know. But why couldn't we just wait east of this shithole since that's where we're going to be anyway?" asked the dark-haired one.

"If we had, we wouldn't have found her," the redhead reminded him.

"True. I hope the others finish up soon. I'd like to get some sleep before I go chasing after some stage."

"I hope we get something this time."

"The boss seems to think we will," commented the dark-haired one. "He's been tracking this load since it left for St. Louis."

"I hope he's right. I don't mind getting shot at if the payoff's good."

"Sure, you just hide behind me," replied the dark-haired one with a wry laugh as they scuffed back inside.

Jim crawled out and walked behind a few huts in the opposite direction from town before making his way onto the road and heading back. He had just passed the hut where the men were when they exited. They followed him into town, though they didn't pay him any mind. The men turned off at one of the cheap boarding houses, and Jim continued to the sheriff's office. When he got close and passed under the streetlights, he started staggering like he was drunk in case someone was watching. He fell heavily against the door to the office as he passed. He continued until he got to the alley, then stopped and leaned against the side of the building in the darkness. As he had hoped, the sheriff stepped outside and looked around. Jim coughed softly to get his attention. The sheriff approached, and Jim told him about the men's plan.

"There's a home station a few miles east, isn't there?" Jim asked, referring to one of the places where the stage stopped overnight. The freight company paid someone to live there, cook for the passengers and freight men, and take care of the horses so a fresh team was always waiting.

"Yes," replied the sheriff.

"They have a telegraph?" Jim asked. He'd seen the wires in his travels.

"Not yet," the sheriff replied.

"I'll ride out and warn them, then."

"What if they've already left by the time you get there? There's more than one route they could take."

"I can get there before dawn."

"You're going to be pushing your horse awfully hard, not to mention yourself."

"I'll be fine, and Ness can do it no problem. Let Sam and Martha know for me, and meet me at the livery with my rifle and shotgun. I have extra ammunition in my saddlebags, so bring them, too."

"OK. But Sam's not going to be too happy with me."

"Would he rather the stage be taken by surprise?" Jim asked.

"I'll be there in a few minutes," promised the sheriff as he turned toward Sam's and Jim trotted off toward the barn.

The sheriff hurried to the stable accompanied by the doctor and endured the physician's scolding the entire way. After a brief argument with Sam during which Jim promised he wouldn't do anything stupid, Jim took off, urging Ness forward into the darkness. He was glad Ness could see the road, because he couldn't. He arrived at the home station shortly before dawn. The station-keeper heard Jim ride up and stepped out of the barn. He listened suspiciously as the young man explained the reason for his presence there at such an early hour, until Jim showed him the badge the sheriff had handed him right before he left. The sheriff hadn't deputized him, so Jim wasn't wearing it. The sheriff gave it to him hoping to add validity to his story.

The station-keeper allowed Jim to dismount and water Ness,

and he even offered a stall for the animal. Jim thanked him and spent the next little while walking the horse to cool him down. It was the first time he'd ridden since he'd been hurt, and from the way Ness covered the ground, he knew the horse was happy to get back on the road. Ness ambled the entire way, nonstop, and, after a drink, tossed his head, ready to make the return trip.

The sun was up by the time Ness was cool enough to stop walking, and the driver and guard were awake by then, so Jim told his story again. They believed him even before he showed them the badge, and asked if he would like to stay for breakfast and ride back with them. Jim accepted their invitation. Then he put his rifle, shotgun, and saddlebags on the stage and got Ness settled into a stall. He gave the station-keeper instructions about Ness's feed and promised to return the next day to retrieve him, but forgot to warn the man about Ness's temperament. Later that day, as the station-keeper was trying to turn him out into the paddock, Ness tossed his head and ran off in the direction the stage had taken. He turned up in town the next morning, standing outside the barn and waiting for the stable boys to come let him in and feed him.

Shortly after breakfast, the stage left the station racing toward Dillard, a town a few hours' ride beyond Clayter, which was where Jim had been staying. Jim sat beside Hap, the guard, in his seat, which was above and to the left of Joe, the driver. Jim rode cradling his rifle in his lap, with his shotgun at his feet.

After the information Jim gave them, both men agreed that the attack would probably come at a gorge through which they had to pass. Jim remembered it from the night before, but it was hard to judge the depth of the gorge in the dark.

At one point, Hap looked at Jim's rifle and smiled. "You must be an awfully good shot," he said.

"I can hold my own. Why?" Jim inquired.

"The motion of the coach makes it hard to aim," Hap explained. "That's why we carry a shotgun. That way *something* will hit them if you point it in the general direction."

"Doesn't that mean they have to get awfully close?" Jim asked.

"Yeah," replied Hap. "But they can't shoot too well on a moving horse either, so things are pretty well matched."

"This stage rides pretty smooth, considering," Jim remarked.

Joe heard his comment and explained. "The Concord coaches are designed to rock back and forth rather than bouncing up and down. Believe me, that makes a big difference on the back."

"I think I'll be able to adjust for the motion of the stage when I aim," Jim assured Hap. Though he didn't mention it, he'd practiced shooting from Ness at a run, and rarely missed, though he had to admit that Ness's gait was smoother than most.

"We'll see," replied Hap, smiling.

"You never know, Hap," said Joe with a laugh. "Jim here might be a better shot than you."

Hap nodded and laughed good-naturedly. He didn't want to discourage the young man. "Give it your best try, son. No one can ever fault you for that," he said.

Two hours later, they stopped at a swing station to change teams. This station wasn't set up for overnight stays and only had a barn owned by the freight company. A farmer and his wife who lived nearby took care of the horses.

Joe mentioned as they approached that the husband had once taken the stage all the way to town when a driver had been hurt. "I don't know if you've ever tried to manage a six-horse team like this," the driver continued, "but with three sets of reins, it takes most of us a week or two just to keep them on the road."

Two hours later, they stopped at another home station to eat lunch and change teams again. When they got back on the road, the men's mood changed. They knew they would be at the ravine within the hour.

"They'll probably hit us as we get to the gorge," Joe warned.

"Yeah," agreed Hap, "that way the sun will be in our eyes."

When they neared the ravine, Jim moved to the top of the stage, where he'd have more room to move around.

They had been passing through forest, breached only by a clearing for a homestead every now and then, but now the trees thinned and totally disappeared. They were at a higher elevation. Low, rocky hills broke the landscape, forcing the road to skirt around them.

As they rounded the final curve and Hap and Joe looked ahead to get their first glimpse of the gorge, Jim saw movement behind them. "I've got two riders back here," Jim announced to the others. "Do I wait for them to fire first or try a warning shot?"

"Are their weapons drawn?" asked Hap.

"Yep," Jim replied.

"Then you can fire on 'em, but you better let them get closer," advised Hap, looking over his shoulder. "There's no way you can hit 'em yet."

Jim rose to one knee, took aim, fired, and one man fell.

"Unbelievable!" breathed Hap.

Jim immediately fired again and dropped the other man. By now, he was hearing gunfire behind him. He turned to see two more riders heading toward them and closing the distance fast. Hap held his shotgun ready, waiting for the men to come into range. One of the men was firing a rifle, though the movement of his horse was interfering with his aim.

Jim stood on the rocking stage and braced his knee against the back of Hap's seat. Fully exposed, he ignored the bandits' oncoming fire. Jim leveled his rifle and took his shot, and the man with the rifle tumbled from his horse. Jim chambered another round and fired on the other rider, and he too fell. Joe glanced over his shoulder at Jim in disbelief. A second later, another shot came at them.

The sides of the gorge were clearly visible now. Jim and Hap saw a man on the rock face to their left perched on a ledge. Jim dropped to one knee, and Hap scooted closer to Joe to get out of his way. Joe heard the ratcheting sound as Jim chambered a round in his lever action rifle, then silence as he took aim. The man was hiding behind some rocks, so Jim waited. A shot rang out and tore through Jim's left side, but to Hap's amazement Jim didn't move. He grunted from the impact but didn't flinch. There was another report and a bullet whizzed by Jim's right arm, but still he didn't move. A moment later, just as Hap was afraid the bandit would center his aim and kill the young man, Jim fired, and the man fell.

"Got you, you bastard!" Jim muttered under his breath.

"My God!" cried Hap.

"What?" Joe asked.

"Jim was just shot and didn't even seem to notice!"

"Are you OK?" asked Joe, glancing back at Jim.

"Yeah, the son of a bitch just winged me," Jim replied evenly.

"Why don't you help him," Joe suggested to Hap, who was staring at Jim in amazement. "And both of you watch your language. No cussing on the stage."

"Oh, sorry," muttered Hap, coming to his senses.

Jim had pieces of cloth in his saddlebags for cleaning his weapons, so he took some and pushed them into the holes made by the bullet, as it had passed through him.

Hap noticed that Jim's jaw tightened as he forced the fabric into the wounds, but was surprised that the young man made no sound.

"We better keep our eyes open. There could be more of the bast—them," Jim advised, catching himself before he cursed again.

The road followed a stream running through the gully. The air became cool as they entered the shadow of the rocks and smelled of damp ground and moss that never saw the full light of day. Jim and Hap scanned the rocks and studied the shadows. Jim ignored the pain in his side as he looked for any sign of movement. A rabbit made its way to the stream for a drink, then froze as the stage passed. Up on the rocks, Jim saw a mountain goat gazing down at them in disdain. The young man knew then that no human was up on that side of the gorge, or the goat would have run. Even so, he stayed vigilant, in case someone was hiding farther down or on the other side waiting for their shot.

A moment later, they burst back into sunlight as the gorge fell behind them. Jim turned to make sure no one was following or hiding up on the sides of the rocks, while Hap checked on the passengers. They all breathed easier when the gorge disappeared out of sight, and were relieved that none of the passengers had been hurt.

"You're still bleeding," said Hap, looking at Jim's side.

Jim pulled out a longer piece of cloth and let Hap tie it around his middle, over his shirt.

"Is that tight enough?" Hap asked.

"It's fine," Jim replied.

"We'll be in Clayter before too long. Why don't you lie down? There shouldn't be any more trouble today," Hap suggested.

"I'm OK," Jim said, wiping the blood off his hands. Then he noticed his hands were bleeding too, so he took a couple more pieces of cloth from his saddlebags and bound the wounds.

"What happened there?" asked Hap.

"I was burned a few weeks ago."

"Wait a minute," said Joe. "Are you the boy I read about in the paper? The one that saved that woman and her children when their house burned down?"

"Do you mean Mrs. Petersen?" Jim asked.

"I think that was her name," answered Joe.

"I remember that, too," added Hap. "Was that you?"

"Yeah, that was me, but I didn't realize it had been in a newspaper," Jim replied unhappily. He had no desire to be well known.

"From what they said in the paper, you were hurt pretty bad," Joe recalled. "Are you sure you're all right? We don't mind if you want to lie down."

"I'm OK. The doctor's hardly let me out of bed since the fire," Jim stated, settling his back against a box.

Hap gave Jim some water, which he gratefully accepted. Joe offered to stop the stage so he could get inside out of the sun, but Jim refused. He promised to let the men know if he needed anything. The men nodded, taking him at his word, but Joe pushed the horses harder. Though Jim seemed unconcerned, Joe was worried the young man could bleed to death before they got to Clayter, and he was glad they'd get to the town before the next swing station.

It was early afternoon when they arrived in Clayter. Jim was still sitting on top of the coach, and hadn't even dozed off or made a single complaint since he had been hurt. The sheriff, Sam, and Martha were all waiting as the stage pulled in.

As Jim started to climb down from the coach, Hap called to the sheriff, whom he had met before. "You should have seen him! One of 'em shot him, but it was like he was made of stone. He didn't even flinch waiting for his shot. I've never seen anyone shoot like that! Five shots, five dead! With a rifle, from a moving stage!"

"I never should have let you go!" admonished Sam as he stepped forward and, along with the sheriff, helped Jim off the stage. Then Sam took Jim's saddlebags and Jim his weapons, which Hap handed down.

"Amazing!" breathed Hap, shaking his head at Jim.

"It's just a scratch," Jim said to the doctor. Then he turned to the sheriff. "There are five bodies east of the gorge. One is up on the southern face, at the far end."

"Take care!" shouted Joe as the stage pulled away.

"Thanks for the help!" cried Hap with a wave.

Jim waved in return.

"I'll get the undertaker," said the sheriff, turning to leave after seeing that Jim could walk. "I'm glad to see you're in one piece."

"He barely is," remarked Sam.

"Don't forget about the men's horses," Jim reminded the sheriff.

"We'll try to find them," the sheriff promised.

"And I'll need to go back for mine," Jim mentioned with a frown.

"Don't worry, I'll send someone for him," the sheriff promised.

"That may not work," Jim stated.

"We'll get him back here if we have to bribe him with apples at every mile," the sheriff assured him as he started to walk away. Then he turned back to Jim. "You killed all those men?" He didn't doubt the guard's word, just found it hard to believe.

"Yes, sir."

"We'll talk later," said the sheriff as he turned away again.

"You going to arrest me?" Jim asked him evenly.

"No. Not at all," answered the sheriff, turning back, surprised by the question. "Get yourself taken care of. You did a good job today!"

Jim nodded and headed toward the doctor's house, with Sam and Martha fussing over him.

"Why don't you let me carry those?" offered Sam, trying to take Jim's weapons from him.

"I'm OK," Jim insisted.

Sam let Jim carry the weapons rather than argue with him in the street.

Martha prepared a bath for Jim as soon as they arrived at the house while Sam examined the wound. Since it wasn't bleeding profusely, Sam bandaged it quickly and let Jim bathe, but the doctor stayed in the room in case Jim had any problems or collapsed. After he was clean, Jim wrapped himself in a sheet, and Sam took him into the operating room. Martha had laid a sheet over the table so it wouldn't be cold. Jim unwrapped himself and used that sheet to cover himself to his waist. Sam had just started cleaning the wound in Jim's side when there was a knock at the front door. Sam and Martha ignored it. If someone needed them, they could step inside and wait in the reception room. They heard the door open and shut. Then there was a knock on the operating room door.

"We're in a procedure!" Sam called out in irritation.

The door swung open partway, and a well-dressed man with a thick, neatly trimmed mustache stuck his head in. "I'm sorry to bother you, but you must be Jim Morgan," said the man, looking at Jim and stepping farther into the room.

Jim was facing the door, so he sat up on one elbow and gazed at the man.

"I'm Theodore Scofield. I run the freight office out of Dillard, and I just crossed paths with the two men you were riding with today. They told me what happened, and since my stage was passing through, I wanted to stop and meet you. That was an amazing bit of shooting you did."

"Thank you," Jim replied, still eyeing the man, whose mustache looked too big for his face. Jim supposed he grew it to look older and command respect.

Sam gently pushed Jim back down onto the table and began cleaning the wound again.

"Doesn't that hurt?" asked Mr. Scofield, watching the procedure.

When Jim didn't answer right away, Sam spoke for him. "It sure does. He just doesn't show it."

"How do you do that?" asked Scofield.

"Practice," Jim replied evenly, without a hint of humor. He wasn't joking.

"Well, as I said, I'm sorry to interrupt, but I only have a minute. I don't want to make my own stage late," Mr. Scofield added with a smile. "Like I said, I work out of the office in Dillard, but I wanted to stop by and offer you a job. I don't have time to go into all the particulars now, but I can tell you the pay is comparable to anything else you can find around here. And with your skills, I'd start you out at the highest rate. If you're interested, that is."

"I'm interested," Jim answered.

"Good!" said Scofield, smiling. "I'll get back this way in a couple of weeks and we can speak further. If you're out and about before then you can talk—"

"He won't be!" interrupted Sam. "He's going to stay in bed

this time if I have to chain him to it. And you better make it three weeks."

"Well, I'll see you here in three weeks, then. Take care, and sorry for the interruption, doctor." Mr. Scofield waved and shut the door behind him.

"Of all the nerve!" exclaimed Martha. "I hope you aren't really going to consider working for that man!"

"Yes, ma'am, I am," Jim replied.

"But you could get yourself killed! You nearly did today! And you're just a boy!" she cried.

"Martha!" said Sam, more sternly than Jim had ever heard him address his wife before. "I need you to concentrate on the job at hand."

Martha turned her attention to assisting her husband.

"This is more than just a scratch," announced Sam as he inspected the wound in Jim's side. "You're lucky. An inch closer to your middle, and there wouldn't be much I could do to save you."

After Jim was stitched and bandaged, Sam and Martha helped him to his room and into bed. When Martha returned a short time later with a light supper for him, Jim was already asleep. He stirred, and his eyes fluttered open, but they immediately shut again, and he didn't appear to wake up. She left the tray on the bedside table. A little while later, she returned and stayed with him through the night.

Jim slept until morning, when the pain woke him. He managed to eat a little breakfast at Martha's insistence. Then Sam inspected his wounds, ordering him to drink some water and telling Martha to give him a glass every hour. As Sam was finishing his instructions, there was a knock at the reception room door. They heard it open and the sheriff's voice asking if he could come in.

"We're in Jim's room," called Sam in reply.

"How are you doing?" asked the sheriff, looking at Jim as he entered. Then he nodded to Sam and Martha.

"Been better," Jim answered.

"We brought all the bodies back to town," said the sheriff, taking the chair Sam offered him. "I must say, you're a heck of a marksman. Each one was shot only once. Where did you shoot from?"

"The top of the stage."

The sheriff shook his head in disbelief. Then he asked, "How did you sleep?"

"Fine."

"Good. I wanted to come by and—well, I've known men much older than you who have had problems after something like this."

"I'm OK," Jim assured him.

"Have you ever killed anyone before, son?" asked the sheriff.

"Once. In self-defense."

"Did it bother you later?"

"Only that I didn't get a clean shot and it took him three days to die," Jim replied.

"With me, it's always something," said the sheriff, shaking his head. "The look in their eye, how they fall. Something. When my boys were little, sometimes one of them would have a bad dream, and my wife would always make them talk about it. That way they wouldn't have the dream again. I've found that helps with the nightmares we have when we're awake, too."

Jim gave him a long look. Then his gaze softened. "Thanks, Sheriff," he replied. "I didn't look at their faces. The one that got me was up on the rocks."

"What about when you were hurt?" asked the sheriff.

"All I could think about was making the shot so he couldn't hurt anyone else."

"Weren't you afraid?" asked Martha.

"No. Not for me," Jim replied. "I don't know why, but I was more concerned that Hap or Joe or one of the passengers would get hit."

The sheriff shook his head in disbelief. "You're an amazing young man." Then he shook Jim's hand and was about to leave the room when he turned back and told Jim about Ness. "He must have traveled all night, but he's safe and sound now."

"Thanks for letting me know," Jim said.

"I'll have your saddle and tack sent on the stage," promised the sheriff. "And I'll check on your horse later, too."

Jim thanked him.

"And I'll make sure he gets another apple," the sheriff added with a smile. "The stable boys gave him one this morning." Then he nodded to Sam and Martha, turned, and left.

Sam followed him out the front door and down the steps. "I'm worried about him," Sam commented after he and the sheriff were far enough from the house that Jim couldn't hear them.

"Why?" asked the sheriff, stopping in the yard and facing the doctor. "He's not healing?"

"Physically, he's fine. I'm worried because he just killed five men and it doesn't seem to bother him."

"Five men who were trying to kill him and everyone on that stage," the sheriff reminded the doctor. "He doesn't feel guilty if that's what you mean, and it's good that he doesn't. I've known men who felt bad even if they killed in self-defense, and they didn't last long in this kind of work."

"I'd prefer Jim not be in 'this kind of work.'"

"I know you're worried about him, but he's old enough to make his own decisions, and whether you like it or not, you're not his father. Unless you had him when you were ten. At least he's good at it. There are very few who could best him. I'll be back later and take him to see the bodies after the undertaker has them cleaned up."

"Do you think that's a good idea?" Sam asked.

"He killed them. He should see them. Plus, I want to know if they're the same men he saw in the saloon last night."

Early in the afternoon, the sheriff returned, and Jim and Sam accompanied him to the undertaker. There were two tables in the center of the room, with a body stretched out on one of them. There were more tables along the sides next to the walls, and these too held bodies. All of the bodies were naked without even a sheet over them. The undertaker was at one of the tables in the center of the room, and looked up as they entered.

"Sloan," said the sheriff, "this is the young man who's responsible for making your fortune this month."

"We'll see about that," Sloan answered. Then he greeted Jim with a nod. "You're a good shot. It looks like all of them died instantly, except the one on the rocks, and he didn't last more than a minute or so," added the undertaker, looking at the body on the table next to him.

"This is the one who shot you," said the sheriff to Jim, indicating the body. "Did you see him in town the night before?"

Jim nodded. He recognized him as the one who had been

dressed all in black.

"Couldn't you even cover them with something?" asked Sam. "Out of respect?"

"You don't have to wash the sheets," answered Sloan. "I won't know if I'll break even until after that sale tomorrow."

"What sale?" Jim asked.

"The sheriff here sells off all their possessions, and with luck it's enough to cover the cost of burying them. At least we found all the horses, that'll help," replied the undertaker.

Jim walked around the room, followed by Sam, and looked carefully at the bodies. "These are the men I saw," he announced, circling back to the sheriff.

"Thanks, Sloan," said the sheriff, turning to leave.

"Nice to meet you," Jim said to the undertaker, just as a matter of form.

"The pleasure was mine," replied the undertaker, with a smile that made Jim's skin crawl.

"I wish I knew if one of them was Carlos," muttered the sheriff when they were back out on the street.

"He wasn't with them," Jim answered. "I heard them talking about their boss."

"I didn't think he participated in this kind of thing," the sheriff remarked.

When they got to the corner, the sheriff took his leave, and Sam turned toward home, but Jim started to go the other way.

"Where are you going?" asked Sam.

"To check on Ness."

"Not today, young man. You're going back to bed."

Jim started to argue with him, but knew it would be useless and disrespectful, so he followed the doctor back to his house.

What no one knew was that Jim had gotten the attention of more than just Theodore Scofield. The loss of five of his men didn't go unnoticed by Carlos, and when he heard there would soon be a new guard riding the stage, he thought with a smile, *More food for the crows.*

5

PREPARATIONS

Jim rested for the next few days until, finally, Sam allowed him out of bed.

"Mind if I tag along?" Sam asked the young man as he dressed to go out to check on his horse.

"Are you trying to keep an eye on me?" Jim asked in return, half-seriously.

Sam smiled. "Do you blame me? I've known you less than two months, and you've already nearly killed yourself twice, not to mention the countless stitches I've put in you."

"Let me know what I owe you before I leave," Jim said seriously.

"Don't worry about that," replied Sam, putting his hand on the young man's shoulder. "Martha says you've paid us back already by helping her with the laundry and things. I should be angry with you," he smiled again. "Now she'll expect me to help, too."

When they got to the stable, Jim walked to Ness's stall, only to find it empty. Then he heard a familiar snort and turned to see Ness's head sticking out of another stall farther in.

"There you are," Jim said, pulling an apple out his pocket.

"He decided he wanted a bigger stall," explained one of the stable boys when he heard someone speaking to Ness. Then he stuck his head out of a stall on the other side of the barn and added, "Don't worry though, Robert said it won't cost you any more. We'll do just about anything to keep him happy."

"So he's been behaving?" Jim asked as he cut a piece from the apple with his pocketknife and fed it to the horse, patting his neck as he chewed.

"He's been great here lately. But he sure was happy to get back and get fed the other morning. Did he really come all that way on his own?"

Jim nodded. "He must have since he's here."

"I've never heard of a horse doing anything like that before, but I've also never taken care of a horse that does half the things he does."

Then they heard a commotion outside the door on the other end of the barn.

"That's Mr. Phelps's horse, Prankster," explained the boy. "Robert is trying to shoe him, but, as usual, he's not cooperating."

Jim fed Ness the rest of the apple and walked over to take a look, followed by Sam. They saw a beautiful and extremely skittish horse throwing his head. A very perturbed Robert stood back, tools in hand, waiting for the horse to calm down, while the animal nearly knocked his owner, who was holding the lead, off his feet.

"Need some help?" Jim asked.

"Only if you know how to shoe a horse," replied Robert, the blacksmith.

Jim turned toward the barn and called for the boy to bring a canvas bag from Ness's stall.

The boy quickly obeyed.

"Well, I'll say," murmured the blacksmith, as Jim took out his farrier's apron and tools. They carried a brand of his initials, like his saddle.

Jim walked up to the horse, talking to him softly, and rubbed his neck. The animal calmed, and Jim had the owner walk the horse around so he could observe his gait. Then Jim walked to the rear of the animal, gliding his hand along the horse's body and then down one of the animal's hind feet. At the pressure from Jim's hand, the horse obediently lifted his foot, so Jim set to work under the critical eye of the smith. When Jim was done with that foot, he moved to the other hind foot. Again he talked to the horse as he moved his hand along the animal's leg, and again the horse cooperated fully.

"I can't believe it," commented Robert, speaking softly. "He nearly killed me the last time I shoed him."

"You know as well as I do, if you're nervous, he will be, too," Jim replied calmly.

"I know, but it's hard to relax when you've nearly gotten the stuffing kicked out of you," remarked the smith.

As Jim was finishing the last hoof, the smith noticed a red stain on the young man's shirt. "You're bleeding. I forgot you were shot a few days ago. I can finish up."

"I'm OK," Jim replied, continuing his work.

"I shouldn't have let you do this," said Robert.

"The animal needed to be shod. I'm OK."

"I bet Dr. Sam will disagree," Robert commented.

The doctor was on the other side of the horse and hadn't seen Jim's side yet.

When Jim was done, the smith turned to Mr. Phelps. "Pay the man," he said, motioning to Jim.

"Thank you," said Mr. Phelps to Jim as he handed him the money. "I've never seen him behave so well before."

"Jim's fearless. That's why," remarked the smith, patting Jim on the back. "He was shot the other day defending that stage."

"I heard about that. I hope you didn't hurt yourself doing this." Then Phelps saw the blood on Jim's shirt.

"Just a scratch," Jim replied, following his gaze.

"It was a little more than that," corrected Sam, walking over, taking out his handkerchief, and stuffing it inside Jim's shirt.

"Just oozing a little," Jim said quietly to the doctor, who shook his head.

Phelps nodded his thanks and led his horse away.

Jim turned to the smith and offered to give him some of the money.

"Keep it. You earned it," Robert insisted. "You know, I could use a good farrier."

"Sorry. I've been offered a job with the freight company," Jim replied.

"Well, if you want to earn some extra money, and the doctor doesn't mind, just come by and I'll put you to work."

"Thank you," Jim said.

They shook hands, and the smith showed him where he could wash up.

Afterwards, Jim and Sam stopped by Ness's stall again so Jim could put his tools away and give the animal another pat. Then, as they headed back to Sam's, they passed the Bowers's clothing shop. Jim indicated he wanted to go inside. Sam peeked at Jim's wound, and, since the bleeding seemed to have stopped, he nodded and followed the young man through the door.

Julietta was behind the counter with her back to them. Even though there was a bell on the door, she didn't look up when they walked in, apparently too absorbed in her work to notice them. Sam pointed to the back of the shop where her husband was cutting fabric on a large table, and he and Jim headed toward him. Albert greeted them with a smile and Jim ordered pants and shirts, two of each.

As he was taking the measurements, Albert noticed the blood on Jim's shirt. "Are you all right?"

"He would be if he'd stay quiet," Sam replied for Jim.

"I'll make you a few more than you ordered and keep them here, just in case," Albert said. "It looks like you'll need them, and I'll make sure to give you room to grow. He is still growing, isn't he?" he asked Sam.

"He'll get a few more inches," the doctor replied. "You might even get taller than me," Sam added with a smile. At six feet, he was taller than most men.

"I'll have them ready in a few days, and I'll give you a discount, too," said the tailor.

"You don't have to do that," Jim replied, taking money from his pocket.

"I insist. So keep your money for now."

Jim thanked him, and he and Sam took their leave. As they left, Julietta still didn't look up.

"Goodbye!" said Sam to her as he shut the door behind them. Then, when they were back out on the boardwalk, he remarked, "That was odd."

"What was?" Jim asked.

"Julietta didn't even speak. She acted as if we weren't even there!"

"Probably because of me," Jim said.

"Why do you say that?" asked Sam.

"I've seen it before, after I've killed someone."

"But you were defending the stage."

"Doesn't make any difference," Jim stated. Then he sighed. "I guess it's because of my age, or she thinks I'm no better than a hired gun."

They heard a child call out to Jim and saw Paul, the youngest Petersen boy, running across the street toward them. Suddenly the child fell, and Jim saw a young rider on horseback racing up the street straight toward the boy. Jim dashed out into the road. He didn't have time to lift the child out of the way of the running animal, so he leaned over Paul, shielding him from the animal's hooves with his own body. The horse balked, rose up on its hind feet, turned, and came down just inches from Jim and the boy. Jim looked up, glaring at the rider. He helped Paul to his feet and gently pushed the boy behind him. He felt the child cling to his leg as he reached up and grabbed the horse's bridle.

"Let go of my horse!" the young rider shouted.

"You nearly killed this boy!" Jim growled, eyes flashing.

The young rider, unfazed, hit Jim on the arm with his riding crop. Still holding the bridle with his left hand, Jim grabbed the youth's wrist with his right and squeezed it until the rider cried out and dropped the crop.

"Willet!" called the sheriff as he strode up. "You can't whip a man like a horse! I've told you before not to ride that animal full tilt through town. Now get down and walk him from now on."

Willet didn't move, so Jim twisted his arm and pulled him from his saddle, then released him, letting him fall onto his hands and knees in the dirt. Willet picked up his crop and flew at Jim. Jim let go of the bridle and turned his body to face his attacker and shield Paul. Jim held the boy against him, keeping him behind him, as he grabbed Willet by the throat. Willet began hitting Jim on the arm with the crop, but Jim refused to let go. Jim held Willet firmly, but he wasn't trying to kill him.

"Willet, I wouldn't mess with Jim here," cautioned the sheriff. "He's already killed five men this week. I doubt he'd worry about a sixth."

Willet stopped hitting Jim, and Jim released him.

"From now on, you walk that animal in town," ordered the sheriff, "or I'll throw you in jail."

"On what charge?" Willett demanded.

"Attempted murder," stated the sheriff.

Willet sniffed and stomped off, leading his horse.

"I feel sorry for that boy's mother," commented the sheriff as Willet walked away.

"I feel sorry for his horse," said Jim, looking at smears of blood, not his own, the crop had left on his shirt. Then he lifted Paul and carried him out of the road. "Are you OK?" he asked the child as he and the sheriff joined Sam back on the boardwalk.

The child nodded mutely.

"Are *you* OK?" the doctor asked Jim, looking at his arm.

"I'm fine. It's not my blood."

"I'm going to follow Willet and make sure he got the message," said the sheriff, taking his leave.

Mrs. Petersen came running up to them. "Someone told me what happened!" she cried, taking her child from Jim's arms. "Thank you!" she said, hugging Paul, who buried his head in her neck and began to cry. "How can I ever thank you enough for all you've done for my family?"

"It was Willet," whimpered Paul, looking up and drying his eyes.

"That boy's always been trouble," replied Mrs. Petersen. "I sent Paul to find you to remind you about dinner tonight," she explained.

"Oh, sorry," Sam sighed with a shake of his head. "I forgot to tell them."

"I'm sorry I haven't invited you earlier, but it's taken us a while to get settled," Uma explained.

"How's that going?" asked Sam.

"Oh, fine. Mrs. Canady is very easy to get along with, and loves the children. It was so nice of her to let us live with her. So can you come tonight, between seven thirty and eight? Mrs. Canady doesn't like to eat too early."

Jim looked at the doctor.

"We'd be delighted," replied Sam. "And I'll make sure to tell Martha this time."

"We'll see you then," said Uma. Then she looked at Jim. "I have a surprise for you. And thank you again," she added, giving his arm a squeeze. Then she noticed the smears of blood on his sleeve, and looked worried.

"I'm OK," Jim assured her.

Uma looked to Sam, who nodded, so she too gave a nod as she turned.

"Thank you!" called Paul, as his mother carried him away.

"Well, Martha will be glad to not have to cook tonight," remarked Sam, smiling. "What's wrong?" he asked, noticing a troubled look on Jim's face.

"This is my last shirt," Jim replied, looking at the dirt and blood on the garment.

"Don't worry, I can loan you a few until yours are ready."

"Thanks. I'll try not to mess them up."

"You *are* hard on clothes," commented Sam with a laugh as they continued toward his house.

When they got back to his office, Sam led Jim into the examination room. "Now, let's see how much damage you've done to those stitches," said the doctor.

After Jim was restitched and bandaged, Sam insisted he rest before dinner. Jim lay down on the bed and was soon fast asleep. Martha woke him late in the afternoon so he could get ready. While Jim took a quick bath, careful to keep his stitches dry, she laid out one of Sam's shirts. Jim thanked her when he saw it and began to dress as she left the room.

The evening was clear, with hardly a cloud in the sky, as they walked toward the house Mrs. Petersen was now sharing with Mrs. Canady. Jim trailed behind Sam and Martha, who were holding hands. He gazed at the rose-colored sun as it neared the horizon and breathed deeply.

Martha glanced behind her. She noticed Jim's expression was peaceful and as close to a smile as she had seen. She nudged her husband, and Sam looked back as well.

"Beautiful sunset, isn't it?" he asked their young friend.

"Yes, sir, it is," Jim replied.

Sam slowed and held out his hand. He pulled Jim to him and continued walking with his arm resting on the young man's shoulder. "I think there's a bit of the romantic in you, my boy," he smiled.

"Why? Because I can appreciate a sunset?" Jim asked.

"Look around you," Sam replied, motioning to the people walking past on the street. "How many of them have even noticed it?"

Jim glanced around them and saw most of the people were

too preoccupied with their own concerns to take time to look at the sky.

"That's because they expect to see another one," Jim stated.

Sam and Martha exchanged a glance and continued walking as Jim kept his eyes on the sunset.

Mrs. Canady was an older woman whose husband had passed away years before. He'd been one of the few honest business-men in the area and had made his money through real estate and water rights. The house was one of the nicest and largest homes in town. It had two stories, with a vestibule leading into what Mrs. Canady referred to as a salon. There was also a dining room, kitchen, and pantry, as well as a small room her husband had used as an office, which she now kept locked. Upstairs were five spacious bedrooms.

Mary, Uma's oldest daughter, answered the door to Sam's knock and showed them into the salon. It was a large room, comfortably furnished, with an overstuffed chair that Mrs. Canady occupied near the fireplace. A small fire was going even though the weather was warm. There was a settee across from the chair and a couch behind that against the wall, and there were various other chairs around the room.

Mrs. Canady waved to Martha and Sam with a smile, but she stood as Mary introduced her to Jim and extended her hand. "It's a pleasure to finally get to meet you, Mr. Morgan."

"Thank you," Jim replied, taking her hand gently, but then strengthening his grip, as hers was as firm and strong as a man's.

She and her husband hadn't always been rich, and her body, though no longer lean, was still strong from earlier years of hard work. Age had softened her middle and shortened her gaze, but she still had her "man sense," as she called it. "Some men have horse sense," she often said, "but I have man sense."

"Please call me Jim, ma'am," he said as Mrs. Canady settled back into her chair.

"All right. I'll call you Jim if you'll agree not to call me ma'am. It makes me feel so old," remarked Mrs. Canady, still smiling.

Jim nodded.

"Sit here where I can see you," she said to Jim, motioning to the settee. "Mary, you sit next to him, it's not right for a young man to sit on a settee alone."

Mary obeyed with a shy smile. "Mama may need me in

the kitchen."

"I told your mother you would be in here this evening. Plus, as organized as she is, I'm sure she has everything under control. She can always ask the boys to help her if she needs it," Mrs. Canady added with a smile and a wink.

Mary laughed.

"Why, you are a very handsome young man," commented Mrs. Canady, turning her attention back to Jim.

"Thank you," Jim replied, looking down.

"I heard you were hurt again the other day. I trust you're healing properly and feeling better," she said, moving her glance from Jim to Dr. Thorne, who was sitting next to Martha on the couch behind Jim and Mary.

"He would if he'd keep his stitches in," replied Sam.

"What happened?" asked Mrs. Canady, looking worried.

"He insisted on shoeing a horse today and tore a couple stitches out of his side."

"Why were you doing that? I thought we had a blacksmith to do such things," Mrs. Canady scolded gently, looking at Jim.

"He was having problems with the animal, so I helped him," Jim replied.

"It looked like the horse was going to kill the smith," remarked Sam, "but Jim here calmed the animal down and got him shod no problem."

"You're a farrier then?" asked Mrs. Canady.

"Not formally, but I know how to do it."

"Smithing too?" Mrs. Canady asked.

"Yes, ma—" Jim stopped himself from adding the appellation, and Mrs. Canady smiled and nodded.

Paul bounded into the room and threw his arms around Jim's neck.

"You look none the worse for wear," Jim said, placing the child on his knee.

Mrs. Canady noticed how tenderly Jim handled the child, but she also noticed that he didn't smile, that only his eyes softened.

"Mama told me to tell everyone supper is ready," announced Paul.

"Jim, would you mind helping an old woman?" asked Mrs. Canady.

Jim set Paul on his feet, helped Mrs. Canady up from her

chair, and escorted her into the dining room. Mrs. Canady took the chair at the head of the table closest to the salon and placed Jim on her right, with Mary next to him and Sam and Martha on her left. The rest of the children chose their own places after much running around. They finally settled down when their mother entered carrying a large tray that she set on a sideboard against the wall.

Then Uma hurried back into the kitchen and returned with a turkey on a platter. The children could hardly contain their excitement as Uma placed the dishes on the table. Jim gazed at the huge turkey, its skin cooked to a golden brown. There were also four large bowls, each filled almost to overflowing with mashed potatoes, green beans cooked with ham, squash steamed with onion, and sweet corn cut off the cob and swimming in butter. Then Uma set two large baskets full of biscuits next to the vegetables. She placed four bowls containing butter whipped with honey down the middle of the table so no one would have trouble reaching one of them.

Jim wasn't accustomed to large meals, and the sight of all the food left him speechless.

"Sam, would you say the blessing?" asked Mrs. Canady.

"I'd be honored," Sam replied.

Then everyone took the hand of the person next to them and bowed their heads. The handholding took Jim by surprise, so Mary and Mrs. Canady had to give him a second. After everyone bowed their heads, Sam proceeded with the prayer.

"Heavenly Father, we thank you that we can be together with friends and family this evening. We thank you for keeping Jim safe so he can be with us, and we trust that you will continue to watch over him in the future. And we thank you for this food, for the nourishment of our bodies and us to your service. Amen."

Mrs. Canady and Mary each gave Jim's hand a slight squeeze before releasing it, and Jim quickly tried to reciprocate so they wouldn't think him rude.

"Dr. Sam, I hope you wouldn't mind slicing the turkey," said Uma. "I always seem to make a mess when I try to do it."

"As a surgeon, I suppose I'm up to the task. You haven't had any complaints, have you?" he asked, looking at Jim and smiling.

"No, sir," Jim replied disconcertedly. He wasn't sure if Sam was just joking or really wanted an answer.

The others laughed. Jim tensed, and Mrs. Canady patted his hand, sensing his displeasure. Jim glanced at her, his eyes flashing for a second, until her warm smile comforted him.

Jim waited until Uma served everyone before he started eating, even though Mrs. Canady had given him the first plate. He was glad Martha had reminded him about manners on the way over, and she had reassured him again that his were quite good, which made him feel more comfortable.

"I hope you'll be staying in town after you're well," said Mrs. Canady after everyone had a plate and a chance to eat a few bites.

"I'm going to work for the freight company," Jim replied.

Mrs. Canady gave him a searching look, then commented, "So you must have talked with Theodore Scofield."

"He came by the day I was shot."

"He barged into my operating room, you mean," Sam interjected.

"Theodore's a good man, if a bit impetuous," explained Mrs. Canady. "I've met him through my son, Willard. He's a lawyer in St. Louis, and Mr. Peck, one of the owners of the freight company, has engaged my Willard more than once. What are you going to do for the P & D Freight Company?" she asked Jim.

"The same thing I did the other day, as far as I know."

"Oh, my!" breathed Mrs. Canady with concern. "Does Theodore know how young you are? Uma mentioned that you are only fifteen."

"He didn't ask my age."

"Well, if this is what you want to do, I wouldn't mention it. But if Theodore asks, tell the truth, or he'll never trust you again."

"I wasn't planning on misleading him," Jim assured her.

"I didn't think you would," replied Mrs. Canady, patting Jim's hand. "But at your age, shouldn't you still be in school?"

"I finished all my lessons," Jim stated.

"So early?" Mrs. Canady asked.

"I lived with a teacher," Jim replied with a slight edge to his voice. His eyes flashed as he lowered them.

"I just hope you're careful," Mrs. Canady said, sensing he didn't want to talk about his past.

"I certainly hope he will be, too," commented Martha. "I keep telling him he's only a boy and should act like one, but he doesn't want to listen."

Jim raised his eyes and met Martha's gaze. "I mean no disrespect."

Mrs. Canady noticed in Jim's eyes the same softness he had displayed to Paul. She patted his hand again. "How do you feel about this, Dr. Sam?"

"Jim and I haven't discussed it yet. I'm not his father, so I don't have any authority over him, but, as his physician, I'm concerned. I'm thinking about accompanying him when he goes to Dillard to make sure they have a good doctor in town. You wouldn't mind that, would you, Jim?"

"No, sir," Jim replied. Then he took a deep breath and spoke evenly. "I appreciate everyone's concern, but I don't plan on getting myself killed. I just want to do some good is all."

"That's very admirable," said Mrs. Canady, giving Jim's hand a squeeze. "You've sure done a lot of good here."

"Yes, you have," added Uma. "I thank God every day that you happened to be riding by that night, or my children and I wouldn't be alive."

"And he saved me today," piped up Paul.

"Yes, he certainly did, didn't he?" Mrs. Canady smiled at the child.

"I'm thankful for that as well," said Uma to Jim. "Also, since you were the reason I was able to sell the goods on the wagon, I'm going to give you most of the money."

"That's not necessary, ma'am," Jim assured her.

"But I insist. It's the least I can do."

Jim looked down and sighed quietly.

Mrs. Canady patted his hand again. "You're embarrassing him, Uma. Let's not talk about this right now," she admonished gently.

Uma nodded.

When they were done eating, Uma and her children cleared away the plates. Then they brought out four pies and set them on the table.

"Two are apple and two are blueberry," announced Uma. Then she looked at Jim and asked him which he would like.

"Either is fine, ma'am" he replied.

"Why don't you give him a piece of each," suggested Mrs. Canady with a smile. "And I'll have the same."

Jim rarely had sweets, so he savored each bite of his slices of pie. He could feel Mrs. Canady's eyes on him often throughout the meal, but, surprisingly, she didn't make him feel uncomfortable.

After everyone was finished and the dishes were cleared away, Jim accompanied Mrs. Canady to the salon. Mrs. Canady had Jim sit on the settee again while Uma and Mary shooed the children upstairs to put them to bed and Sam and Martha stepped outside to get some air. This left Jim alone with Mrs. Canady.

She gave him another searching look, and Jim met her gaze.

"I can see that you've had a difficult life already," she commented after studying him a moment.

Jim's brow wrinkled in confusion.

"Forgive me, it's a talent—or curse—that I have. My late husband always said that I could see right into a person's soul. He never did business with anyone until I had met them first. I could always tell who to trust. That's one reason I'm fairly well off today."

Jim nodded.

"It's a shame you didn't have a mother to fuss over you."

"How did you know?" Jim asked, his voice low.

Mrs. Canady took his hand and replied, "You looked embarrassed when I complimented you on your looks. If you'd had a mother, she would have told you every day how handsome you are and probably made you vain," she added with a smile.

Jim looked down.

"Don't be ashamed of your past, Jim. It's what's made you who you are today."

Jim looked at her, his eyes starting to flicker. She gazed into them and felt as though she was staring into a fire. For the first time, she saw through the wall of anger and distrust that shielded his soul, and sensed something that troubled her deeply. She saw a chasm, a darkness in him, a depth of pain and hopelessness. The flame in his eyes came from something lying in a torporific state at the base of the abyss. Something he hadn't faced himself, something that could destroy him if he ever did.

She remembered reading about the angel called Apollyon,

Abaddon in the Hebrew. The angel who held the keys to the bottomless pit. *What is more to hell than the soul of this man?* she wondered. She prayed her instincts were wrong, or that whatever it was would remain dormant, imprisoned, so this man before her, this boy who truly only wanted to do good, would thrive rather than wither in his own despair.

His eyes were bluer than any she'd ever seen, and she looked deeply into them as she spoke, hoping to soothe the blackness and quell the torment. "You'll always have friends here, never forget that. I've always said that actions are the only truth in this life. Words mean nothing. You've shown all of us the good in you, and we'll always be thankful for what you've done."

All Jim could do was nod. He was unaccustomed to kind words, as well as the emotions they stirred within him.

Then the others joined them, and Mrs. Canady released his hand.

"Uma, I think I'll take some sherry," announced Mrs. Canady, smiling. "Dr. Sam?"

"Why, thank you," Sam replied.

"I know you're a little young, but would you like some?" she asked Jim.

"Thank you," Jim answered, still thinking about what she'd said.

"Is that all right with you, Doctor?" Mrs. Canady asked Sam.

"Sure. From the way I saw him drink whiskey a few weeks ago, I'd say he's had alcohol before."

"May I have some, Mrs. Canady?" asked Mary.

"That's up to your mother, dear."

Uma shook her head.

"Martha?" asked Mrs. Canady.

"No, thank you."

"Get a glass for yourself as well, if you'd like some," said Mrs. Canady to Uma as she left to go into the kitchen.

Mary sat on the settee beside Jim, trying to hide her embarrassment over her mother treating her like a child.

Mrs. Canady grinned at her conspiratorially and whispered. "I'll give you a sip of mine when your mother isn't looking."

Mary smiled.

Uma returned a few minutes later with the bottle and glasses. After serving Mrs. Canady, Sam, and Jim, she poured a glass for herself.

Mrs. Canady watched Jim as he tasted the sherry. "Do you like it?" she asked him.

"Yes, thank you. It's sweeter than whiskey."

Mrs. Canady laughed.

Light conversation filled the rest of the evening. Sam told a few funny stories. One of them was about an unnamed patient who had hurt himself running just for enjoyment.

"I can't imagine anyone running like that for no apparent reason," commented Martha.

"I do sometimes," Jim replied quietly.

"Do you?" asked Mrs. Canady. "My husband used to as well. He said it cleared his head."

"Why do you do that?" asked Martha, looking at Jim. "Is it fun?"

"Not really," Jim replied. "Sometimes I just have to, and when I'm on the road, it saves my horse."

"Do you run in those?" Mrs. Canady asked, looking at his boots.

"Yes," Jim answered softly. They were all he had, and he realized with surprise that he felt ashamed because they were worn.

"That's got to be hard on your feet," remarked Mrs. Canady.

"I'm used to it, I guess," Jim said, glancing at the door and wishing for escape. He felt a tightness in his chest and longed to be outside where he could breathe.

"I'll have the cobbler make you something more suitable for running. They'll be better for your feet," stated Mrs. Canady.

"Thank you. But it's not necessary," Jim replied softly. Then he took a deep, quiet breath, and wondered if he should explain that he considered food and shoes for his horse more important than having either for himself.

Mary sensed his unease and brushed his hand with her own.

Jim pulled away slightly and then realized he'd been gripping the settee. He glanced down, hoping no one would see the impressions his fingers left in the velvet.

"I insist," said Mrs. Canady. She too noticed Jim's discomfort, and an expression of worry crossed her face. Then she brightened and changed the subject. "I've heard the children talking about your horse."

This led into another series of stories as Sam told about Ness and had everyone, except Jim, laughing.

Mrs. Canady noticed that, even though he was amused, Jim never laughed or smiled. The only sign of his amusement was a change in his gaze.

When it was time for Sam, Martha, and Jim to leave, Mrs. Canady took Jim's hand. "Remember what I said earlier."

"Thank you," Jim replied.

Then she insisted on giving him a hug.

Uma hugged him too and then held out an envelope. "This is for you," she said.

Jim shook his head. "No, ma'am."

"But I insist," said Uma. "For all you've done."

"No, please," Jim stated softly but firmly in return.

Mrs. Canady saw rigid determination in the young man's eyes, but underneath that, something resembling fear. She took Uma's arm as the younger woman started to force the envelope into Jim's hand. "Let him be for now. Don't let the evening end disagreeably."

Uma nodded. "Thank you again for all you've done," she said to Jim, and he nodded in return.

Sam and Martha thanked her for a wonderful meal, and they took their leave.

Later that night, after he was alone in bed in the dark, Jim thought about what Mrs. Canady had said about his past. He recalled Paul Townsend, the teacher he'd lived with, scolding him about his language. Paul had even made a list of the words he was never to utter, and Jim had used it to learn to read. He remembered all the afternoons he'd spent sitting at the kitchen table doing his lessons after finishing at the blacksmith's. He'd completed eight years of school in just under four by studying every day, including weekends and through the summer.

After that first day of school, when he'd gotten in a fight and everyone had found out about his scars, he'd never gone back. The parents were afraid he'd hurt their children because, along with the scars, Paul and the children had seen the knife he kept hidden in his clothes. Hiding it was easy, because his clothes were always too big. Everything he wore had been cast off by men where he'd lived before.

He remembered all the times he'd dreamed of shoving the blade into the chest of the man who hurt him. He never did because of what the man told him. "You use that on me, boy, and the other men will skin you alive with it." He had no reason not to believe him.

He sighed and shook his head as he pondered the things Mrs. Canady had said to him. *If she only knew,* he mused. Then he drifted off to sleep.

The cobbler came by the next day and took some measurements. When he returned a few days later, he had a pair of flat-soled running shoes for Jim and a new pair of boots, compliments of Mrs. Canady. Jim wanted to thank her. He stopped by to see her, but Mrs. Canady was out, so he left his message with Uma, who insisted he take some biscuits back with him.

A couple of nights later, Jim awoke with a gasp, sucking in air as though he'd been underwater or nearly suffocated. This happened every now and then, and he always felt an uncontrollable urge to get outside. Then he felt compelled to run.

He put on the new running shoes and quietly made his way through the kitchen and out the back door without awakening Sam or Martha. As soon as he was outside, he breathed in deeply, relishing the sensation of air in his lungs. It was the middle of the night, so there were no lights in any of the windows. The lanterns used to light the streets were out as well.

Jim had become familiar with the town from his walks with Martha, and he headed straight out through the backyard. He picked his way carefully through the darkness, lit only by a partial moon, until he reached the open area around the edge of town. Then he turned west so the moon would be in front of him and began to run, following the contours of the town. His side still hurt from the bullet wound, but the pain wasn't enough to deter him. He had no idea what distance he would have to cover to make a full circuit, but was confident he could manage it with ease and get back before daylight.

He enjoyed the exercise, and didn't contemplate what could drive him to get up in the middle of the night and go out for a run in the dark. The movement of his body lulled his mind, freeing it from emotion and memory, and the night forced him to use his full concentration to make his way relatively safely through the darkness. He ran for over an hour, continuing to run even after the pain in his side became excruciating, pushing himself to complete the circuit, willing himself not to stop. He arrived back at Sam's an hour before dawn, dirty and bloody from falls he'd taken in the darkness and sweating from exertion. He returned to his room, stepped through the door, and froze, sensing something in the shadows.

"Where have you been?" Sam's voice asked from a chair in the corner.

"I went for a run," Jim replied, still out of breath.

Sam lit the lantern he had set on the end table next to the chair. He believed the young man when he saw the state of his clothes and his person.

"I'll get my bag while you get cleaned up," Sam sighed, rising.

When the doctor returned, Jim had stripped and was washing at the basin. After the young man had cleaned and dried himself, Sam examined his gunshot wound first and then turned his attention to the damage done during the run.

"Next time, run during the day," Sam advised.

"I never want to then."

"So you prefer running into things or tripping over them in the dark?"

"I just have to get outside sometimes, and running helps me sleep."

As Sam bandaged the last of the wounds, Jim thanked him and apologized for waking him.

"I usually listen outside your door at some point in the night to make sure you're OK," Sam replied as Jim climbed into bed. Then the doctor pulled the covers up to the boy's chin, returned to his own bed, and they both slept for a little while.

Later that day, Albert arrived with numerous suits of clothes for Jim, along with a riding coat that was warm and repelled water as well. Jim protested that he had not ordered the extra clothes, but Albert told him Mrs. Canady had ordered them for him. Jim immediately dropped by to thank her, but again she was out, and this time he returned with an apple pie Uma nearly forced on him.

Since Mr. Scofield had returned and he was leaving for Dillard the next day, Jim left her a note and bade Uma and the children farewell. To his relief, Uma didn't try to give him anything other than the pie. He didn't like feeling as though he owed anyone anything. He wasn't happy that Mrs. Canady had put him in that position, but, for some reason, her kindness only mildly annoyed him and, like Sam and Martha's, didn't frighten him.

What Jim wouldn't discover for another few days, when he walked in to deposit his first paycheck, was that Mrs. Canady had opened an account in his name at the bank in Dillard and deposited five hundred dollars into it. He immediately wrote her and thanked her for her generosity, though he supposed there had been some mistake about the amount. A few days later, he received her reply, in which she assured him the amount was correct and told him that if at any time he needed more, or anything else she could provide, to let her know. Jim realized she must have sensed his suspicions, because she added a postscript: "I expect nothing in return, young man. Think of me as the generous aunt you never had." If he'd been able, Jim would have smiled.

6

DILLARD

The next morning, Jim and Sam left for the town of Dillard, where the freight office was located. Sam and Theodore rode inside the stage while Jim rode Ness and kept an eye out for any signs of trouble. The trip was short and uneventful. They arrived in Dillard in late morning, and while Theodore showed Jim around the office and introduced him to the men working there Sam ventured out to see the local doctor.

When Sam arrived at the man's small office, the doctor was out, but a sign on the door said he would be back shortly and to go on in and sit down. Sam entered. The office was really the front room of a small house. Though this in itself wasn't unusual, the office was cluttered and grimy, with what looked like a barber's chair in the middle of the floor, a few shelves along the walls, and a small desk in the corner. Sam decided to see if there was a separate treatment room, and, finding none, he amused himself by looking around the office.

He found one outdated medical book that contained general anatomy and guidelines for a few procedures, most of which had been abandoned twenty years before. The only medicines he discovered were a bottle of laudanum and a stomach remedy like that sold by traveling merchants. He saw no instruments or other equipment of any kind. Finishing his inspection, he settled into a chair to wait.

The doctor arrived a little while later. The man was young, too young to be a doctor, Sam thought. His urgency of manner and the somber ostentation of his dress, which, other than his white shirt, was all black, suggested a person more concerned with appearing to be a doctor than actually working as one.

"Can I help you?" asked the young man.

"I'm Dr. Samuel Thorne," said Sam, offering his hand. "I traveled here with a friend and patient of mine who is taking a job with the freight company, and I thought I'd stop by and see who is representing the medical profession in this town."

"Dr. Crane. Jack Crane," replied the young man, forcing a smile and shaking Sam's hand. "Pleased to meet you."

"Is this where you treat your patients?"

"Either here or in their home."

"Do you have any patients you're treating now? I'd like to see them. Maybe learn something," added Sam tactfully.

"I have three here in town right now," replied Jack. Then he scurried to his desk and nervously rummaged through some papers, as though he was looking for something important. "I just got done with them and they're resting now. Perhaps if you come back after lunch I can take you to them."

"That would be fine. Around two, then?"

"That sounds good," replied Jack, trying not to look relieved. "I'd stay and chat, but I have an appointment out of town. I'd invite you to come, but I have to treat her for hysterics, so another doctor would make things—awkward," he concluded with a wink, hoping to appear nonchalant.

"I understand," replied Sam, putting on his hat. "I'll see you at two. Thank you, Doctor."

Jack nodded as Sam left.

Sam walked back to the freight company, wondering if Dr. Crane was really a doctor at all. He sat and waited in the front office until Jim and Theodore came down the steps.

"Well, did you meet our Dr. Crane?" Theodore asked Sam.

"Briefly. I'm going to meet him at two and take a look at a few of his patients."

"They're probably my men," said Theodore. "If you get to see them, let me know how they're doing. He keeps their doors locked and doesn't let anyone in. Maybe it's just me, but that has always struck me as a bit odd."

"It is odd," replied Sam, his concern deepening. Theodore showed them to the outside door. "Give me a minute and I'll take you two to lunch," he said. Then he strode to one of the windows, spoke to the man behind the counter about a schedule change, and rejoined them. "One of the saloons has the best food in town, and it has a two drink maximum during the day, so respectable people can eat in peace," Theodore stated as he opened the door and they stepped onto the boardwalk. "No dancing girls either to anger a wife," he added with a smile.

They had a pleasant lunch with Theodore, who insisted they call him Ted. While they ate, he and Sam, who had both lived in large cities, enjoyed swapping stories comparing that to small-town living. After lunch, Sam and Jim left to keep Sam's appointment with the doctor, while Ted returned to the freight company. At the doctor's office, they found the door standing open. They were about to go in when a man called to them.

"Looking for the doctor?"

"Yes," replied Sam.

"He rode out of town about an hour ago. Looked like he'd packed a bag and was in quite a hurry," said the man, joining them outside the office.

"Did he say when he would be back?" asked Sam.

"No, I just saw him as he rode by."

"Thank you," replied Sam as the man gave a nod and continued on his way.

"I better let Ted know," said Jim. "Something doesn't seem right about this."

A few minutes later, Jim returned with Ted, and all three of them entered the doctor's office.

"It looks to me like he isn't coming back," remarked Ted after looking through the desk drawers and examining the few remaining items in the room.

"Same here," Sam replied.

"All the drawers are empty in the bedroom," announced Jim as he stepped out a door at the back of the house. "All he left was some rags on the floor."

"Do you know where his patients are?" asked Sam.

"They're in their rooms," answered Ted. "I'll take you to them. It'll be a good chance for Jim here to see the rooming houses."

They walked outside and followed Ted down the street.

"There are three rooming houses in town besides the hotel, which is where I live. And the brothels, of course," Ted explained. "To be honest, the first house we'll go to is cheaper than the hotel, cleaner, and the food is better, too. One of the other rooming houses is for respectable women only, and the third you'll see in a few minutes."

"If the rooming house is better than the hotel, then why don't you move?" asked Sam.

"I was planning to. I've built a house, but my fiancée wrote me a few months ago and called off the wedding. She decided she didn't want to move from Kansas City, and since the freight company doesn't have an office there, we've parted company."

"I'm sorry to hear that," Sam sympathized.

"Sorry," Jim said.

"I'm not as upset as I should be, I suppose," Ted admitted. "To be honest, it was more her parents' idea than mine. I just wish she'd decided before I spent all that money on a house I won't be using."

"Why don't you just live there?" Jim asked as they walked.

"I don't have time to cook and clean for myself," Ted replied with a laugh. "I practically live at the freight office, so I'm planning to stay at the hotel for now. Maybe I'll be able to sell it. The town is growing, so someone will want it one day."

He stopped in front of a neat, two-story house with a fenced yard and a sign on the door that read, "Mrs. Harraday's Respectable Men's Rooming House." Ted knocked on the front door, and a small but sturdy woman answered. She looked to be in her sixties, but her posture, agility of movement, and the twinkle in her eye suggested someone younger.

"Good day, Mrs. Harraday," said Ted. "This is Dr. Sam Thorne. He's here to see Colby."

"Pleased to meet you," replied Mrs. Harraday, with a hint of an Irish accent.

"And this young man is Jim Morgan," Ted added, indicating Jim. "I've just hired him as a guard, and he might be interested in that empty room you have."

"Don't you want it?" asked Jim.

"Mrs. Harraday wouldn't tolerate my hours, I'm afraid," Ted grinned.

Mrs. Harraday nodded and replied with a smile. "I expect my boarders to be on time to supper." Then, still smiling, she turned to Jim and looked him up and down. "And it's a pleasure to meet you, Mr. Morgan. A bit of Irish in you as well by your looks and name."

"I wouldn't know, but pleased to meet you," Jim replied a little uncomfortably.

"Come in, gentlemen, and I'll get the key to Colby's room," said Mrs. Harraday, stepping aside so they could enter. She disappeared into the dining room and returned a moment later holding a set of keys.

"Where's Dr. Crane?" she asked. "He hasn't checked on Colby since yesterday."

"We think he's left town," answered Ted.

"Well, I can't say I'm sorry," commented Mrs. Harraday as she led them upstairs. "He wouldn't even let me in to give Colby proper meals or see if he needed anything."

She stopped at a room on the second floor at the back of the house and knocked loudly.

"Colby!" she shouted. "I have some men here who want to see you, and one of them is a doctor! Are you decent?"

When there was no reply, she unlocked and opened the door. The smell of rotting flesh immediately caused all of them to turn their heads. Sam quickly blocked the door with his arm and told them to stay where they were. Then he entered the room holding his handkerchief over his nose and mouth, leaving the others to gaze in horror from the hallway. Colby was lying in a filthy bed, still fully clothed except for one pant leg cut to expose a wound covered by a dirty bandage.

He slowly turned his head as Sam entered. "Who are you?" he asked in a weak voice barely above a whisper.

"I'm Dr. Samuel Thorne, and I'm here to help you." Then Sam turned to Mrs. Harraday. "Would you please get this man some water?"

Mrs. Harraday nodded as she turned and disappeared down the hall, too horrified to speak.

"How long ago was this man hurt?" Sam asked Ted.

"Three weeks ago. But I didn't think it was that serious. He scratched his leg while getting down from the stage. It was deep, but I didn't expect...." Ted let his words trail off. He didn't want to voice what each of them was thinking.

Sam set his bag on a chair, pulled out a mask, and tied it behind his head to protect his face. Then he rinsed his hands in alcohol and carefully removed the cloth on Colby's leg. "Let me know if I hurt you."

As soon as he removed the bandage, the wound began to ooze a dark, foul-smelling liquid.

Mrs. Harraday returned with a pitcher and glass but, at a motion from Sam, stopped at the door. Sam took the glass from her and helped Colby drink. The man guzzled the water as though he'd been in a desert for days.

"The poor thing," whispered Mrs. Harraday, watching from the doorway.

After examining Colby and assuring him he would return shortly, Sam stepped back into the hallway and shut the door behind him. "This man has been horribly neglected!" Sam growled softly through clenched teeth. "I'm afraid he will have to lose the leg if he's to have any hope of surviving. Is there somewhere clean I can use for an operating room? Also, I'd like to be able to keep an eye on him for a few days."

"Let me think about it," replied Ted, his voice hollow from shock.

"I'm so sorry!" sobbed Mrs. Harraday. "Dr. Crane told me to stay out—"

"It's not your fault," Sam assured her. "You were just doing what you were told, but don't go back in there."

"No one blames you, Mrs. Harraday," added Ted. "Everyone knows you wouldn't have let him lie in his own filth like that."

"Where are the others?" asked Sam. "Crane said he had three here in town."

"They're across the street," answered Ted.

"How long have they been in that man's care?" Sam inquired as he and Jim followed Ted down the stairs and out of the house.

"Well, Will Parker was hurt a few weeks ago. He fell off the top of the stage while unloading it. He's not really one of my men. He tends to drink a lot, but I try to find things for him to do when he's sober enough to earn a little money. The other is George Tait, one of my guards. He was shot in the arm last week."

"Take me to Tait first," suggested Sam. To himself, he guessed the young doctor was less neglectful of his female patients. He just hoped, for their sakes, he used only his hands therapeutically.

Ted led them up the front steps of the other rooming house, which was a long, one-story structure. A middle-aged woman answered his knock, wearing what had once been an attractive dress but was now a grimy, stained garment, worn smooth and shiny under the arms.

"Mrs. Kent," said Ted. "We need to see Tait and then Will. Could you let us in their rooms, please?"

Mrs. Kent stomped to a small end table next to a threadbare couch and withdrew two keys from a drawer. Then she led them down a dark, narrow hallway past two doors, stopping at the third. She knocked, then opened the door. Sam told them to wait in the hall. A few moments later, he returned.

"Where's Parker's room?" asked Ted of Mrs. Kent.

She showed them to a room across the hall and one door down. Again, she knocked and unceremoniously opened the door.

Sam thanked her. "Mrs. Kent?" he asked before entering the room. "Would you be so kind as to get Mr. Tait some water?"

Mrs. Kent grunted and stamped off.

Again, Sam entered the room alone. He was still in with Will Parker when Mrs. Kent returned with a glass. She stood in the hall outside of Tait's room, waiting indignantly.

Jim noticed her and walked back to where she stood. "Thank, you. I'll give it to him," he offered, taking the glass.

Mrs. Kent grunted again and stamped back down the hall.

Jim found Tait in a similar state to Colby, though he didn't yet appear to have succumbed to infection. Jim held the man's head and the glass to keep Tait from choking as he gulped the water. He was just draining the glass when Sam returned.

"Thank you," Tait managed to say.

"Yes, thank you," said Sam to Jim. "I thought the landlady might do that."

Jim gently laid Tait's head back onto the soiled pillow, and Sam motioned him into the hall. "Let's go outside. I feel like the walls are closing in," said the doctor softly.

Jim shut Tait's door and followed Sam and Ted out to the street.

The doctor turned to face them. "All of these men are in

deplorable condition. I can save Tait, and probably Colby. I'm not sure of Parker. Have you come up with a place where I can operate?"

Ted thought for a minute. "Would a brand new, two-story house with five bedrooms do?"

"Yes," answered Sam.

"Then follow me." Ted led them down an alley that intersected the street they had been on, turned onto another street, walked a ways down it, and stopped at a house that was just as he described. "This was supposed to be my house, but I would be glad to let you use it, Dr. Thorne, as long as you need it."

Sam was dumbfounded. "Are you sure?"

"It would be my pleasure," answered Ted, opening the front door. "As you can see, it's already furnished. I'll get Mrs. Harraday to freshen it up. Also, I think the windows in the dining room will provide you with enough light for an operating room."

Ted showed them into a spacious room with a large table, but the most amazing feature was the windows. The back wall of the room jutted out in a semicircle from the rest of the house, and the glass windows on that wall stretched from floor to ceiling. It was an amazing show of wealth considering most people counted themselves lucky to have one or two glass windows in their home.

"If we move the table over here," suggested Ted, walking over to the windows, "you should have enough light. Shouldn't you?"

"I should say so," Sam replied in awe. "These windows are even larger than the ones we had in the operating room in medical school. Ted, this is amazing!"

Ted smiled. "Thank you. I'm not one for ostentation myself, but I thought my bride-to-be would like them. Though I must say, I'm more pleased by the prospect of this being an operating room than I ever was about it being a dining room. Now, Dr. Thorne, let me show you the rest of the house, and then you can tell me what else you're going to need."

After seeing the house, Sam gave Ted a short list of items.

"What can I do?" asked Jim after Sam had finished speaking to Ted.

"It would be a big help to me to have Martha here," replied

Sam. "Is there another stage she could catch?" he asked Ted.

"Not until tomorrow, I'm afraid," Ted replied.

"I could take Ness and get her here by this evening," offered Jim.

"You've already ridden him all that way once today. Why don't you take a wagon?" suggested Ted. "You can use mine, and I have a strong, fast team to go with it."

Jim looked to Sam, who nodded. "I know she'd prefer a wagon to a horse," said the doctor.

Within the hour, Ted had Mrs. Harraday and some other women working to rid the house of dust and get it ready, men lined up to move the patients, and Jim on the road to fetch Martha. Sam had sent her a telegram, in which he had mentioned the procedures he would be performing, so she was waiting and ready to go when Jim arrived. Just in case though, Sam had given Jim a detailed list of the things he would need. Before they left, Martha took a moment to look over it and make sure she had everything.

Ted's wagon was a stylish black surrey with a canopy to protect the riders from the weather. It had removable doors, and, since the weather had been warm, the sides were still open. The team was a handsome, high-strung, matched set of grays. At first, they tried to take charge, but Jim firmly took control, and they cooperated beautifully the rest of the trip.

Martha was always nervous around horses, and, as Jim helped her onto the wagon, she hesitated because one of the animals snorted and stamped his foot. Jim calmed the animal with his voice. The other horse tossed his head, so Jim spoke to him, too.

"Are you sure about this?" she asked.

"They're fine," Jim assured her. "They just want to get back on the road, and one gets jealous if the other gets more attention." He held the reins and her arm until he had her settled. Then he took his place on the seat beside her. He gave the reins a slight flick, and they took off at a smart trot. The horses itched to go faster, so as soon as they were out of town, and since the road was firm and smooth, he urged them into a jog.

Martha smiled seeing the animals enjoying themselves so much, even as she clung to Jim's arm, afraid the bouncing carriage would throw her off. She also couldn't help but notice the feel of his muscles under her hands as he manipulated the reins. She thought back to the night her husband and the sheriff had been forced to restrain him, and wondered how much power was really stored in them. She remembered how gentle he'd always been with the Petersen children, and the contrast struck her. Then she thought about the job he had taken, its inherent dangers, and what a tragic waste it would be if some outlaw killed him. This caused her involuntarily to give him a squeeze, not as a romantic gesture but a motherly one, even though she was only old enough to be his sister.

Jim simply thought she was still a little nervous and paid her no mind.

Martha wondered about his past and why he didn't seem to have any family. She felt that any woman should be proud to have such a man for a son. She thought about the scars on his back and shuddered, wondering again how anyone could have treated him so.

As they rode, the shadows lengthened, and the sunlight turned from yellow into gold. After about an hour, Jim slowed the horses back to a fast trot. He didn't want to anger Ted by running his animals too hard. The slower speed made conversation easier, so Martha asked Jim questions about Dillard, whether he liked it and the man he would be working for. Jim replied that Ted's concern for his men had impressed him, as had his generosity in letting Sam use his house.

"I must admit," replied Martha, "he's turned out to be more pleasant than he had seemed at first."

Jim nodded.

"I'm sorry about his broken engagement," she remarked. "I was worried when Sam expressed an interest in going west shortly after medical school. But he was my husband, and I trusted him, so we loaded up what little we had and left. Sam said that people needed good doctors out here, and, from what you've told me about this Crane person, he was right."

Jim nodded again and replied, "I hate to think what would have happened to me if Sam was as bad a doctor as that man is."

"You were lucky to have him. And we were lucky to meet you," Martha added with a smile.

She gave his arm another squeeze. This time he reacted in his usual manner when touched. He tensed and drew slightly away.

"Just try to be careful with this new job of yours," she added seriously. "I'm sorry, but I can't help worrying about you."

Jim glanced at her. "I'll do my best."

"I know you will."

It was late July, so there was still an hour of daylight left when Jim and Martha arrived in Dillard. Jim guided the horses to Ted's house, helped Martha down from the carriage, and took her bags from under the seat. Ted heard them drive up and opened the front door. As they stepped inside, Jim looked over his shoulder to make sure a livery boy was going to take care of the horses. He saw one of them running toward the house, having seen them arrive.

"Your husband is already in the operating room with Colby, the patient," Ted explained. "You can wash up in here, and I have a kettle of water boiling for the instruments," he said, leading them into the kitchen.

Martha thanked him, then took out the instruments Sam would need and put them in the boiling water. One of the instruments was a saw, and she noticed Jim and Ted exchanged a glance as she dropped it into the kettle. After the instruments had boiled for a few minutes, she washed her hands up to her elbows, donned an operating robe and mask she had brought, and draped another over her arm for her husband. Then, using two clean towels as potholders, she carefully carried the kettle with the instruments in it into the dining room. There was a sheet hanging in front of each entrance to give privacy and keep out dust. Ted held the sheet back for her and then let it drop, leaving him alone in the kitchen with Jim.

After setting the kettle down on a stand next to the operating table—the dining room table covered with layers of newspapers and old blankets—Martha helped her husband with the gown, then rinsed her hands in alcohol.

"Did you have a good trip?" Sam asked.

Martha nodded and inquired about the patient, who was lying unconscious, thanks to chloroform, on the table. Sam filled her in on the procedure and then began.

In the kitchen, Jim and Ted sat down at the table and waited.

"Is the man really going to have to lose his leg?" Jim asked.

Ted nodded gravely.

"I hope Sam gave him something for the pain," Jim remarked.

"He did. He already had him unconscious when you got here. Poor Colby, he was pretty upset when Sam told him. He kept saying that it had only been a scratch. He couldn't understand how it had gotten so bad. It wouldn't have either if that bastard of a doctor had known what the hell he was doing!"

"Are the other men here already?"

"They're upstairs. Sam said Tait is going to be fine, but he doesn't think Will Parker is going to last much longer."

"What's wrong with him?" Jim asked.

"Sam said he must have hurt his back when he fell, and if he'd gotten to him soon enough he would probably have been OK, but now he can't move. We brought him in on a board to keep his back straight, and Sam had us leave him on it."

"Is he in a bed?" Jim asked.

"Yes. We set the board on it. The poor cuss hadn't had anything to eat or drink in I don't know how long, and I suspect that's one reason Sam thinks he's going to die."

"I'm sorry," Jim said sincerely.

"I am, too. I wish I'd known, but I trusted that ass of a doctor. I'm glad your friend Sam came with you today or all of these men would have been dead before long."

"Should I go check on them?" Jim asked.

"Mrs. Harraday's up there now. She'll let us know if they need anything," Ted replied.

Not able to just sit and wait, Jim rose and set about fixing a pot of coffee.

A little while later, Martha came back into the kitchen with something wrapped heavily in a towel. "Is there somewhere this can be buried or burned?"

"Is that Colby's...?" Ted couldn't bring himself to say it.

"I'll take it," Jim offered.

Martha carefully handed it to him. "Thank you."

"There's a shovel out back if you want to bury it somewhere," said Ted.

"If you bury it," instructed Martha, "make sure it's good and deep."

Jim nodded as Ted opened the back door for him. Jim found the shovel and carried it and the bundle out of town. They had gotten some rain recently so the ground wasn't too hard. In a short time, he dug a hole over five feet deep and large enough for the bundle. After he buried it, he walked on the ground to pack it down. Then he scraped the dirt level with the shovel and replaced the sod over the hole so no one would notice the grave. When he returned, he helped Sam and Ted carry Colby upstairs and settle him into a bed.

Sam introduced Martha and Mrs. Harraday. Then Martha assured her she would take over the care of the patients for a while so Mrs. Harraday could get back to serve supper for her boarders.

"Would you like me to bring something by for you and the others later on?" Mrs. Harraday offered.

"We wouldn't want to put you to any trouble," Martha replied.

"Oh, don't you worry yourself about that. It won't be anything fancy tonight. Probably just bread, cheese, and some smoked ham. I think my boarders will forgive me for not having a hot supper for once."

"Well, if you have enough, it would be appreciated," Martha acknowledged, touching the older woman's arm.

Mrs. Harraday nodded, then bustled downstairs and out the front door.

Sam, Jim, and Ted came out of Colby's room, and Martha told them about Mrs. Harraday's kind offer. Then Sam informed her of the conditions of the other patients, and the two of them checked on the men, with Ted and Jim waiting in the hall in case they could be of any assistance. After Sam was satisfied that all the patients were resting as comfortably as possible, he led the others downstairs to the kitchen. The coffee was hot, so Jim poured a cup for all of them. Martha thanked him as she sank heavily into a chair and the others joined her at the table.

"I appreciate everyone's help today," sighed Sam. "Ted, I hope you'll thank your men for carrying the patients."

Ted nodded.

"Jim, I'd appreciate it if you would stay here for a few days with Martha until I get back. Unless that's going to interfere with your plans," Sam continued, looking at Ted.

"He's scheduled to go out on his first run day after tomorrow, but I could have one of the townswomen stay with her while he's away," replied Ted.

"I'd appreciate that. Do you mind staying here?" Sam asked, turning to Jim.

"No, sir. But how are you going to manage a practice in two different towns?"

"There's a doctor fresh out of medical school who's written to me. He said he'd be here at the end of this month. I wasn't planning at the time to turn my practice over to him, but if I find that he's competent, I think that's what I'll have to do. If you don't mind, my dear," Sam said, looking at Martha.

"So we would live here?" she asked.

"I think this town needs a good doctor. I know we'll miss our friends, but they won't be that far away, and we'll meet new people here."

"Where will we live?" Martha asked.

"You could just stay here," offered Ted.

"Oh, no!" exclaimed Martha. "We couldn't. This is your house!"

"I wasn't planning to live in it, anyway."

"I couldn't afford it, I'm afraid," remarked Sam.

"I'm sure we can work something out," Ted assured him. "I'd rather see you make good use of it than have it sit here empty."

"That's very generous of you," replied Sam.

"Now, I need to get back to the office. There are a few things I have to get done," said Ted, rising. Then he turned to Jim. "I'll see you tomorrow."

"When do you want me there?" Jim asked, also standing.

"My morning is going to be very busy, so come in after lunch. We'll go over a few things, and I'll introduce you to the men." Ted started to leave, then turned back. "Oh, and bring your weapons. I know you can shoot, but there are some things I make all the new guards do. I plan to have as many of my men there as I can round up so you can show off," he added with a smile.

"I'd really rather not," Jim replied sincerely.

Ted looked at him for a moment. "You're serious, aren't you?"

"Jim's always very modest," explained Martha.

"OK," Ted replied, "but word has already gotten around, so don't be surprised if there are quite a few people there to watch."

Jim nodded, and Ted patted him on the shoulder. Then he held up his hand and shook his head as Jim started to follow to show him out.

A little while later, Mrs. Harraday returned with a light

supper for Sam, Martha, and Jim and some broth for the patients.

After supper, Sam and Martha saw to their patients again. Then they settled into what was supposed to be the master bedroom upstairs, and Jim settled into the one room left. He noticed that Sam had graciously given him a corner room with two windows. As he went to sleep, he thought about the next day and hoped he wouldn't disappoint Ted. He was exhausted and didn't hear Sam get up a couple of times during the night to check on his patients.

Jim awoke early and busied himself by bringing in wood for the kitchen fire and making coffee. When they came downstairs, Martha and Sam were surprised to see him already up, since this was really the first time he hadn't been under doctor's orders to stay in bed and rest.

Sam poured himself a cup of coffee. "This is good," he said after taking a sip. "Martha, I think Jim makes better coffee than you do."

Martha smiled. "Do you cook, too?" she asked Jim.

"I can, but I don't like to."

There was a knock on the front door. Jim rose to answer it, and Sam followed out of curiosity.

"I hope I haven't come by too early?" asked a young woman when Jim opened the door.

"No, ma'am," Jim answered.

"I brought over some biscuits and gravy so you all would have something for breakfast," she said, holding up a basket and offering it to Jim.

"Thank you," Jim replied, taking the basket.

"Are you the doctor?"

"No, ma'am," Jim answered, stepping back so the woman could see Sam.

"I'm Dr. Thorne," said Sam, stepping forward.

"Pleased to meet you," said the woman, holding out her hand, which Sam took. "I'm Olivia Henson. My husband, daughter, and I live on the other side of Main Street, in the older section of town."

"Won't you come in?" Sam asked.

"I don't want to be any trouble, and I have to get back in just a minute."

"It's no trouble. I'd like to introduce you to my wife," Sam said, showing her into the front sitting room.

"I'll get her," Jim offered.

A moment later, Jim returned with Martha. He had left the basket on the kitchen table. He stood back so as not to intrude. Sam introduced the two women, then motioned for Jim to join them and introduced him, too.

Martha offered Olivia a seat, but she insisted she needed to get home, so Martha invited her to come back again later on. Olivia agreed smiling.

"See, I told you you'd meet new people," commented Sam to Martha after Olivia left.

After breakfast, Sam and Martha checked on the patients while Jim sat in the kitchen and cleaned his weapons. He had just finished when there was another knock on the front door. When he opened it, he found Ted standing on the porch.

"I got done early and thought Sam and Martha might want to join us if they can," said Ted, as Jim stepped back to let him enter.

Jim was just about to shut the door when he saw Mrs. Harraday coming through the front gate. Then Sam and Martha came back downstairs. Since Mrs. Harraday agreed to stay with the patients, they followed Jim and Ted to the freight office. Ted took them around behind the building, where they found quite a crowd gathered in the alley. Many of them looked to be freight employees, but there were children running around and even a few women, all waiting to see if the new freight guard was really as good a shot as they'd heard. Jim saw Hap and Joe, and they smiled and waved to him.

Ted motioned to a man, who then approached them. "Jim, this is one of our drivers, Hank Wilson," said Ted, introducing a large, muscular man who looked to be around thirty. Hank stood six feet four inches tall and was a good six inches taller than Jim. Then Ted introduced Jim to Hank, and the two men shook hands. "Hank, bring the stage around and we'll see if Jim here is as good as Hap and Joe say he is."

Hank disappeared around the side of the building and returned a few minutes later, driving an empty stage pulled by the usual six horses.

"Well," said Ted to Jim, "climb on up. The targets are over there away from the people. Hank will drive you by, then bring you back here, and I'll go see how you did."

Jim turned and gazed at the targets. They were placed along the edge of a field that stretched out beside the building across the alley from the freight company. People had already gathered and were milling around in front of the building, and more were arriving and spilling out into the field.

"All those people will need to be on this side of the street," Jim said to Ted.

Another guard heard him and half-laughed. "Why?" he asked. "Afraid you'll miss?"

Jim eyed him a moment, then replied evenly, "Just thought it impolite to shoot over their heads."

The other guard turned, looked at the targets, then shook his head as he spoke to the guard next to him. "How in hell would he think he'd be shooting over their heads?"

The other man shrugged.

Jim climbed onto the stage. Instead of sitting in his seat above and behind Hank, to the driver's left, he climbed on top of the coach as he'd done when he was with Hap and Joe. The crowd murmured, because they'd never seen anyone do that before. Then they murmured again as the young man readied his lever action rifle, not his shotgun.

Hank urged the horses into a jog, guided the stage down to the end of the alley, and turned onto a side street. He had to go around the block so they would be heading in the right direction on their return. "We can make more than one pass," he explained to Jim as he turned onto the street that ran parallel to the alley.

"Shouldn't need to," Jim replied. He noted Hank's skill as the driver chose the most efficient course through the curve, slowing just enough to make the turn and urging the horses faster as they passed the apex. Jim understood that meant Hank had to manage the speed of the inside horses separately from that of the outside horses, and the technique could mean the difference between life and death in an attack.

"I can put the horses at a walk," Hank offered.

"Set the usual pace."

"Well, that depends," Hank said. "Will we be stopping at a swing station after two hours, or home station after four?"

"We were at a full gallop on Joe's stage," Jim stated.

Hank passed one street, then turned onto the next.

"I thought I'd give us an extra block," Hank said, smiling. "Why not make a grand entrance?"

He glanced over his shoulder when Jim didn't laugh and saw the young man scanning the rooftops and the street with his eyes. He'd have thought the man's vigilance an affectation to impress Ted and the crowd, except they were still on a side street that appeared deserted.

They turned back into the alley and saw Ted standing in the road a few feet from the boardwalk that ran behind the freight building. He had gotten everyone to move to that side of the street and was standing there to prevent anyone from stepping out or trying to cross back.

Hank gave the reins a shake and urged the horses into a gallop. Jim balanced on one knee and chambered a round. He kept his gaze on the road ahead as they approached, trying to ignore the crowd and the uneasy feeling he always got when someone was watching him.

The men in the crowd eyed the new guard, skeptical about what they'd heard about his marksmanship.

The women in the crowd found him attractive and noticed how his blue eyes shone in the morning sunlight.

Ted stepped back onto the boardwalk, noting how the young man positioned himself on the coach and the serious concentration on his face as the stage raced toward them.

All noticed how still the young man appeared as he sat ready, weapon in hand. Then, just as the lead horses reached the edge of the block, the young guard raised his rifle.

Jim began firing, pumping the lever up and down without lowering the weapon from his shoulder. He hit all of the targets before the stage finished its pass.

"Done," he said to Hank, lifting his hat to shake off the spent shells and then resettling it firmly on his head.

Instead of driving past the targets, the driver pulled the animals to a stop in front of Ted and the crowd.

Ted walked across the alley, inspected the targets, and returned. "That was impressive," he smiled. "You didn't miss once, and with a rifle, no less."

The crowd murmured again.

"How about one more time," suggested Ted.

Jim nodded and reloaded his rifle.

Ted spoke to Hank. "Go back around and come in the same way."

Hank urged the horses forward.

As the stage pulled away, Ted turned to the guard who had questioned Jim. "Now you know why he wanted the people on this side of the street."

When they reached the alley again, Hank urged the animals into a gallop. Jim fired, and for the second time Hank was able to pull the team to a stop in front of Ted.

"Well, you did it again," announced Ted, after inspecting the targets. "Is there anything else you'd like to do to show your abilities?"

As he walked across the roof of the stage to climb down, Jim noticed a particularly beautiful redheaded woman in the crowd and felt a strange urge to impress her. "Do you have some silver dollars?" he asked Ted.

Ted took three out of his pocket and showed them to Jim.

"I have a couple," Hank offered, taking out two.

"I'll need someone to help me with this," Jim said as he walked out into the street toward the field, positioning himself so there was no one in front of him.

"I'd be glad to," said Ted, following.

"I'll just need you to throw the coins up as high as you can, one at a time," Jim said.

"How fast?" Ted asked.

"Well, keep in mind I have to aim," Jim replied.

Ted tossed the first coin. Jim drew his revolver and fired. Ted tossed the rest of the coins, one after the other, pausing slightly in between. Jim fired five more shots. Then Ted walked to where the coins had fallen and picked them up. He held them up high, one at a time, so everyone could see the hole through the middle of each. When he held up the last coin, the hole wasn't round. Jim had hit it twice. The crowd gazed at the coins in silence for a moment, then someone started clapping, and they all joined in. Sam strode to Jim's side, smiling, and patted him on the back. Martha shook her head in amazement.

"I think we have our next freight guard!" announced Ted after the clapping had subsided, and the crowd cheered again.

Jim didn't smile, just calmly reloaded his weapons.

The young woman Jim had noticed was immediately interested in him as well. She found him quite good-looking, and that, combined with the easy grace of his movements, captivated her. The intensity of his eyes struck her, too. Even from the back of the crowd, she could see a flash of blue when he glanced in her direction.

After the demonstration, Ted took Jim inside and introduced him to some of the employees he had yet to meet, including the guard who had questioned him.

"Good job," said the man as he shook Jim's hand. Then he looked at Ted. "I hope you don't mind, sir, if the rest of us stick with our shotguns."

"Of course not, Tom," Ted replied. Then he spoke to the guards and drivers who had gathered around them. "As you all know, the safety of our passengers is our number one concern. We have seen the number of attacks increase here recently. All of you have performed admirably in the face of the dangers you've encountered on the road. Jim Morgan, here," Ted said, putting a hand on Jim's shoulder, "will help us not only keep the passengers safe but the rest of you as well. Using a rifle, Jim killed five bandits when he rode with Joe and Hap. Though I don't wish him to run into trouble on the road, if he does, I feel certain more dead bandits will be left in his wake."

"I sure hope so," said Hank from the back of the group. He had returned from taking the coach and horses back to the stable just as Ted started speaking. "Maybe Jim here will give the bandits something to think about, and they'll stop waylaying our stages."

"We can only hope," Ted said. Then he led Jim and Hank up the stairs and showed them into his office. He walked to the far side of the desk, sat in his high-backed leather chair, and motioned for Jim and Hank to sit in the chairs on the other side. "Well, what do you think?" asked Ted, turning to Hank as he opened a desk drawer and drew out a bottle of whiskey and three glasses.

Hank smiled, looked at Jim and back to Ted. "I think we'll have the bandits on the run."

Ted filled the glasses, handed one to each of his men, then raised his own and took a sip. Hank sipped his as well. Jim tasted the whiskey and then downed his in one swallow.

"We've been having at least one robbery each week," Ted stated, gazing at his new guard to gauge his reaction.

"Do you think it's the same people?" Jim asked.

"I don't know," replied Ted. "The robberies aren't all the same. Sometimes they just take the freight and any money and valuables that the passengers have and leave. Other times they murder everyone on the stage, even when it didn't appear that anyone resisted. That's why the US Marshals told me to order my men to shoot first rather than just in self-defense. If you see someone approach the stage and they have their weapon drawn, go ahead and shoot."

"And he'll hit 'em, too," added Hank, smiling and taking another sip.

"I can't believe you hit all those targets with a rifle," remarked Ted. "All the other guards use a shotgun because it's so hard to aim from a moving stage. How do you do it?" He held out the bottle, offering to refill Jim's glass.

Jim shook his head, refusing the whiskey. "I don't know. I just aim and shoot," he replied.

"Though I didn't mention it downstairs, I'm going to have the other men try it, too," said Ted. "I doubt any of them will be able to hit much, but it's worth a try."

"When do we leave?" asked Hank, also refusing a refill.

"Tomorrow morning," Ted replied as he stood. Then he spoke to Jim. "The runs usually last six days to a little over a week." He slid a map out from under some papers on his desk and turned it so Jim could see. "I'm going to have you passing through what we call Hell's Playground." He pointed to an area on the map. "It's where most of the attacks occur, because it's remote and the bandits can hide behind the rocks. It'll take you a day and a half to get there and three days to pass through it."

Jim studied the map as Ted continued.

"On your first trip, I'm only sending you halfway through, so you'll be gone six days. Three days out and three back. On your next trip, you'll go practically all the way through, so it'll take eight days. The next time you'll go halfway again, and so on."

Jim nodded.

"I know eight days is a long trip, but with Hank here, you don't have to change drivers every four hours or so at a home station. He's the only man who can drive eight hours straight."

Jim glanced at the big man. He'd sized the driver up when they first met, and he figured that, though Hank was at least ten years older, the driver was probably stronger even than him.

"So, though your trip will sometimes be longer than most, your days will always be only a little over eight hours," Ted continued. "The other guards sometimes have to wait two hours while their driver rests in the middle of the day. We try to have a fresh driver waiting at the station, but that doesn't always happen."

Hank laughed quietly and shook his head.

"With Hank, your day will always be shorter than everyone else's," Ted added.

Jim and Hank exchanged another friendly glance.

"That day you rode with Hap and Joe," Ted explained, "Joe was supposed to rest for two hours at the home station since he didn't have a relief. We don't have all of the stations built yet, so sometimes we get behind. Joe broke the rules by starting out early after lunch. I didn't reprimand him because by doing so he was hoping to prevent the attack."

"The driver's in charge of the stage," Hank stated, quoting company policy.

"And I'm in charge of the drivers," Ted responded, though not harshly. "You'll always spend the night at a home station," Ted informed Jim. "With all the attacks, we don't run the stages at night."

He looked Jim in the eye as he concluded. "You'll be traveling the most dangerous part of our route, but right now you're the best shot I have. You're allowed to refuse, and we can part friends," he added, as Jim glanced down at the map again.

The young man looked up and met Ted's gaze. "I'll do it," he replied evenly.

Ted nodded. "Hank can tell you what to bring." Then he added, "I expect all of my men to stay clean, both in language and body. What you do here in town is your business, but when you're on the stage, you represent the P & D Freight Company."

"Yes, sir," Jim replied.

"Yeah," said Hank with a laugh, "he expects us to bathe every day and keep our clothes clean."

"Do you have a problem with that, Mr. Wilson?" Ted asked.

"No, sir," Hank said. "I just wanted Jim here to understand, that's all."

Jim thought for a moment. He wondered if he'd have any privacy, because of his back, but decided he could bathe outside after dark if he had to. "I don't have a problem with it either, sir," he assured Ted.

"Good," Ted said. "Take care." He shook Jim's hand.

Jim and Hank left Ted's office, shutting the door behind them. When they got to the street, both men turned in the same direction.

"Aren't you staying with the new doctor?" Hank asked.

"I want to talk to Mrs. Harraday about a room," Jim explained.

"I live there. She's a great cook," commented Hank with a smile.

As they walked, he told Jim what he would need for the trip. When they arrived at Mrs. Harraday's house, Hank strolled on in and called for her. Mrs. Harraday answered from the kitchen, so the two men stepped through the house and found her kneading bread on the table.

"Have you met Jim?" Hank asked her.

"I sure have," replied Mrs. Harraday with a smile. "And I hear he's a pretty good shot, too. Dr. Thorne and Martha told me all about this morning."

"I'd like a room if you still have one available," Jim said.

"I do," she replied, still kneading.

"Do you need help with that?" Jim asked.

"You know how to knead bread?" Mrs. Harraday asked in return.

"Yes, ma'am."

"Well, wash your hands, roll up your sleeves, and you can take over."

A moment later, Jim was kneading the dough while Mrs. Harraday explained the house rules to him. Never idle she began peeling potatoes. "I don't care what you do somewhere else, but I don't allow my boarders to have members of the opposite sex in their room. Also, I understand needing a nip every now and then, but I don't want someone coming back late, blind drunk, falling down, and waking everybody up. You can drink in your room as long as you don't make a mess."

She motioned to Hank, and the big man hefted a large pot of water from the sink and set it on the stove. Then he reached for the potato she'd just peeled. She wrinkled her brow, so Hank washed his hands and then began dropping the potatoes into the pot, as she continued to peel more. She let the skins fall into a bowl to be roasted and served with the soup later.

"I change the sheets once a week and tidy the room," she informed the young man. "I empty the chamber pots every morning, unless you tell me you want to do it yourself. But if you do, I expect it to be done every day. Also, there is a warming stove in every room. It's for heat in the winter, not cooking, though I don't mind if you want to heat water on it for shaving, coffee, or tea. I don't charge extra for the wood, but I do appreciate help carrying it upstairs. Speaking of which, there's some outside," she motioned to Hank again.

The driver nodded and obediently began carrying in wood that had been stacked in a neat pile by the back door. He filled the woodbox near the stove as Jim continued kneading the dough.

"My rates are reasonable," Mrs. Harraday continued as she began chopping an onion. "They're lower than the hotel, and a little higher than the place across the street, but you'll find my house is cleaner than both and the food is better, too. You get three meals a day, and since you boys with the freight company are gone so much, I don't charge you as much each month, provided you help with the chores when you're here. Also, if you tell me when you should be back, I'll have water hot for a bath. I have two tubs. I'll save something warm on the stove for you, too, if you're late for supper because of your work. Does this sound good to you?"

"Yes, ma'am," Jim replied, still kneading the dough.

Mrs. Harraday checked a watch she kept in her pocket. "Thank you. You can stop now."

"I'll be staying at Mr. Scofield's house tonight because Sam will be away," Jim explained, wiping the dough off his hands with a damp towel Mrs. Harraday handed him. "But I'd like to put some things in the room if that's all right?"

"I'll have it ready in just a few minutes, after I get this dough warming."

Jim thanked Mrs. Harraday, and Hank shook his hand. Then Jim returned to Ted's house, sorted through his things, and set aside what he would need for the trip. The rest he put back in his bag and took over to Mrs. Harraday's. She had readied the room, which was on the second floor at the front of the house, bright and cheery with the window open to air it out. Jim put his things in the chest of drawers and sat on the bed. The mattress was of good quality and firm, and the pillows were plump with goose down. Satisfied with his room, Jim took his empty bag, stopped at the store to buy some apples, and walked to the livery stable to check on Ness. Since he had time, he set out for a ride.

It was mid-afternoon when he returned. He gave Ness over to the care of one of the boys, grabbed his bag, and headed back to Sam's new house to fix something to eat. He still had some apples but wanted to save them for the trip. He was chewing on some bread and cheese he found on the counter when Martha came into the kitchen.

"You'll spoil your supper," she scolded playfully.

"Is there anything I can do to help you?" Jim asked.

"No. Sam just wanted me to have you rest this afternoon. You've still got some healing to do." Then her smile faded as she added, "He reminded me that you will be leaving tomorrow on the stage."

Jim saw concern in her eyes, and it made him uncomfortable. "I'll be OK," he assured her.

Martha nodded but turned away, obviously unconvinced.

Jim retreated to his room, cleaned and readied his weapons for the next day, and was about to lie down when he noticed a book tucked under his pillow. He pulled it out and found it was a Bible with a note inside from Sam that read:

> *I know you're not religious, but I noticed you keep books in your saddlebags and thought you could add one to your collection.*
>
> *Take care of yourself,*
> *Sam*
>
> *PS: I don't want to have to put more stitches in you.*

As Jim flipped through the book, another few sheets fell out. They were in Sam's hand, but he had transcribed them from something else. The title of the first sheet caught Jim's eye, so he read it.

HOPE

One day, the Father conceived of a being created to glorify Him. This being would be beautiful to behold, graceful in proportion and movement, a delight to the eye. This being would be capable of great works of art, music, and literature, as well as curious about science and his surroundings. The Father conceived of creating a beautiful world for His creation to enjoy, full of good things to eat and other creatures for companionship. He smiled at the wondrous beauty and harmony of this pleasant world and looked forward to creating an entire universe, not only to interest His creation but to impress on him the wondrous power and love of the Father.

Then He decided to give His creation not only intelligence but, like Himself, a will of his own, the power to choose. In that instant, because He saw all that would be, in all its convolutions, He dropped his head in sadness. He saw that His beautiful creation, whom He would love more than the creation would ever be capable of understanding, would one day choose the wrong way. When this happened, even the Father, in all His power and might, would be incapable of gathering up His creation and returning him to his former state, because the creature had sinned. Then His creation would be forever cut off from Him, separated from the Father by a chasm impossible to bridge. He sighed as His heart broke. He could not create a creature that would have no hope, no future except to endure eternal damnation, exiled to the outer darkness, where the worms never die.

He felt a hand on His arm, and looked up to see His Son, His eyes shining with the power of everlasting light and the determination of an iron will. The Son had seen all that His Father had conceived, for, though separate, They were One, and in that moment, the Father understood His Son's intent. The Son would be the bridge, the way of retrieval, so the Father's creation would have hope and a chance for everlasting communion with the Father.

In that second, as soon as they conceptualized the thought, both Father and Son understood the scope of

*the sacrifice. The Son instantly felt all He would have to
endure. The Father mourned for Him, His heart crying out
for His Son, but His Son's hand remained firm. His will
never wavered in its inestimable love for the creation. The
Father looked into the eyes of His Son and gave Him the
choice. Though He knew the answer, the Father left the
final decision with the One who would perform the great-
est act of love the universe would ever witness. The Son
nodded. Not only did He nod, He smiled in that quiet way
of His, His eyes gleaming with the hope of the world. He
had made His decision.*

*The fall of Lucifer followed. He took a third of the
angels with him, and he would be the source of the fall
of man. Lucifer looked forward to the time of the Son's
sacrifice, always striving to defeat the Father and the Son
but never truly succeeding.*

*Though the Son saw all that would be, one has to
wonder if He fully appreciated the true cost of becoming
His own creation. For, in that instant when He offered
Himself in place of His creation, though sensible to all
that would occur, He was still holy and undefiled, unen-
cumbered with the weaknesses of the flesh. During the
last three hours on the cross, when He fully took all man's
sins into His body and mind, our sins completely separated Him from the Father, leaving Him abandoned, alone
in His suffering. What force of will was necessary to con-
quer not only His own human weaknesses, but to prevail
against all the horrors Lucifer inflicted, no human will
ever be able to fully understand or appreciate. We must
never forget, He did this by choice, so even the least and
worst of us has a chance.*

S. B. Kelly

Jim sighed and thoughtfully tucked the sheets back in the
book without reading farther. He appreciated Sam's concern as
well as the gift, but he wasn't interested in learning more. He lay
down and dozed for a while.

When he awoke and walked downstairs, Martha had food
on the table that one of the townswomen had brought. They ate

in silence. Martha was too tired and worried to talk, and Jim wasn't one to make idle conversation.

As Jim was about to leave the kitchen, Martha grabbed his hand. "Please be careful!" she begged, fighting back tears. "I know I'm not your mother, but I do care about you, and so does Sam."

Jim gazed at her for a moment. He was unaccustomed to having anyone worry about him, much less a teary-eyed woman. "I won't do anything foolish."

"I know you won't," she said, giving his hand a squeeze.

Jim got up shortly before daylight and was gone before Martha awoke. When he arrived at the freight office, he offered to help the men load the stage, but Hank stopped him.

"Save your strength for the trip," the driver advised.

Ted stepped out as they were about to leave and wished them well. He watched as his new guard climbed over his seat to sit amongst the luggage. He waved and his new guard returned the gesture. Then, Ted noticed Jim's expression and manner change completely as soon as Hank urged the horses forward. The young man's back straightened, his brow wrinkled, and his right hand moved closer to the trigger of his rifle.

Ted had seen other men become suddenly serious when the coach started to move and they knew they were officially on duty, but it was the change in Jim's eyes that struck Ted. Their expression turned cold as though with deadly intent, but at the same time their color seemed to burn as though with an inner flame. Ted found himself staring at his new guard. Then he felt Jim's eyes on him as the young man gave a quick nod, just as the horses found their stride and the coach tore away.

7

THE WORK

Jim's first trip was uneventful. Other than getting tired of the dust and dirt and having to bathe outside after dark for privacy, he found the work tolerable. He fell into the habit of checking on the horses when they stopped for the night. The men at the home stations appreciated his help and skill. He started keeping his tools on the stage so he was able to care for the animals' feet and prevent problems that could have caused them to become lame. Otherwise, a horse might have to stay at a station for days until the regular farrier hired by the freight company could travel to care for it.

Jim soon became familiar with the people working at the home stations. All of them greeted him warmly right from the start. The old man who ran the first station when they were heading toward Hell's Playground was the quietest of all the station-keepers. He lived there with his half-Mexican grandson. When the boy learned the name of Jim's horse, he offered to teach Jim Spanish. Jim accepted, mainly out of curiosity, but also to occupy his mind. He was surprised it came to him relatively easily. He'd refused to learn Latin or Greek years before, and realized he liked Spanish because he was simply learning how to speak, not read, write, or conjugate.

A husband and his wife ran the next home station, and they had three children. The oldest, Lizzie, helped with everything from baths to horses, depending on what her parents needed her to do. She was eleven, and Jim worried some of the men were starting to see her as a woman rather than the child she still was.

The Professor ran the next station. The men called him that because he'd been a teacher. He lived there with his woman, Elena, and two boys he'd taken in. All the freight men liked Elena. She was very friendly, and the Professor didn't mind sharing because Elena kept certain things only for him.

On their longest trips, Jim and Hank traveled to the next station and spent the night before turning around and heading back to Dillard. Two men ran this station, Kevin and Alvie. Kevin took care of the horses, and Alvie took care of everything else. Alvie's was the cleanest station in the district, and he was the best cook as well. Though he and Kevin said they were cousins, some of the men had their doubts.

Kevin and Alvie had only been with the company a couple months when Jim started. During his first visit, a stray dog wandered to the station. Someone had shot the poor animal, and Alvie had cared for her. Seeing the man's concern for the dog softened Jim's opinion, and he became their staunchest defender whenever any of the other men made any derogatory comments. One word from him was all it ever took to silence the men, and they soon accepted Kevin and Alvie and looked forward to the best meal they ever got, even when in town.

Though the people manning the stations were friendly, Jim kept his distance, and they respectfully kept theirs as well. They had all heard about the new guard before they met him and knew he'd killed five men before officially joining the company. Some admired him for it and dismissed his reticence, while others wondered if something was wrong with the quiet, reserved young man. Even the other guards were somewhat aloof. Though Jim didn't seem to notice, the men made way when he approached, and even those who suspected he might not be their elder addressed him as "sir". Everyone noticed Jim was polite as well and often helped with household chores, even though no one dared to ask.

Things continued to run smoothly for the next few weeks, and Jim and Hank got along well. Neither was much of a talker, so much of the time they rode in silence. Both men were glad the other wasn't afraid of quiet as so many other people seemed to be. It was also advantageous that when one of them spoke, the other listened.

Jim even tolerated Hank's gentle teasing. Jim always kept apples with him unless none were available and usually ate one in either the late morning or early afternoon. Then he'd throw the core away from the road to avoid leaving any sign they'd passed. He'd given Hank a standing offer if the driver ever wanted one.

"Maybe I should call you 'Jimmy Appleseed,'" Hank jokingly suggested one afternoon when he heard his young guard bite into the crisp fruit. "You hoping all those cores will sprout?"

"Nope," Jim replied.

Hank waited for a further explanation but after a minute realized the single word was all the response the young man was going to give.

"It'd be nice though, wouldn't it?" Hank asked.

"Yep," Jim replied.

Hank smiled and shook his head. He'd become fond of his new guard and remembered how, on the previous trip, Jim had offered to give him his last apple when he'd mentioned he was hungry. The young man had even offered to cut it into pieces and feed it to him while he drove. He doubted there was another man in the company who was as generous and considerate.

They enjoyed the tranquility of the road but knew it couldn't last, since the trend of a stage robbery a week continued. Then one afternoon, as they headed southeast toward Dillard and were almost out of Hell's Playground, Jim heard the call of a crow and sensed something. He tossed away the core of the apple he'd been eating and looked around. They were still in the dry lands, where the trees fell away to be replaced by large rocks. The rumbling stage kicked up a cloud of dust in its wake. Jim was sitting on top of the coach and, through the haze, thought he saw the glint of sunlight on metal. He gazed intently behind them, trying through force of will to make his eyes penetrate the swirling brown turmoil, then readied his weapon.

Hank involuntarily shuddered at the sound of Jim's rifle as the guard swung the lever down then brought it up, forcing a round into the chamber.

"Damned dust," Jim muttered. He stood so he could see over

the roiling dirt and steadied himself against the luggage.

Hank heard him. He would normally gently chastise the young man, but he didn't want to break the guard's concentration. The company forbade the use of foul language on the stage. His mind shot back to the first time he'd had to scold Jim. The stage was rounding a sharp curve, and it was his new guard's first trip. Jim, not realizing how much the coach could sway in a turn, had reached for his bag and nearly been thrown off. "God damn it!" Jim had growled loud enough for the passengers to hear. Hank couldn't help but smile as he remembered Jim's response when he'd reminded his new guard not to swear. "Sorry. Profanity was my first language."

Jim saw two riders following them, and they had their weapons drawn.

Hank heard the report of Jim's rifle, and his smile faded.

Before either of the men could get off a shot, Jim fired twice and both men lay in the road dead. Jim heard gunfire behind him. He turned as another shot rang out and felt a sharp pain in his right arm. He saw two more riders coming toward the stage, apparently using the same tactic as the men he'd killed when he rode with Hap and Joe. The riders, approaching at a gallop, didn't know their comrades were already dead. Jim fired and dropped them both before either could get off another round. Then he scanned their surroundings for other attackers as the stage rolled on, leaving the bodies in the dust.

"You OK?" Jim asked Hank.

"Fine, and you?" Hank replied over his shoulder.

"They winged me," Jim answered, tying his bandana around his upper right arm.

Hank then knocked on the coach, and one of the passengers stuck his head out of the window. "Anybody hurt in there?" asked the driver.

"No, we're fine," replied the man. "Are they gone?"

"They're dead," Hank answered.

The man nodded and disappeared back into the coach.

It was early evening when they arrived at the next home station. This was the one tended by the old man and his half-Mexican grandson. The old man took care of the horses while Jim and the boy unloaded what luggage the passengers would need for the night. This done, everyone but Jim left the barn, which was attached to the living area for security reasons.

That Jim remained behind wasn't unusual, because he often checked on the horses one last time. Though the company deemed human life important, and one of Jim's duties was to protect it, the horses were of more monetary value to the freight company than the passengers were. There would always be more passengers, the company reasoned, but good horses were hard to come by.

This time, however, Jim remained in order to tend his wound. He walked to the far side of the coach and opened his bag, which he had tossed down with the passengers' luggage. Then he lit a lantern and took out a bottle and some bandages. He stripped to the waist and poured some of the contents of the bottle on his arm. He grimaced from the pain as the liquid soaked into the wound. Then he began to bandage it.

When Jim didn't return after a few minutes, Hank decided to look for him. As he entered the barn, he saw a light on the other side of the coach and approached it. He found Jim with his back to him attempting to wrap a cloth around his arm. What caught Hank's attention, and caused him to stop dead and shiver as if his blood had turned to ice, were the raised scars across Jim's back. The driver felt his breath escape his body and a deep ache in his chest as shock wrapped its cold fingers around his heart. He shook off the sensation and approached Jim, trying to pretend he hadn't noticed anything.

"Here, let me help you," Hank offered.

Jim spun to face him, his eyes flashing and his breathing short.

Hank realized the young man considered just his presence a form of attack at that moment. He ignored Jim's reaction and the possible danger to his person that came from Jim still being armed. "Did you wash this?" he asked, inspecting the wound.

Jim just glared at him for a moment, then shook his head.

Hank strode over to a water pump in the barn and filled a bucket. Then he took a bar of soap, washed his hands, and returned to Jim.

The driver's deliberate manner calmed the young man, and he stood patiently as Hank carefully washed and rinsed the wound.

The big man noticed that Jim hardly reacted to the pain. "Is this what you want on it?" Hank asked, picking up the bottle Jim had set on the coach step.

"Sam gave it to me," Jim stated, his voice low, almost a growl.

Hank smelled it and shook his head. "That's strong stuff."

"It's alcohol, but don't drink it. Sam said it could kill you," the guard replied in the same tone as before.

Hank held Jim's arm out and carefully poured the liquid over both sides of the wound, since the bullet had passed through. He noticed that again Jim's only reaction to the pain was to tense his jaw. Then Hank took a fresh bandage, and, with Jim's arm bent to flex the muscle, he began to wind the cloth around the injury.

"I've never seen stripes like that on a white man before," Hank commented as he worked. He was holding Jim's right arm where he couldn't grab his gun, but he felt the young man tense. "I didn't much like seeing them on a black man, either. Anything you want to talk about?"

Jim shook his head.

"It's your own business," Hank said as he tied the bandage. "It doesn't change what I think of you, Jimmy."

"Thanks." Jim noticed the nickname, but decided he could tolerate it as long as Hank was the only person who used it. And as long as the nickname didn't reference apples.

Hank wasn't sure whether Jim had thanked him for tending his wound or for what he said, so he decided it was for both. The driver helped his friend put on a clean shirt, which the young man only buttoned partway and didn't bother to tuck in. Then, with Hank carrying Jim's bag and Jim his weapons, they trod into the house through the side door that led from the barn. Hank put Jim's bag beside the bed farthest from the front door, which wasn't where Jim usually slept. He liked to take the bed closest to the door, so if there were any trouble he'd be the first to face it. However, Hank decided he didn't want to chance the guard catching a chill.

Jim laid his rifle and shotgun under the bed within easy reach.

"Lie down for a while," Hank suggested. "Your bath can wait."

Jim nodded, took off his gun belt, and drew the pistol. He set the gun belt under the bed and slid the pistol under his pillow. Then he removed his boots and stretched out on his back. He hadn't realized how tired he was, and he fell asleep almost immediately. Though he'd wake anywhere else if someone entered his room, he could sleep soundly if he had to share a room as long as the people were already in it when he lay down. There were only four passengers on this trip: two men traveling together and a woman traveling with her young daughter. While the old man and the boy prepared supper, the two men played cards, their voices rising with the excitement of the game. At one point, Jim stirred in his sleep, and Hank shushed the men, who quieted out of respect for the young man who had saved their lives earlier that day.

When supper was ready, the woman was about to pat Jim's arm to let him know when Hank stopped her. "Don't touch him when he's sleeping, ma'am. I learned that the hard way on our first trip." He grinned, rubbing his jaw as he recalled the blow from Jim's fist.

He said Jim's name and the young man opened his eyes. There was an expression of pain on his face for a second until he masked it. Then he slowly got to his feet.

The old man had a hearty beef stew and cornbread ready and shuffled around the table serving everyone. Jim only took a small piece of the cornbread and one ladle of stew, which he ate with his left hand. He wasn't hungry but forced himself to eat. He finished first, rose from the table, took his pistol, gun belt, rifle, and coat and stepped outside. He leaned his rifle against one of the posts for the small porch. Then he painfully put the gun belt on over his still untucked shirt, buttoning it against the wind. He eased on his coat, grabbed the rifle with his left hand, and began his usual walk of the perimeter. As darkness fell, he watched for any campfires in the vicinity or movements of men and horses that would indicate someone was following.

After making his circuit, he stood in the shadow of a large bush a short distance from the front of the house. The others had finished eating by now, and the two male passengers and Hank walked out onto the small front porch. The passengers rolled and lit cigarettes while Hank enjoyed the cool night air. After tucking her little daughter into bed, the female passenger stepped outside as well and strolled out into the yard looking up at the stars.

"Shouldn't be out here alone, ma'am," cautioned a male voice from the darkness.

"Is that you, Mr. Morgan?" she asked with a slight start.

Jim stepped out from the shadows. "Yes, ma'am."

"I just had to get away from those two men for a few minutes," she replied in exasperation.

"They been bothering you?"

"Not directly. They both just keep staring at me, one of them with a strange grin on his face." She shivered and wrapped her shawl more tightly around her shoulders.

"I can say something to them if you'd like."

"No, thank you. I'll just continue to ignore them." Then she took a deep breath and gazed at the sky. "I'm going to miss beautiful nights like this when my daughter and I get to Philadelphia. You don't see stars like this in a big city."

"Why don't you stay?"

"I've tried. My husband died two years ago, and my daughter and I were doing fine until the copper mine came in. Ours was a nice little town where everyone knew each other, but the mine brought all sorts of people and suddenly ours wasn't a safe little town anymore. For my daughter's sake, we're going to live with my parents."

Jim gazed up at the stars with her for a few minutes and for some reason felt comforted by them. "Would you like me to walk you back?" he offered.

"Yes, thank you. And thank you for saving us this afternoon. I hope you weren't hurt too badly."

"I'll be all right."

As they headed back toward the others, they heard Hank arguing with one of the men.

"Is there a problem?" Jim asked as he and the woman approached.

Hank didn't answer but looked at the man he'd been talking to, whose companion also looked at him, forcing him to speak.

The man swallowed hard and faced Jim. "How can you protect the stage tomorrow if you can't even eat with that arm?"

Jim eyed him a moment. He still held the rifle in his left hand. He turned away from them. "See that rock?" he said, pointing to a small stone lying on the ground about twenty feet away, just visible in the moonlight. He swung the rifle down to cock it, snapped it level, and fired. The blast threw the stone and dust into the air. Jim turned back to the man, his eyes flashing in controlled anger. "I can shoot with my left hand. If I couldn't do my job, I'd say." Then he stepped by them and followed the woman through the door.

"It's not like it's the first time you've been shot," Hank commented as Jim passed.

The others stayed on the porch a while longer.

The woman stepped behind the screen the old man had set by her bed to give her privacy. Then she slipped out of her dress, hung it on a hook, loosened her corset a bit, and went to sleep. The screen was the one for the chamber pot, and she was so tired she hardly stirred as Hank lifted it and put it back in its usual place.

Jim sat at the table, cleaning and reloading his weapons. Then he placed them under the pillow and bed as he had before, removed his boots, and lay down under the covers. Though it was against company policy for a freight man to go to bed without sponging off at the least, Jim was too tired.

The two male passengers came in after a short while.

The old man and the boy had already climbed into their loft to sleep. Before long, the house was dark and quiet.

Jim awoke later in the night. His arm hurt, and he realized he must have tried to roll onto it in his sleep. He was about to doze back off when he heard a rustling sound coming from the woman's bed, then a thud as if someone had been struck. As a precaution, he took his revolver from under his pillow and crept toward the noise. There was one bed between his and the woman's, where one of the male passengers was supposed to be sleeping. As he passed it, Jim patted it gently, feeling for its occupant. It was empty. The rustling was louder now, and he thought he heard a muffled cry. He straightened, faced the woman's bed, and raised his weapon.

"Whoever's moving, hold still!" he commanded and cocked his gun.

The rustling stopped.

"Hank!" Jim called. He heard the driver stir. "Hank!" he called again. "Light the lantern!"

Hank sat up groggily. As he fumbled in the darkness for the matches, the man who had been on the woman's bed launched himself at Jim and the two fell to the floor. Jim quickly uncocked his gun and used the butt to hit the man on the side of the head, knocking him unconscious. Then Jim roughly pushed the man aside and jumped to his feet. The lantern flared, and Jim saw the other man start to move.

"I wouldn't try it!" Jim growled, cocking his weapon again and aiming it at the male passenger.

He had been leaning over the headboard of the woman's bed, restraining her.

The man froze.

"What in the—" Hank uttered in disbelief, looking at the other male passenger lying on the floor.

"Get some rope," Jim ordered.

The one on the floor regained consciousness as Jim grabbed him. Hank took hold of the other. Jim and Hank tied the men with their hands behind their back. Then the freight men looped and tied the rope around the men's feet and left them lying hog-tied on their sides in their bunks.

After making sure both men were secure, Jim walked to the woman. "Are you all right?" he asked, kneeling beside her bed.

The woman sat clutching the covers to her chest, shivering and gazing at her daughter still sleeping beside her. She opened her mouth and blood dripped out.

Jim caught it with his hand so it wouldn't stain the bed.

The woman paled at the sight.

"Hank, bring the lantern over here," Jim ordered. Then he asked the woman, "May I touch you?"

She nodded.

With Hank holding the light, Jim gently curled back each lip and looked inside her mouth. "You're not missing any teeth, but you have a cut on your upper lip. Did he hit you?"

She nodded and glanced at the man Jim had knocked unconscious.

"You bastard!" muttered Hank in a rare use of profanity, turning to the prisoner so the woman wouldn't hear him.

"Untie me and say that!" the man retorted.

"Do you really think you can take me?" Hank asked threateningly, looming over him.

The man didn't reply.

"Did he do anything else?" Jim asked her softly.

The woman shook her head and began to cry. She leaned against Jim's shoulder and he put his arm around her to comfort her.

"They won't be hurting you now, ma'am," Hank assured her. "Jimmy here saw to that."

"Stay with her," Jim said to Hank as he gently freed himself from the woman. He stepped to the sink, washed his hands, and filled a glass. Then he grabbed a bowl and returned. He sat next to her on the bed and offered her the water. "Don't drink it," he instructed. "Just swish it around in your mouth then spit it out."

She obeyed.

Jim had her do this two more times and then he had her hold the water in her mouth. A few minutes later, the bleeding stopped.

"Thank you both," she whispered.

"Try to get some sleep," Jim suggested, standing.

She nodded, scooted down in the bed, and pulled the covers up to her chin.

"It's a good thing you woke up," Hank said to Jim as the guard took the glass and bowl to the sink.

Jim nodded.

"Did your arm wake you?" Hank asked in concern.

"It was either that or the noise."

"You going to be able to sleep?"

Jim nodded again.

The next morning, the old man and the boy were surprised to see two of the passengers tied up. They had slept through the incident. Jim let the two men eat, but he kept their feet tied and his gun handy. To get them on the stage, he and Hank tied their hands behind them, released their feet so they could walk, and retied them after they were in their seats.

Jim took two potato sacks from the house, cut a hole in them with his knife, and put a sack over each man's head to cover their eyes. The hole, revealing the nose of one and the mouth of the other, was cut only so they could breathe easier.

"What are you doing this for?" asked one of the prisoners as Jim put the sack over his head.

Jim didn't answer, but the woman nodded her thanks. Her daughter laughed, and the woman shushed her.

They arrived in Dillard late that afternoon, and Jim and Hank took the men to jail. Then Jim intended to help unload the freight, but Ted insisted he go to Sam's to have his arm treated.

"Hank did a good job," Sam said as he examined the wound.

"There's no sign of infection."

Since the wound had begun to heal, Sam couldn't stitch it, leaving Jim with a large scar. Jim didn't care. He was just thankful it healed.

The sheriff asked the woman, Sylvia, to stay in town until she could speak with the judge hearing the case against her attackers. She agreed, and Ted secured a room for her at the hotel at his expense. Then he invited her and her daughter, Laura, to have dinner with him. Sylvia accepted, and they dined together every night thereafter. A few weeks later, Ted asked her to marry him, and Sylvia agreed.

One afternoon, the sheriff overheard his prisoners talking and informed Ted that they planned to plead not guilty. The prospect of a trial and having to testify frightened Sylvia and angered Ted. Jim was on a stage run, but as soon as he returned, Ted called him to his office and told him about the men's plan, as well as its effect on Sylvia.

Jim's jaw tightened at the news, and his eyes flashed. "I'll handle this!" he growled and strode out of the office.

Ted had to stop to tell his chief clerk he was leaving for a while. Then he followed Jim to the sheriff's office.

"Give me a minute alone with your prisoners," Jim said to the sheriff as he laid his gun belt and knife on the man's desk.

"Sure," the sheriff replied, grabbing his keys.

Jim and the sheriff had just reached the cell when Ted rushed in from the outer office.

The sheriff unlocked the cell door. Jim stepped in, much to the surprise of the prisoners, and the sheriff locked the door after him.

"Why don't you step outside," Jim said over his shoulder to the sheriff without taking his eyes off the men.

"That's OK," the sheriff replied with a smirk. "I'd like to watch." Then he stepped back and casually leaned against the opposite wall.

Ted stood near the door to the office, where he could see the prisoners but they couldn't see him because of the shadows.

"What do you want, Morgan?" asked the leader of the two, standing to face Jim while his friend remained seated on his bunk.

"I hear you plan to plead not guilty," Jim replied.

"That's right."

"You really think that'll do you any good?" Jim asked, stepping close to the man, who was slightly taller and somewhat heavier.

"We didn't hurt her," the man insisted. "It was all just a misunderstanding."

"I was there," Jim replied, his voice low and menacing. "I know what you intended. And if you know what's good for you, you'll plead guilty."

"But then we'd hang!" whined the other man, still seated.

"That's right," said the leader. "We've been accused of attempted rape."

"That can change," mentioned the sheriff. "You agree to plead guilty, and I'll change the charge to assault. You'll go to prison, but you won't hang."

"No!" insisted the leader, glancing at his companion, hoping the man would stand up and face the guard with him. Instead, the other man seemed to shrink back against the wall.

Before the one standing could react, Jim grabbed him and shoved his back into the bars hard enough to knock the wind out of him. The man found himself gasping, one arm pinned by the guard's iron grip, the other by Morgan's elbow, with the guard's fist pressing crushingly on his chest.

The man inhaled sharply, struggling, but the pain in his chest and arms stilled him.

"Plead guilty!" Jim growled softly in the man's ear.

"No!" the man grunted, again struggling uselessly against greater strength.

The prisoner tried to bring up a knee. Jim was quicker and shifted his weight against the man, pushing his own knee into the prisoner's groin.

"Plead guilty!" Jim growled again. "Or I'll start doing real damage."

"Help me!" the man cried to his friend.

The other man shook his head, refusing to move. He sensed a malevolent power to the guard's anger. He remembered once when he was a child cowering under a wagon as a terrible storm broke over him. He felt the same dreadful tingle on his skin as he had just before the sky darkened, the thunder ripped the air, the hail began to fall, and the wind almost lifted the wagon off him. It was as though all the malice of the world had been unleashed. He stared at the guard. Though Morgan was of average build, he rendered his friend helpless with ease. The guard wasn't even breaking a sweat, and his friend was struggling with all his might. The guard's eyes shone as though lightning were in his soul, the man a lethal force of nature all his own.

The leader fought until the pain in his groin, arms, and chest became too excruciating to endure. Then he relaxed, capitulating to the superior might.

"Plead guilty!" Jim repeated. "Save everyone the trouble of a trial."

"But we might be found innocent!" the man gasped.

"Doubt it," Jim scoffed. "You go to trial, either you'll hang, or I'll kill you both. Either way, you die."

The man looked into the guard's eyes. The intensity of Jim's gaze disconcerted him and assured him of the guard's unwavering intent. He glanced at the sheriff. "He threatened me! You heard him!"

"What?" the sheriff asked. "I didn't hear a thing."

The man looked back at the guard and slumped against the bars. "OK."

"You change your mind," Jim warned, "I'll come back." Then he threw the man aside like an unwanted doll.

The sheriff unlocked the door, and Jim stepped out.

Ted didn't say a word until they were back on the street. "Thank you, but I can fight my own battles."

"I know you can," Jim responded. "But why should you when I can save you the trouble?"

"I was just planning to do it in court," Ted stated.

"I didn't want to have to testify either," Jim replied. "Oh, and I heard about your engagement, congratulations."

"We're not planning to get married for at least a year."

"Why?" Jim asked.

"Her mother has been ill, and won't be able to travel until next spring at the earliest."

"Why not just go ahead and marry her now? You won't be living with the in-laws."

"To tell the truth," Ted replied, "I don't mind. I know I was engaged before, but having a woman here in town—I need time to get accustomed to the idea."

Jim nodded, then noticed Tait coming toward them. He had been the only one of Sam's adopted patients to live, and he had quit the freight company to work for the wheelwright.

"How are you?" Ted asked his former employee, looking the man up and down.

Ted's genuine concern for his men still surprised Jim.

"I'm doing well, thank you," Tait replied. "Guess who my boss's wife heard from the other day?"

Ted and Jim shook their heads.

"That jackass, Crane!" Tait growled. "I overheard her talking to one of her women friends. Apparently, our Dr. Crane decided to seek his fortune in the Far East, and from what he wrote her should be on a ship on the high seas by now. That's one man I'd like to see swallowed by a whale but never spit back up."

Jim nodded.

"Well, I hope he's not planning to practice medicine," Ted commented.

"Me too," Tait replied with a nod. Then he bade them good-bye and headed back to work.

After picking up his rifle, shotgun, and bag, which he'd left in Ted's office while he dealt with the prisoners, Jim walked to his room. He wished he could go for a ride on Ness, but he knew there wasn't enough time for that. Instead, he took a quick bath and, since there was still some daylight left, strolled over to see how the work was progressing on Sam's house.

Sam had started building his own house even before Ted announced his engagement. To the freight man's credit, he never complained or asked the doctor to move. On the contrary, Ted offered to build himself a new house and let Sam and Martha stay in the old one, but Sam insisted on building his own. His new house was to have two treatment rooms, an operating room with windows to rival those of Ted's dining room, and plenty of rooms for guests or patients.

Since there had been a gold shipment on this stage run, it had been a nine-day trip. Due to the recent robberies, Jim and Hank now had to go all the way through Hell's Playground when the stage was carrying the gold. The gold mine also always had three of its own guards protecting the shipment. Though this lessened the chances of an attack, it made the home stations more crowded, and that always played on Jim's nerves. He hoped the walk would calm him so he could sleep.

As he sauntered up to where the men were working, the ones on the roof saw him, called down, and waved. He waved in reply and circled the structure, nodding his approval.

"What do you think?" asked the foreman, striding up to him with a smile.

"Looks good," Jim replied. "You sure you'll have enough support on that back wall for the glass for the operating room? It's going to be heavy."

"We're not quite done with it yet," said the foreman. He was always surprised at Jim's eye for detail. "We should have all the supports up by the end of the week."

Jim nodded. "Let me know if you need an extra pair of hands." He wanted some way to repay Sam for all he'd done for him. The doctor had yet to charge him for any of his medical care and became offended when he tried to force money on him.

"Thanks," said the foreman, "but I think the smith needs you more. I just put in another order for hardware."

Jim nodded. "I'll go by there tomorrow. I just got cleaned up, and knowing him he'd put me to work in the dark."

The foreman laughed and nodded, noting Jim didn't smile, as they parted with a wave.

Jim stopped by the stable to see Ness. Though it was too late for a ride, he gave him a good brushing and an apple, then headed back to his room.

Jim earned the respect and admiration of most of the people in Dillard, though from a distance. His natural reticence, combined with his unwitting intensity, which others often perceived as ferocity due to his reputation, kept most of the townspeople from attempting any sort of closeness. To the few who made the effort to get to know the man rather than the impression, they found him surprisingly kind and gentle. He possessed a quiet, soft-spoken manner that could put people, as well as animals, at ease.

However, if any of the townspeople ever questioned for a moment whether he deserved his reputation on the stage or it was just an exaggeration, all they had to do was look into his eyes. The fire was always there, smoldering just below the surface like hot coals in an oven concealed by the ashes. A quick stir and the fire would burst forth. To those who still may have doubted, the opportunity arose for Jim to prove himself much closer to home.

8

SARAH

In late spring of 1871, Sam and Martha's house was finished. They were happy and thankful to Ted for all he had done for them.

Ted insisted on paying a large part of the expense for the operating room, treatment rooms, and the patient rooms as well. "You'll be taking care of my men," he explained to Sam as justification for his generosity.

Martha had quickly learned to like the new town, and she and Olivia Henson became close friends. Olivia was often at Martha's house, either visiting or helping with household tasks so Martha could attend to patients, and Olivia's eight-year-old daughter, Sarah, usually accompanied her. Since Jim was often at the house helping with chores that Sam didn't have the time or the expertise to perform, he and Sarah became friends.

Sarah liked to watch Jim chop wood or work on something that needed repair. She loved to walk with Jim to the barn to check on Ness, though she usually ended up riding on Jim's back or shoulders. Then she would beg Jim to put her on Ness's back and lead her around. Sarah's short legs tickled Ness's sides, and she would giggle when he shivered in response. Ness apparently didn't mind the tickling, because he always perked up when he saw her, and Jim noticed he paid careful attention to where he put his feet when she was perched on his back.

One night, shortly after dark, Jim had just returned from an afternoon ride to give Ness some exercise. As he entered town, he saw a group of men on horseback holding torches and gathered in front of the sheriff's office. He rode up and asked what was happening. One of the men told him that Sarah and her father had gone fishing and not yet returned.

"I just saw them a couple of hours ago at their favorite spot," Jim replied.

"Can you lead us there?" asked the sheriff.

Jim nodded and turned Ness. The sheriff handed Jim a torch, and he led them out of town to the place beside a stream where he had seen Sarah and her father. The bank was flat on that side but rose sharply on the other, and the stream was shallow.

Jim dismounted and, using the light of the torch, examined the ground. "Sarah and her father were on foot," he explained. Then he waded across the stream and looked at the opposite bank. "It looks like two horses went up here. There are some footprints, too, maybe Mr. Henson's."

"Any sign of the girl?" asked the sheriff.

"No, sir," Jim replied, surprised by the dread he felt surge within him.

"Do you think you can track them?" the sheriff inquired as he crossed the stream.

"I can try," Jim replied.

He tied Ness's reins around the saddle horn and, holding the torch near the ground, followed the tracks. "Ness, come," Jim ordered the horse, and the other men were surprised that the horse obediently followed him without Jim needing to lead him.

A few yards from the stream, the ground hardened. Eventually, Jim lost the tracks, but he was able to see from broken twigs and branches which way the horses had traveled. They'd gone almost a mile into the woods when they heard a cry. All of the men froze and listened.

"Let me go on ahead," Jim said softly to the sheriff as he handed his torch to another man. "All of us together make too much noise."

The sheriff nodded. "But I'm coming with you." Then he dismounted and whispered to the other men, ordering them to remain where they were.

Jim pulled his rifle from its saddle holster and cocked it. Then he motioned to Ness to stay, and the two men headed deeper into the woods. They hadn't gone far when they heard another cry. Jim was sure it was Sarah, and his jaw tightened. After a few more yards, they saw a glow.

"Better let me go first, Duncan," Jim whispered to the sheriff. "No offense, but I'm a better shot."

The sheriff nodded.

Jim came to the edge of a clearing and saw two men near a fire. One was standing with his back to him. The other was kneeling on the ground next to a small form wrapped tightly with ropes.

"Just kill her," said the one standing. "Her hollering is giving me a headache."

"I'll kill her soon enough," replied the one on the ground. "Remember, the boss wants it to look like Indians. Don't forget that you still need to scalp the man."

"Why Indians?" asked the one standing.

"So the cavalry will start going after them and leave us alone," said the one kneeling. Then he drew something out of the fire and moved it toward the helpless victim before him, who began to squirm and beg.

Jim recognized Sarah's voice. He stepped out from the trees, rifle leveled and ready. "Put that down!" he commanded.

The man on the ground looked up in surprise, and the one standing reached for his weapon as he turned. Jim fired. As the one who'd been standing fell dead, the other reached for his gun. A second later, he too was lying by the fire, his eyes staring toward the sky but not seeing.

Jim ran to the small bundle bound cruelly on the ground. Sarah's head turned, their eyes met, then hers closed as she lost consciousness.

Jim was cutting the ropes as the sheriff ran up. "Is she OK?" he asked.

"I don't know," Jim answered, removing the last of her bonds.

The others joined them.

"Sheriff, you should see this," said one of the men, who had noticed something and crossed to the other side of the clearing. "I think it's Henson."

The sheriff ran to where the other man was standing.

Jim glanced in that direction but was more concerned with

getting Sarah back to town. He saw Ness on the edge of the glade with the other horses. He called him, and Ness came trotting up and tossed his head.

"Shouldn't you wait for a wagon?" asked the sheriff as he turned back from viewing what the others had found.

"Ness rides smoother than any wagon," Jim replied, slipping his rifle back into its holster.

He mounted, holding Sarah gently in front of him. Then he took a torch from one of the men and gave Ness a slight kick. He guided the horse carefully through the woods, using his legs since he held Sarah in one arm and the torch with the other hand. When they reached the road, he dropped the torch and unwrapped the reins. "Take us to Sam!" he commanded as he urged Ness into a run. Within minutes, he was back in town. At the sound of his horse people stepped outside.

One man shouted to him, and Jim told him to get Sarah's mother and meet him at Sam's. When Jim arrived at the doctor's house, he leapt off almost before Ness had stopped, and Sam met him at the threshold. Jim had just handed Sarah to him, and Sam and Martha had taken her into a treatment room and closed the door, when Olivia ran into the reception room. Jim grabbed her arms to keep her from following them.

"Let go of me!" Olivia screamed as she struggled against Jim's grasp.

"Let Sam take care of her," Jim said softly, not releasing her but trying not to hurt her.

Olivia calmed and stopped struggling. "Is she all right? What did they do to her?"

"She's alive. That's really all I can tell you. I just picked her up and brought her here."

Olivia collapsed in tears.

Jim caught her and held her as she cried.

"My husband?" she asked, after a few sobs.

"I don't know."

Olivia continued to cry for a few minutes. Then she took a deep breath and tried to stop.

They heard noise outside, and the sheriff entered, followed by his wife and a few townswomen.

Olivia looked up expectantly, but when she saw the sheriff's face, she started to cry again.

"I'm sorry," said the sheriff, shaking his head.

Olivia held onto Jim as she wept, gripping his shoulder to keep from drowning in her grief.

"Is the little girl OK?" the sheriff asked him.

"Sam's with her now," Jim replied.

"Who did this?" Olivia asked through her tears.

"We don't know yet," answered the sheriff. "But they won't hurt anyone again, thank God. Jim here made sure of that."

Olivia glanced up at the young man, then lowered her head, weeping.

Jim moved her to a sofa. Olivia continued clinging to him, so Jim sat beside her.

A while later, Sam opened the door to the treatment room and stepped out, shutting it behind him. "She's going to be fine," he assured Olivia.

"Thank God!" Olivia breathed. "Can I see her?"

"Martha's getting her settled. I gave her something to make her sleep." Then he turned to the others and said, "If you all will excuse us, I need to talk to Olivia in my study."

They nodded, and the women assured their friend they'd still be there when she returned.

Holding on to Jim, Olivia followed Sam down the hall to his study. After getting her seated, Jim turned to leave, but Olivia wouldn't let go of him. Sam nodded, so Jim knelt beside her chair.

"Like I said," Sam began, "she's going to be all right."

"What did they do to her?" Olivia asked, fright evident in her voice.

"They burned her legs with something," said the doctor evenly. He didn't want his own emotions to upset the frightened woman before him any further. "Probably a piece of metal of some kind," he continued. "She'll recover and be able to do everything she could before, but she will be scarred."

Olivia stared at him in disbelief, then started to cry again. A moment later, she looked up and asked, "They didn't do anything *else*, did they?"

Sam knew to what she was referring and shook his head. "Would you like to see her now?"

Olivia nodded.

Sam led them back down the hallway to the room where

Martha had settled Sarah.

"She's sleeping," whispered Martha as they entered. She stepped to the foot of the bed.

Olivia fell to her knees at the bedside and gazed at her daughter.

"There's a daybed right here," Martha said, motioning to a small bed behind her. "It's made up, so why don't you try to get some rest, too."

"I can't sleep. What if she needs me?"

"She'll sleep until morning," Sam assured her. "Now drink this, and so will you." He handed her a glass of water mixed with laudanum.

Olivia gazed at Sarah another minute, then drained the glass.

Jim and Sam stepped out of the room as Martha helped Olivia prepare for bed.

"Mr. Henson?" asked the doctor.

Jim shook his head.

Sam sighed. "And the men who did this?"

"Dead."

"Good. What they did to that child was inhuman."

"I have to take care of Ness," Jim said, turning toward the door to the reception room where the townswomen were waiting. "Should I come back?"

"They should both sleep, but it might not hurt to have you here if one of them does wake up. Olivia seemed to really rely on you earlier, and I know you're close to Sarah."

Jim nodded and followed Sam back to the reception room.

The doctor assured the women that Olivia wouldn't need them until morning. Then Jim followed the women outside and was surprised not to see Ness waiting for him.

"My husband had one of the stable boys take him," explained the sheriff's wife.

Jim was again surprised that Ness had allowed someone to lead him away, but asked her to thank her husband for him and walked back inside. He returned to Sarah's room just as Martha was leaving it.

"Now they're both asleep," she whispered.

They stepped into the kitchen and found Sam eating some bread and cheese. After their snack, they all went to bed. Jim didn't have a permanent room, but he was there often enough to know which room was his. It wasn't one of the patient rooms but one of Sam and Martha's guest rooms. It was on the front corner of the house, across the hall and one door down from where Martha had put Sarah and her mother.

Jim was very tired. He had just gotten back from a stage run the night before and had spent the day working for the blacksmith before taking Ness out for a ride. He had been working for the freight company for almost a year, and the stallion had adjusted well. Ness didn't seem to miss him nearly as much now that he had taken up with a pretty little filly owned by the smith. Jim and the smith hoped they would breed. With Ness's strength and intelligence and the filly's good looks, they knew they could get a good price for the foal.

Jim was worried about Sarah but managed to fall asleep. He awoke during the night and heard something, so he stepped into the hall. The sound was coming from Sarah's room. He silently walked to her door and opened it noiselessly. Sarah and her mother were sleeping, but Sarah was restless and whimpering. Jim crept to her bedside and took her hand. She stirred and looked up.

"You're safe now," Jim whispered to her.

"Jim?" the child murmured.

"Yes, Sarah. I'm here."

The child closed her eyes and drifted back to sleep, resting peacefully.

Jim held her hand for a few minutes. Then he slipped free, intending to go back to his room. As soon as he let go of her, though, Sarah became restless again. He took her hand and she calmed, so he remained another little while. Then he tried to leave again, and again she stirred and almost awoke. There was an armchair a few feet from the bed. Jim quietly moved it over, took the child's hand, and settled in for the night.

A short time later, Martha peeked in to check on Sarah and Olivia and was surprised to see Jim sleeping in the armchair holding Sarah's hand. She started to wake him but decided against it. She was about to close the door when she saw Jim's eyes looking at her in the dim light of the lantern she'd left burning earlier. Martha nodded silently to him, shut the door, and went back to bed. She was always amazed at how he could wake up at the slightest sound within the room. She tried not to think about the environment he must have endured that required such vigilance in order to survive.

She returned the next morning accompanied by Sam and found Jim awake, still holding Sarah's hand.

"Did you get any sleep?" Martha whispered.

"A little," Jim replied softly.

"Have you been here all night?" Sam asked, also speaking quietly.

"Almost."

"Why didn't you sleep in your room?" inquired the doctor.

"Every time I let go of her hand she gets restless and wakes up," Jim explained.

Olivia looked up, woken by their whispered voices, and heard Jim's last reply. She arose, walked to him, and patted the young man on the shoulder. "I'll hold her hand now. Go get some sleep."

"I slept in the chair," Jim said. "But I'll let you take over."

He slipped his hand out from under Sarah's and was about to leave the room when the child stirred and mumbled something in her sleep.

Olivia took her daughter's hand and talked softly to her, but the child became more agitated. Sarah cried out, looking around in terror. "Where's Jim?"

"Mama's with you," Olivia whispered.

"They'll hurt us!" Sarah cried. "Only Jim can protect us! Where is he?"

"I'm right here," Jim replied, returning to the bedside.

"Those men! They hurt me and Papa!" Sarah shouted, almost hysterical. She reached for his hand. Jim gave it to her and she clung to him. "They killed Papa!" she screamed. Then she fell silent and gazed around, her eyes wide with fear. She looked up at Jim and whispered, "They killed him, didn't they?"

Jim nodded silently.

Sarah started to cry, and so did her mother.

Jim held the child as she wept, with Olivia resting her head on his shoulder.

After a few minutes, Sarah looked up. "Jim?"

"Yes?"

"What happened to the men who hurt me? Did you kill them?"

"Yes, Sarah."

"To protect me?"

"Yes."

"Thank you," Sarah breathed, laying her head against his chest. Then she fell back asleep.

Jim stayed with her the rest of the day. Now just his presence was enough, so his hands were free. He spent his time whittling a piece of wood he found outside, using his pocketknife and leaning over a waste bin so as not to get wood chips on the floor. Sam let Sarah wake up for meals but other than that kept her medicated to reduce her suffering, so she never saw what Jim was making.

By that evening, Jim was done with the initial shape of the object, and he spent part of the next day doing some detail work. That afternoon, he took a few minutes to go to the carpenter's shop and asked the carpenter's permission to sand the piece smooth and stain it. The carpenter agreed and refused money for the supplies. The man smiled when he looked at the small object, admiring the work. Then he asked Jim if he would be interested in doing more for sale.

"I really don't think it's all that good," Jim replied.

"It looks fine to me," insisted the carpenter. "It's not supposed to be a work of art or anything. I'm sure I could sell any you make, especially if you can do other figures, too."

"I'll think about it."

The object was dry by the next afternoon, and Jim returned to retrieve it. Then he stopped by the freight office and found that Ted had scheduled him to leave the following day.

That evening, Sarah paled when Jim told her he would have to leave on a stage run the next morning and that he'd be gone for a few days. He had spent almost every moment with her, even eating his meals in her room to encourage her to eat as well. When Sam tended to her burns, Jim did his best to comfort her, cradling her in his arms and talking to her.

Though he always refused any medication for pain for himself, Jim was surprised Sam couldn't give her something to make her unconscious so she wouldn't have to suffer. The doctor assured him he wished the same thing, but to medicate her so strongly every day would be extremely dangerous.

At night, Jim slept on the floor by Sarah's bed so she could reach down and touch him if she got scared. Whenever he left the room, she became anxious, and every few minutes would ask whoever was with her when he'd be back.

"Can't you stay?" Sarah asked him.

"I have to do my job, you know that," Jim replied.

"But couldn't you stay here just this once?" Sarah pleaded.

"I have something for you to keep with you while I'm gone," Jim said, taking the small object he'd made from his pocket and giving it to the little girl.

It was a horse, adequately carved and darkly stained.

"It's beautiful!" Sarah exclaimed. "And it looks like Ness!"

"I made it so you'd have something to hold when I'm not here."

Sarah gave him a hug. "I still don't want you to go," she whimpered, gazing down at the toy horse.

"I know, but now you'll be brave, won't you?"

Sarah nodded.

"I have to go back to my room at the boarding house so I'll be ready for tomorrow. OK?"

Sarah nodded again. Then as he was about to leave, she called, "Jim?"

He turned back to her from the doorway.

"Be careful," she said.

Jim nodded and left.

As he walked to the boarding house, he vaguely remembered another little horse he'd made many years before for another little girl. Then he shook his head slightly, shut the memory behind one of the doors in his mind and, by doing so, protected himself from the pain.

9

THUNDER CROW

By the next afternoon, Jim was miles from Dillard, sitting atop the stage and scanning his surroundings. He and Hank both knew that trouble could appear in the form of bandits at any moment. Jim heard the call of a crow and glanced up at the black spec in the sky. The crows were always around it seemed, either sitting on branches in the forests or circling overhead looking for a meal. Sometimes he saw a group of them harassing a hawk, and seeming to laugh at the larger bird as it flew away. Once he saw a crow drop down where he'd thrown an apple core then lift off again holding part of it in its beak. He started leaving more for them after that.

What Jim didn't know was that the crows followed his stage. They had learned that this one particular featherless, two-legged creature with the loud stick often provided them with an easy meal, one that was more filling than apples. The other featherless, two-legged things with the same sticks, who sat on the dust-maker like the apple-giver, didn't usually kill with their sticks. The predators on the flying-footed grass-eaters would ride away after attacking. That is until the apple-giver, the predator disguised as prey, killed them.

The Indians noticed this as well. They dubbed Jim "Thunder Crow," after the sound the stage made as it rumbled over the road, the birds that followed him, and the blackness of his hair, which shone blue in the sunlight when he removed his hat like a bird's feathers. The Indians admired his marksmanship, nerve, and ability to withstand pain, and they wondered at the stupidity of the white men who went up against him.

Jim was so successful at protecting the stage that sometimes Ted had to change the route he and Hank took because the bandits learned to avoid it. Other times, though he didn't tell Jim, it was because a passenger had paid extra to have Jim protect his stage. Ted kept this knowledge to himself, but put the amount into a special account he used to pay Jim when he couldn't work because he'd gotten injured on the stage. The gold mine also paid to have Jim on the stage when they were transporting the gold, and Ted added that amount to the fund as well. He felt gratified that Mr. Peck, the main owner of the company, agreed with him that these revenues should be passed on to the man who made them possible.

Jim and Hank were on the eastern run this time. It was late afternoon, and the stage was passing through one of the forests. The trees were so close together they cast a gloom over the way, darkening the day with dusky shadows. The stage was negotiating a curve around a low hill when Hank suddenly pulled the horses up short, nearly toppling Jim off the roof of the coach.

"What the f—" Jim said, stopping himself before he uttered the profanity as he regained his balance. He rose up onto his knees and saw a tree across the road.

Four armed men stepped out from the forest and surrounded the stage.

"You were saying," said Hank softly.

One of the men told Jim to drop his weapons. Jim eyed the man for a second. Then he complied, dropping his rifle and then his handgun over the side of the coach. Hank didn't carry a weapon so as not to be a target, and the men left him alone. One of the bandits opened the coach door and disarmed their only passenger, a businessman traveling east from Bridgetton. Apparently satisfied that the passenger was no longer a threat, the bandit closed the door. Then he walked to the front of the stage and tugged on the strongbox kept under Hank's seat.

If the boxes weren't full, Ted always had his men fill them with bricks or anything heavy they could find. He reasoned that a three hundred pound box was harder to steal than a seventy-five pound box, and the horses would hardly notice the difference. The single bandit couldn't budge the box, so he called for help, and another man came to the front of the coach. The two of them still could hardly move it, so they called for the third. This obviously annoyed their leader. He still had a weapon trained on Jim, but glanced angrily at his men.

What the bandits didn't know was Jim kept his double barrel shotgun lying beside him on the top of the stage where no one could see it. As soon as the three men were engaged in trying to remove the strongbox and the other man looked away, Jim grabbed the weapon. He fired one barrel at the man guarding him, nearly cutting him in two. The second barrel he fired at the other three, wounding them all.

Then Jim tossed the empty shotgun aside and leapt from the top of the stage. The men fired at him as he fell. He grunted softly when a bullet tore through his right side. As soon as his feet touched the ground, Jim grabbed his rifle and rolled to control his momentum as well as escape the gunfire of the men. He came up on one knee, chambering a round as he moved. He fired three times in quick succession, finishing the men off. Then he stood and watched the bandits for a moment to make sure they were all dead. Jim kept his rifle trained on the men as Hank climbed down, gathered their weapons, and stowed them in the rear boot with the mail.

A horse snorted in the woods. Jim assured Hank he would be back in a minute and jogged off looking for the animals. He returned a few moments later leading four horses. He tied three to the rear of the stage and used the remaining one to remove the fallen tree from the road. Then he walked to the front of the stage after securing the fourth horse to the back, and the passenger spoke to him.

"You're bleeding," said the man as he nonchalantly stepped over one of the bandits after retrieving his weapon from the dead man's belt.

"One of them got me," Jim replied, unconcerned.

"Shouldn't that be tended to?"

"We'll be at the next home station before long," Jim explained, pushing the strongbox back into place by himself.

Jim's nerve, strength, and skill impressed the passenger, and he would remember Jim later when he needed someone with the young man's abilities.

"You sure you're OK?" Hank asked as Jim climbed back up on the coach, and the passenger stepped in and shut the door.

Jim nodded, then reached for his bag.

Hank gave the reins a shake, and the coach lurched forward. Jim was still standing. The movement caught him off balance. He dropped to his knees to keep from falling and cursed softly as his wounded side hit a piece of luggage.

"No more of that now," Hank scolded gently.

"Sorry, Captain," Jim replied as he wrapped a bandage around his middle.

Hank glanced back at him and was relieved to see a twinkle in Jim's eye in spite of the pain. He knew the young man was reading *Moby-Dick*. Though he hadn't read the book, he understood the reference and realized Jim was teasing him.

When they arrived at the home station, the station-keeper was surprised and unhappy to have four more horses to care for. His mood improved when Jim explained that he might get a bonus from the company from the sale of the animals.

This particular station had enough rooms for Jim and Hank to have a room to themselves. Hank was relieved he would be able to care for Jim's wound in privacy, and he winced when he looked at it.

"That bad?" Jim asked calmly.

"It looks like the bullet grazed off your side, but it tore the skin up pretty bad and may have cracked a couple ribs," Hank stated as he cleaned it. "Though I guess you're lucky it didn't go in you, or you'd probably not still be amongst the living."

Jim tensed as Hank poured alcohol on the wound.

"Sorry," said the driver.

"Just get it clean," Jim replied, his voice slightly strained.

"I think you should keep this dry," Hank advised as he finished treating the wound. Then he had Jim inhale and hold his breath as he bandaged him so as not to get it too tight. The driver noticed Jim's jaw tighten as he wrapped the bandage around him.

"Does it hurt to breathe?" Hank asked as Jim exhaled.

The young man nodded as he took another breath. "I won't tell Ted you ordered me not to bathe this trip," Jim promised.

Hank could tell he was teasing, even though he didn't smile.

The driver grinned. "You can sponge off at least," he suggested. "Otherwise, someone may think you're dead when you're just sleeping."

Jim shook his head at the remark.

Even though the days were warm, the nights were still cool. Since Jim insisted on bathing outside after dark, Hank didn't want him catching a chill.

After supper, Jim took his usual walk around the perimeter, carrying his rifle with his shotgun slung over his shoulder.

Their passenger met him on his way back.

"How are you feeling?" asked the passenger.

"All right."

"That was some pretty impressive shooting."

"Thanks."

The passenger fell into step with Jim, glancing at him as they walked.

"I've never seen someone put a strap on a shotgun before," the passenger commented with a laugh. He sensed Jim bristle, and when the young man made no reply, the passenger continued. "Let me introduce myself. Max Baier, US Marshal." He drew his badge out of the breast pocket of his suit coat and showed it to the guard. Then he returned it to his pocket and held out his hand.

"Pleased to meet you," Jim replied, giving the man's hand a shake.

"I've heard about you, and I'm glad I got to see you in action. Sorry you got hurt, though."

"Part of the job."

"Indeed it is. I've lost more than one man through the years," commented the marshal with a sigh.

"You're not dressed like a marshal."

"And you have a strap on a shotgun," Max laughed. "Who says a marshal can't be well-dressed?" he asked grinning and playfully tugging on his silk vest. "Besides, my men and I aren't your typical marshals. That's why I don't always wear my badge. Maybe one day I'll have the opportunity to explain it to you." Then he laughed again. "I suppose I should thank you for saving me the trouble of arresting those men."

"You're welcome," Jim replied without a smile.

They had reached the house, and Jim strode in and immediately went to bed.

The next morning he felt worse but concentrated on his job and made it through the day. That afternoon, they arrived at their farthest point east and unloaded the mail, the freight, and Max. Along with more mail and freight, they took on four passengers: a man, his wife, and their two children. Then they headed back to the same home station at which they had stayed the night before. The room Hank and Jim had shared was given to the family, since it was the only one large enough to accommodate them, so the two men settled into a smaller room.

"It doesn't look angry or anything," Hank assured his friend as they readied for bed. "It's still swollen, though."

All of the rooms had bunk beds. Though Jim usually took the top, Hank offered to sleep there this time. Jim declined, because he wasn't sure the top bunk could hold the big man. He would have slept on the floor if the room had been larger, but instead he had to climb up to the bed. He was in much more pain than he had been the night before and collapsed into his bunk, gritting his teeth to keep from groaning. Though he said nothing, Jim was glad they only had two more days to go before getting back to Dillard.

In the morning, Hank had to wake Jim, which was unusual. As the day wore on, the driver saw grim determination in the young man's eyes as he continued to function in spite of the pain. That evening, they were at the smallest of the stations and didn't have a room to themselves. Hank didn't want to try to treat Jim's wound in the barn, so after a whispered argument between the two men, during which Hank reminded his guard that the driver was in charge of the stage, Jim finally glared at him but nodded. Jim removed his shirt and lay on his left side facing the room. The woman offered to help, but Hank refused her when he caught the look in Jim's eye. She did see the wound, however, and shuddered. Hank was respectful of Jim's wishes, and no one saw his scars as the driver treated and bandaged the injury.

"I'm glad you'll be able to see Sam tomorrow," Hank commented as he tied the bandage.

"I hope Sarah's done OK."

Hank nodded, knowing Jim was more worried about the little girl than he was about himself. This amazed Hank, since the young man had obviously been mistreated when he was a child.

Jim was barely able to climb up onto the coach the next day. Hank considered making the passengers wait for another stage, but the young man insisted he could do his job. Jim compartmentalized the pain and managed to stay alert through force of will.

When they arrived in Dillard, Ted took one look at Jim and had Hank take him to the doctor. By the time they arrived at Sam's, Hank was practically carrying the young man, and was glad Ted had ordered someone else to bring his friend's bag and weapons later. Martha showed them into the treatment room while Sam washed his hands.

Sarah was still there, and Martha had Olivia assure her Jim was going to be all right.

Hank waited in the reception room until Sam was through, and was relieved to hear that he had taken good care of his friend. Sam also told him that the swelling came from Jim having sustained a few cracked ribs when the bullet hit him.

"He'll be in a lot of pain for a while, but he'll live," Sam explained to Hank. "I'm going to keep him here for a few days so he can rest."

"Will he be able to work next week?" Hank asked.

"No. I'm surprised he was able to function at all."

"You know Jim," stated the driver.

Sam nodded. He noted later in his journal that it was amazing the bullet hadn't entered Jim's body, for if it had it would most assuredly have killed him.

Late the next morning when he awoke, Jim wasn't sure where he was for a moment. Then he recognized the room at Sam and Martha's. Since he was alone, he allowed himself to react to the pain. He shut his eyes and gritted his teeth against a groan. When he heard someone coming down the hall, he steeled himself, so he was composed when Martha peeked into his room.

"Good morning!" she said with a smile. "Are you hungry?"

"No, ma'am."

"There's a certain little girl who's anxious to see you. Do you need a few minutes?"

Jim nodded.

"Do you need any help?"

"I don't know."

Martha stood by as he painfully got out of bed. He was naked, but she had seen him so often he no longer cared.

"I'll be all right," he said softly after he was on his feet. She nodded and left.

A little while later, Martha knocked on his door, and he told her to come in. She stepped into the room followed by Sarah, who was walking but followed closely by her mother. Jim was surprised and pleased to see Sarah walking, but he still didn't smile, though Martha noticed his expression softened when he looked at the little girl.

"You look like you're doing better," Jim said to Sarah.

Sarah smiled.

"She's been looking forward to showing you," Olivia announced, smiling as well.

"How are you feeling?" Sarah asked, touching Jim's arm, the smile leaving her face.

"I'll be fine."

"But you were shot," whimpered Sarah.

"It's not serious," Jim said.

"Can I see?"

Jim looked to Martha and shrugged slightly to show he didn't care, but he didn't want to encourage it if Martha or Olivia thought Sarah shouldn't.

Olivia nodded, so Martha pulled the covers down to Jim's waist and removed the bandage, since it needed changing anyway.

Sarah looked at Jim's side and began to cry.

"It looks worse than it is," he assured her.

Olivia tried to comfort her.

Martha moved a chair close to the bed.

Olivia sat down and held Sarah in her lap.

"But you could've been killed," Sarah said through her tears.

"But I wasn't."

"But if you had been, then there'd be no one to protect me and Mama!"

"Protect you from what?" Jim asked.

"Bad men. You're the one who saved me."

"Sarah, I wasn't the only man in the woods that night. The

sheriff was there, along with at least a dozen others. I just got to you first."

"But the sheriff said you got those men because you're the best shot, and the quickest."

"The results would have been the same if I hadn't been there," Jim explained. "The men who hurt you were outnumbered. You would have still been rescued, and the men killed."

"But I don't want you to die!" Sarah cried, tears rolling down her cheeks.

"I don't plan to," Jim answered, as he reached out to touch her arm.

Sarah slid off her mother's lap and gave him a hug. Though it was painful, he leaned toward her so she could put her arm around his neck.

"You look tired," Jim commented as he released the child.

"It's time for her to take a nap," Olivia explained.

"Can I take it in here with Jim?" Sarah asked.

Olivia didn't know what to say.

"I don't mind," Jim replied, "but I think your mother should stay too in case you need anything."

Olivia agreed.

Martha had Sarah and her mother step out while she cleaned and bandaged Jim's wound. Then she got Sarah a pillow, and Olivia helped her daughter settle in under the quilt but on top of the sheet. Martha gave Sarah some medicine to help her sleep, and a few minutes later the child was dozing contentedly beside Jim. She started out on her back, but soon turned over onto her right side. She brought her knees up, hitting him in the ribs, and he was glad she was on his left side. He managed to doze off while Olivia sat in the chair and busied herself with some hand-work. After about an hour and a half, Olivia rose and walked around the room to stretch. As she returned to the chair, she was surprised to see Jim watching her.

"I'm sorry if I woke you," she whispered so as not to disturb her daughter.

"That's OK," Jim said just as softly. "I'm a light sleeper."

"Let me get you some water," Olivia offered, going to the pitcher on the bureau. She poured a glass, brought it to Jim, and helped him lift his head to drink.

"Thank you," he whispered, after a few sips.

"You've been awfully good to Sarah and me," said Olivia, setting the glass on the bedside table and sitting back down. "I don't know how to thank you."

"No need." Then Jim winced slightly as he tried to sit up.

"Let me help you," offered Olivia, rising.

"No!" Jim responded too harshly. "I need to do it myself," he continued, moderating his tone.

Olivia stood by just in case, surprised by the level of his insistence.

"Sarah's worried about how she'll look," Olivia frowned after Jim had the pillow at his back against the headboard.

"She shouldn't be." Jim winced slightly again, trying not to show pain in his voice. He shifted his weight, trying to get comfortable.

"Why shouldn't I?" asked Sarah, looking up at him.

"How long have you been awake?" Jim asked the child.

"A few minutes. But why shouldn't I worry about having scars?"

"Everyone has scars," Jim replied. "Yours won't be any to be ashamed of."

Olivia had left the door open, and, hearing Sarah's voice, Martha walked down the hall. At Jim's words, she stood at the door as though transfixed. Hank had informed her and Sam about Jim preferring to bathe outside after dark, even in the cold of winter, rather than let anyone see his back.

"You don't have that many scars," Sarah said, sitting up and looking at his chest and arms.

"I have more than these," Jim replied, dropping his voice.

"Where?" asked Sarah.

"Sarah!" Olivia scolded her. "He might not want to talk about them."

"It's OK," Jim said softly, glancing at Martha. "I have some I don't like people to know about."

"Why?" Sarah asked, wrinkling her brow in concern.

"Because of what people think they mean."

"When did you get them?" asked the child.

"Starting when I was about your age."

Martha caught her breath and Olivia looked at her, then turned her attention back to Jim.

"Where are they?" Sarah asked.

"My back," Jim replied, his voice soft but intense.

"Can I see?" asked the child.

"Only if you promise not to tell anyone."

"I promise," Sarah said. "Do Sam and Martha know?"

"Yes, and Hank too, but that's all."

"Can Mama see them?"

Jim nodded.

Olivia crossed to the other side of the bed and stood near her daughter. Jim turned his back to them. At the sight of the scars, both mother and daughter caught their breath. Jim tensed. Sarah reached out and touched his back, causing him to draw away as though he'd been stung.

"How did you get those?" Sarah asked, fighting back tears.

Jim settled against the pillow again, his eyes resting on the bed to avoid everyone's gaze, his own burning as the fire within him kindled. "A man with a whip," he answered.

"Oh my God!" Olivia breathed.

"So see, Sarah?" Jim growled, his eyes flashing, though not in anger toward her, as he continued staring at some indeterminate point on the bed. "You have nothing to be ashamed of!"

"Neither do you!" Sarah insisted.

"Like I said, it's what people think they mean."

"What's that?"

"Prison, or worse," Jim replied, his voice even but covering intense emotion.

Sarah threw her arms around his neck. She understood, even at that young age, why he'd shown them to her, and what it had cost him.

Jim patted her back.

Olivia returned to the other side of the bed and put her hand on his shoulder. *So much power in him,* she thought, feeling his muscles under his skin, *and so much pain.* "You said you got those starting when you were Sarah's age?" She exchanged a horrified look with Martha.

Jim nodded.

"How long did this go on?" she asked.

"Few years. Don't like to talk about it."

Olivia gave his shoulder a squeeze. "I'm so sorry," was all she could think of to say, glancing at Martha again.

"Still have the horse I gave you?" Jim asked Sarah, anxious

to change the subject.

"Of course. I keep it by my bed and hold it every night when I say my prayers so you'll be safe. Though I guess it didn't help," she added, touching his bandage.

"I lived, didn't I? Guess it helped, then," he replied, giving her a tickle.

She laughed.

"Do you want to have lunch with me?" she asked. "Martha lets me eat on the back porch so I can get some air."

"Whatever you want," Jim replied, still looking only at the child, avoiding meeting either of the women's gazes.

"Sarah, why don't you help me fix it," Martha suggested, holding her hand out for the child.

Sarah climbed off the bed and walked on her own to the door, and she and Martha disappeared down the hall.

"Thank you," Olivia breathed. "I don't—"

Jim held up a hand to stop her, still not looking at her.

Olivia leaned over and gave him a kiss on the forehead. Then, embarrassed, she left the room, not noticing him shake his head slightly in a refusal to entertain any more painful memories.

Jim spent a few more days at Sam and Martha's, mainly because Sam didn't trust him to take it easy. When Martha told him how Jim had revealed his scars to Sarah to comfort her, Sam shook his head and commented that their young friend continued to amaze him. Later, he made note of it in the journal he'd started keeping on the young man.

As soon as the doctor allowed, Jim took Sarah to see Ness. Sam told him not to even think about riding, and told Ted that Jim would need at least three weeks to heal before he could return to work. Jim would have tried to ride anyway, but Hank stayed with him to make sure he obeyed the doctor's orders.

The knowledge of Jim's mistreatment as a child haunted Olivia, and she discussed it with Sam and Martha. All they could tell her was that the scars were old and that Jim refused to say where he'd gotten them. She tried to talk to Hank as well, but he told her he respected Jim's silence on the subject.

At night, Olivia would often think of Jim, out of concern for his safety when he was on the road, disbelief that one so ill-treated could be so kind, and admiration for how he'd saved her daughter. She knew he'd saved the lives of countless others on the stage, but she couldn't know that Sarah would only be the first of the ones he would save there in Dillard as well— though not necessarily with his gun.

Jim sometimes thought of Olivia at night as well. She was a beautiful woman, but, though he was attracted to her, he didn't allow himself the indulgence of either courting her or imagining what it would be like to be with her. He instinctively knew she couldn't be happy with someone who would always be gone, and she couldn't live with the very real possibility he wouldn't come back.

Sometimes, he thought about the beautiful redhead he'd seen his first day with the freight company. Again, he kept his thoughts to only what he could see and didn't let them torture him by imagining what he couldn't. He often saw her walking by when he worked for the smith, but he never spoke to her. He was greatly attracted to her, but he also knew where she lived, and, though he'd learned she didn't do what the other women in that house did, he still suspected she was like the women he'd known as a child.

10

NATALIE

In the fall of 1871, a young woman came into town on the stage. She had been traveling to St. Louis, but her money was about to run out, so she stayed in Dillard. She didn't have sufficient funds to secure a room in the respectable women's rooming house, so she got a room at one of the less respectable places, which came with the job of dance hall girl and prostitute. She was able to delay the latter by hinting to the saloon owner that it was the wrong time of the month, but she knew it was only a matter of days until he forced her into service.

She hated dancing in the saloon. All of the men ogled her, and some were very free with their hands. If she or any of the other girls protested, the saloon owner was quick to punish them, and he was an expert at delivering pain without leaving any marks where the men would see them. At least, not until they were already alone with them in the room, and then the men were thinking about something else and didn't care about a few bruises or cuts. He also made a point of trying out all the new girls to make sure they knew what they were doing, and the thought of the big, sweaty, smelly saloon owner touching her made Natalie sick to her stomach.

She was on her way back to her room one night after taking a walk to get some air when one of the regular customers recognized her and followed her. He grabbed her as she was walking through an alley lit only by a single lantern hanging from a chain. She tried to resist, but, even drunk, the man was too strong for her. He was in the process of unbuttoning his pants as she struggled against him when someone called out to them.

"Do you need help?" she heard a man ask, stopping as he was passing by on the street.

"Get him off me!" Natalie screamed.

The man approached, grabbed the drunk by the arm, and pulled him away from her.

The drunken man started to protest, but in the dim light recognized the face of the man holding him. "Sorry, Mr. Morgan," apologized the drunk, quickly buttoning his pants. "No harm done, sir." He turned and ran off as fast as intoxication would allow.

Natalie took off in the other direction.

Jim followed her and saw her duck behind some casks by the back door of one of the saloons. He walked up to them. "Why don't you come out? I'm not going to hurt you, miss," he assured her.

Slowly, Natalie stepped where he could see her.

"Are you OK?" Jim asked.

She nodded, then started to cry.

"Why don't you let me walk you home, miss," Jim offered, gently taking her arm.

Natalie walked with him until they were back on the street.

"You look a little young to be a saloon girl," Jim commented, looking at her face as they passed under a light.

Natalie was frightened and didn't want this stranger to know where she lived, so at the first opportunity she broke away and ran into the darkness.

Jim decided not to pursue her, assuming she was older than she looked and more experienced.

Natalie remembered the name the drunk had called her rescuer, and the next day asked the other girls about him.

"Was he young and incredibly good-looking?" one of the girls asked, who was a strawberry blonde.

"He was young, and yes, he was good-looking," Natalie replied.

"It had to be the same Jim Morgan. I keep hoping he'll take

me upstairs," said another one, a brunette.

"You and me both," added Ruby, a redhead. "I'd do him for free."

"And get beaten for it," laughed the strawberry blonde.

"It'd be worth it," replied Ruby with a smile.

The other two giggled.

"I've never heard of him having any of us," commented the brunette. "You think he likes boys?"

"No," answered Ruby. "I've seen how he looks at us, or one of us at least."

"Who?" asked Natalie.

"Rose," Ruby replied. Secretly, she hoped one day he'd take her friend Rose away and give her a good life. The life she deserved. "I just think he's a nice man, and shy."

"So he's nice?" Natalie asked.

"Honey, you couldn't do any better in this town," Ruby stated.

That afternoon, Natalie went looking for Jim. She found him at the stable brushing his horse, but she hung back in the shadows, not wanting to interrupt.

"Why don't you come out where I can see you?" Jim asked her without turning around.

Natalie jumped. He hadn't even glanced in her direction. She slowly stepped toward him. "I'm the girl you helped last night."

"I know."

"How? You haven't even looked at me."

"I recognize your perfume," Jim explained, turning and looking at her for the first time.

"We have to wear it," she muttered, looking down.

"You don't have to thank me," Jim replied, turning back to Ness.

"I'm not here—" She stopped, realizing she was about to be rude. "What I mean is, you asked if I needed help, and—" She started to cry and turned away, ashamed.

Jim put down the brush. He walked to her, took her arm, and led her toward the back of the barn. "Finish up for me, will you?" he asked one of the stable boys as they passed.

"Yes, sir," the boy answered as he trotted to Ness's stall.

The horse snorted and stomped his foot in protest.

"Easy, Ness," Jim said over his shoulder. Then he led the girl outside where they could talk more privately. "What's wrong, miss?" Jim asked, leading her to a bench where they sat down.

"I'm sorry to bother you," said Natalie wiping her eyes, "but I don't know anyone here, and I don't know what to do. You were right last night. I am too young to be a dance hall girl. I told the saloon owner that I was sixteen so I'd have a job and a place to live. I didn't know that I'd have to—" She stopped, not knowing how to put it politely.

"How old are you?"

"Fourteen," she whispered.

"Why are you here alone?"

"My mother died years ago, and my father died a few months ago. I tried to get a job in our town, but everyone said I was too young, and no one had the money to pay someone to watch children or clean. I thought I had enough money to get to St. Louis, but I'm almost broke, and I don't want to be a whore. I told the saloon owner that I couldn't right now," she explained, looking up at him to see if he understood, and was relieved to see him nod. "But tomorrow or the next day he's going to, you know, break me in." She shuddered involuntarily. "Can you help me? I'm sorry I ran from you last night, but I didn't know who you were. The other girls all say that you're a nice man and they all like you. Ruby even said that she'd do you for free, and Tina said that—"

Jim held up his hand to stop her rambling. "Come with me," he said, rising.

"You're not taking me back?" Natalie cried, drawing away from him.

"Of course not. I'm taking you somewhere you can stay, with someone I think will help you."

"What if they don't?" she asked, almost too frightened to breathe.

"Don't worry," Jim stated, his voice firm with resolve. "I won't let anyone hurt you."

They stopped by her room and got her things, which fit in a small carpetbag. The other women looked on, smiling and winking at Jim. One of them came close and leaned against him, trying to seduce him, but Jim politely refused.

"You don't like boys, do you?" the woman asked.

"No, ma'am," Jim replied, "but I don't like loose women, either."

"Pity," she said with a smile. "You don't know what you're missing."

As they were leaving, a woman passed them carrying a load of wash. Jim recognized her as the pretty woman he had seen in the crowd his first day with the freight company and then on the street near the smith's many times. He knew her name and thought about speaking to her, but something inside him balked at the thought of trying to get close to a woman.

She looked up as they passed.

Jim nodded to her and thought he saw a look of sadness on her face when she saw Natalie with her things. He asked Natalie about her when they returned outside, but the girl hadn't noticed her. She was too worried about the saloon owner catching her.

Jim took Natalie to his boarding house, told Mrs. Harraday her story, and asked the older woman if she could use some help.

Mrs. Harraday thought for a moment. "This could cause trouble with some of my male boarders," she worried.

"Tell them she's my sister," Jim suggested seriously.

Mrs. Harraday nodded. "Good idea. They'd have to be a fool to mess with her then. I guess I could put a cot in the pantry for now, unless you and your sister are going to share a room?" she asked with a smile. As well as having been married, she'd been around the men at the rooming house long enough to know they had needs that would be met one way or another.

Jim gave her a look of understanding tolerance, showing he got the joke but didn't appreciate it.

"Just kidding, my boy," Mrs. Harraday apologized, still smiling. "Though it's not healthy for a young man like yourself to live like a monk and never have any fun. Even Hank has a lady friend. I bet she has a friend or two you could meet."

"I'm sure she does," Jim replied. "But they're probably a little old for me."

"They might teach you a thing or two," Mrs. Harraday suggested.

"That's what Hank said. But I think I'm a little young for that sort of thing, don't you?"

"What are you? Twenty-five, twenty-six?" asked Mrs. Harraday.

"About sixteen," he replied.

Mrs. Harraday and Natalie both looked at him in surprise.
"Well, that does change things a bit," said Mrs. Harraday.
"You can wait a couple years to start sowing your wild oats."
She turned to Natalie and looked at her dress, which was low-cut and falling off one shoulder. "Let's get you into something more appropriate. I can't pay you much, but I won't turn you out on the street, either."

"Thank you!" breathed Natalie, smiling and taking her hand. "Thank you both." Then she looked scared. "But what if the saloon owner comes looking for me?"

"I doubt he'll want to mess with Jim here," replied Mrs. Harraday.

All the other boarders except Hank, to whom Jim told the truth, believed that Jim's sister had come to live there. The saloon owner believed it too and didn't pursue the girl. He was even thankful Natalie had found Jim before he'd given her brother reason to kill him.

Natalie proved a hard worker and earned her keep. Jim offered Mrs. Harraday extra money for the girl's care and board, which Mrs. Harraday tried to refuse. She did take the money when Jim insisted strongly, giving it to the girl as a bonus and, per Jim's wishes, never telling Natalie that it came from him. Natalie was like the daughter she never had, and she truly learned to love the girl as her own.

One of the boarders, Marcus Livingston, a young man who worked in the freight office, was immediately attracted to the pretty young girl. He was respectful, however, and waited until she was older and they knew each other better before voicing his intentions.

Jim never got close to the girl. Natalie soon realized he never got close to anyone, as far as she could tell, and didn't take it personally. In truth, Jim didn't know how to get close to a woman. The few times he had been attracted to one, such as Olivia or the pretty woman from the brothel, he buried any feelings that might have developed. Like so much else, he compartmentalized his attraction to a woman and shut the door on his feelings. Though at night, when he was asleep, sometimes the feelings broke through: love, hate, anger, bitterness. Then he'd wake, and, when he wasn't on the road, he'd either drink or run.

On the road, he just had to lie awake and endure, but in town he could do what he preferred: run. When he ran, he would return hours later, exhausted and often bleeding from falls, but he would be able to sleep without the dreams that haunted him. When he drank, sleep would come, but so would the dreams, though not as vigorously. He never remembered the details of the dreams whether drunk or sober, but the remnants of the dreams left him filled with agony and despair. He would wake up, in either the night, unable to breathe, or the next day, still as exhausted as though he hadn't slept at all.

Though a man's pain is his own, sometimes he needs another to help him face it. Even Christ needed the solace of his friends in the Garden. Just as the body craves water to survive, a soul craves companionship. When the will of man is too stubborn, sometimes a Greater One needs to step in and take control. Using fate as His guise, He can force even the strongest and most determined man to capitulate to the most basic of human needs: love.

11

ILLNESS

The winter of 1871 was relatively quiet for the freight men. As Jim and Hank were about to head to a saloon to get a start on their winter break, Ted called them to his office.

"I was wondering when this was going to happen," Jim muttered as they climbed the steps.

"What?" Hank asked, looking at his friend in concern.

"My spare weapons and ammunition have added weight to the stage," Jim explained. "Marcus takes it into account when booking passengers. Ted's probably not happy about it."

"You did that months ago," Hank stated. "If Ted didn't like it, he would have let you know already."

Jim nodded. "Then maybe he wants to send us on another run before the first of the year."

"The stages never run the two weeks before or the two weeks after Christmas," Hank reminded him. "They don't want men dying over the holiday."

Jim sighed.

Hank patted him on the shoulder, remembering the difficulty his friend had experienced the year before. He also noticed that Jim never used the words "holiday" or "Christmas," apparently giving the day no significance.

When they stepped through the door, Ted greeted them with a smile. He had a bottle of whiskey on his desk and handed each of them a glass.

"I thought I'd give you gentlemen a jump on the holiday," he said. Then he turned to Jim. "You've been with the company a little over sixteen months, and, though you've been shot three times, counting the time when you rode with Hap and Joe, you've also killed fifteen men, counting that time as well. That's almost one dead bandit for every month!" he cried, raising his glass.

Hank smiled and drank.

Jim drank but didn't smile.

"That's some record!" Ted continued. "There's not a man in the company who's come close to doing the same. And since you've done such a remarkable job, my superiors in St. Louis have authorized me to give you and Hank an extra two weeks off!"

"Now that's something to drink to!" Hank laughed, raising his glass and taking another sip.

Ted followed suit, and again Jim took a drink but still didn't smile.

Hank looked at Jim and shook his head. "You should be happy, Jimmy."

Jim nodded. "I guess I should be glad it'll give me more time to work for the smith," he said, still looking nonplused.

Ted and Hank both shook their heads at him.

"I want you to rest," Ted said to him. "Even though it's been months since you were last hurt, I know it still pains you."

Jim looked at him with as much surprise as he ever demonstrated.

"You do a good job of hiding it," Ted said, "but those of us who know you can tell."

"Then I'll have to do better at hiding it," Jim stated evenly.

"You need to relax," Ted said, refilling the young man's empty glass. He noticed that Hank just sipped his, but that Jim drank his whiskey like water. "You need to have some fun." He looked up and met Jim's gaze. "That's an order. And like last year, I'll expect you both to my house Christmas morning."

Hank smiled and took another drink.

Jim drained his glass, but to Ted it seemed more out of desperation than celebration.

Ted gazed at his young friend and employee. "There's nothing for you to worry about. We're your friends and want you with us. Don't worry about all the trappings."

Jim knew what he meant. "Thank you for the whiskey, sir," he said, standing and turning to leave.

"There's plenty more here," Ted offered, holding up the bottle.

"Someone needs to help Mrs. Harraday with the firewood," Jim stated, making the only excuse he could think of to explain his exit.

He gathered his belongings from where he'd left them at the bottom of the stairs, including the oilskin bag that held his two spare rifles and an extra shotgun. They were all fully oiled and slid into their own sleeves. As he hoisted the bag and settled its strap onto his shoulder, he almost regretted not waiting for Hank. He knew his friend would offer to carry it for him and smile when he seemingly grudgingly let him. He turned and purposely avoided meeting the gaze of any of the other men as he walked quickly out of the office and headed to the boarding house. He wanted to avoid any seasonal well-wishing, and he didn't want to give Hank a chance to catch up with him. He knew his friend would try to appease him with his humble wisdom, and, though Hank usually could, he wasn't in the mood for it.

Mrs. Harraday heard him enter. With Natalie and Marcus's help, she got the tub and buckets of water to his room within moments of his arrival. Being true to his word, Jim offered to help bring in firewood before he bathed, but Mrs. Harraday said Marcus had already done it.

Jim bathed quickly. He had just stepped into the hall carrying the buckets and empty tub to return them to the kitchen when Hank came shuffling up the stairs. The big man stumbled on the last step and laughed when Jim dropped the tub and grabbed his arm in alarm.

"Thanks, Jimmy! I guess I had a little more than I realized."

Jim nodded, leaned the tub against the wall, and continued downstairs with the buckets, thankful he hadn't spilled any of the water. When he got to the kitchen, he informed Mrs. Harraday Hank was in his room and offered to help carry the water for his friend's bath. Since Mrs. Harraday insisted she and

Natalie had Marcus to help them, Jim headed out the back door.

"Be back in time for supper, young man!" Mrs. Harraday called after him.

"Yes, ma'am," Jim replied as he closed the door.

She remembered he'd just bathed, stepped to the door, and opened it again. "Is your hair still wet? You'll catch your death!"

He heard her but chose to pretend he hadn't. He needed the chill to help clear his head, and he was accustomed to bathing outside, even in the winter, to hide his scars. He knew Ted meant well, giving him more time off and inviting him to his house, but he didn't want to be reminded about his embarrassment from the year before.

When he'd arrived at Ted's house that Christmas morning of the previous year he'd seen a table piled high with packages but assumed they were gifts from Sam to Martha since they were still living there. They'd all shared a meal, prepared by Martha and Sylvia. Then Sam asked Laura, Sylvia's daughter and the youngest among them, to distribute the gifts. She'd given him the first one. Maybe if he'd walked over with Hank instead of going to the stable and checking on Ness first he would have had time to think, because he'd have seen the gifts Hank brought. Instead, the situation caught him completely by surprise, and all he could think of was escape. He excused himself and found himself heading back to the stable. He stopped in his room, got his weapons, money, and saddlebags, and then jogged to the barn.

He remembered riding out of town and considering never returning, but realized that would be disrespectful to Sam and Ted. Instead, he stopped at the next town of any size where he could buy things for his friends. He didn't mind spending the time or the money, but he was frustrated no one told him about gifts. He knew that was what families did at Christmas, but he'd never had a family. He'd always ignored the days others considered special. To him, each day was just a day, nothing to celebrate.

Paul hadn't earned enough to cover his own expenses, much less buy Christmas gifts for him. Since he'd kept the man fed and a roof over his head with the money he earned working for the smith, he felt no obligation to give him anything else.

Sam and Martha, though, he owed more than he cared to

admit, and they deserved the best things he could buy. Ted had given him a job, even though he'd earned it, so he didn't mind buying something for him. Hank had helped him when he was hurt and hadn't told anyone about the scars, so he deserved something, too. He didn't mind buying something for Sylvia just to be polite, and Laura was a child, so she deserved a good Christmas.

By the time he got to the town, he knew what he wanted for each person. A man in one of the saloons told him the shops wouldn't reopen until two days after Christmas. He thought about trying to get the shop owners to let him in early, but he didn't want to appear desperate, so he waited. He spent the time riding, exploring the area, and sleeping in the open so he could use his money for gifts. He kept himself fed from game, and there was enough grass for Ness until they got back. He also realized how lucky he was to have a room and a job. He'd forgotten how much work it was living by what you could kill and how hard it was to sleep when you were freezing.

After he was able to make his purchases, he rode back to Dillard. Ted and Sam had all of them over again that night for supper. When he got to the house, he saw most of the gifts still piled on the table. Only Laura had opened her gifts after he left. Then he wasn't sure which was worse: not having anything for anybody the first time, or having to admit he hadn't, and that was why he'd left.

He still remembered how surprised he'd been when he realized everyone was just happy he was back, and that they didn't appear to hold it against him. They seemed pleased with the gifts, but the happiest was Laura. He'd given her a doll very similar to one for sale in Dillard that she'd been disappointed not to get on Christmas day.

Though he had gifts for everyone this year, he still didn't like the thought that his friends would feel obliged to give him things as well. He'd never received gifts before and didn't like feeling obliged to anyone for anything. He'd read Shakespeare, and agreed with the words, "neither a borrower nor a lender be." He kept himself out of debt. He'd even told Sam about the money Mrs. Canady gave him, and that he wanted to send it back. Sam said that would only offend her, so he'd kept it but not spent it. He'd tried to give Sam money towards the construction of his house, but Sam had refused. "You're not giving that money to me," he'd said, laughing.

Jim stopped and gazed out over the fields surrounding Dillard, enjoying the quiet of a winter's evening. He'd wandered almost halfway around the town and decided to cross through on his return trip so he wouldn't be late for supper. He was walking down one of the side streets lined with shops when he saw a little girl looking in the carpenter's window. He stopped to see what had caught the child's interest and found her gazing at the wooden animal figures he'd carved.

The carpenter had been so impressed with the horse he'd made for Sarah that the man had insisted he make more. Though there were still two more weeks until Christmas, most of the figures had sold. All that was left of the two dozen he'd made were a turtle, a bear, a goat, and a swan. He was most proud of the latter, especially since he'd only seen one in pictures, and people like Sam, who had seen the real thing, said it looked exactly like the actual bird.

"Which one do you like?" Jim asked the child.

She looked up in fright and turned to run away. She tripped on an uneven board and would have fallen had Jim not been quick enough to catch her.

"I'm sorry if she was bothering you, sir!" cried a woman, running up to collect the child. "We mean no harm, sir!"

The woman looked up at him. In the light of the shop window, Jim saw fear in her eyes.

"I just wanted to know which carving she liked," Jim said.

"Oh, sir," said the woman, shaking her head. "She knows she can't have anything like that."

"Why, ma'am?" Jim asked.

"Her father was hurt months ago," the woman replied. "I manage to keep us fed cooking for the hotel, and they let me have the leftovers, and Doctor Sam hasn't asked to be paid." She recognized Jim and knew of his friendship with Sam. She knew Jim by his reputation and was truly afraid her daughter might have angered him.

Jim nodded. Then he dropped to one knee before the child. "Which one do you like?" he asked again, speaking softly.

The girl shrank from him.

"It's OK," he assured her. "I made them. You can have

whichever one you want."

"Really?" the girl asked, her voice barely above a whisper.

Jim nodded again.

"The swan," said the child, smiling.

Jim stood and knocked on the shop door. Though the carpenter had closed for the evening, Jim could see him inside sweeping.

The carpenter looked up, his brow wrinkled in annoyance until he saw who was at his door. Then he smiled and ran to open it. "Sorry, Mr. Morgan!" he said, swinging the door open wide. "I didn't see you!"

"Can you give me the swan, please?" Jim said to the man.

"Of course!" said the carpenter smiling. "You made them." He walked away, and they saw his head and then his arm in the window as he picked out the carving. He looked up at Jim and smiled through the glass before stepping back and reappearing at the door. He handed the figure to Jim, still smiling.

Jim held it down to the child.

She started to reach for it, then looked up at her mother, who nodded. The girl carefully took it from Jim. "Thank you, sir!" she breathed.

"That's very kind of you, sir!" said the mother, genuinely surprised by the man's thoughtfulness.

"Thanks, Frank," Jim said to the carpenter. "Sorry to bother you so late."

"No trouble, Mr. Morgan," said the carpenter. "A good evening to you, sir. And if you have the chance to make any more carvings before Christmas, I'm sure they'll sell. I just put the last batch in the window yesterday, and, as you can see, I've sold three already."

"I'll see. Thanks, Frank," Jim said again.

The carpenter nodded and shut the door with a smile.

Jim turned to the woman.

"Thank you again, sir," she said. "Bless you!"

Jim reached into his pocket and pulled out a few bills. Not happy with what he found, he reached in the breast pocket of his coat and drew out a money pouch. He pulled out a bill and held it out to the woman. "Take this, ma'am," he said. "Buy yourself and your family some proper food."

"Oh, I couldn't, sir!" said the woman, drawing away, frightened by the man's sudden generosity. She smelled whiskey on his breath and was now afraid he was drunk and might want something immoral in return.

"Ma'am, I know what it's like to go hungry," Jim stated, his eyes shining in spite of the dim twilight. "If you won't take it, then I'll have to buy the food for you myself."

Not wanting to offend him, the woman took the bill, which she noted was a twenty. "God will truly bless you, sir!" she said as she folded it and pushed it into the cuff of her sleeve. "Thank you!" She then hurried away, hoping she could get to the general store before the owner locked the doors for the night. Now she could feed her family for the next month without worry.

Jim simply nodded and turned. As he did so, he saw a woman watching from where she stood just within the light of a lamp across the street. She was the pretty redhead he'd admired since the first day he arrived. The woman, realizing Jim had seen her, turned and walked quickly away. Jim thought about asking Frank for another carving to give her. He turned back to the window. Seeing only the turtle, the bear, and the goat left, none of which he thought appropriate for her, he shook his head at his own folly and returned to the boarding house. As he walked, he wondered what figure would be appropriate for the woman. What could he give her to express his admiration? For her own beauty was perfection itself.

The year ended with the usual festivities, which Jim grudgingly tolerated since he couldn't ignore them. The smith was glad to have his services for a couple extra weeks. Since the smithy was on the same end of town as the brothel, Jim was glad to get to see the beautiful redhead as she walked back and forth doing errands. Ted and Sam kept a close eye on him, and one of them usually visited him at the forge almost every day. On one of these occasions, the woman walked by. Though Jim didn't notice his own distraction, Sam did. The doctor smiled out of amusement and relief to know his young friend was human after all.

Their break over, Jim and Hank were back on the stage by the end of January 1872. To Jim, it seemed that every day on the stage was cold and wet due to rain or snow, depending on the elevation, but he just had to ride. The wet weather made the driver's job challenging at the least. Rain in the morning meant there would be ruts in the road by afternoon. A wheel caught in a deep rut could be broken and destroyed. Two stages had been lost in this manner, and in one of the accidents a guard was crushed when the stage rolled over him. Under these conditions, Hank sometimes envied Jim because he didn't have to concentrate every second on the road. Avoiding every rut was impossible. The trick was judging the safest track in which to place the wheels.

One afternoon, Hank made a minor miscalculation, and the stage bumped over numerous large ruts, hurling Jim into the air. To prevent flying off, Jim grabbed for the rail surrounding the top of the coach. His hand slipped as he caught it and he crashed down on the bar, landing on his right side. The fall reinjured his ribs, bruising them where the bullet had torn across them the year before. This injury still bothered him, as Ted had noted before Christmas. Hank glanced back when he heard his friend gasping and remarked to Ted later that it was probably good Jim had got the wind knocked out of him. Otherwise the passengers would have heard cussing for sure.

As for Carlos, he had apparently ordered his men to avoid the stages during the fall of 1871, perhaps because of Jim. Instead, his men seemed to concentrate on stealing livestock, killing many homesteaders in the process. The cavalry rode in before the end of the year. After more than one encounter, the bandits returned to attacking the stages that spring of 1872, and the cavalry trotted back to Indian Territory.

There'd been rain all week, and the roads were muddy, making travel difficult and miserable for man and horse alike. It was mid-May, and Jim was on another stage run, the last of many since he'd been hurt in his fall. Though it had been over two months since he'd reinjured his ribs, they still hurt, and the vibration of the stage made them ache even more.

Late in the afternoon of the first day, the stage came to what was usually a shallow stream but was now a raging, swirling mass of angry water. Jim noticed an Indian following them but wasn't worried. He had gotten a glimpse of the boy and figured he was probably from one of the nearby villages. The Indians often followed the progress of the stage. Jim knew they didn't consider the stage a threat since Ted didn't allow the passengers or freight men to indiscriminately kill game along the way.

There was a large rock in the middle of the stream, and, using it to gauge the water level, Jim and Hank could tell the stream wasn't too deep for the stage to cross. Hank gave the reins a shake, the horses reluctantly entered the water, and they crossed easily. The road immediately curved, so after only a few yards, they were out of sight of the stream.

Jim was worried the boy might try to cross as well, so, breaking with protocol, he asked Hank to stop. He climbed down and returned to the stream just in time to see the boy's horse stumble. The water swept the child from the animal's back, leaving him desperately clutching his horse's mane. Jim dropped his rifle and tore off his boots and gun belt. As he was about to dive in, the force of the water ripped the boy loose, sending him tumbling downstream. Jim ran along the bank and sprang into the water ahead of the struggling child.

With a few powerful strokes, Jim reached the boy and grabbed him under an arm. The boy clung to him with the strength of a frightened animal, almost tearing Jim's shirt off his body. Jim made it to the bank, took hold of a large root, and swung the child up onto the grass. As he did so, the current caught him and smashed his right side against a rock, nearly knocking the breath out of him. The pain almost caused him to lose his grip, but Jim hung on, summoned his strength, and pulled himself onto the bank beside the boy. Then he lay on his belly gasping and choking.

"You all right?" Jim asked when he could speak between coughs.

The boy looked him in the eye and nodded, coughing as well. Then he crawled to where Jim lay.

Jim looked up to see the child kneeling beside him, staring at his back. His shirt had torn, revealing the scars. He rolled over and tried to sit up, but the pain stopped him. "Damn it!" he muttered as he fell back, coughing some more.

The child looked at him with worry in his eyes.

"It's not you," Jim assured him. Then he rolled onto his stomach again and pushed himself to his knees. "You sure you're OK?" He guessed the boy was around twelve.

Jim put his hands on the outside of the child's shoulders. "No broken bones?" he asked, feeling down the boys arms and scanning his person for injuries.

The child shook his head without meeting Jim's gaze. Then

the boy lifted off the necklace he was wearing and slipped it over Jim's head.

"You don't have to do that," Jim replied modestly.

The child showed him the medallion hanging from the thin strip of leather. It was made of silver and bore an engraving of what looked like the head of a crow in a line drawing. The boy pointed to Jim, though he refused to look him in the eye. "Thunder Crow," he announced.

"What?"

"Thunder Crow," the boy insisted, pointing at Jim again with his eyes still lowered.

What the boy didn't realize was that the bird his people had in mind might actually have been a raven. Both birds followed the stage, but the smaller crows usually outnumbered the larger ravens. The crows needed the raven's strong beak to tear into the carrion, and the raven used the crows as sentries. Though the Indians made a distinction between the two birds, most white men referred to any black bird of that type as a crow. Therefore, "crow" was the only English word the boy and his people knew. They considered this just another indication of the inadequacies of the white men. There were a few, though, whom they learned to respect.

Jim would remain unaware of any misunderstanding until much later. Then, knowledge of the possible intent of his name would seem inconsequential compared to something else he would learn.

The boy said again, "Thunder Crow." Then he realized the white man wouldn't know the name his people had given him and kept his eyes lowered, now in embarrassment.

"Thank you," Jim replied, examining the medallion.

They both looked up as the stage rumbled around the curve toward them. Hank had become worried when Jim hadn't returned after a few minutes, so he turned the stage around to look for him. When he saw Jim and the boy, he pulled the horses to a stop, hopped down, grabbed two blankets from the rear boot, and ran to them.

"You both look half-drowned!" he said as he put one blanket around the child and the other around Jim's shoulders.

Jim shook his head, then turned to the boy. "I hope your village is on this side of the water?"

The child nodded, still averting his gaze.

Jim noticed that the boy looked Hank in the eye. Then he remembered he'd heard somewhere that, to the Indians, looking down was a sign of respect. "Let's get you back on your horse," Jim suggested as he turned and walked to where the boy's horse was waiting patiently, having managed to cross the stream.

Hank held the animal as Jim swung the boy onto the horse's back one-handed, gritting his teeth against the pain. He didn't want to drop the blanket and run the risk of the passengers getting a glimpse of his scars.

The child started to remove his blanket, but Jim told him to keep it.

"You're not going to try to cross back over as soon as we're out of sight, are you?" Jim asked the boy.

The child shook his head, his eyes still lowered in respect.

"Take care of yourself!" Jim called as the child turned his horse.

The boy nodded and rode off.

As soon as he was gone, one of the passengers, an older woman with a pinched face, stuck her head out of the coach window. "You risked your life and held up the stage for a savage?" she asked.

Jim flashed her a look. The fire in his blue eyes frightened her, so she disappeared back into the coach.

"You need to get out of those wet clothes," Hank ordered as he climbed onto the stage and handed Jim's bag to him. Then he climbed down and held up the blanket so the passengers couldn't see Jim while he changed.

"What happened there?" Hank asked when Jim removed his shirt.

There was a bad scrape on Jim's right side, obscuring the bullet scar from the year before.

"A rock," Jim answered.

"Did you break anything?"

"Don't think so."

"It hurts, though, doesn't it, Jimmy?" Hank commented, reading his friend's face. "You'll let me know if you're not going to make it, won't you?" Hank asked, referring to the rest of the run. They still had five and a half days to go.

Jim nodded.

When they arrived at the home station where they would spend the night, Hank treated and bandaged Jim's wound. They had to do it in the barn for privacy, but the added support of the bandage helped relieve some of the pain. There weren't enough beds at this station, so Jim slept on the floor, giving his up for one of the passengers, who were all female. Traveling with the older woman were her daughter and two granddaughters, and, luckily for Jim and Hank, they were of a more agreeable disposition.

Hank offered to give his bed to Jim. The guard, however, insisted on obeying company policy, which dictated that the driver always got a bed, even if that meant God himself had to sleep on the floor.

The next afternoon, Hank was worried about Jim, but the younger man assured him he was OK. "Besides, I've gotten used to it," he stated, referring to the pain in his ribs, which he'd been enduring for almost a year.

The next few days were uneventful. Their only adversary was the weather, as it rained some each day. When they returned to the stream that had nearly drowned Jim and the Indian boy just days before, the water was wider and faster but, luckily for them, not much deeper. Hank gave the reins a shake, but the near leader, the lead horse on the right side of the coach, balked. Jim removed his boots and gun belt and climbed down.

Hank noticed his friend's movements were slow and stiff from pain.

Jim grabbed the animal's harness and led the horses into the water. About halfway across, the horse stumbled and lurched, causing Jim to lose his grip. Hank watched helplessly as the young man was pulled under the swirling water. He had no option but to continue across the stream, hoping he wasn't crushing his friend in the process. As soon as the coach was safely up on the bank, Hank set the brake and jumped down. He ran to the brink and shouted for Jim, hoping the water had only swept him downstream and he'd been able to swim to the side. There was no answer. Hank called again. Still no answer. He ran down the bank a little ways, hoping to see some sign of the young man.

"Jim!" he cried. "If you can hear me, answer me, damn it!" He never even realized he'd cursed. He turned back toward the coach, fighting tears. "God, please!" he begged. Then he saw his friend lying face down under the wagon. "Oh my God!" Hank breathed, running back to the stage.

He dragged Jim out and hit him hard on the back a few times, hoping to rouse him. He knew if he turned the young man over he could choke to death as he tried to breathe. He had hit Jim three or four times when finally the young man coughed then pushed himself up onto his hands and knees and vomited. A moment later, he vomited again. Hank brought him a flask of water from the coach. Jim took some, rinsed his mouth, and spat. Then he drank a little, and, when that stayed down, he drank a little more.

"Thank God you're alive!" Hank cried. "You sorry son of a bitch, I thought I'd lost you for sure."

Jim just nodded, raised his forefinger, and wagged it at his friend for cussing.

Later, Hank realized what must have happened. The stage was moving forward, so when the current caught Jim it pushed him under the coach. Just by the grace of God, Jim had some-how avoided the crushing force of the two sets of turning wheels and managed to grab onto the undercarriage and let the stage pull him out.

"Let's get you home," Hank sighed.

He helped Jim to his feet, but the young man immediately collapsed, so Hank lifted him and carried him like a child. Since Jim was too exhausted to change clothes, Hank simply wrapped him in one of the blankets and sat him in the coach with the passengers, ignoring the guard's weak protests. Then he hurried the horses toward Dillard.

When they arrived, Jim was feeling better and could walk. Hank told Ted what had happened, and Ted gave Jim per-mission to leave, thinking he would go straight to Sam's. Jim, however, decided to drop his things off in his room first. When he got there, he was so exhausted he locked his door and col-lapsed onto the bed without even removing his boots. It was late by the time Hank finished at the freight office, and he hurried back to the boarding house so he wouldn't miss supper. He wasn't surprised not to see Jim, since he thought he was at the doctor's, and neither Mrs. Harraday nor Natalie had seen Jim when he arrived.

It wasn't until the next morning, when Hank went to see

Sam, that they realized something was terribly wrong. Sam ran to Mrs. Harraday's, followed by Hank. They had her open Jim's door and found him still collapsed on the bed. The room was cold. He hadn't even lit the stove or changed clothes. Sam felt for a pulse and was relieved to find one, but Jim's body was burning up. Sam instructed Mrs. Harraday to get the tub, and she returned moments later, followed by Natalie. The doctor told them to fill the tub with lukewarm water. Luckily, they had water already heating on the stove for dishes, so the tub was ready in minutes. Then, since Sam and Hank were still working on undressing Jim, the women stepped into the hall and shut the door.

"Careful, he's heavy!" cautioned Hank as they lifted Jim to put him into the tub.

"He's all muscle," Sam replied, his voice strained from the effort.

Jim had only been in the water a moment when he came to and thrashed, nearly hitting Sam in the face.

"You're OK," Sam assured him. "You're in a tub."

Jim then settled back, nearly unconscious again.

After a few minutes, the young man groaned and began to shiver. Sam and Hank managed to get him to stand up so they could dry him. While they were doing this, Sam called Mrs. Harraday. She opened the door a crack, just enough to hear the doctor, who asked for at least two more pillows. When she returned with them, Sam and Hank had Jim in the bed. Sam expertly placed the pillows and settled Jim onto them.

Then the doctor took his stethoscope, listened to Jim's chest, and frowned. "Just as I thought. Pneumonia."

"Is it contagious?" Mrs. Harraday asked.

"Shouldn't be, if you're healthy to start with," the doctor replied.

Jim tried to look at the doctor, but his eyes didn't want to stay open. "How?" he asked, his voice barely above a whisper.

"Well, your lungs may not have fully recovered from the fire. Then you nearly drowned, twice, from what Hank said, so it's really not too surprising."

"How long?" Jim gasped.

Sam knew he wanted to know when he would be able to work again. "At least four weeks."

The young man shook his head.

"Jim, I'm not going to lie to you, this could kill you," stated the doctor as he took out his thermometer and shook it down.

Jim nodded.

"Someone's going to have to stay with him twenty-four hours a day for a while," Sam announced, putting the thermometer under Jim's tongue and then turning to the others.

"Aren't you taking him back to your house?" Hank asked.

"I think it would be best if he stayed here," Sam replied, looking at his watch as he took Jim's pulse. "I don't want to have to carry him through town. I'll need help from any of you who are willing."

"I'd be glad to," offered Natalie.

"Now, miss, you know that wouldn't be appropriate," Mrs. Harraday scolded her gently.

"Why?" Natalie asked.

"Because you've never been married or had any brothers," the older woman replied.

"You forget that I worked in a brothel for a week. I didn't do what the other women did, but I did see things, like naked men for instance."

Mrs. Harraday looked to Sam for support, but he turned to Jim.

"If Jim doesn't mind, I don't," Sam replied.

"Martha," Jim managed to whisper around the thermometer. Then he coughed.

"Unfortunately, you're not my only patient," Sam replied. "I need her at home. So will you allow Natalie to help me?"

Jim shrugged to show he didn't care. Then he had to hold the thermometer in his mouth as he coughed, wincing from the pain.

"Why would he mind having a pretty face around?" Hank asked, smiling and trying to cheer his friend.

"I know some other women who might be willing to help also," suggested Natalie.

Sam looked to Jim, and his reaction was the same. He was too weak to care and groaned as he started coughing again.

"I'll have to talk to them first," Sam instructed, lifting Jim's head and cradling the young man in one arm as he continued coughing. "And to you and Mrs. Harraday as well. There are things that you'll need to know and agree to."

They both nodded.

As he held Jim, Sam looked at his watch, only glancing at the young man's face. The doctor knew his worry showed in his eyes and had learned to keep them averted so as not to alarm his patients. After five minutes, the doctor gently pulled the thermometer from Jim's mouth and settled him back on the bed. Then Sam took the thermometer to the window to read it.

"Much higher and you'd be in convulsions," Sam said to his patient as he shook down the thermometer. Then he wiped it with alcohol and returned it to its case, which he set in his bag. "Now I need to go back to my office and get a few things," he said, walking to the door.

"I'll stay with him while you're gone," offered Natalie.

"Keep a cool cloth on him, and get him to drink some water," the doctor advised.

Natalie nodded.

Mrs. Harraday asked Hank to help her make the room more comfortable and accommodating. When Sam returned, there was an overstuffed chair and a writing desk in Jim's room, as well as two more lanterns. Sam then took Natalie and Mrs. Harraday aside and explained about Jim's back and the need for privacy.

Later that afternoon, three women Natalie had known in the brothel stopped by Sam's office. After he told them they would have to commit to at least two nights a week and respect his patient's privacy, two of them left. The woman who stayed agreed to all of Sam's conditions and assured him she would act respectably toward his patient.

"So I'll be alone with him all night?" she asked. She was worried she might have to lift the man, who was at least six inches taller than she was.

"Yes," Sam replied.

"How do I—?" She didn't know how to put it politely. "How do I keep him clean?"

"He never soils himself," Sam explained.

She looked surprised.

"I don't know what was done to him," Sam continued, "but no matter how weak or delirious he gets, he never does. I'll be by in the evening and again first thing in the morning. If there is a need during the night and you don't feel comfortable, Hank or Marcus can help you."

"Marcus," she replied thoughtfully. "He's the boy who works at the freight office?"

Sam nodded. Then he half-smiled. "Marcus is twenty. He's three years older than Jim."

"Really?" she asked. She had thought Jim was older than she was, not two years younger.

Sam then took her to Jim's room.

Jim recognized her as the beautiful redheaded woman he'd seen in the crowd his first day with the freight company, and on the street before Christmas, and many other times, most recently while working for the blacksmith. He would have caught his breath if he'd had any. Instead, he tried to force his eyes to focus and not start coughing again.

"My name's Rose," she said, extending her hand to Jim and nodding to Hank, who had been sitting with his friend.

Jim already knew her name, though she wasn't aware of this. He took her hand politely, and when she smiled the whole room seemed to brighten.

"I can stay with him this evening if you'd like," she offered, turning to Sam and continuing to smile through force of will. The young man's hand was hot, and his remarkably blue eyes lacked their usual clarity and seemed to glow from fever.

"That would be appreciated. I'm still trying to work things out with people," the doctor replied, noting the fear the young woman tried to hide with her smile. He also noticed that, rather than drawing away from his patient, she moved closer to him, and realized it wasn't her person she feared for but Jim's.

As Sam left Mrs. Harraday's that evening, one of the women he'd talked to earlier stepped out of the shadows and called to him. "You know Rose isn't one of us," she mentioned.

"I guessed as much," replied the doctor.

"Then shouldn't you send her back? Or is it that, because she works at a brothel, you don't care about her reputation?"

Sam looked at the woman in surprise. "I appreciate your concern for her, Ruby, but her reputation is already questionable to most."

"You don't have to make it worse. Why keep her?"

"Because I've seen how Jim looks at her. One time at the

smith's, he stopped in mid-sentence as she walked by. He's never reacted like that to any woman before."

Ruby smiled. "You devil. You hope he's in love with her."

"She could do a hell of a lot worse," commented the doctor.

They both laughed and went their separate ways.

Rose stayed with Jim the next night as well. Tired of sitting, she rose from the armchair next to his bed, walked to the door, and turned, studying her surroundings. The bed was to her left, with a night table beside it. In the wall to her right were hooks with coats and Jim's hat hanging from them. A folding cot was leaning against the wall in case she wanted to lie down in the night. On the opposite wall across from her, near the corner, was the chest of drawers. Beside the bureau and across from the bed was the only window, with the writing table under it. Mrs. Harraday said she had the table brought up from downstairs so Sam would have somewhere to set things. The armchair was also a new addition, she'd been told. On the other side of the bed against the far wall was a bookshelf and, beside that, in the far corner by the window, was the chamber pot, now hidden by a screen.

She smiled as she remembered Jim's insistence that Hank find a screen for it. Jim had said to his friend that if the woman helping him had to go downstairs in the night then he would too, to be polite, and Hank would have to carry him. "A screen's a hell of a lot lighter than I am," he had managed to say before he started coughing again. Hank had agreed, and, luckily, Mrs. Harraday had one she kept folded up in a closet.

She remembered Mrs. Harraday mentioning there had been a wardrobe along the wall where the hooks now were. She smiled again. Mrs. Harraday told her Jim gave it to Natalie when she moved into the room he had added off of the kitchen for her downstairs. Then, after getting Jim's approval, Mrs. Harraday explained that Natalie wasn't really Jim's sister, but that Hank was the only boarder who knew the truth.

I wonder if he would have helped me too if I'd asked, she thought as she gazed around the room again. Other than the weapons, saddlebags, and travel bag stored in the corner next to the bureau, the things hanging from the hooks, and a surprisingly large number of books on the bookshelf, there were no personal items in the room. Everything he owned had a utilitarian purpose. Even the books, since they were all either Shakespeare or some other author read as much to appreciate skill as for entertainment, seemed more for education than simply to pass the time. Mrs. Harraday's china pitcher and basin on the bureau, with their dainty floral print, looked out of place in the otherwise sparse, masculine environment, and were only present for their usefulness.

She noticed that every now and then Jim reached for the revolver he usually kept under his pillow and sometimes became agitated when he realized it was no longer there. Sam warned her he might ask for it and ordered her not to give it to him under any circumstances, unless the Devil himself was coming through the door.

"A delirious Jim Morgan with a gun could be lethal to us all," Sam had said.

On the third evening, she relieved Natalie and began sponging Jim's forehead and chest. Jim was still in a great deal of pain, especially when he coughed, but Rose was able to adjust the pillows so he was more comfortable.

She was wearing a low-cut dress, and when she noticed Jim looking at her, she smiled. "You like it? I just finished making it, though I think it makes me look fat."

"No it doesn't," he replied weakly.

"Thank you!" she smiled again.

"Why are you here again so soon?"

"What? Don't you like me?" Rose asked playfully.

"I just thought you had to work."

Rose started to turn away sharply, but Jim caught her arm. He was too weak to hold it, though, and his hand dropped back to the bed. "What I mean is, I don't want you to get in trouble." He knew the saloon owner beat his women if they weren't making enough money. Though he'd learned Rose wasn't a prostitute, he didn't want her to be mistreated either, especially since he was in no condition to do anything about it.

Rose turned back to him and smiled wearily. "I come here after I get done." She didn't know he knew the truth.

Then she cradled him in her arms as he began coughing again. Speaking always caused another coughing fit. As a mother instinctively learns to sense her child's wants even before the little one learns to talk, Rose learned to sense Jim's. Whether it was adjusting his pillows, giving him a drink of water, or just holding his hand so he knew she was there, Rose somehow knew what he needed.

As she held him, Jim looked up at her between coughs. He sometimes found himself gazing at her as she moved about the room. Though he'd found her attractive from the first moment he'd seen her almost two years before, he'd never let himself really notice everything about her. To combat the fever, he forced his rambling mind to cling to her. Sometimes it took all his concentration to focus on her face, or her hands, or the intriguing way her breasts moved as she breathed. He found himself looking at the curve of her waist, the way her hair fell on her shoulders, or how the light played in her eyes. He took pleasure in looking at her, but what he wasn't aware of was how much he needed her in a way he couldn't yet understand.

Though Jim tolerated the summer heat during the day when doors could be left open to facilitate the breeze, at night he was restless and uncomfortable. He dozed off and on, and his fever would rise in the early evening and not diminish until the morning, even then staying at least two to four degrees above normal.

One time, Rose tried to put a damp cloth on his head while he slept, and he grabbed her arm. Sam had warned her to speak to him first, but she had forgotten. She spoke softly to him, and he let go. The next time, she spoke to him first, and he allowed her to touch him, seemingly without waking. She often stayed through the morning and helped Sam get Jim into the tub to cool him down.

One day, while Jim was still in the tub, there was a knock on the door, and a man summoned Sam away to an emergency. Rose assured the doctor she could manage Jim, and she did. When Sam returned later, his patient was back in bed and asleep, though still feverish.

Mrs. Harraday took over late that morning, and Rose offered to return that evening and stay through the night. When she arrived, Jim's fever was raging, and he was restless. Rose talked to him softly and he quieted, much to Mrs. Harraday's amazement. She hadn't been able to quiet him at all.

Jim's response to Rose surprised Sam as well. The doctor had treated the young man enough over the last two years to know how Jim typically reacted when in pain and delirious. Sam had noticed that his patient seemed to retreat into himself, steeling his will against pain and shunning human contact when delirious. There had been more than one occasion when Jim had nearly struck Sam simply for trying to take his pulse, even after the doctor spoke to him first.

"Sorry," Jim would say later when told about the incident. "I probably thought you were someone else."

"Who?" Sam would ask.

Jim would simply shake his head slightly in reply.

Because of these incidents, Sam found it highly unusual one night when he entered the young man's room and found him clinging to Rose's hand as she sat by the bed. Jim was coughing painfully and burning with fever.

"He woke up a little while ago," Rose explained. "I was just about to send someone for you." She started to stand so Sam could examine his patient and give him medicine, but Jim refused to release her.

"No!" he groaned.

"I'll be right here," Rose said softly, caressing his cheek.

Jim reluctantly let go and began coughing harder as she walked away.

Rose excused herself, left the room, and trudged downstairs.

Sam examined Jim, then prepared the medicine. He stirred quinine and codeine into a glass of sugar water to mask the bitter taste of the former and get some nourishment into the young man.

Rose found Natalie in the kitchen, and the girl offered to take some broth to Jim while Rose stepped outside. Natalie assumed the other woman was going to the outhouse, and walked on up to Jim's room.

Rose closed the back door behind her, then leaned heavily against it. She needed a minute alone. She stood in the darkness and allowed herself to cry. Finally, she was with the man she'd fallen in love with almost two years before, but now not only was he ill, she was truly afraid he was going to die. She only allowed herself a few moments of weakness before she dried her eyes, prepared some sage tea for his throat, and returned to his room. When she entered, she found Natalie and Sam standing back as Jim groaned and thrashed on the bed.

"I don't want to restrain him," Sam explained softly to Rose's questioning look, "but he won't let either of us near him. If he won't take the medicine, I'll have no choice." The doctor stepped to the bedside. "Jim! You need to drink this!" he stated firmly. Then he tried to lift his patient's head, but Jim pulled away and pushed at the doctor's arm with a groan.

"Let me try again," offered Natalie. She too spoke to him before touching him, and again Jim pulled away.

Sam turned to Rose. "He let you touch him before."

Rose nodded and set the tea on the bureau. She was sure Jim hadn't known who she was earlier and had simply been in pain, but she spoke his name softly as she stepped to the bed.

At the sound of her voice, Jim stopped thrashing and seemed to listen.

"You need to take the medicine," she continued as she gently lifted his head.

To everyone's surprise, the young man didn't struggle. Instead, he leaned toward her, apparently wanting to get closer to her.

Sam handed her the glass, and Rose put it to the young man's lips.

Jim grimaced from the taste and turned away.

"Is it that bad?" Rose asked him, forcing a smile.

Jim nodded slightly.

"Too much sugar?" she asked, having previously watched the doctor prepare the medicine.

Jim nodded again.

"I'll use less next time," Sam promised, but Jim didn't seem to hear him.

"Drink this," Rose said softly, "and it'll be better the next time."

Jim took a few more sips, then turned away again.

"You have to drink all of it," Rose insisted gently.

Jim glanced up at her.

"For me?" she asked.

He drank the rest.

Rose handed the glass to Sam as she settled Jim back onto the pillow. Before she could move away, Jim reached for her, and she took his hand. He coughed and groaned, then began coughing heavily, his body wracked and twisting. Rose wrapped her arms around him and sat on the bed cradling his head in her lap. Natalie handed her the tea, and Rose managed to get him to sip a little. Then she stroked his forehead, and just her touch seemed to soothe him. A few moments later, the medicine calmed him. He rolled onto his side, his head still resting in her lap, and drifted off to sleep.

She tried to stand, but Jim had an arm around her waist. He groaned and refused to release her.

"Is he hurting you?" Sam asked in concern.

Rose shook her head.

Sam shook his head, too.

"What?" Natalie asked the doctor softly.

"He's never wanted anyone to touch him before."

Rose looked up in surprise, then down again at the face of the man she loved as he slept.

Natalie excused herself and went to bed.

Sam stayed, settling into the overstuffed chair. He was worried about Jim's unusual behavior and didn't want to leave Rose alone with him in case he became violent. After about an hour, Rose was able to slip off the bed. Jim became restless but calmed at her touch and voice.

Sam rose and walked to the door. "I'll be back in the morning," he promised. "Don't hesitate to send for me if you need me. Hank isn't here, but Marcus Livingston is just down the hall, and he'll come get me."

"Is he the one who likes Natalie?" Rose asked.

Sam smiled and nodded. "But he hasn't said anything to her yet. Poor chap doesn't realize it's no secret to anyone, except maybe to Natalie." Then he stepped out, leaving Rose smiling.

The wee hours of the morning were always the worst time for Jim. Rose worked tirelessly, sponging him with water and sometimes rubbing alcohol to cool him. As soon as she heard Mrs. Harraday moving around in the morning, Rose would get the tub and bathe Jim in the cool water.

Almost against his will, Jim found himself enjoying her touch. His conscious mind took longer to realize what his subconscious had known immediately. He also noticed that when she wasn't with him he found himself missing her and looking forward to her return. This was a new sensation for him. Though he had friends, his feelings toward her were different. They seemed to emanate from somewhere deep within him he never knew existed. He realized she had captured his entire consciousness, body and soul.

When she wasn't with him, every heartbeat was in hopeful expectation of her return. When she was there, she filled every breath with the sweetness of her presence. He found her comforting, like warm sunshine on a winter's afternoon. He came to understand that she was the reason for his existence. All he desired—love, happiness, comfort—all were possible only in her.

Had he been well, he would have fought these feelings, but pain and illness taxed most of his will and endurance as he endeavored to recover. His emotions were closer to the surface and could no longer be ignored or denied. They overwhelmed any resistance he could muster. Since love had never before inoculated him with its touch, it relentlessly infiltrated his heart, mind, and soul. Never having suffered love, he had no defenses against it.

His fever finally broke a little after a few weeks, but it was many more weeks before it broke completely. Then it left him weak, and he still needed someone with him at night. Rose had been helping with Jim for over two months when one evening, as she was sponging his chest and arms, she noticed his body react to her touch. Jim shifted in the bed, trying to make it stop, but his body seemed to have a mind of its own. Though he was covered, his reaction was obvious.

"Don't be embarrassed," Rose said softy, still acting the role of a whore. The situation made her uncomfortable, but since this had happened before when he wasn't fully conscious, she was able to mask her discomfiture. Then, still playing her part, she reluctantly offered. "I can help you, but—"

"No!" Jim insisted.

"It's OK. I can step outside if you want to do something about it."

Jim looked at her and shook his head.

Something about his reaction struck her. "Don't you know what I mean?" she asked.

"Of course I do. I just don't do it."

"Why not?" she asked, surprised. "It's only natural for boys."

Jim looked away. He had been tempted to a few times, but as soon as he started, he felt sick. He didn't know why, because it wasn't a moral issue with him. He sensed the answer lay locked behind one of the doors in his mind he refused to open. Then he remembered the time Elena had offered to please him with her hands. He'd wanted her to, but he'd felt sick then, too, as soon as she touched him.

"From what I've heard, men do it all the time," Rose remarked.

Jim just shook his head.

"Why don't you ask the doctor?" she suggested.

"I can't ask Sam something like that. I'm a little young for that sort of thing, don't you think?"

"No. I know you're a boy in age, but you've been doing the work of a man, you've suffered the consequences as a man, and you take the pain as a man. I'd have to say that you're more of a man than many twice your age."

Jim gazed at her.

"What is it?" Rose asked, smiling at him.

"I grew up around women in your profession," he said, playing along with what she wanted him to believe. "But you're different."

"In what way?"

"You actually seem to care."

She smiled. "What were these other women like?"

"They were dirty, coarse, and often cruel."

"Where was this?"

Jim tensed. "You don't need to know," he replied, his voice low, almost a growl.

"Is it where you got the scars?" she asked softly.

Jim dropped his eyes and tried to control his breathing.

Seeing him upset made Rose want to cry, but she remained calm so as not to further agitate him. "Did these women hurt you?" she asked.

"They seemed to enjoy pouring whiskey on me when I was cut up."

Rose bit her lip. The thought of anyone doing that to him made her want to scream. "Did they do anything else to you?"

"I don't want to talk about it," Jim muttered without meeting her gaze.

Rose gently brushed some hair from his forehead and he flinched involuntarily. "I hope one day you meet a woman who will show you that touch can be a good thing."

"I'm sorry. I don't know what made me." He truly didn't understand his reaction. He liked her touch.

"It's OK," she replied gently, noting the pain in his eyes. "I understand bad memories. Now you should get some rest."

Later that evening, Sam came in to check on Jim before returning home for the day.

"I think there was something Jim wanted to ask you," Rose mentioned, still playing her part. She was concerned for the young man.

Sam looked at Jim, but Jim shook his head, remembering what she was talking about.

"We were having a discussion," Rose continued. "And we wanted your opinion."

"What would you like to know?" Sam asked, confused by Jim's apparent discomfort at the subject.

Rose took the doctor aside, whispered in his ear, then stepped into the hall, shutting the door behind her.

"I take it you have questions about masturbation," Sam stated without embarrassment. He had no hesitation about discussing the subject. He wished more people asked about it. Then maybe he would never have to treat a woman for hysterics again.

"I didn't, but Rose was concerned because I've never—" Jim didn't want to finish the sentence.

"From a purely medical point of view, there's nothing wrong with it," stated the doctor. "For either men or women. Some animals even engage in the activity. I'm sure some theologians would disagree. I mean, some people think that sex should only be performed in one position. But she's not taking advantage of you, is she?"

"No! Of course not!" Jim replied indignantly. "I can take care of myself."

"Apparently not," Sam responded, smiling. "As far as I'm concerned, there's nothing wrong with it, and most everybody does it at some point." The doctor then turned, still smiling, and opened the door. "Just, if you're going to do something like that, use the lock." He gave Rose a nod and left.

"Do you want me to stay out here?" she asked, placing her hand on the knob.

Jim shook his head.

She returned to his bedside and touched his cheek. Then she smoothed the stubborn lock of hair that always fell across his forehead. His hair was so black, she felt she could lose herself gazing into it, and imagined it would be like wandering through a soft darkness, chasing shining blue shadows. "You've had so much pain," she said. "Don't you think you deserve some pleasure?"

Jim gazed at her. Then he lifted her hand to kiss it, but Rose pulled it away.

"You need some more water," she said, rising and snatching the glass off the bedside table. She walked to the bureau and stood with her back to him for a moment.

Jim watched her and thought he saw her shoulders shaking. He got out of bed, followed her, and pulled a pair of pants from one of the drawers. He slipped them on, leaning heavily against the bureau and causing the pitcher to rock noisily in the basin. Even though she had seen him naked many times before, he felt uncomfortable. He fumbled with the buttons, getting the middle two fastened and giving up on the rest.

Then he put his hands on her shoulders and turned her toward him. She quickly wiped her eyes, looked up, and forced a smile. Jim kissed her cheek. Then, with a will that didn't seem his own, as he was about to kiss her mouth, she pulled away, nearly knocking him over in his weakness.

"No, you shouldn't!" she insisted.

"Rose," Jim uttered, his voice low and husky with emotion. "I think I love you."

Rose looked up at him in surprise. Then she felt his forehead. "Your fever must be up again. You should lie back down."

"Rose, I—" He stopped and took her hand.

"You're just infatuated. If you'd just take care of that," she said, motioning toward his groin, "you'd be able to think more clearly."

"I don't need that. I need you with me, always. Will you marry me?"

"I can't."

"Why?"

"Because you should find yourself a nice, respectable girl."

"Rose—"

"No! You can't! If nothing else, what would people think?"

"I don't care what people think."

"If you'd just—" she pleaded, pointing to him again.

Jim pulled her close. "Rose, I love you, and not just for that.

You're beautiful, and any man would want you." He glanced from her face down to her ample breasts and then back up, looking deeply into her eyes. "But I love you for what's in here." He lightly rested a finger on her breastbone.

His touch sent a thrill through her body. "You don't understand—"

"Rose, if you don't want me or don't like me, that's fine," Jim said, still holding her. "But don't base your decision on what other's may think or do."

Rose gazed into his eyes. They seemed to burn into her soul, as though they were lit by a flame churning somewhere deep within him. He was holding her tightly, and she could tell there was more to the fire than just desire. Feelings generated above the waist were the basis of his words. "You can't mean it," she breathed, hardly above a whisper.

"I do," Jim replied softly. "Well?"

"You need to get some rest," she said, pushing him toward the bed. "We'll talk about this later."

Jim got back in bed with her help and soon dozed off, exhausted by just having walked across the room.

He awoke a while later to find Natalie sitting in the chair next to his bed.

"Rose had to leave, so she asked me to stay with you," Natalie explained.

"Did she say why she left?" Jim asked without looking at her.

"No, but she seemed upset."

Jim turned away and tried to go back to sleep.

In her room at the brothel, Rose buried her face in her pillow to muffle her sobs. Though she was alone, she didn't want any of the other women or their customers to hear. She turned her head to the side, took a shuddering breath, and whispered as she prayed in the darkness. "I love him so much, but he can't love me! He deserves a respectable woman. A woman he can be proud to have on his arm, not one everybody thinks is a whore!"

She cried so hard her body writhed in her anguish, wrenching sobs from the innermost depths of her soul. "I just want him to be happy," she prayed. "Even if that means I have to die in misery. Oh God! I want him so bad! I love him and always will! Why couldn't I be worthy of him?"

Then another thought struck her. One she knew wasn't true,

though she tried to convince herself otherwise. "He only wants me because he thinks I *am* a whore," she whispered. "He thinks I know all the tricks and will pleasure him in ways he can't even imagine!" Then she cried all the more, her bitter tears burning her face. Though she knew deep in her heart that this was false, she clung to the belief, holding it up as her beacon as she descended into the abyss of despair.

Rose didn't return that night, but Jim's fever did. He was restless and often delirious and refused to eat or drink. Sam had Olivia stay with him the next night. When the doctor arrived the following morning, Jim was in horrible shape.

"Were you able to get him to eat or drink anything?" Sam asked.

"No," replied Olivia, almost in tears. "Every time I got near him he lashed out. I wasn't even able to put a cool cloth on his head."

Sam called to Mrs. Harraday for the tub, and she helped the doctor and Olivia get Jim into it. Almost as soon as the cool water hit him, Jim became agitated, and they all had to stand back to keep from getting hit and splashed.

"I don't know how Rose put up with this," Sam muttered as they waited for Jim to calm down.

"Get me out!" Jim ordered after soaking in the tub for a few more minutes.

Sam helped him stand up and dried his front while the women dried his back. Then Jim made his way to the bed with Sam's help. Before she left, Sam asked Olivia if she'd be there that evening, and she shook her head, fighting back tears. Natalie offered to stay with him that night, and Mrs. Harraday stayed with Jim during the day so Natalie could rest. Though they tried, neither Mrs. Harraday nor Sam could get Jim to eat or drink anything.

That evening, Jim's fever raged again, and again he was difficult. Natalie managed to get a cloth on his head only to have him toss it on the ground, and she too was unable to get him to drink. In the middle of the night, she sent Marcus to fetch the doctor.

When Sam arrived, the young man was so weak Sam knew he wouldn't be able to get him in and out of the tub, so he tried sponging him with water and alcohol. Jim fought against the doctor, throwing the cloths on the floor and even grabbing Sam's arms more than once. After hours of struggle, Jim's fever still hadn't lessened. Sam too was unable to get Jim to take any water and was physically and emotionally exhausted. Finally, the doctor just stood back, eyed the young man on the bed, and shook his head. Though it was now morning and bright sunlight shone in the window there was the gloom of death in the room.

"What is it?" asked Natalie.

"He'll be dead by tomorrow at the latest if I can't get his fever down, or at least some water in him," Sam replied softly, his frustration evident in his voice. Then he looked at Natalie. "Stay here until I get back."

He left the room at a run. A few moments later, he was at the brothel where Rose lived, knocking on the door.

Rose was in the kitchen. She heard the knock, walked to the front room, and opened the door. When she saw it was Sam, she started to shut it again.

"Rose!" Sam insisted, blocking the door with his foot. "I need to talk to you! I need your help!"

"You can manage without me," Rose replied, still pushing on the door.

"Rose! He's dying! I need your help!"

Rose slowly opened the door a little. "What? He was doing better when I left."

"His fever came back that night, even higher than it was before, and now no one can get him to eat or drink. He won't even let me put a cloth on his head."

"Why did you come to me?"

"You've managed him alone almost every night. I thought you could help. I realize you must've left because you're needed here, but I don't know what else to do. I just don't want that boy to die!" Sam pleaded, leaning heavily on the doorframe, trying to control his emotions.

"Let me get my shawl." She disappeared into the darkness behind her. She'd left the curtains closed because everyone else was still asleep even though it was late morning.

She rejoined Sam a moment later and they hurried back to Mrs. Harraday's, running through a summer shower that had swallowed the sun. When they arrived at Jim's room, they found Natalie cowering in a corner as Jim thrashed on the bed, sending a plate and bowl crashing from the night table to the floor.

"Get the tub now!" Sam shouted to the girl, and she ran out of the room. "His fever's so high he's having convulsions," he explained to Rose.

Rose tried to grab one of Jim's arms.

"Careful!" Sam cautioned. "He could hurt you."

"I know. But he could also hurt himself," she insisted as she held one of Jim's arms, only to have him tear it away. "Jim!" Rose said loudly. "Jim, we're trying to help you!"

"He can't hear you," Sam explained, trying to prevent his patient from throwing himself off the bed.

Mrs. Harraday and Natalie arrived with buckets and the tub, followed by Hank, who had heard the commotion. He had returned from a freight run late the day before and had still been sleeping. Mostly with Hank's assistance, Sam, Rose, and Mrs. Harraday managed to get Jim into the tub, while Natalie waited in the hall, too upset to help. Jim continued to thrash as Sam gently poured water over him. Rose knelt behind Jim's head, held it in her hands, and talked to him softly. After a few minutes, the young man calmed.

"Jim?" she asked, her face close to his.

He felt her hand touch his cheek and turned toward her.

"Please. Can you hear me?" she asked.

He breathed in as her breath caressed him, sending life into his lungs.

He nodded, then started to shake from the cold.

"Do you think you can walk?" Sam asked him.

Jim tried to stand but couldn't, so Hank pulled him to his feet and held him while Sam, Rose, and Mrs. Harraday dried him. Then Hank scooped him up and carried him to the bed. Rose had Sam help her arrange the pillows under Jim's head so he could breathe easier. Then she gave him some water and he drank.

"Thank God!" the doctor whispered.

"When did he last eat?" Rose asked Sam.

"Days ago. He hasn't eaten or drunk anything since you left."

Hank caught his breath at the news. Natalie had told him the night before about Rose's abrupt departure.

"Can you help me, please?" Rose said to Mrs. Harraday, leading the older woman out of the room.

Rose returned with a tray. She fed Jim some cool broth, and even got him to eat a little bread.

"Amazing," Sam breathed as he watched her with his patient.

"What is?" Rose asked as she continued to feed Jim.

"In less than an hour, you've accomplished more with him than the rest of us have in three days," the doctor replied.

"Were you difficult on purpose?" Rose asked Jim.

Jim shook his head weakly. "Yours was the only voice I knew," he replied, barely above a whisper.

"What?" Rose asked, not understanding.

"He probably thought everyone was trying to hurt him," Hank explained. "He told me about it once. When he's asleep or in pain, he thinks he's back with the people who hurt him when he was young."

Jim nodded weakly.

Rose fought back tears and managed to get him to drink some water mixed with the medicine.

"Will you be here when I wake up?" he asked her.

"I won't leave you again. I promise," she replied.

At her words, the sun broke through the clouds and streamed through the window. Jim felt its warmth on his face and shut his eyes.

After the young man was asleep, Rose asked Sam to step into the hallway so she could talk to him without waking Jim. They left Hank to watch him.

"What is it?" Sam asked, shutting Jim's door behind him.

"I can't keep coming here, or I'll lose my job," Rose replied. "I'm not a prostitute. I make their dresses, cook their meals, and clean their rooms."

"But—"

"I wanted you to think I was so I could stay with Jim. I wanted to help him because I saw how he helped Natalie, and I hoped he would help me, too. I want to leave the brothel, but then I'll have nowhere to go. I tried to get a room at the women's boarding house when I first got to Dillard, but they found out I was traveling with Ruby and wouldn't take me. Do you know of anyone who needs someone to cook and clean for them? And wouldn't mind a woman with a tarnished reputation?"

Sam thought for a minute, then asked, "Why don't you just stay with me and Martha?"

"Won't your wife be offended at having someone like me in her home?"

"I'm sure she won't mind. I'll go talk to her now. You stay with Jim, and I'll be back in a few minutes."

"Thank you," Rose replied as she stepped back into Jim's room.

Hank left to get something to eat. While he was gone, Sam returned and informed Rose that Martha would be happy to have her. Rose left Jim with Sam while she went to collect her things, and she took Hank along to help carry them.

"I knew you weren't one of them," Hank informed Rose as they walked.

"How?" Rose asked.

"I may not go to one, but I can tell a woman who is one."

"So why didn't you tell Sam?"

"He already knew, and both of us saw how Jimmy looked at you the first time you came to his room. We thought you might be good for him's all. A woman can give a man the will to live."

Luckily, the owner of the brothel and saloon was away, so they were able to avoid any difficulty he might create. After taking her things to Sam and Martha's and graciously thanking Martha for her generosity, Rose headed back to Jim's room. She knew Sam needed to leave to attend to other patients. Hank stopped by the freight office on the way back, so Rose returned alone. Jim awoke when she entered the room, and Sam left her sitting at Jim's bedside sponging him with a damp cloth.

As the afternoon wore on, Jim's fever began to rise again, and Rose worked tirelessly to try to keep it down. Mrs. Harraday brought a tray for both of them that evening, and Rose nibbled as she tried to feed Jim. He wasn't hungry because of the fever, but Rose managed to get him to drink some water and broth. After the meal, she helped him clean his teeth and take care of other necessaries. She smiled to ease his embarrassment, and, when she returned to the bedside after washing her hands, kissed his cheek. Then she arranged the pillows under him so he could rest.

"Thank you. I never thought...." His voice trailed off.

"Thought what?"

"I never thought I'd feel this way about anyone."

Rose kissed his forehead, and he went to sleep.

Over the next few days, Jim's fever would break early in the morning, only to rise again as the day wore on. One night, he was very agitated and knocked a glass of water out of Rose's hand as she was trying to get him to drink. Her exclamation as he hit her woke him. He opened his eyes to find her on her hands and knees drying the floor with a towel.

"What happened?" Jim asked groggily.

"As if you didn't know!" Rose snapped. "You purposely knocked the glass from my hand!"

Jim's only response was to get out of bed, ignoring his nakedness, go to the bureau, and return with two towels. He reached down and helped Rose up, nearly falling over himself from weakness. Then he began drying her with one of the towels.

"You need to lie down," Rose ordered, grabbing his arms and turning him toward the bed. "I don't need you collapsing on the floor."

Jim let her pull him to the bed, but he pushed a pillow up behind him and sat leaning against the headboard instead of lying down.

"I'm sorry," he said as Rose finished mopping up the water with the towels.

"I might believe that if you hadn't looked me straight in the eye as you hit me," Rose replied.

"Where did I hit you?"

Rose held out her right arm and showed him.

Jim took her arm and, remembering what he had once seen a woman do for her child, kissed her where she indicated he had hit her.

His gesture was so tender and unexpected she began to cry.

"I'm sorry I hit you," Jim said, thinking that was why she was crying. "I would never do anything like that on purpose."

"But you looked at me as you did it," she replied through her tears. Then she realized she had forgotten to speak to him before she touched him. She told him this and apologized.

"I would never hurt you on purpose," he stated. He reached up and caressed her cheek. "I love you, Rose, and I want to marry you." He raised her hand to his lips and kissed her palm.

"Why me?" she asked, barely above a whisper.

"Because I knew it was you when you spoke to me and put the cloth on my head and sponged me to cool me down. And it was your voice that calmed me when I was delirious and your lips that kissed my forehead as I went back to sleep."

"You remember?"

Jim nodded. "Everyone else is a blur, but I remember you." He kissed her hand again.

"I just want you to know that this wasn't my intention," she said.

"What do you mean?" he asked.

"I never intended for you to fall in love with me. I just hoped you would help me is all."

"I never intended to fall in love, either." Then he gazed at her, his eyes burning into her. "I admit, I don't know much about it, but I know I want you with me. After you left the other day, I—I've never cared if someone left before. I'd rather get shot a dozen times than for that to happen again."

"I promise I'll never leave you." She kissed his forehead. As she stood up, she looked at him in surprise. "You're smiling!"

"So?" he asked, still smiling.

"I wasn't sure you knew how." Then, on an impulse, she kissed him on the mouth.

Jim pulled her to him, and, when she didn't resist, he kissed her deeply and passionately. He pulled her closer and felt her melt against him. As their lips parted, she shifted her weight so she was closer to him. He could feel her body against his, and he felt his start to react to her warmth and proximity. He pulled the covers up more, shifting in the bed, and when she looked up at him he looked away.

"It's OK," she said with a smile. "It means you're getting better."

"It's embarrassing," Jim replied, still not looking at her.

"Do you want me to leave?"

"No. I'll be fine. It should go away before too long."

"With me here? Close to you?"

"Well, maybe you better sit in the chair," he suggested.

Rose walked to the door, locked it, and returned to the bed. She sat next to him and slipped her hand under the covers, but Jim put his hand on hers and stopped her before she could touch him.

"I'd rather wait until I'm healthy and not in pain," he said. He wondered if her touch would be different and not cause his stomach to turn, but he wanted to treat her with respect.

Rose smiled and asked, "Are you sure?"

Jim nodded. "Promise me something."

"What?"

"Don't let me go too far. I respect you too much to treat you any other way. So don't let me get carried away." He was concerned about what he wanted to do to please her, since he wasn't sure if he could be pleased at all.

"What if I get carried away?"

"We'll both have to try and behave," he said, smiling again, pulling her to him, and kissing her on the mouth.

After their lips parted, Rose smiled, gazing at him. Then she stood, gave him some water, helped him lie down, and he slept straight through to morning.

During the day she returned to Sam and Martha's to rest but was always back by Jim's side after supper to help him through the night. They kept to just kissing so as not to be tempted to do what they had promised each other they wouldn't.

Since Jim refused to wear underwear and was now healthy enough for his nakedness to embarrass him, she made him some pants from soft cotton cloth. They were loose-fitting and kept up with a drawstring around the waist, since he hadn't looked happy when she'd mentioned buttons.

"Do you like them?" she asked when he tried on a pair for the first time.

Jim nodded. "Thank you."

"I could make you underwear from the same fabric."

"No, thanks. I never had any as a child, and now I doubt I'd ever get used to them."

Rose just smiled and shook her head.

After another two weeks, Sam announced that he thought Jim was well enough to go out for a little while the next day. "Since you won't stay in bed, you might as well get outside," the doctor stated with a smile.

"Will you marry me now?" Jim asked Rose after Sam had left.

"When?"

"In the morning. We can go talk to a preacher and find us somewhere to live."

"Preacher?"

"For the wedding."

"You want to marry me in a church?" Rose asked, astonished.

"I thought that's what you'd want. I'm not religious, but I heard you praying when I was sick, so I thought—"

"Do you really think a preacher will let a woman like me get married in a church?"

"Why not? You were never a prostitute," he replied.

Rose looked at him in disbelief. "You knew?" she whispered.

"I knew a long time ago."

"Why didn't you tell me?"

"I didn't think it was important."

"But I thought that was one reason—" She stopped. Then she looked down and asked, "Would you still want to marry me if I was?"

Jim stepped closer. He lifted her chin, and gazed into her eyes. "Without question." Then he saw them fill with tears. He gently kissed her lips.

"I swear I've never been with a man," she whispered.

"And I've never been with a woman," he replied.

"Do you really think we can be married in a church?"

"Never hurts to ask," he said as he settled into bed.

Rose kissed him, then sat in the chair so he could sleep. Even though the cot was still folded up and resting against the wall, she never used it. This evening she wouldn't have been able to sleep anyway. Her mind was too preoccupied as she contemplated her future. Then she marveled at how quickly it had changed, all due to the man sleeping near her. She smiled and gazed on him lovingly, her soul rejoicing in his every breath, as he meant love, safety, and a life of happiness.

12

ROSE

The next morning, Jim was up and getting dressed when Sam arrived to check on him.

"Where are you going?" asked the doctor.

"I have some things I need to do today. You said I could start getting out some."

Sam looked at Rose, who was beaming.

"You two look like you're up to something," Sam said.

"You haven't told him?" Rose asked.

Jim shook his head.

Sam looked confused.

"May I tell him?" Rose asked.

Jim nodded as he put on his gun belt.

"Jim asked me to marry him!" Rose announced, smiling. "And I accepted."

Sam was stunned and sat down on the bed. "Isn't this rather sudden?"

"We've spent most of the last three months together," Jim replied. "How long did you know Martha before you proposed?"

"I courted her for months."

"How long before you knew you wanted to marry her?" Jim asked.

"I guess I knew from the moment I saw her."

Jim gazed at him evenly.

"I guess it's not so sudden, then," Sam replied, reading Jim's look. Then Sam smiled and stood. "May I be the first to congratulate you?"

"Thank you," Rose said, still smiling.

"I'm sure you'll both be very happy," Sam stated, smiling back at her.

"We're going to find a preacher this morning," Jim mentioned.

"Pastor Brown is a good man, and does a fine service," Sam remarked. "Would you like me to go with you and introduce you?"

Rose looked at Jim and nodded. Sam accompanied them to Pastor Brown's house, observing his patient on the way. Sam noticed that even though Jim didn't smile, the young man appeared happier than he ever had before.

The pastor had just finished breakfast when they arrived. His wife showed them into a quaint sitting room, and Pastor Brown joined them after only a short wait. Sam made the introductions and they all sat down.

"So you two want to get married," the pastor said, looking at Jim and Rose and balancing his Bible on his knee.

"Yes, sir," Jim replied.

"Have you set a date?"

"Not yet, but we'd like it to be as soon as possible," Jim answered.

Sam started to speak but held his tongue.

"Marriage isn't something you should rush into," the pastor cautioned, glancing at the doctor. "How long have you two known each other?"

Jim looked to Sam, and the doctor and Rose took turns explaining the circumstances surrounding their acquaintance.

The pastor nodded. "So you haven't had the opportunity to really get to know each other when you're both healthy?"

"We can do that after the wedding," Jim replied.

The pastor looked thoughtful. He'd heard of Jim and was concerned that his hurry was due to the dangers of his job. He wasn't intimidated by the young man's reputation. He agreed with Oliver Cromwell: "If you fear God, you have no one else to fear."

"If she can put up with me when I'm sick, doesn't it follow that I can make her happy when I'm well?" Jim asked.

The pastor nodded again and looked at Jim and Rose as they sat on his couch holding hands. "How old are you, Mr. Morgan?"

"Seventeen."

"And you, Miss Calloway?" he asked Rose.

"Nineteen."

"I can vouch for Jim that he's very mature for his age," Sam assured the pastor. "As his doctor, I can't go into the details, but he's been through a lot in his short life. Though I agree, it would be better for them to court, at least for a little while."

"And you, Miss Calloway, have you been through a great deal as well?" Pastor Brown asked.

Rose blushed and looked down. "I was working at a brothel until I met Jim," she replied in a voice just above a whisper. "The owner thinks I'm three years younger than I am, so I wasn't a prostitute, but I guess you want us to leave now." She started to rise.

"Sit down, miss," Pastor Brown said compassionately.

Rose sat and looked up at Jim with tears in her eyes. "If I hadn't lied—"

"I'm glad you did," Jim stated. Then he kissed the hand he was still holding.

"I know people, especially women, are sometimes forced, by necessity, to do things they aren't proud of," the pastor said.

Rose looked at the pastor and a tear fell to her cheek.

"How about four weeks from Saturday?" the pastor suggested, referring to a small calendar he had tucked in his Bible. "That'll make it the last Saturday in September, the twenty-eighth."

Rose smiled and looked at Jim.

"That will give you time to prepare and get to know each other a little better," Pastor Brown explained. Then he smiled and added, "I had only known my wife for two weeks before I married her, and it's been over fifteen years now."

"Thank you, sir," Jim replied.

They stood, and Jim and Rose shook his hand. Then they made an appointment to see the pastor the next week to go over the ceremony and details.

When the three of them were back outside, Sam headed to his office after cautioning Jim to take it easy. Then Jim and Rose turned and walked toward where the respectable working people lived to see if they could find a house. They strolled up one street and down another and were about to turn up the next when they saw a little house on the far corner set off from the others. The door was unlocked so they stepped inside.

The house was small, with a kitchen area to the left, the living room to the right, and the only bedroom behind it. There were no full walls, just supporting beams between the rooms, so the house was open and seemed larger than it really was. The only interior wall jutted out a few feet from the back of the house and ended in a four-by-four beam. The wall had been placed between the bedroom area and the back door to keep out the draft. For privacy, there was a frame around the bedroom for curtains. The house also had front and back porches that ran the length of the structure. On the front porch was a swing so the occupants could sit and greet their neighbors on a warm summer evening.

Jim inspected the sink and water pump and looked closely at the ceiling and floor for leaks. Then he walked to the fireplace, which was on the front of the house in the living room area. Holding a lit match for light, he leaned in and inspected the chimney as best he could.

"What do you think?" Rose asked him.

Jim nodded. "It'll do," he replied, shaking the match to extinguish it and dropping it into the grate. "I'd like to get a look at the roof, but it wouldn't be the first one I've replaced."

Rose walked to him and kissed his cheek.

As they stepped back outside, Jim took the notice off the door and read it. "We better go to the bank," he suggested.

When they arrived at the bank, they asked to see the man named on the notice. A few minutes later, a clerk showed them into a small office. The bank representative stood and shook their hands as they introduced themselves, and Jim handed him the notice.

"We'd like to buy this house," Jim stated.

"Let me get the journal," replied the man. He stepped to a cabinet in the corner and removed a ledger. After thumbing through it, he settled on a page and turned it for Jim and Rose to see.

"We require a third down with a third—" he started to say.

"I'd like to buy it outright," Jim informed him after looking at the figure written on the bottom of the page.

The man looked at him in surprise.

"You can check my account. There should be enough to cover it," Jim stated, meeting his gaze.

"I'll be right back," replied the man.

"You can pay that much?" Rose asked.

Jim nodded. "I've been saving my money. Ted still pays me if I'm hurt on the stage, and I work for the blacksmith on my days off."

"That must pay pretty well."

"I can sometimes make as much in a few days as I do in two weeks on the stage."

"Then why don't you just do that?"

"Because they need me on the stage," Jim answered.

"Well, Mr. Morgan," said the man, when he returned a few minutes later. "It appears that you do have sufficient funds for this purchase. Would you like me to prepare the paperwork right away?"

"Yes, sir. But since I'm paying for it outright, do I have to pay that amount, or can I get a discount?"

"Let me talk to the bank president. I'll be right back."

"You're so smart," Rose beamed, giving Jim's arm a squeeze after the man left.

"It never hurts to ask," Jim replied.

The man returned and handed Jim the ledger again. There was a new figure written at the bottom.

"That's as low as we can go," the man announced. "Is that to your liking?"

Jim looked at the amount, thought for a moment, then nodded.

"Mr. Talmadge, the bank president, gave you the most generous discount I've ever encountered," explained the man. "He told me to tell you that it's in honor of the work you've done with the freight company and all the money you've saved the bank by preventing robberies on the stage. He's in a meeting right now, but he'll see you on your way out. I'll start preparing the paperwork immediately."

"Thank you, sir," Jim replied. "When will we be able to take possession?"

"I'll have the necessary forms ready for you to sign by three this afternoon, and you can take possession right after that if you'd like. Now, if you'll just sign this form stating that you are over twenty-one, I can get started on the other ones."

"What if I'm not twenty-one?" Jim asked.

The man raised his eyebrows in surprise but recovered quickly and remained professional. "Then you will need someone to co-sign for you. I hope that won't be a problem."

"Shouldn't be," Jim said. "But does that mean the person who signs also owns the house?"

"His name will be on the deed," the man replied, "and he will be held responsible for the property until you are twenty-one. Though, considering your line of work, Mr. Morgan," the man added, "you might want to consider leaving this person's name on the deed even after you come of age."

"Why?" Jim asked.

The man glanced at Rose. "Maybe we should continue this in private," he suggested. "I don't want to upset the young lady."

"You mean if I'm killed," Jim stated bluntly.

The man caught his breath and glanced at Rose again. He saw a pained expression cross her face.

Jim kept his eyes on the man, not noticing. "She knows the dangers of my job," Jim added evenly.

The man nodded. "Yes, sir. If your co-signer is someone you trust he could safeguard the property for her in the case of your death."

"Wouldn't the property go to her anyway?" Jim asked. "After we're married, of course."

"A woman can't own property, sir," the man explained.

Jim gazed at the man in surprise. "You mean even after we're married I can't add her name to the deed?"

"No, sir," the man replied. "The law doesn't allow it."

"Can I leave it to her in a will?" Jim asked.

The man shook his head.

Then Jim shook his as well in disbelief and exchanged a glance with Rose.

"A woman can't be burdened with such things," the man stated, "and I'm sure you agree she shouldn't be. Leave it to a relative or trusted friend to care for her should there be any unpleasant events in the future."

Jim nodded again.

"Is there anything else I can do for you folks today?" the man asked.

"I think that's it," Jim answered, still surprised by what he'd learned.

"Well, let me see you out, Mr. Morgan. Mr. Talmadge would like to meet you. Though he knows you by sight, you have never been formally introduced."

The man took them by the bank president's office. Mr. Talmadge stood, shook Jim's hand, and thanked him for all his hard work on the stage. After his employee told him Jim and Rose were getting married, Mr. Talmadge took the ledger from his clerk, wrote another figure at the bottom, and signed it.

"Consider it a wedding gift," Mr. Talmadge said, showing the figure to Jim. "I'd give it to you for free, but a man appreciates what he has to pay for."

"Thank you, sir," Jim replied in surprise. "That's more than generous."

"It's the least I can do, my boy," smiled Talmadge, patting Jim on the shoulder.

"What did he do?" Rose asked when she and Jim were back outside. "He held it up too high for me to see."

"He took off another fifty percent," Jim replied.

"So you got it for next to nothing?"

"*We* got it for next to nothing," Jim corrected her. "Regardless of the law, it's your house, too. I'll ask Sam to sign the papers, and he'll make sure you get to keep it regardless."

Rose smiled and squeezed his arm. "I can't believe this. You know, I have some money of my own. I can help with the furniture and things."

"We'll see."

"You look tired," Rose commented, gazing at him worriedly. "Let's head back."

Jim nodded, and they turned toward Mrs. Harraday's.

"I'll have to talk to Sam and see if he'll go to the bank with us later," Jim said as they walked.

When they arrived at the boarding house, Mrs. Harraday was thrilled to hear about the engagement, and she invited Rose to eat with them that evening. Rose accepted. Then she walked back to Sam and Martha's so that Jim could rest and she could tell Martha about her dinner plans. Sam was out, so she didn't speak to him.

Later, after he had rested, Jim ate an apple as he walked to Sam's to meet Rose and talk to the doctor. Sam had just gotten home and was eating in his study while making notes in patients' charts. He waved Jim in as he was about to knock on the open door. The doctor agreed to meet them at the bank at three. He also promised to provide for Rose in the future, seeming surprised Jim felt he needed to ask. Then Sam suggested Jim write a will.

"I know it's not something you want to think about," said the doctor, "but it avoids questions later. It also shows your wife you love her and want her to be cared for."

Jim nodded. "Do I just write it out myself?" he asked.

"Before you go out on the stage again," Sam replied, "get Hank or Ted over here. I'll help you with the wording, and one of them and I can be your witnesses."

After talking to Sam, Jim took Rose to the furniture makers. They ordered a bed, a table and chairs, and two other chairs to put in front of the fireplace. The furniture maker gave them a price, and Jim promised to return later that afternoon with the first payment and pay the remainder upon delivery.

Then Jim and Rose headed to the bank. Sam arrived a few moments later and signed all the necessary papers. Jim thanked him, and the doctor left. Jim stepped to one of the windows and withdrew the money for the furniture from his account. With Rose at his side, he returned, paid the furniture maker, and gave him the address for the delivery.

The furniture maker's shop was near the carpenter's shop, and the carpenter met them as they stepped back out onto the street.

"I hear congratulations are in order," said the carpenter, smiling.

Jim's brow wrinkled, but he shook the carpenter's hand.

"If there's anything I can do," the carpenter offered.

"Maybe there is," Jim replied. "Give the place a look-over and let me know if there's anything wrong or that I need to keep an eye on. He can give you the address," he added, motioning toward the furniture maker, who was just inside his open door pretending not to listen.

The carpenter nodded and bowed to Rose as they passed.

Jim wanted to keep the news quiet, but Mrs. Harraday was so excited she couldn't help mentioning it during supper that night. Everyone was already glad to have Jim join them for the first time in months, and the news of his engagement brought congratulations from all.

"I didn't know you had it in you," Hank smiled, clapping Jim on the shoulder.

Everyone else laughed, apparently thinking the same thing.

"It's always the quiet ones that surprise you," Hank added.

After supper, Jim took Rose with him to the stable to check on Ness. He hadn't seen the animal since before his illness.

"I've always thought he was so pretty!" Rose exclaimed as Ness came trotting to the fence.

Ness nuzzled Jim's shoulder, knocking his hat off as he patted the horse's neck.

"Do you ride?" Jim asked her.

Rose shook her head, smiling as she patted the horse.

"I could teach you," Jim offered.

"Horses are beautiful animals, but sitting on one scares me."

"What if you're with me?" Jim asked, stepping close to her.

"Only if we're on the same horse," she replied and kissed his cheek. "Can he hold both of us?"

"I don't think he'd mind. You weigh nothing to him."

"That's why they scare me," Rose laughed.

Ness snorted as though he understood and was offended.

"It's OK, boy," Jim assured him. "She likes you, you're just too much horse for most, and you know it."

"Kind of like his master," Rose commented. Then she smiled as Jim talked to the horse, apologizing for his absence while feeding him an apple. "Do you think he understands you?"

Jim looked at her and nodded. Ness looked at her and seemed to nod as well.

Rose gazed at the two of them and laughed. "You two even look alike. You both have a stubborn lock of hair that insists on falling into your eyes," she said, reaching up with both hands and trying to smooth the hair of the man while doing the same for the horse.

"It's our forelock," Jim stated. "And one reason I wear a hat," he said, retrieving his and setting it firmly on his head.

Ness nuzzled the hat again, and Jim smiled and rubbed his neck. "I could get a hat for you, too."

Ness snorted and shook his head.

"He really understands you!" Rose laughed.

"He's a smart one," said one of the stable boys, stopping to admire the horse. He had overheard the question. "He'd been fidgety when you didn't come around like usual, Mr. Morgan, until I told him you were sick. Then about once a week or so, he'd run up to the fence when he saw me and kick up a fuss until I told him you weren't well yet. The other boys didn't believe me at first when I told them until they saw it for themselves."

"Thanks for letting him know," Jim replied. "And thanks for taking such good care of him. He looks great."

"You're welcome, sir. He's been a dream since you explained that you'd have to be away a lot."

"What did he do before that?" Rose asked.

"Oh, all sorts of stuff, ma'am," the boy replied. "He'd throw his head every time we tried to put a line on him and tear around the paddock causing all kinds of ruckus. Or he'd nearly run us down if we had to go out there to get one of the other horses. That is, until this one time when one of the boys just stood still and he ran past him. Then we realized he wasn't really trying to hurt anyone."

Rose looked at Jim, amazed.

"He's done worse, believe me," Jim replied to her look. Then he turned and threw the apple core into the adjacent field.

"Heard you're getting married, sir," said the stable boy.

Jim looked at him, his brow wrinkled.

"It's all over town, sir," explained the boy. "It being so unexpected and all."

"You must mean sudden," Rose corrected.

"No, ma'am," insisted the boy. "Unexpected. No offense, sir," said the boy, looking at Jim, "but I guess you're so good at killing no one even thought you'd be interested in the opposite."

Jim gazed at the boy as he turned and disappeared into a stall. Then he gave Ness a final pat and they headed back.

Jim walked Rose to Sam and Martha's. Before he knocked on their door, he took Rose in his arms and kissed her.

"Are you sure you'll be all right tonight by yourself?" Rose asked him.

"Sam said I should be."

"I'll miss you," Rose said, resting her hands on his waist.

"I'll miss you, too," Jim whispered, leaning close to her and kissing her again.

Then he knocked and Martha answered the door.

"Did you want to come in?" Martha asked Jim.

"No, thank you."

Sam came out of his study and joined them. Then he insisted on walking Jim back to the boarding house.

"Jim, I'm not trying to pry, but do you think that maybe you're moving a little fast?" asked the doctor as they walked.

"What? About Rose?"

Sam nodded. "She's a beautiful woman, and that can make a man do things he might later regret. You could just court her for a while. Then, when you're sure, marry her."

"It sounds like you don't approve," Jim replied evenly.

"I didn't say that. I just don't want you to make a mistake, that's all." Sam stopped walking and looked Jim in the eye. "As I've said before, I know I'm not your father, but I care about you. As your friend, not just your doctor, I feel I should say if I think you're doing something wrong."

"So you think my wanting to marry Rose is wrong?" Jim asked, meeting Sam's gaze, the fire in his eyes beginning to kindle.

"No, I don't think it's wrong," Sam replied, noticing the flicker. "But what do you really know about her?"

"What do you mean?"

"Jim, she lived at a brothel."

"She wasn't a whore!" Jim growled, his eyes flashing.

"That doesn't mean she's never been with a man."

Jim glared at the doctor. "She hasn't."

Sam faced him without wavering, and the two men stood in the fading light of evening gazing at each other. Sam noticed Jim had grown and could almost look him straight in the eye. "If she hasn't, then she'll let me examine her," stated the doctor.

"What?" Jim asked in angry surprise.

"That way you'll know for sure."

"I know because she told me."

"She wouldn't be the first woman to lie about such a thing."

"You're calling her a liar?" Jim growled again, and his hand instinctively moved toward his gun, though he had no conscious intention of using it on his friend. "They all lie about their age, and with less reason than she had!"

Sam noticed the slight movement but stood his ground. "Jim, my main concern is you. As your physician, I don't want you to catch something you'll never get rid of."

"She said she's never been with a man, and I believe her!"

Sam nodded and gently rested his hands on the young man's shoulders, hoping to calm him, but felt Jim tense instead. "I just want you to be sure this is what you really want. At your age, it's difficult to conceive what the rest of your life really means, and that's what marriage is—for the rest of your life. Jim, I want you to be happy and not spend most of your life regretting a boyish mistake." He wondered if his young friend's determination to get married so quickly was due to his strength of feeling or because he didn't expect to live through an extended courtship. He decided it imprudent to ask. Then he was relieved to feel Jim relax and see the young man's expression soften.

"How did you know you loved Martha?"

"I found myself thinking about her every second I wasn't with her," the doctor replied, releasing the young man but, in his heart, wanting to hold him close like a father does his child. "When I was with her, I felt whole. Like part of me had been missing all of my life. I couldn't imagine a future without her."

"That's how I feel about Rose," Jim stated. "I know it's sudden, but I've never felt like this about anyone before. I know we don't know each other all that well yet, but even when I was at my worst during the last few weeks, when I looked at her, all I saw was acceptance."

Sam gazed at Jim for a moment. Then he nodded, turned, and they started walking again.

"When it gets closer to the wedding, I'll tell you a few things about women," Sam offered.

"No offense, but I grew up around whores. I doubt there's much you can tell me."

Sam glanced at his young friend and wondered if he would ever hear anything about Jim's past that didn't shock or appall him. When they arrived at the boarding house, Sam gave Jim some final instructions and informed him that Mrs. Harraday had agreed to check on him later. Jim nodded, and Sam took his leave.

When he got to his room, Jim found a note slipped under his door. It was from Ted, congratulating him on his engagement and promising him he wouldn't have to go out on a stage run until after the wedding.

The next morning, Sam took Rose aside and talked with her privately. If she had been with other men, as a physician he was concerned with her health as well as Jim's. Rose informed him that she was still pure and agreed to let the doctor examine her. He did and found she was telling the truth.

"Are you going to tell Jim?" she asked the doctor.

"I can't," Sam replied. "As your physician, I'm bound by confidentiality."

Rose nodded thoughtfully. She decided that, since Jim believed her, she wouldn't mention the examination, because she wasn't sure if he would be upset by it or not.

What no one in Dillard knew, or even suspected, was that Carlos had decided to eliminate the freight guard who had been killing so many of his men. What even Carlos didn't know was that one of them had already tried.

13

DECEPTION

In early July 1872, about eight weeks before Jim and Rose visited the Pastor and bought their house, Carlos had decided to put his plan into action. He knew that if he just started killing all the freight men, he might never know for sure if he killed the one he was looking for or not and that the man might decide to go into another line of work. He also didn't want to have to deal with the cavalry again.

Before starting his attacks on homesteads the year before, he'd tried to distract the cavalry by making it look like the Indians were on the warpath. He'd planned, beginning late in the spring of 1871, to let his men rape, murder, and scalp their way through to the fall. He'd started near Dillard, hoping to incite the freight men. *If I can get Morgan or one of the other guards to shoot at the Indians who always follow the stage,* he thought, *then maybe they really will go on the warpath and save me some trouble.* Morgan had stopped this plan as soon as it began, though, by killing two of his men. *It still might have worked,* he mused, *if a damned newspaper hadn't reported that my men were planning to take scalps to throw the blame onto the Indians.* How they'd figured that out he didn't know.

Carlos wasn't just concerned with his business. He was also out for revenge. This freight guard, this Jim Morgan, had not only killed some of his best men, but was now creating problems with the men he had left, not to mention interfering with his revenue. He'd already had to shoot one man for refusing to rob a stage, and he didn't want to have to kill any more. It was bad for morale. So he came up with a plan. The only problem was, since Morgan had killed every man who rode against him, though all of them knew the guard's name no one knew what he looked like. That needed to change.

He'd kept his men in check that spring of 1872, only allowing them to sporadically rob, rape, and murder. When they complained, he'd just smiled and reminded them that only a few months before they'd complained because he'd wanted them to attack stages again.

He used their frustration to gauge the freight men's complacency. Now it was time "to unleash the dogs," as his brother put it. He broke his men into groups and assigned a few men in each group to rob the stages. The one or two others in the group were to watch the robbery take place. That way there would be someone left who would be able to recognize the guard later. Then the men were to switch jobs before the next attack.

Carlos knew the schedule of every stage and, over the next few weeks, systematically robbed a stage protected by each guard that rode out of Dillard. His men would have considered it a suicide mission to go up against the man they were looking for, but Carlos convinced them their chances of attacking his stage were no greater than before. He also promised a healthy bonus to any man who got a good look at the guard, agreeing to pay even if the robbery wasn't a success.

His men understood his orders to mean that once they knew they were up against Morgan, all they had to do was see his face and then they could ride away, saving their own lives.

They kept the robberies to no more than one or two a week to avoid having the military brought in. All the robberies went smoothly, and none of the men were lost. Therefore, they knew they still had not found the man they were looking for.

"He couldn't have quit," muttered Carlos in frustration when the last group reported to him.

"Maybe he's out of commission for some reason," suggested one of his more intelligent men.

"But we haven't shot anyone here lately," remarked one

of the others.

"We haven't needed to," commented another with a laugh.

Carlos thought for a few minutes, then nodded. "You," he said pointing to the one who had spoken first, "ride into Dillard and find out what that cocksucker Morgan is doing."

"Why didn't you just do that in the first place?" asked one of the men with a laugh.

The others froze and stared at him.

Carlos eyed the man for a minute. "What happened the last time I sent some men into a town on a mission?" he asked.

The others exchanged a glance, afraid to speak. Then they began to slowly move away from the man.

"The sons of bitches couldn't keep their mouths shut," Carlos stated, answering his own question. "Morgan learned what they were up to, and they all ended up dead."

The man suddenly realized he was standing alone before his boss.

Carlos gave a slight nod to his other men.

"I was just—" the lone man started to say as he reached for his weapon.

He wasn't fast enough. A dozen bullets tore into him before his hand touched his pistol.

"I'll find out what's going on with Morgan," the man Carlos had ordered into Dillard promised as he holstered his weapon. "And I won't let anyone know why I'm there," he added to impress his boss.

Carlos didn't seem to hear as he walked away, leaving his men to clean up the mess.

When the man arrived in the town, he drew no attention. He just looked like a road-weary traveler who had decided to take a few days to rest and enjoy the pleasures the town had to offer. The man was smart, and one of the first things he did was to determine where most of the freight employees lived. He figured this man earned more than most, so the first place he watched was Mrs. Harraday's.

He soon realized that something wasn't quite right. The sign on the house said that it was a respectable men's boarding house, but he noticed women entering late in the day and not leaving until the next morning. He also noticed that a light was kept burning in one of the rooms all night. After watching for a couple of days, he decided to follow one of the women when she left in the morning.

The woman stopped by the general store on her way home.

The man followed her in but kept his distance to avoid undue attention.

The woman walked through the store for a few minutes, then took the items she wanted to the counter.

"Oh, hello Olivia," said the female shopkeeper to the woman. "How's Jim?"

"About the same," Olivia replied, obviously exhausted after her night's work. "I'm just glad Sam only needs me to stay one night a week now. I don't know how Rose does it the rest of the time," she concluded with a yawn.

The man stood near enough to hear their conversation, glancing admiringly at the shopkeeper. The first thing he noticed was her breasts, but then he worked his way up and decided that, other than her breasts, there wasn't much else to look at. He also wondered why she had what looked like a sheet tied around her head and hoped she didn't think it made her look any better.

"Don't get discouraged. He's young and strong. I'm sure he'll be fine," said the shopkeeper.

"Thank you, Norma," said Olivia. Then she walked back outside.

The man had been pretending to look at something on one of the tables. After the woman left, he took a pouch of tobacco to the counter.

"Did I hear you ask about someone named Jim?" the man asked.

"Yes," answered the shopkeeper.

"The one who's the freight guard?"

"Yes, why?"

"I met him the last time I was in town a few months ago. What's his last name?"

"Morgan," the shopkeeper replied. "Jim Morgan."

"What happened to him? He didn't get himself shot, did he?"

"Oh my, no! He has pneumonia."

"I'm sorry to hear that. I'll have to stop in and see him. Is he still at Mrs. Harraday's?"

"Yes," she replied with a sweet smile.

The man smiled in return, thanked her, and left.

By the next afternoon, the man had reported everything to Carlos, who grinned at the news. Then, since he knew the man could draw, he sent him back to Dillard to try to find out what Jim looked like and sketch his likeness. "But don't do anything else without orders," Carlos growled.

As the man rode out of camp, he saw his boss speaking privately to someone, but the other person was behind a rock. He hardly noticed the mule grazing nearby as he urged his horse into a canter.

When the man arrived in the town again, he thought about claiming to be a friend of Jim's and just going in to see him. Then, after getting a good look at him, he could claim he'd mistaken him for someone with the same name. However, he figured the guard might get suspicious, so he continued watching the boarding house.

He was engaged in this activity from a bench across the street when an old man on a mule rode up. He sat slumped in the saddle, his body bent from age. The old man pulled his mule to a stop in front of Mrs. Harraday's and dismounted, almost falling. The bearded old man untied a large leather bag from his saddle and slowly climbed the porch steps, struggling under the weight of the sack. Then he knocked on the door. The young maid answered and, seemingly reluctantly, showed the man inside.

"My mistress is out," said Natalie to the old salesman.

"I won't keep you but a minute," promised the old man. "I have just the thing you might need."

"Me?"

"I bet there's a young man in this town you admire."

Natalie lowered her eyes shyly, thinking about Marcus Livingston. He hardly spoke to her, but she'd seen him watching her sometimes, and he seemed to want to stay close to her when he was helping in the kitchen.

The salesman noticed her blush and, as though reading her mind, asked, "Has he paid you any mind?"

"A little." Natalie looked up in surprise.

"Well, put a few drops of this in his tea or coffee," said the man, taking a vial from his bag, "and he'll find you irresistible. Only two dollars."

"Really?" asked Natalie, looking at the vial in awe.

The man nodded.

Natalie took the vial from the man, reached in her apron pocket, and brought out a single dollar. "I only have one dollar. I'm sorry," she said disappointedly, holding out the vial to return it to the old man.

"That's quite all right, my dear," said the salesman, gently pushing her hand back toward her. "I'll sell it to you for one dollar."

Natalie smiled and handed the man the money.

"Now is there anyone you can think of who might need anything? A cure-all, perhaps?" asked the salesman.

"A cure-all?"

"It gets a person over sickness. I discovered it while studying herbs with the Indians," explained the man, taking another vial from his bag. This one was smaller than the one he had given Natalie, and made of dark-colored glass with strange writing on it. "It's a wondrous thing, miss. I've seen two drops from this very bottle bring a man back from death."

"He was dead?" Natalie breathed.

"On the very brink, miss. Was just about to breathe his last, but two drops of this and he was dancing a jig the next day. On my word," swore the man, holding up his right hand. He noticed the girl glanced toward the steps. "Do you know someone who might need this?"

Natalie nodded. "How much?"

"Oh, miss, I don't sell this one. I keep it for extreme cases only."

"Can I use it and give it back to you?" she asked, obviously desperate to help someone.

"No, miss. This wonder here has to be administered by one who knows how to use it," replied the man gravely.

"But you said it just takes two drops."

"But they have to be given in the proper way," explained the salesman. "Is the person who needs this nearby? I could examine the patient and see what needs to be done."

Natalie thought for a moment. She was watching Jim that afternoon and, reasoning she needed to check on him, didn't guess it would hurt to let the nice man see him, especially if he could help.

"Is the person you're taking me to see the one you need the

other potion for?" asked the salesman as Natalie led him up to Jim's room.

"Oh, no, sir," answered Natalie, blushing again.

When they arrived at Jim's door, she peeked in. Jim was sleeping, so she motioned to the man to be quiet, but as soon as they stepped into the room Jim stirred, awoke, and started coughing.

"I have someone here to see you," Natalie explained to him softly as she helped him drink some water. "He has some medicine that can help you."

Jim eyed the man suspiciously and forced himself to stop coughing.

The salesman gazed at Jim and his eyes narrowed. "You're a very ill young man."

"I have a doctor," Jim informed him, coughing again.

The salesman nodded, then bent over Jim and sniffed at his face. "Pneumonia."

"How did you know?" Natalie asked in awe.

The salesman didn't answer but continued his examination of Jim. "May I?" asked the man, indicating that he wanted to touch the young man.

Jim nodded hesitantly.

The man felt Jim's throat. Then he placed his hands lightly on Jim's chest, noticing the wound in the young man's side but not saying anything about it. The man seemed lost in concentration, as though he was feeling the illness inside Jim's lungs with his hands. Jim started to say something, but the man motioned for him to be quiet, and Jim reluctantly obeyed.

"Yours is a strange case," announced the salesman. "There's more that needs to be healed than just pneumonia."

"His lungs were hurt in a fire," Natalie mentioned.

"A fire!" exclaimed the salesman, looking at Jim in wonder. "How long ago?"

"Two years," answered Natalie when Jim only gazed at the man and didn't respond.

The salesman nodded, then stepped to the window and looked out. He could see his mule waiting patiently for him to return, as well as the man across the street. He turned abruptly. "There's a man sitting on a bench across the way. Do you know him?" he asked Natalie.

Natalie walked to the window, saw the man and shook her head.

"Good. Go get him," he commanded her.

"Why?" Natalie asked.

"For this to work, I need someone who's never met this man before."

"What?" Jim wondered as Natalie ran from the room.

"Trust me, young man," the salesman assured him. "I've healed worse cases than yours."

Jim shook his head but waited patiently for Natalie to return. He knew he always had his gun under his pillow if things got out of hand and was glad Sam had reluctantly given it back to him just days before.

A few minutes later, Natalie returned with the stranger in tow.

He stepped into the room as though entering a church. He couldn't believe his luck, and knew the boss would be pleased—and probably laugh his ass off—when he told him.

"This is Mr. Colt," said Natalie to the salesman.

Jim figured it was the name of the manufacturer of the man's gun rather than his name, but stayed silent to humor Natalie. The girl had been kind and helpful during his illness, and he didn't want to hurt her feelings.

"Thank you for coming," the salesman said to the stranger. "Though what man could resist the plea of so charming a messenger," he added, smiling at Natalie, who blushed.

"Pleased to be of assistance," replied Colt, eyeing Jim closely.

"Now I need all of you to do exactly as I say," ordered the salesman gravely. "It's a matter of life and death."

Natalie nodded solemnly, and the stranger gave a nod as well.

"You don't believe in this stuff, do you?" Jim asked Natalie.

"Quiet, young man!" the salesman commanded. "I'm trying to save your life."

"And how much are you charging her?" Jim asked, becoming annoyed.

"Nothing, young man, nothing," answered the salesman seriously. "How can one put a price on human life?"

Jim looked at Natalie. She nodded, so he relaxed and let the man continue.

The salesman took the bottle he'd shown Natalie earlier and held it up to the window. The vial looked like a glowing purple star in the old man's hand. Then the salesman said words in a language none of them could understand and gave the vial a shake. It went dark. He stepped next to the bed, held the vial over Jim, and placed his other hand on Jim's chest. He said more strange words, and the vial seemed to vibrate.

"What are you doing?" Jim asked, his right hand touching the gun under his pillow.

The salesman said some more words and then gasped. "Water!"

Natalie ran to the bureau, grabbed a clean glass, filled it from the pitcher, and brought it to him.

"Not me, child! Give it to Mr. Colt. But don't drink it!" commanded the salesman to the stranger.

Natalie handed the man the glass.

He too was amazed at what he was seeing.

Then the salesman removed the tiny stopper from the vial, and a faint white smoke wafted up from it. He held the bottle over the glass the stranger was holding and very carefully poured a few drops into the water. The liquid turned green. "Give it to him, quickly!" the salesman ordered.

Colt rushed to Jim, but Jim held up his hand and stopped him.

"Drink it quickly!" commanded the salesman.

"This has gone far enough," Jim replied.

The salesman frowned, grabbed the glass, and drank some of the liquid, pouring it into his mouth so Jim could see he was actually swallowing it. "Now will you drink it?" he asked, handing the glass back to the stranger.

Jim nodded and let Colt lift his head and hold the glass as he pretended to drink. If the man noticed he wasn't really drinking, he didn't say anything.

Colt took the opportunity to study Jim's face closely. Whether the man drank the medicine or not made no difference to him.

"Well?" Natalie asked Jim after Colt stepped back.

Jim just shrugged.

"It will take a few minutes for the potion to begin to take effect," the salesman explained. "Give him more water, but use a different glass."

Natalie took the glass Jim had been using all afternoon, filled it, and brought it to him.

"Thank you," the salesman said to the stranger. "You have

helped save this young man's life."

Colt nodded. With a motion from the salesman, the stranger turned to leave the room, pausing at the door and gazing at Jim for another moment so as to better memorize his features. He knew he could reproduce Jim's likeness for the boss. Then he left, laughing to himself at his good fortune and the irony of it.

Jim drank from the second glass of water.

"How do you feel?" the salesman asked.

"About the same."

The salesman smiled. "It may take a while before you notice any difference."

"What's it doing?" Natalie asked.

"He's feeling stronger," stated the salesman.

Jim nodded slightly, veiling sarcasm to appease the old man.

"You'll feel even better by tomorrow," continued the salesman. "But you still need to take it easy. You may feel like you can get up and run around, but don't try it, at least not until tomorrow afternoon. Give your body twenty-four hours to heal."

"Thank you!" breathed Natalie. "How can I ever repay you?"

"Just remember me in your prayers, my dear," said the salesman, gathering his things together. "I'll see myself out. And dispose of this," he added, taking the glass containing the green liquid. "Wouldn't want it to fall into the wrong hands," he stated with a smile as he closed the door behind him.

Natalie sat at Jim's bedside, beaming.

"I didn't drink it," Jim stated after the salesman left.

"What?" asked Natalie in angry surprise.

"I don't trust that man. There could have been poison in that glass."

"But he drank it himself!"

"I appreciate the thought, but never trust one of those salesmen."

When the salesman got outside, Colt was standing beside his mule, intending to thank him. Colt knew the salesman would think he was thanking him for helping the young man upstairs. However, he would know he was really thanking the salesman for saving him countless days hoping to get a glimpse of the guard. Colt was surprised when the salesman told him in a hushed voice to meet him at the livery stable on the other end of town. Colt looked confused, but something about the way the man said it caused the stranger to obey.

The younger man turned back as he walked away, and the old man motioned for him to hurry along. After Colt was out of sight, the old man drew a bottle from one of the packs hanging from his mule. He took two swallows, ran to the side of the house, and vomited in a bush. He then poured the green liquid over the vomit and left the empty glass on the porch.

Mrs. Harraday would never know why one of her favorite flowering shrubs died suddenly that summer.

When the old man arrived at the livery stable, Colt was waiting for him.

Colt watched as the salesman dismounted, almost hopping from his animal's back. Then the old man turned abruptly and faced him.

"Now that you know what he looks like," the old man said, in a voice different from what he'd used before—harsher, younger, and more menacing—"You can kill him." He'd noticed the guard had only pretended to drink from the first glass. He'd been tempted to grab the guard and, with the other man's help if necessary, force him to drink it. Then he could have watched the guard writhe and squirm until he drowned in his own juices.

Colt looked at the old man, confused, realizing the man was much younger than his gray hair and beard had led him to believe.

"We both have allegiance to the same man," explained the salesman. "Me by blood, you by oath," he said, touching Colt on the left shoulder.

Colt realized only one of the initiated would know about the oath and the pain inflicted on the left shoulder as it was given. "Do you want me to just go up there and shoot him?" he asked.

"No, he's got a gun under his pillow. Even ill, he's faster than you. Wait until you can catch him by surprise. He'll be up and about before too long, and you'll be able to get him when he's outside."

"What did you give him, some sort of poison?"

"No," lied the salesman, not trusting the man. "That would be too obvious. I gave him something the Indians use before battle to get their blood pumping. Your boss wants this one to die violently!" he growled as he mounted.

Colt noticed the man moved with ease and vigor, and now sat straight in the saddle. He watched the man ride off at a gallop. Then he stood, smiling and shaking his head.

Colt immediately returned to his room and sketched Jim's face. Then he had a good meal and spent the night with one of the women. The next day, he left to deliver the drawing.

Carlos smiled when he looked at the picture, but gave no reaction or explanation when told about the salesman. Carlos then sent Colt back to Dillard to kill the guard.

Colt could enjoy his stay now that he knew what Jim looked like, and he turned toward the saloons that offered more than just liquor. He ended up on a two-week bender since he needed to wait until he could catch the guard outside anyway. By the time he came around, circumstances had changed, so he watched and waited.

Rose arrived at Jim's room the afternoon after the salesman's visit. She looked annoyed when Natalie told her about the nice man and the medicine. Rose was worried the man might have tried to give Jim something harmful.

Sam had the same concern when he arrived later on, and he scolded Natalie.

"I'm glad you didn't drink it," Sam said to Jim. "But you shouldn't have even let it touch your mouth."

"When the old man drank some himself, I figured it couldn't hurt to fake it."

"Jim, there are poisons that can kill almost instantly with only one drop, or simply by getting on your skin," Sam explained.

"Then that salesman and I both would be dead," Jim stated.

Sam could never argue with Jim's analytical mind. He looked sternly at Natalie. "But don't ever take anything from one of those salesmen again," Sam ordered. "If there was some miracle cure, don't you think I would have used it?"

"But it came from the Indians," Natalie explained.

"I know the Indians have some good remedies," Sam replied, "but if they have one for pneumonia I've never heard about it."

That evening, Natalie told Rose about the potion she'd bought from the salesman. She asked Rose if she thought she should give it to Marcus Livingston, the young man with whom she was in love. Rose smiled and informed her that she didn't think he needed it. She went on to explain that everyone in the house had noticed how he looked at her. Natalie smiled, thanked her, and promised not to give him the potion.

Two days later, Jim and Rose bought the house. They spent the next few days making it livable. Sam was worried Jim was doing too much, but every time he checked on him the young man looked healthier and was stronger.

"You must be taking good care of him," Sam commented to Rose during one of his visits to their house. It was the following Monday, and they had only owned the house a week, but the doctor noticed that Jim had already made all necessary repairs, painted the walls, and had even had the chimney cleaned.

Rose smiled. "I try to keep him quiet, but once he decides on something there's no stopping him."

Sam nodded.

Jim motioned for the doctor to follow him out back. When they were alone outside, Jim asked him to be his best man at the wedding.

"I'd be honored. Who's going to give the bride away?" asked Sam.

"Hank. He even promised to clean his boots."

Sam laughed. "Martha and Mrs. Harraday are enjoying planning the reception. Have you heard from Mrs. Canady yet?"

"She'll get here a couple days before the wedding."

"I bet she was surprised," Sam replied, smiling as he headed back toward the road.

Jim nodded and walked with the doctor.

"Martha wanted me to remind you to invite the Bowers," Sam mentioned.

"Why should I do that?" Jim asked.

"They had you over for supper," Sam reminded him.

"Then Julietta wouldn't speak to me."

"Still."

"OK, for Albert's sake," Jim sighed. "But I doubt they'll come."

Sam nodded and walked away with a wave.

When the stage arrived that afternoon, Rose's former boss, Smythe, was on it. He had been away for weeks. He was surprised and displeased to hear Rose had left the saloon and was now living with the doctor. *Morgan's meddling again,* he thought, growling audibly and stomping back and forth in his office and frightening the associate whom he'd left in charge. The whole reason he'd gone out of town was to get bids on Rose.

"How could you let this happen?" he shouted at his employee. He now regretted not letting the man in on his plan. "Rose has worked here for years, and I never touched her or let anyone else! Even though she's always looked older than she is. Didn't you wonder why?"

The other man shook his head as he cowered, afraid of Smythe's large fists.

"I had hoped to get a very large sum of money for her virginity, you idiot!" Smythe shouted. "And she's just now the perfect age!"

The other man caught his breath. He'd never thought of such a thing.

"Get out of here before I kill you!" Smythe screamed.

The other man ran out of the room.

"What if Morgan's already screwed her?" Smythe wondered aloud. Then he shook his head. It really didn't matter. Unless he sold her to a doctor, whoever bought her wouldn't know. He'd gotten some bids, but the men wanted to see her first. He couldn't blame them. Even though he'd assured them of her beauty, they had no reason to believe him.

He smiled. He had it all planned out. The bidders were just waiting for his telegram. He knew the men would be willing to pay a lot after they saw her. "They'll take one look at her and come in their pants before they even touch her," he said aloud, rubbing his hands together with a grin.

He couldn't let Rose know about the money. He'd have to make sure the buyer understood that. He'd slip her some laudanum and then, when she was groggy, he'd let the man into her room and lock the door. He'd have to warn the man that she might still have some fight in her. Or, if the man wanted, he could tie her up.

Then, after the bastard had had his fun and left, he, her beloved Smythe, who'd always been her protector, would find her. He'd pretend outrage as he dried her tears. She'd be scared, so he'd comfort her, and she'd give herself to him willingly out of gratitude. She was the prettiest girl he'd ever owned. He smiled and felt himself move in his pants at the thought of the pleasure he'd have with her. "And I won't even have to force her," he grinned.

He was still smiling when he stepped out into the saloon. He saw some regulars who looked like they'd just ridden into town. After a word with his bartender, who assured him the men had just arrived after a three-month absence, Smythe's smile broadened. *Now to yank the cunt from the prick,* he thought.

14

CONSUMMATION

Later that evening, Jim and Rose were taking a walk near the edge of town. Jim gazed at Rose as the setting crimson sun shone in her hair, accentuating its hues until it matched the glow of the sun itself. Her ivory skin gleamed in the golden light, and her laughing blue eyes mirrored the color of the clear, late summer sky. They were on a seemingly deserted street, and Rose had Jim so preoccupied he didn't notice the men watching them.

A man ran up behind Jim and struck him on the back of the head with the butt of a rifle. The blow glanced off but stunned Jim, knocking him to his knees. The man took Jim's gun.

Rose screamed. Another man grabbed her and clamped a hand over her mouth. She struggled, but the man was too strong and she couldn't break away.

Jim staggered to his feet. Two others grabbed his arms and held him while another punched him in the stomach. After the second blow, Jim came to his senses and looked up.

"He doesn't look so dandy, now," grinned the man who had hit him with the rifle as the one punching Jim landed another blow.

Jim quickly recovered and noticed the man with the rifle was still holding it by the barrel, with the revolver he'd taken in the other hand. Jim also noticed that, since he hadn't struggled, the men restraining him weren't gripping him tightly. He realized these weren't professionals, probably just ranch hands sent to do someone's bidding, so he decided not to kill them.

Though still weak from his illness, Jim summoned his strength and tore away from the two men holding him. Then he swung his arms out, hitting the men and knocking them to the ground. Now free, he punched the one who had been beating him, first in the stomach and then in the face, dropping him as well.

The one who had smiled was so surprised he forgot about the weapons he was holding and ran toward the young man.

Jim grabbed the rifle. Then, using the man's own momentum, Jim swung him around and threw him on top of the first two, ripping the weapon from the man's hand. Jim saw his own gun sail to the ground well out of the men's reach, so he left it and drew his knife as he ran to the man holding Rose.

The man tried to keep Rose between he and Jim, but Jim was too quick and got behind him. Then, pointing the rifle at the men on the ground with one hand, Jim held the knife to the man's throat with the other.

"Let her go!" Jim growled in the man's ear.

The man released Rose and she ran behind Jim.

"Try anything and you all die!" Jim warned as he swung the lever-action rifle down and back up with one hand to cock it. Then he aimed it at the others as they painfully got to their feet.

The sheriff and one of his deputies ran up with their guns drawn, summoned by Rose's scream.

"What's going on here?" asked the sheriff.

"These men attacked us," Jim answered.

"Get their weapons," the sheriff ordered his deputy.

"The one on the ground is mine," Jim informed them, removing his knife from the man's neck and stepping back as he sheathed it. Then he held out an arm to Rose and she threw herself against him.

Jim spoke softly to her to make sure she wasn't hurt but kept the rifle trained on the men.

The sheriff picked up Jim's revolver and held it out to him.

Jim stepped away from Rose, took the gun, and handed the rifle to the sheriff. Before holstering his weapon, Jim checked the barrel to make sure it was clear. Then he held Rose and kissed her cheek.

"Let's go to my office and sort this out," said the sheriff.

One of the men started to speak, but the sheriff stopped him. "Let's not handle this on the street, unless Jim here wants to settle it himself." He saw one of the men shrug to another. "You don't know who this is, do you?" the sheriff asked, motioning to Jim. "Heard of Jim Morgan?"

Though the men didn't know Jim by sight, they were aware of his reputation and exchanged glances. Rumor was it took him longer to count the men he'd killed than the years of his life, and most believed he was close to thirty.

After they were in the office, one of the men spoke. "We're sorry, Mr. Morgan. We didn't know it was you. We were just trying to help Rose," he said, lowering his eyes before Jim's glare.

"Help Rose? Why?" asked the sheriff.

"We know Rose from the broth—the saloon," the man corrected quickly, noticing Jim's hand was resting on his pistol and not wanting to anger him further. "Her boss, Smythe, told us that a rich young dandy gave him some money, took her away, and now wouldn't let her come back." He looked pleadingly at Rose. "We thought we were helping you."

"He's my fiancé," Rose stated.

They all turned at the sound of the office door closing behind Jim.

"Damn it!" muttered the sheriff, hurrying out the door. But Jim was already out of sight.

The sheriff rushed back into the office and ordered his deputy to watch the attackers. He told Rose to stay there. Then he ran, hoping to catch up with Jim.

When Jim arrived at Smythe's saloon, he wasn't even out of breath from the run. He walked in, and his purposeful bearing caused heads to turn. He saw Smythe sitting at a table at the back of the room and marched up to him.

Smythe appeared to be unarmed and, though he tried to hide it, looked worried as he stood to face Jim. He thought the men he'd sent would have either killed the young man or died trying, and no one would have ever known he was involved.

Jim grabbed Smythe by the throat and pushed the saloon owner up against the wall. Though Smythe weighed considerably more than he, Jim lifted him effortlessly, until only his toes were touching the floor. "Don't ever mess with me or mine again!" Jim growled menacingly, his eyes flashing blue fire.

"Unless you're ready to die!"

The sheriff ran in and, when he saw the two men at the back of the room, shouted, "Jim!"

Jim dropped Smythe. He turned, but saw the sheriff's hand go for his weapon. In one movement, Jim spun back around, drawing his gun and firing.

Smythe had reached for the pistol he kept in the small of his back. Jim's bullet tore through Smythe's heart, and the saloon owner crumpled to the floor, dead.

Jim turned again and strode out of the saloon.

The sheriff stopped and told a man to get the undertaker, then followed Jim outside.

"How'd you know?" the sheriff asked when they were on the boardwalk.

"I saw you reach for your gun," Jim answered. "Then I saw his hand behind his back."

"So you hadn't planned to kill him?" The sheriff hoped no one noticed Smythe was lying dead on the floor before their sheriff had even gotten his weapon out of his holster.

Jim gazed evenly at the sheriff. "No, sir."

The sheriff nodded. "What do you want me to do with the men in my office?" he asked as they walked back the way they had come.

"Don't care."

"I guess I'll let them go, then, since Smythe lied to them to put them up to it."

Jim nodded.

When they reached the office, Rose was giving the men a stern talking-to. She turned as they entered and, seeing the grim expression on Jim's face, ran to him.

The sheriff explained what had happened and told the men they could go. They apologized to Jim and Rose as they left.

"Do you need me anymore?" Jim asked the sheriff.

"No. And congratulations on your engagement," he added as the couple walked out the door.

Jim just nodded in reply.

"Do you need to see Sam?" Rose asked him after they were outside.

He shook his head.

"I think it would be a good idea," she urged.

"I'm all right," Jim answered, wanting to continue their walk. He turned toward the stable.

"Are you sure you're OK?"

"Yes. I'll let Sam look at me later. You sure you weren't hurt?"

Rose shook her head. "I'm sorry that happened."

"It's not your fault."

"Still," Rose said and began to cry.

Jim stopped and held her gently.

"I'm sorry," she whispered, wiping her eyes. "Even though I never did what the other women do, the men still know me. Does that bother you?"

"Rose, we both have a past. If you can accept mine, I can accept yours." He kissed her cheek.

Rose pressed against him, and Jim inhaled sharply.

"Did I hurt you?" she asked, concerned.

"No. It's just—" He paused, not knowing quite how to put it. "Woman, I'll tell you if you do."

"I like that."

"What?" he asked.

"What you called me," she replied.

Jim gazed at her, then led her into the barn. He lit a lantern and turned it low.

"Easy," he said softly to the horses as the animals stirred, disturbed by their presence. The horses quieted as Jim drew a key from his pocket and unlocked the door to the tack room. The livery stable owner trusted him and allowed him to keep his saddle and other tack there. He led Rose inside. Then he hung the lantern from a chain, locked the door behind them, and turned to find her looking around the small room.

In the near-darkness, she saw saddles sitting on wooden stands and bridles hanging from nails in the walls. The room smelled of horses and leather. Then she noticed a cot in the corner. "Why is there a bed in here?" she asked.

"It's for the stable boys to use if they're waiting for a mare to foal," Jim answered, stepping close to her.

"Are you planning to take advantage of me?" she asked playfully.

"Never." He really wasn't sure why he'd taken her there. Something inside him made him want to be alone with her, but he had nothing particular in mind.

She moved closer until her body pressed against his, and he caught his breath again.

"What's wrong?" she asked.

"Sometimes, when you touch me," he replied, gazing into her eyes.

Rose understood.

Jim took her in his arms and kissed her. Their tongues touched and explored each other's mouths. Then Jim released her. "Maybe this wasn't such a good idea," he said, his voice low and tense with pent-up emotion. When he'd been alone in his room with her, due to illness as much as decorum, he'd managed to keep himself restrained. Plus, they'd never known when Mrs. Harraday would pop in, even in the middle of the night.

"You know, there are things we can do. Things that I'm sure most couples do before they're married," Rose said. As they kissed again, Rose pushed Jim against the door. "Take off your gun belt," she whispered.

Thinking it was hurting her, Jim obeyed. Then she slipped her hand into his pants, but he stopped her. "Not 'til we're married," he breathed.

"Are you sure?" she asked. "I could please you."

Jim gently removed her hand. "I'm sure."

"It's not like I haven't seen you before," Rose smiled.

"Not like this, though." He was so hard he thought the buttons on his pants were about to burst.

"Don't be too sure."

"What?" Jim asked, holding her away from him and staring at her.

"It happened sometimes when you were ill," Rose explained.

Jim released her. He tried to choke down a blush and walked to the other side of the room, turning his back to her.

"It's nothing to be ashamed of," Rose said, walking up behind him.

"What caused it?"

"It was usually when we were giving you a bath."

"'We?'" Jim asked, turning to face her.

"Sam and I. Though it only happened when I was touching you. The first time I had to smile to hide my surprise. I was supposed to be a whore, after all. And Sam said it was perfectly normal."

Had she asked, the doctor would have affirmed that only her touch elicited such a reaction.

Jim looked away and shook his head.

"What's wrong? Sam's a doctor, and I'm going to marry you."

"But you weren't the only ones taking care of me," he stated, turning toward her again.

"But Sam and I were the only ones who bathed you," Rose assured him.

"What about Olivia?"

"She's been married, so if it happened, she knows about such things. Why?"

Jim looked away again. "It's embarrassing."

Rose stepped around in front of him, looked up into his eyes, and smiled. "It doesn't have to be now," she whispered, pressing her body against him.

"We should get back."

"So soon?" she asked.

Jim gazed at her, then kissed her passionately, and felt her hand touch him through his clothes. Rather than cringing as he always had, his body seemed to swell even more in anticipation of Rose's grasp. He caught his breath and let her push him up against the door again. She slipped her hand inside his pants, but this time he didn't resist. He felt paralyzed by her touch and stood enrapt as her hand enveloped him and began to move.

"Stop or I'll—" he said a few moments later.

"It's OK," she whispered, using her other hand to untie his bandana from his neck.

He felt the sensation build until he exploded in her hand with a gasp. Rose smiled, carefully removing her hand and wiping it off. Jim turned, leaning his forehead heavily against the door. Rose ducked under his arm, came up in front of him, and kissed his lips. Jim returned her kiss, pressing his body against hers.

"I can do the same for you," he whispered in her ear.

"But I've never—" she started to say.

"Me neither."

"I know you told me you never pleased yourself, but you must have come at some time," Rose insisted. "Men do it in their sleep, according to the women I lived with."

"Yeah," Jim said, kissing her neck. "And a couple of times when I was half awake, but it was never like this."

"Thank you," she replied, smiling.

"So do you want me to please you?"

"I thought you wanted us to stay pure?" she asked.

"I'm still a virgin, aren't I?"

"Of course," she replied.

"So—" he said.

"OK."

Jim lifted her, carried her to the bed, and laid her down. He slipped his hand under her dress. Rose gasped as she felt him touch her through her clothes. Then she caught her breath as his fingers made their way through them. They both sighed as he touched her.

"Let me know if I hurt you or do something you don't like," Jim whispered in her ear. "If you want me to stop, just say."

Rose nodded, then gasped again as he touched her gently. A moment later, she began to moan softly. He continued touching her, gazing at her face.

Her body tensed. The sensation built until she gasped and shuddered. "Stop," she whispered.

"Did I hurt you? I know my hands are rough."

"No," she said smiling. "But how did you know what to do?"

"I grew up around women who didn't leave much to the imagination. Remember?" Then he kissed her. "We better get back."

Rose nodded as she adjusted her clothing.

Jim walked her back to Sam's and let the doctor examine him.

"You'll have a headache for a while, but other than that you're fine," Sam said.

Jim thanked him, and Sam let Rose show him out.

At the door, they kissed again, and Jim gave her a long look before he left. He walked back to his room thinking about Rose. He'd never imagined it could feel so good to be touched. He was so preoccupied that he didn't notice the man in the shadows following him. He walked straight up to his room and went to bed. He longed for the time he would have Rose beside him and fell asleep thinking of her.

The next morning, he awoke later than usual. As he dressed, he realized that, for the first time in his life, he was looking forward to the day because he would be with Rose. He smiled.

Mrs. Harraday and the others were having breakfast when he descended the stairs, but Jim told her he had errands to do and left without eating. He stopped at the store to buy a few things, including an apple. Then he continued to his house, eating the fruit as he walked. He threw the core into the yard, hoping one of the seeds would sprout. Then he set his purchases inside and headed toward Sam's to get Rose, taking his accustomed route.

He was passing through an alley leading to the main street when suddenly he felt a sharp, intense pain in the lower right side of his back. He turned as he crumpled to the ground, but there was no one in sight. A man passing by on the main street saw him and ran to help. He immediately sent a boy to summon Sam. The doctor ran to Jim, followed by Rose. They found the sheriff and one of his deputies already there when they arrived. The deputy was kneeling beside Jim pressing on his back with both hands.

Hank had finished his breakfast and was walking toward the freight office when the boy sent to fetch Sam ran past on his return to the alley. The child told Hank that Jim had been hurt, so Hank arrived shortly after the others. He and some other men lifted Jim onto the stretcher the doctor had brought and started for Sam's office. Sam had the men lay Jim on his stomach so he could keep pressure on the wound as they walked, but he didn't pull up the young man's shirt to examine him.

Rose took Jim's hand as she comforted him, and he squeezed it gently to reassure her.

"Did you see who did this?" the sheriff asked as they walked hurriedly.

"No," Jim replied.

"Damn!" the sheriff muttered under his breath.

"Get Pastor Brown for me," Jim said to the sheriff through gritted teeth.

The sheriff paled but left to obey.

When they arrived at his office, Sam had the men put Jim on the operating table. Then he told all of them except Hank to leave.

"Wait for the preacher!" Jim ordered as Sam and Hank began to remove his clothes.

"Since when are you religious?" Sam asked as he worked.

"I want him to marry me and Rose, just in case," Jim

explained. "That way you can make sure she gets everything I have."

Sam paused, eyeing Jim for a moment. He gave a nod, then continued removing his clothes. He covered Jim with a sheet, reaching under to keep pressure on the wound. When Pastor Brown arrived, Hank asked him to come into the operating room and bring Rose, who started to cry when Sam told them what Jim wanted.

"Just in case," Jim said, reaching for her hand.

Pastor Brown hesitated but started the ceremony after noting the intensity in Jim's eyes. He used Sam, Hank, and Martha as witnesses, and completed the wedding in minutes. Rose bent down and kissed Jim on the mouth at the end. Then Sam immediately dismissed her along with the pastor so he could begin the procedure.

"I need you," Sam said to Hank as he started to leave. "Keep pressure on it for me," he ordered the driver.

Hank obeyed, causing Jim to groan. "Sorry, Jimmy," Hank said to his friend.

Martha began to gown.

"Don't bother," Sam said to her. "I'll have to use chloroform. You can't be in here because of the baby."

"What?" Jim asked.

"Martha's pregnant," Sam explained.

"Congratulations," said Hank, and Jim nodded in agreement.

"Thank you," replied Sam as he continued to lay out his instruments.

"If I don't assist you, he could die," Martha stated. "If I get lightheaded, I'll leave."

Sam didn't argue with her but had her step out as he prepared to administer the drug.

"Don't use it!" Jim insisted, grabbing his arm.

"I have to," Sam stated. "This could take a while."

"I won't move. Martha! The baby!" Jim gasped.

"It'll be fine," Sam assured him. "Let me do my job. Trust me."

Jim released Sam's arm.

Since Martha was going to assist, Hank walked through the door to the kitchen. After washing Jim's blood from his hands, he waited with Rose and the pastor, who both prayed continuously for the young man.

Someone had stabbed Jim, and the knife had gone almost all the way through. The man hadn't taken the time to twist it as he pulled it out, though. Miraculously, it hadn't sliced through anything crucial.

"I'll be damned," Sam muttered as he examined the wound.

"What?" Martha asked.

"There's no real damage in here. I could have just sewn up the outside and not bothered with the chloroform," he said as he sutured the wound closed. Then, as a matter of form, he checked to see if Jim was breathing. He wasn't.

"Open all the doors and windows!" Sam barked to Martha. "And get Hank in here!"

Martha obeyed, motioning for Hank when she opened the door to the kitchen.

Sam was hitting Jim hard on the back between the shoulder blades as Hank entered. Rose stood at the door, frightened, not understanding what was going on. Martha walked over and put her arms around the young woman.

Pastor Brown had stood when Martha opened the door, but when he realized what was happening he fell to his knees and continued praying.

"Help me turn him over!" Sam ordered Hank.

Hank helped Sam turn and lift Jim, sliding him onto his back. Then Sam hit the young man hard on the chest. He waited a second and hit him again. "Come on Jim, breathe!" Sam begged.

Rose heard him and leaned heavily against the doorframe for support. At Sam's words, it was as though something inside of her broke.

"Sit him up!" Sam ordered.

Hank obeyed.

Then Sam hit Jim on the back again. "Lay him down! You try," he said to Hank, when they had Jim flat.

Hank landed a powerful blow on Jim's chest, waited a second, and, at a signal from Sam, hit him again.

"Sit him up!" Sam ordered, then motioned for Hank to hit Jim on the back between the shoulder blades.

Hank obeyed using all his strength.

"He'll break his back," breathed Rose.

"No he won't," Martha replied quickly.

At their words, Pastor Brown looked up and saw a creature standing at the head of the operating table. The creature had the form of a man and was clothed in a white robe that seemed to glow from within. The creature looked at him, its face stern but its eyes loving. Then the creature spoke, its voice filled with the authority of the One who had sent it.

"'For what shall it profit a man, if he shall gain the whole world, and lose his soul?'"

The pastor blinked, and the creature was gone.

"Lay him down! Now hit him on the chest!" Sam ordered.

Hank hit Jim with such force his body lifted off the table.

"Again!" Sam said after a second.

Hank struck Jim again and raised his hand for another blow when Jim inhaled sharply. He took another breath and opened his eyes.

"What's going on?" he asked groggily.

Sam looked at him and smiled, tears shining in his eyes. "We thought we'd lost you. Luckily for you, Hank here is big and strong. It was him hitting you that brought you back."

"What did I do to you?" Jim asked weakly, looking at Hank.

All of them but Jim laughed through their tears.

Rose ran to him and kissed his cheek.

"Let's get him into a bed," suggested Sam.

Pastor Brown offered to help, but Sam assured him he and Hank were more than capable. The pastor spoke briefly to Jim, wishing him well. Then he whispered to Rose before leaving. He hurried to his study and looked up the passage the angel had quoted. Though he'd never seen one, he was sure that's what the creature was. The verse was Mark 8:36, and Christ had spoken the words shortly before the transfiguration. He wanted to tell all his parishioners about the vision but felt in his heart he should wait. God would reveal to him the proper time. However, he knew he could tell the one man who was as good at keeping secrets as he was, and the next day he met with Sam. It was then Pastor Brown realized that, though he'd heard the creature, its mouth had never opened.

Since Jim and Rose were now married, Martha had them put Jim in a room with a double bed.

Jim dozed off shortly thereafter. When he awoke a few hours later, Rose was sitting in a chair at his bedside. She saw him stir, wince, then open his eyes. He was lying on his stomach and tried to turn over, but she stopped him.

"How are you feeling?" she asked.

"It hurts, but it's tolerable," Jim replied.

"I need to go get Sam. He's been sitting here the whole time you slept and only just now left to get some coffee." Rose ran from the room, and Jim heard her calling to the doctor.

Jim heard Sam answer, then the sound of his feet as he ran up the hall.

"I imagine you're in a lot of pain," Sam said to his patient as he entered the room and walked to the bed, followed by Rose.

"Not as much as I'd expect."

"I can give you something if you'd like."

"Laudanum?" Jim asked.

"Yes," the doctor replied. "Or morphine."

"No thanks."

"You can turn over on your back if you want. But it will hurt more," Sam warned.

"I hate lying on my stomach," Jim grumbled as he slowly turned onto his back.

"You need to lie as still as possible so you don't tear out the stitches," ordered the doctor. "But you can get up when you have to. You were lucky. The blade was thin and didn't do any serious damage."

"How long do I have to stay here?"

"At least a week."

Jim sighed. "Damn!"

"Don't worry, if you do as you're told, you should still be able to get married three weeks from Saturday. Unless you're just going to skip it now."

"No," Jim replied, looking at Rose. "I promised you a real wedding."

Rose took his hand.

"Get him to drink some water," Sam said to Rose and left the room.

A little while later, Sam came back in and smiled when he realized they'd been kissing. "The sheriff is here. Do you feel like talking to him?"

"Sure," Jim replied.

Sam showed the man in.

"Can you tell me what happened?" the sheriff asked, sitting in the chair Rose had vacated for him.

"I had gone by our house to drop some things off," Jim said. "On my way back, I cut through the alley. It felt like something hit or stung me. I turned around but no one was in sight. It was like whoever stabbed me just disappeared. Believe me, if I'd seen the bastard he'd be dead." He glanced at Rose, but she didn't seem to care about his language.

"My deputies and I searched the alley, and there's a door into a storage room right where we found you. He must have gone in that and then out the back. The owner wasn't there, and none of the doors are kept locked. We've spent the better part of the day asking everyone who either lives nearby or would have reason to be near there if they saw anyone, but no one did."

"Well, he didn't kill me, so if he tries again, maybe we can get him the next time," Jim remarked.

Rose and Sam caught their breath.

"Are you joking?" the sheriff asked, incredulous at Jim's attitude.

Jim gazed at him evenly, and the sheriff saw he was serious.

"Any idea who might want you dead?" the sheriff asked.

"With my work on the stage, it could be a relative of one of the men I've killed. Or Carlos, of course."

"How many men have you killed?" the sheriff asked.

"A dozen or so I guess," Jim replied. "Ask Ted. He keeps track of all that."

The sheriff shook his head. He had heard the rumors too and suspected Jim was just being modest. He stood. "If we find out anything, I'll let you know."

"Thanks," Jim said.

Sam showed the sheriff out, and, when he returned, Rose was kissing Jim on the mouth. She looked up and smiled when he entered.

"You need to take it easy," Sam cautioned Jim. "I remember what it was like to be young and in love, but you're going to have to stay still."

"Completely?" Jim asked.

"It would be best, but if you do anything, be careful. I don't want to have to re-stitch you." Sam noticed then that Rose had her hand under the covers. "Like I said, take it easy," said the doctor with a smile, motioning toward her hidden hand. "Just don't put any weight on him."

"Yes, sir," Rose replied, blushing.

Sam smiled again. "Like I said, be careful. And this door locks." Then he stepped into the hall.

He met Martha coming toward Jim's room, and they both heard the bolt slide closed.

"What's going on?" Martha asked. "I was just going to see if Jim wanted anything to eat?"

"Maybe in a little while," Sam answered, still smiling.

"Did I hear the door lock?"

"They don't want to be disturbed."

"But he was just nearly killed!" Martha said in surprise.

"Exactly," Sam replied as he took her in his arms. "Our room has a lock on it, too."

Martha smiled. Since she had gotten pregnant, it seemed like she wanted to have sex all the time. She wasn't showing much yet, so she and Sam didn't have to be careful about positions, and they had been enjoying each other as often as possible. She took her husband's hand and led him to their bedroom, which was on the other end of the house. After they were undressed, Sam started to touch her to get her ready, but she pushed him onto his back and climbed on. Sam smiled in surprise and then found himself trying to think about anything but how good she looked and felt.

He wondered about Jim and Rose and if they were enjoying each other, too. Then he looked up at Martha on top of him. *I think her breasts are already getting bigger,* he thought. *I'm glad Jim has someone now. Look at her breasts! I love to watch them bounce! I wonder how many people will be at Jim's wedding?* He desperately tried to distract his mind from the pleasure his body was receiving. He wanted her to be pleased first. *God, she feels great! I wonder what dress Martha will wear? She looks so good!* He reached up and cupped his hands under her breasts.

Martha smiled.

Then Sam dropped his arms to the bed and grabbed the sheet, desperately trying to hold off. *I hope it doesn't rain for Jim's wedding. It'd be awful for everything to get muddy. I hope I can last. Go Martha! Go! I wonder if I should get*

*Martha flowers? I haven't given her flowers in a long time. I'm going to give her something now if she doesn't hurry up. What are her favorite flowers? What's in season? My cock's in season. Oh God, Martha, hurry. Please! I wonder if I could get it up if I was in as much pain as Jim? I'm up now! She feels so good, sounds good too. Oh, don't get tighter. I can't stand it! The curse of being a gentleman. Ladies always come first. Good, I think she's coming. She's not slowing yet! Oh God! Not yet, Sam. Not yet. Just a little longer. Hurry up, Martha! You're killing me! Oh God, I hope she's almost done. Good Martha, that's right, start slowing. No, don't speed up again! What's her favorite color? Blue? My balls are blue, and my cock too by now. God, she's getting even tighter, and listen to her! I love it when she yells. Hold on Sam, not yet man, not yet. Good, she's slowing again. Women and their numerous orgasms. I just want one, and it's going to be a big one. Good Martha, slow down. Please, don't get faster again. Good, she's still slowing. Oh God! Every inch of me wants to. Is she done? She's got to be done. I can't hold it. **I can't!*** Sam gripped Martha's hips and came deep inside her.

She moved a few more times, and he jumped and twitched. Then she looked down and smiled.

"Did you come?" Sam asked breathlessly.

Martha nodded, still smiling. "Twice." Then she kissed him, and he held her in his arms as their heartbeats slowed.

"Was it good?" Martha asked.

"It was great. Almost too good."

"I wonder if Jim and Rose are done?"

"Are you done?" Sam asked in return.

"For now. I'll probably be ready again by bedtime, though."

Sam kissed her. Then they held each other and dozed for a while before they got up and dressed.

In Jim's room, Rose locked the door, then stepped to the bureau and took out her nightgown. She had moved her things into the room while Jim slept. Luckily, perhaps because of the chloroform, he hadn't woken when she entered with them. Now she wanted to get her corset off for a few minutes. When she opened the drawer, the sight of his things next to hers made her smile.

"Hank brought you some clothes," she said over her shoulder.

"They're here in the top drawer with mine." Then she turned her back and began to undress. "Don't peek," she ordered, smiling.

Ignoring the pain, Jim sat up on the edge of the bed.

"I said not to peek," she laughed, turning when she heard him move.

"I'm not," Jim replied, and he wasn't. He had his eyes closed. "I just want to be ready to enjoy the view." He waited patiently until he heard her fussing with her corset.

As she tried to undo the last few laces, she looked up to find him standing close to her. He took a shirt from the drawer, slipped it on, then grabbed her corset by each side and ripped it off her.

"Hey! I need that!"

"Not anymore," Jim said, looking at her. She was nude to the waist. "I don't want you wearing one of those things again."

"But—"

"Sam says they're not healthy," he explained.

"But I'll look fat!" Rose insisted.

Jim put his hands around her waist, his fingers easily touching. "You're not fat," he said softly.

He brought his hands up to her breasts and lightly touched them. He kissed one and then the other. Then he pulled her to him and kissed her on the mouth as he slid his hands under the rest of her clothes and began to ease them down. She took over and tore them off, leaving her fully naked. Jim stepped back and gazed at her. He imagined she was every man's dream: full breasts, small waist, round hips, and incredibly smooth skin. Then he stepped close again and dropped to one knee before her. He gently pulled her to him and rested his head against her belly.

"What's wrong?" Rose asked as she smoothed his hair.

"I don't deserve you," he breathed, his voice low with emotion. Then he kissed her belly and gazed again at her body as he lightly touched the mound of hair between her legs.

Rose caught her breath.

Jim noticed a drop-leaf table at the back of the room under the window. He stood and told Rose to help him take the things off it and pull it out from the wall. He left the leaf closest to them down but lifted the back one, and Rose pushed the table leg into place to hold it. Then Jim found a blanket in one of the bureau drawers and they spread it over the table.

"Hop on," he said, patting it.

Rose smiled and sat on the table, and Jim stood in front of her between her legs. Rose lightly took him in her hands and looked up in wonder. Though she'd seen him in that condition before, she was sure he was larger now than he had been then.

Jim gasped, then leaned close. "You first," he whispered as he laid her back onto the table. He felt his stitches pull and a sharp pain deep inside, which subsided when he straightened. He wasn't able to follow her all the way back, but he let her hold onto his arm so she wouldn't fall. Then he scooted her hips to the edge of the table and knelt. Rose caught her breath as he gently parted her folds with his hands. He paused and gazed at her.

"Something wrong?" she asked.

"No," Jim replied, his voice low. "It looks like a rosebud."

"What does?"

Jim lightly touched her clitoris, causing her to gasp. "That does."

Then she felt something warm and moist touch her.

"What are you doing?" Rose breathed.

"Do you like it?"

"Yes!" she gasped again, lifting her head to see.

Jim looked up and smiled. "Then lie back and enjoy it." He began to touch her with his tongue and his hand.

A moment later, she was moaning and writhing in pleasure.

Her scent was almost sweet. It filled his head and made him desire her desperately, but he wanted her to be pleased first. He tasted the mild saltiness as her body prepared for penetration, and this too excited him. Her moans turned to wails as she began to peak. She filled all of his senses now, as he smelled, tasted, heard, felt, and saw her when he opened his eyes. As he continued, her wails became more intense.

"Yes!" she breathed.

He kept doing the same thing and noticed her body begin to tense. A few moments later, she came, screaming, lunging, and clutching at him. He didn't stop until she begged him to so she could breathe. He stood and gazed at her, lying with her limbs spread, a smile of deep satisfaction on her face.

"May I?" he asked.

Rose looked up, still smiling, and nodded.

He pulled her to him and, as gently as he could, entered her body for the first time. The sensation was overpowering, but he felt her tense and knew he had probably hurt her. So, though it took great force of will, he withdrew. "You OK?" he breathed.

Rose nodded.

"Do you want me to put it back in?" he asked.

"Yes," she whispered.

He penetrated her again, and this time he felt her body willingly accept him. She pushed against him and groaned. He paused, reveling in the amazing, deep comfort. Though only a small part of him was inside her, it felt as though she engulfed all of him. He had never imagined anything could feel so wonderful and satisfying. He began to move, and he felt pleasure build within him until he exploded inside her, gripping her firmly. Rose looked up to see him smile again, his eyes closed. He didn't withdraw right away. He wanted the sensation to last as long as possible.

After a moment, he left her body, and she reached up so he could pull her to him. With his back straight, the pain was tolerable enough to hold her.

"You should lie back down," Rose whispered.

"Only if you join me," he replied.

Jim stepped back and helped her off the table. Then he hobbled stiffly to the bed and lifted the covers for her. Rose climbed in, and he lay beside her, pulling her close.

"I don't want to hurt you," she said.

"You won't. I want to feel you next to me," he whispered.

She rested her head on his shoulder and her leg on his.

"I hope I didn't hurt you," he said softly.

"Only for a second," she assured him, kissing his cheek.

Jim could feel the warmth of her body and her soft fur against his leg. It was moist from what they'd done. He sighed.

"Am I hurting you?" she asked, raising her head.

"No, this is nice."

They rested for a while. Then he felt himself getting hard again.

"Why don't you get back on the table?" he suggested.

Rose smiled as he took her hand and helped her from the bed. She lay back down on the table. He started to kneel.

"Just put it in," she whispered.

The insistence in her voice aroused him even more, and he entered her again. He felt her body grip and release him as she too became more aroused. He began to move, and this time it lasted longer. It was as though she enwrapped his entire being in a wonderful, soft, warm place of joy, peace, and comfort. He realized this was truly a gift, one of the few really good things life offered. Moments like this made all the hard work and pain fade away to a distant memory as pleasure took over. Greater than the pleasure was the wondrous connection with Rose. Though he was inside her, it was as though part of her entered him as well. Had he any faith in anything spiritual, he would have understood their union was more than just physical. He sensed it but didn't consciously acknowledge it.

He felt her body tense around him, and she began to moan again. He was thankful for all his years of self-discipline, as he was able to keep moving and hold off until she had come once more. Then he pounded against her, coming with a sound he'd never uttered before, and her body accepted the very essence of him. He forgot about his injury for the moment and leaned over to kiss her. As the pleasurable sensation abated, the pain returned with a vengeance, forcing him to withdraw. He staggered to the bed and lay down, dropping his shirt on the floor in his haste.

"Are you OK?" Rose asked, rushing to him.

Jim looked up at her and forced a smile. "Are you?"

Rose smiled too and nodded. "You were amazing."

"So were you," he said, reaching up and touching her cheek. "Thank you."

"For what?"

"For letting me," he replied, looking deeply into her eyes.

"I'm your wife, that's what I'm supposed to do."

"You never have to if you don't want to."

She kissed his mouth softly and licked his lips. "Did it help with the pain?"

"Until I leaned over," he replied, caressing one of her breasts. "It's better now."

Rose kissed his cheek and turned toward where her clothes lay on the floor.

"Don't get dressed yet," he said.

She smiled and sat on the bed beside him.

"I like just looking at you," he whispered, motioning her to come closer.

Rose leaned over him, and he touched her breasts, cupping his hands beneath them.

"Climb on," he suggested, his voice tense.

"Again?"

Jim nodded.

"But I might hurt you."

"I'll let you know," he replied, watching her as she straddled him.

She positioned herself over him and slowly came down, taking him inside of her. Then she paused, watching to see if she was hurting him.

"That's nice," he breathed.

"I'm not too heavy?"

"How could you be?"

"I mean because you're hurt. Do you hurt more with me on top of you?"

"It hurts anyway. You're not making it any worse, just more worthwhile," he smiled, gazing up at her.

"You have a nice smile. You should do it more often."

"I probably will now that I have a reason," he replied, still smiling.

Rose began to move. "Let me know if I hurt you."

Jim nodded. He watched her breasts bounce as she strove against him. Then he felt himself getting close, so he shut his eyes. He reached out and grabbed the bed as he tried not to come.

"I'm hurting you, aren't I?" Rose asked, slowing her movement.

Jim shook his head.

"Then what's wrong?"

"I want you to get done before I do," he replied through gritted teeth.

Rose increased her pace and after a few moments came with a cry. Jim gripped her hips, thrust against her a couple of times, and came himself. Afterward, he tried to hold her as she lay on him gasping and catching her breath, but she climbed off quickly.

"If I hurt you you'd tell me, right?" she asked.

Jim gazed at her and nodded. "As long as you'll always do the same for me."

She bent down and kissed him. "I better get dressed."

Rose cleaned herself and brought Jim a damp cloth.

A few minutes later, there was a soft knock on the door.

"Come in!" Rose called, now fully dressed except for her corset.

The knob turned, but the door didn't open.

"Sorry!" Rose laughed, running to the door and unlatching and opening it.

Sam and Martha were standing in the hall, waiting.

"I thought you two might be hungry," Martha said as they entered.

Sam immediately noticed the table and grinned.

Martha followed his gaze and smiled.

"I hope we didn't interrupt anything?" Sam asked.

Jim glanced at the table, which he and Rose had forgotten to put back. It still had the blanket on it, but Rose had folded it over.

"You got up, didn't you?" Sam asked, scolding Jim playfully.

"You said I could if I needed to," Jim replied, smiling.

"And you needed to, right?" Sam asked, patting his shoulder.

"I knew you knew how to smile," Martha said to Jim with a laugh.

Rose looked down, but Martha beamed and hugged her.

"Don't be embarrassed," Martha said to Rose. "We were doing the same thing. How was it? All that you expected?"

"Martha!" Sam scolded playfully.

"Just girl talk, dear."

"More," Rose whispered smiling, in answer to her question.

"Just remember to take it easy. I don't want you tearing those stitches," Sam cautioned Jim.

Martha and Rose prepared a light supper while Sam left to check on a patient. After he returned, he and Martha ate in the kitchen, and Rose ate in Jim's room with him. When they finished, Rose took the plates to the kitchen and Sam followed her back to check on the young man. He found Jim sitting up in bed against a pillow.

"I'd order you to stay in bed, but I know it wouldn't do any good," Sam said. "Just remember to be careful. You might be feeling all right now, but tomorrow may be another story. Do you need me to help you lie back down?"

"No, I can manage when I get ready," Jim replied.

Sam bade them goodnight and left.

When he was gone, Rose gave Jim a kiss and began readying for bed.

Jim watched her as she undressed. "Why don't you get back on the table," he suggested, getting up and donning his shirt again as she slid off her last item of clothing. Then he looked at the window behind her and frowned.

"What's wrong?" Rose asked.

"I have the feeling we're being watched."

"We don't have anything to feel guilty about," Rose assured him, smiling.

She hopped on the table and lay back, thinking she would soon feel Jim inside her. Instead, she felt his lips kiss the uppermost part of her thigh. He worked until he was sure she had come. Then he continued until she came again.

As the sensation ebbed, she looked down. "Your turn."

He entered her and began moving slowly. Her moans excited him, and he found himself moving faster. The pain was still with him, but, for a few moments, the pleasure was stronger. He came with a deep, rumbling cry that thundered out of him. Then he stopped but stayed inside her, enjoying the final pleasant throbbing as Rose looked up at him.

"That took longer," she said breathlessly. "You're smiling again."

Still smiling, he lifted her to him and kissed her.

"You better get some rest now," she suggested.

He kissed her one more time, then slipped off his shirt and lay down as the pain took over his sensations again. He soon managed to fall asleep, his exhaustion stronger than the discomfort. He didn't wake until early the next morning when the pain intruded and roused him. His stab wound hurt, and he ached where Sam and Hank had hit him as they worked to revive him the day before. Rose was still sleeping, and Jim lay still, not wanting to wake her. He managed to doze lightly until Sam came in.

"How are you feeling?" asked the doctor softly, not wanting to disturb Rose. She still stirred at the sound of his voice and woke.

"You're the doctor. You tell me," Jim replied.

"That doesn't sound good," Sam stated. "The pain's worse today, isn't it?"

Jim nodded.

"It usually is. That's why I wanted you to take it easy yesterday," said Sam as he removed the bandage. Jim rolled over so the doctor could examine the wound.

"How does it look?" Rose asked.

"It's healing. But he needs to stay as quiet as possible."

"Don't worry," Jim replied as he turned back over.

Rose kissed his forehead. "I should go help Martha," she said and left the room, wrapping her robe around herself while Sam turned his head out of decorum.

Sam listened to Jim's lungs and was relieved they still sounded clear. "If you promise to stay quiet, I won't bandage you."

Jim nodded.

"Good," said the doctor. "That's better for your lungs, too."

Rose returned carrying a tray, and Sam helped Jim sit up. Then he left them and went in the kitchen to eat breakfast with Martha.

Jim rested after he ate. Rose tried touching him, but he stopped her. "Sorry."

"It's OK," she said reassuringly. "I just want to help you if I can."

Jim kissed her hand, then tried to sleep.

As Sam walked in and out during the day, he never noticed the man watching from across the street in the shadows.

15

EXECUTION

The man was willing to wait as long as it took. He'd told the boss he had business to take care of and didn't know when he'd be back. The boss hadn't seemed to care, but this would show him. He knew there was another in town. From what he'd seen of the guard's face the day before, the other man was a pretty good artist. The "artist" was sleeping it off at a brothel, while he was there watching the guard.

He'd wanted to shoot the guard that night he followed him home, but there were too many people on the street. The next chance he'd had had been ruined by some stupid cowhands. *I'd be surprised if those boys could grab their nuts with both hands*, he thought, *much less grab the guard.*

Now he was ready to do whatever he had to, even if it meant killing everyone in the house. He didn't understand how the guard had lived through his first try, but this time he'd get the bastard. It wasn't just about money. He wanted revenge. It had to have been this bastard guard who'd killed his best friend. They'd been closer than brothers, and he still missed him.

He'd still been watching last night when the doctor came home for supper. He'd been hungry, too, but hadn't wanted to miss his chance. He'd hung around and even watched as the bastard guard screwed his wife. Afterwards, the woman had turned the lantern low but left it lit. He'd waited for almost two hours hoping she'd turn it out. She hadn't, so he'd left, glad instead to have been able to find a decent whore. Not as good-looking as the guard's woman, but in the dark, who cared? One cunt was as good as another.

He looked in the window again this night and wondered if he'd get another show. The bastard guard didn't seem interested. *Too bad*, he thought. He wanted to watch them again. He wished he could screw the guard's woman before his eyes and then kill him. That would be a treat. He wondered if she'd really mind. After all, a woman wants a man who's alive, not half dead. If she liked it, that would be even better. That would make the bastard cocksucking guard squirm.

He thought about waiting until the guard and his woman were alone at their house. That way he could take his time with her before he killed her. He could even kill her while he was screwing her. He'd always wanted to do that. He'd heard their cunts got really tight when they died, better even than a virgin. He felt himself move in his pants. *Maybe if I'm quiet, I can still take the woman.* He decided he'd use his knife again—that way, he could kill the man, take the woman, and slit her throat when he got close. She was so pretty. What a waste for a woman like that to be with that bastard cocksucking cold-cocked guard when she could be with him. He smiled. *At least she'll get a whole man before she dies. Maybe more than once if she acts like she likes it.*

He took a piss as he looked through the window. Though he could see in, he knew that with their lantern lit the guard and his woman couldn't see him as long as he stayed back a little ways. The woman began to undress. He held himself as he watched her. He got hard and began moving against his hand as he thought about what he was going to do later. She had her back to the window and dropped something, so he got to see her slit as she bent over. He came as he gazed at it. He smiled again, realizing he'd last longer now and she'd really get a chance to enjoy it. Too bad he'd have to kill the guard first. It would be so perfect for the last thing he'd see to be his woman having fun with another man. He watched as the woman turned down the light by the bed and got in next to the bastard guard. He'd hoped she'd turn it out, and was about to leave for the night when he decided to wait a little longer.

About an hour later, the room went dark. The stupid bitch hadn't filled the lamp.

Now was his chance. He jogged to the back door and opened it as quietly as he could. He stood for a minute until his eyes got used to the dimness inside. He remembered his friend had always had him lead when they robbed a house. He could see almost as well in the dark as in the day. He walked through the kitchen and into the hall. To his left, he heard the doctor and his woman screwing and smiled. At least he didn't have to worry about them hearing anything. He turned to his right and crept down the hall until he got to the last door. The guard and his woman were in the last room at the back of the house. He pulled up on the knob so the door wouldn't scrape and opened it without a sound. He stepped into the room and pushed the door to. He paused but heard nothing, not even a snore. A chill ran through him, but he swallowed and drew his knife. One thrust under the breastbone and into the heart and the bastard would be done for, and he could take the woman.

He felt his cock stir, but first things first. Slowly, he moved toward the bed. He was glad the floor felt new and didn't creak. Still, he put his weight carefully on each foot, just in case, walking on his toes so his heels wouldn't click or thud. He couldn't see the guard in the darkness and didn't dare touch the bed, but he was closer now. He could hear them, and followed the sound of the guard's breathing. It was slow and steady, while his own heart felt like he'd just run a mile. He loved the thrill of it!

He'd seen from the window that the guard was on his back on the far side of the bed. *A man would have stayed on the side closest to the door, even if it did mean she might hit his wound in her sleep.* No matter, he was almost there. He tightened his grip on the knife. He'd be on the guard's right, but he'd kill the bastard before he could open his eyes. Two more steps and the guard would be a dead man. He held his breath. He could hear a sound in his ears like fast-moving water. *I love it!* He was shaking, but he wasn't scared. The sound in his head got louder. He slowly put weight on his right foot. The woman moved. He froze. He didn't even dare breathe. He held the knife so tight his fingers felt like his foot did when it went to sleep. He licked his lips. He was about to do what every man he knew wanted to do. In seconds, the guard would be dead. He smiled. He brought his left foot forward and slowly, carefully put his weight on it. He drew back the knife and held it there, not daring to breathe. He always thought it funny that nothing ever stopped him before he killed someone. *And some people believe in God.*

As fast as he could, he swung with all his might at the man's chest. Something stopped him. He felt the knife hit something hard, but it wasn't what he expected. Then hands as strong as iron grabbed him. Something heavy moved toward him, knocking him down. He dropped the knife. He kicked and struggled, but it had him pinned. He felt pressure on his neck, then between his legs, and froze. The light went on. *How?* It blinded him for a second. Then he saw there was another lantern on the chest of drawers. The man had him. He tried to throw him off, but the man pressed so hard on his balls he had to lie still.

Sam and Martha heard a loud thud, then a scream, and ran to Jim's room to find him on the floor holding down another man.

"Get his knife!" Jim shouted to Sam. "And get the sheriff!"

Sam picked up the bloody knife that was lying on the floor, laid it on the bureau, and ran out. A few moments later, he returned, followed by the sheriff and his two deputies. The sheriff let the younger of the two cover the intruder as he removed some twine from his pocket and handed it to the older and much larger deputy.

"You can let him up now," the sheriff said to Jim.

Jim released the man and rose to his feet.

The intruder rose also.

"Drop your gun!" the sheriff ordered.

The man carefully drew out his weapon. He started to drop it, but suddenly raised it, pointed it at Jim's chest, and fired.

The young deputy, though caught by surprise, fired in return a second later, and the man fell. The larger deputy picked up the man's gun. Then everyone looked toward Jim. As the smoke cleared, they saw him crumpled, naked and bleeding on the floor.

"Martha! Get the stretcher!" Sam shouted. "Help me with him!" he called to the sheriff. Sam glanced at Rose, who was staring at Jim's body as though transfixed.

The sheriff looked at the doctor in confusion. He couldn't

hear anything. The gunfire had temporarily deafened everyone in the room and was causing them to cough from the smoke.

Sam was glad Martha had been in the hall because of the effect it could have had on the baby. When she returned, Sam motioned to the sheriff and his deputies, and they lifted Jim onto the stretcher. Then Sam led them back down the hall and into the operating room, which was at the back of the house next to the kitchen.

To the doctor's surprise, they were soon joined by Hank and Ted. They had been in front of the freight office and were late leaving because Hank's stage had been delayed. A passerby told them Sam had summoned the sheriff. Then they heard the shots. Alarmed when Ted drew a gun from under his coat and tore off toward the doctor's, Hank followed him. He was both concerned for Jim and hoping to keep Ted from getting himself killed.

"Let's get him on the table. But sit him up so I can see his back," Sam ordered. He spoke loudly so everyone could hear him. "It didn't go through," he announced after his examination.

The sheriff and his deputies had only gotten a glimpse of Jim's back, and Ted hadn't seen it at all. The men exchanged glances as Sam laid Jim down on the table. The movement caused him to groan and open his eyes.

While Hank kept pressure on his friend's wound, Sam and Martha stepped into the kitchen and quickly scrubbed.

"Gentlemen, I may need your help during this procedure," said Sam when he and Martha returned.

Martha quickly bandaged Jim's arm where the man had cut him while Sam prepared his instruments.

"Remember, this is an operating room," stated the doctor. "Nothing that happens in here is to be discussed with anyone. Am I understood?"

Everyone, including Rose, nodded.

"May I ask Jim something?" the sheriff asked Sam.

The doctor nodded as he examined the wound.

"Jim, did you know the man who shot you?"

Jim shook his head.

"Ever seen him before?"

"No," Jim replied through gritted teeth.

"What can I do?" asked Rose. She had come to her senses

and was standing behind Jim's head, stroking his forehead.

"Get that leather strap over there," Sam ordered, pointing to a table against the wall. "And hold it in case he needs it in his mouth."

"I don't want her here," Jim insisted, choking down a groan as Sam poured alcohol over the wound.

Rose returned with the strap.

"Why don't you wait in the kitchen," Sam suggested.

"I want to stay with you," she pleaded as she stroked Jim's cheek.

"I can't—" Jim replied through clenched teeth. He shut his eyes as the alcohol burned into him.

Sam nodded toward the entrance to the kitchen, and Rose left Jim's side. As she stepped across the threshold, Sam caught her eye. Jim couldn't see her there, and something made her understand what Sam meant, so she stood in the open doorway.

"At least I married her before I died," Jim gasped.

"I don't intend to let you die at all," Sam stated. "You're lucky he hit you towards the right and not in the center of the chest."

"That's what he aimed for," Jim replied. "But I moved."

"Damn, you *are* fast," muttered the sheriff.

"I was going for my gun," Jim explained.

Sam was about to begin the procedure when he looked up. "Why don't all of you wait in the kitchen, but keep the door open in case I need help."

The men filed out past Rose, who stood still, not making a sound.

"Jim, I know I don't have to tell you, but this is going to hurt even worse than it does now," Sam said, holding the forceps. "And I can't give you anything. Enough morphine to kill the pain would probably kill you too right now."

"OK," Jim replied as he braced himself.

"Put that strap in his mouth," Sam said to Martha.

"No!" Jim growled, his voice strained from the pain.

"Even you won't be able to keep from screaming this time," Sam replied without pausing in his work.

"Yes I will. I haven't screamed since I was young, the first time they whipped me."

Sam didn't respond, and Jim's head fell to the side.

"Stay with me!" Sam ordered him.

The young man stirred.

"Who whipped you?" Sam asked.

"A man, with help from two others," Jim replied in a strained voice.

"Where were you?"

Jim glanced at the doctor, but Sam was concentrating on his work. Jim caught Martha's eye and she nodded, so he decided to answer. "A mining camp."

"Why did they whip you?" Sam asked, motioning to Martha for another instrument. He wanted to keep Jim talking so he'd stay conscious and therefore alive, but he didn't pause in his work.

"We'd just gotten there. I hadn't eaten in days. I took some food," Jim replied, trying to lie still while Sam probed for the bullet.

"Where were your parents?" Sam asked.

Jim tensed and shook his head slightly but didn't answer.

"How old were you?" Sam inquired, trying to keep his patient's attention.

"I feel sick," Jim grunted, trying to turn over.

"I need some strong men in here! Now!" Sam called to the sheriff and the others. "Rose!" Sam pretended to call to her as if she was in the other room.

"Yes?" she answered.

"If he gets sick, turn his head!" Sam ordered.

The men came in and Sam motioned to where he wanted them. He put the sheriff and his deputies on Jim's left to hold his arm and keep him still. He put Hank and Ted on Jim's right. Sam had Hank stand at Jim's shoulder next to Rose to give himself room to work.

"If he gets sick, he'll try to sit up or turn over," Sam explained. "Don't let him do that."

They all nodded, and Hank placed one hand on Jim's upper arm and the other firmly on Jim's shoulder.

"Am I hurting you, Jimmy?" the driver asked, but Jim didn't answer.

"How old were you the first time they whipped you?" Sam asked, speaking sternly to get his patient's attention.

"Seven or eight," Jim replied through clenched teeth. Then he tried to turn as he felt vomit come up his throat.

"Damn! He's strong!" muttered the big deputy, he and the others having trouble holding Jim down.

Jim swallowed hard and lay still without vomiting. "If I'd known I was going to get shot, I wouldn't have eaten."

"So you stole some food and these men tied you up and whipped you?" Sam asked.

"They didn't tie me that time," Jim gasped. "They stood on my arms."

"What happened next?" Sam asked.

"The one with the whip hit me. I screamed, and they laughed," Jim replied, his voice strained and distant, as though he was back in his horrible past. "They hit me again, but I didn't scream. Then I passed out. They hit me more the next time, and more the time after that, trying to get me to scream, but I wouldn't give them the satisfaction."

"How many times did they usually hit you?" Sam asked.

"I don't know, I couldn't count past ten."

"They hit you ten times?" Sam asked in disbelief.

"Sometimes."

"With a bullwhip?"

"No. It was a leather, knotted thing."

"The strand had knots?" Sam asked as he worked.

"Strands. There were ten or so of them I guess."

"So it was like getting hit ten times at one blow," whispered the big deputy.

"A cat-o'-nine tails," growled Hank under his breath. He shook his head with a shudder.

"What?" Jim asked, looking around. Then he moved slightly. "How long is this going to take?"

"Sorry," Sam replied. "I haven't found the bullet yet. I could cut you more, it would hurt less, but it would take you longer to heal. So I'm trying to find it with a probe and my fingers."

Jim's head fell to the side again.

"So you wouldn't scream," Sam said to keep him conscious.

"No," Jim breathed in response.

"But you were just a child," Sam continued. "How you must've cried."

Jim shook his head. "Can't."

"I wish I could give you something," Sam said, thinking Jim was complaining about the pain.

"I can't cry," Jim gasped through clenched teeth.

"Jim, other than a few rare medical conditions, none of which you have, everyone can cry."

"I can't," Jim insisted, shutting his eyes against the pain. "Something bad will happen."

"What?" asked the doctor.

"Don't remember, but something terrible."

"So you've never cried?" asked Martha, exchanging a glance with Rose.

Jim shook his head. "Never tears."

Jim's head fell to the side.

Sam was concentrating on his work, so Hank spoke.

"Where was the camp, Jimmy?"

Jim didn't respond.

"Jim!" Sam said sharply.

Jim stirred and choked down a groan. "Up in some mountains. Nothing else there."

"Were there other children?" Martha asked.

"Just miners, whores, and me."

Hank shook his head again slightly. "How'd they get the coal out?" he asked.

"Train."

"Then why didn't you just get on one and leave?" asked the younger deputy.

"I tried," Jim answered through gritted teeth. "The rail men brought me back."

"Did the man whip you again?" Sam asked.

Jim nodded. "It wasn't the first time I'd run."

"Did you try again?" Rose asked softly.

Jim shook his head. "He told me if I did, he'd cut off a toe for each time."

Rose gasped, and the others caught their breath.

"You don't need your toes," Sam muttered. He couldn't help but think it would have been better for the young man to lose them than have to endure the continued abuse.

"No," Jim said, trying not writhe. "But he said if that was too hard because of the bone, he'd move up."

Sam looked at Jim's face, taking his eyes off his work for the first time.

The young man met his gaze.

Sam understood and shuddered.

"You mean your fingers?" Rose asked in horror.

Jim shook his head.

The men instantly understood exactly what Jim meant and found themselves staring at him to see if everything was still there. It was. Then they each caught themselves and glanced around to see if anyone had noticed their interest.

Hank just shook his head. He'd seen Jim enough he didn't need to look.

Jim's body began to shake.

"Hold still!" Sam ordered.

"I am!" Jim growled as he felt his muscles tense against his will. He gasped, unable to catch his breath. He jerked his right arm away from Hank and Ted and grabbed Sam's wrist.

Though Hank was strong, he hadn't wanted to hurt his friend and so hadn't been holding him tightly.

"Gentlemen, you have to hold him!" Sam ordered sharply.

Hank and Ted pulled Jim's arm off the doctor, and both realized Jim had let them. The other three men renewed their grip and held Jim's left arm and shoulder firmly.

"Just give me a minute!" Jim gasped. Then he pulled against the men holding him, and the shaking stopped.

"Did he pass out?" Sam asked, pausing for a moment but without looking up.

"No," Ted answered, his voice strained.

"At least he's still now," Sam replied, continuing the operation.

"But I'm probably killing them!" Jim grunted, referring to the men holding him.

"Is he struggling?" Sam asked.

The men nodded as they began to sweat from the effort.

"It's the only way I can keep from shaking," Jim explained. "It's freezing in here."

"I'm so sorry!" Martha said. "I was so concerned about your wound I didn't even think to cover you." Then she looked at Rose and nodded toward a cabinet. "There's a blanket in there."

Rose stepped to the cabinet, returned with the blanket, and spread it over her husband, covering him to the waist.

"Nothing like being naked in front of everyone," Jim muttered as Rose laid the blanket over him.

"You were just making everyone jealous," Rose replied, going back to the head of the table and stroking Jim's cheek.

"I'm sure you were making Martha jealous," Sam remarked.

"I thought you said size didn't matter," replied Martha, trying to lighten the mood. As a nurse, she'd seen nearly every man in town.

"We all say that," responded Sam.

The sheriff and the older deputy smiled. Both were married. Hank had lost his wife five years before, but he made no reaction.

Suddenly, Jim jerked.

"Damn it!" Sam shouted. "Hold him, gentlemen!"

"What are you doing?" Jim asked through clenched teeth, trying not to writhe.

"I have to go deeper."

Jim took a long, shuddering breath, and forced himself to relax. "It's amazing," he murmured, as Rose stroked his cheek.

"What is?" Sam asked.

"How different people can be," Jim replied, his voice distant. He had stopped pulling against the men, concentrating on Rose's touch, trying to let the pain wash over him. "Rose isn't like the women I knew when I was young."

"The prostitutes?" Sam asked.

Jim nodded.

"What were they like?" asked Sam.

"They were cruel. They liked to hurt me, too. And do other things."

The men exchanged glances.

"Damn it!" breathed Sam as Jim began to shake again.

"Can't help it!" Jim explained, gritting his teeth.

Sam paused in his work to give Jim a moment. The young man took another deep, shuddering breath. Then he began straining against the men holding him again as Sam continued with the procedure.

Martha motioned to Rose, nodding toward the cabinet again. "Why don't you get a sheet?"

Rose obeyed and slid the sheet over her husband as she removed the blanket. Then she pulled the sheet up over Jim's knees from the bottom, leaving his groin covered, as sweat began to bead on his forehead and roll off. The moisture from his body mingled with that of the men holding him as their silent struggle continued. It was five to one, and yet the men involved wouldn't have wagered on a winner. Jim was accustomed to strenuous physical labor, as was Hank, but the others soon began to wince from the aching burning in their muscles. While they weakened, Jim's pain seemed to give him strength. The young deputy especially was suffering, and finally Sam told him to let go because he was shaking and interfering with the procedure.

"How much longer?" Jim asked, his voice strained.

"I don't know. I'm still looking for the bullet," Sam replied.

Jim turned his face away and whispered something.

"What?" Rose asked, leaning down to him.

"Leave," Jim replied, just loud enough for her to hear.

"But—"

"Please," Jim begged.

Rose obeyed, but she only walked as far as the doorway.

"Is she gone?" Jim asked.

Sam looked up and nodded. He hated lying to the young man but under the circumstances thought it for the best.

As Sam continued to probe for the bullet, Jim ground his teeth against groans. He was beginning to weaken. After the young deputy recovered, the men holding him started switching off so each of them could rest for a few minutes. All of them took advantage of this except Hank, who continued to hold Jim's right arm and shoulder in place so Sam could work.

Jim's breathing changed as his suffering increased. He would breathe normally for a few minutes and then gasp or catch his breath so violently it sounded almost like a hiccup.

Sam hated to see him suffer so, but he had to find the bullet or Jim would die. He worked as quickly as he could, but the operation seemed to go on forever. He couldn't imagine what it was like for Jim. When Jim began shaking his head, his breaths coming in sharp gasps, Sam became worried he might lose the young man simply from the strain the pain was putting on his body. Then Jim began to mumble and mutter under his breath as he continued to shake his head, and Sam knew the young man was in agony. Jim's body continued to react to the pain, but his mind had separated itself from the rest of him in order to prevent its own destruction. That he still had enough self-control not to scream was remarkable, and frightening in its implication.

"What is he saying?" Sam asked.

Ted leaned close to Jim's face and listened for a moment. "'Not again. Oh God, make it stop. Make it stop.'"

"That's what he often says when he's delirious," Martha whispered.

Sam nodded.

The sound of Ted's voice roused Jim, and he looked up at Sam. "Stop!" he demanded.

Sam paused, looking into Jim's eyes and seeing recognition.

"Just for a minute," Jim said, his voice weak.

Sam removed the probe and motioned to the men to release Jim's arms. Then Sam motioned to them again and they stepped away from the operating table.

As soon as they released him, Jim gasped for air as though he had just come up out of deep water, and his body jerked as his muscles tried to relax.

"Are you hurting anywhere other than where I've been working?" Sam asked.

Jim nodded and pointed to his right side. "I must have hit something when I fell."

Sam examined him. "I'll be damned," he muttered. "There it is!"

"What?" asked Ted.

"The bullet. It must have slid along his ribs and finally stopped here," announced Sam, pointing to a lump on Jim's right side. Then he looked the young man in the eye. "Hold on just a little longer, Jim. This won't take long now."

"How did that happen?" asked Ted.

"The Grace of God," the doctor replied.

"Amen," whispered the sheriff and Hank.

Since the bullet had traveled so far, Sam made an incision and removed it from the outside. Then he cleaned and stitched up both wounds.

"OK, let's take a look at that arm," Sam sighed, pointing to the cut on Jim's left forearm. Martha removed the bandage she had put on it earlier, and Sam began to stitch it up.

Jim's arm began to shake from exhaustion, and when each of the other men tried to hold him, they were shaking, too. Even Hank shook, though his tremors were more from emotion than fatigue. So Sam asked Rose to assist.

"You didn't leave," Jim whispered as Rose took his arm.

"No, I didn't. I'm sorry, but I wanted to be here in case you needed me."

Jim tried to reach up with his right arm to touch her, but he was too weak. His hand fell back to his side, so he just gazed at her.

"I'll get another room ready," offered Martha as Sam finished bandaging Jim's arm.

Then she and Sam exchanged a glance.

"Oh, yeah," Sam said. "We still have a body in Jim's room."

"Robert, why don't you run and get the undertaker," suggested the sheriff to the younger deputy.

The young man left, and by the time he returned, the others had Jim settled in another room.

"This is the last one with a double bed," Martha mentioned as she helped Rose settle Jim's head on the pillow.

"This doesn't mean you can do as you please, though," cautioned Sam, mainly to Jim. "I want you still and quiet until further notice. Understand?"

Jim nodded.

"I think he expects you to listen this time," Hank said to Jim, touching his arm. Then he looked at Sam. "Sometimes I think he makes a point of going against your orders."

"I know," Sam stated. Then he turned back to Jim. "If you ignore me this time, you'll be sorry. Not only do I not have to fix any stitches you tear out, I can make Rose leave and only allow you to see her under supervision."

Sam had never been so firm with Jim before.

"That could be interesting," commented Hank with a smile. He had seen Jim's eyes flash at the doctor and wanted to diffuse the situation. "Sam only wants what's best for you."

Jim took his eyes off Sam, glanced at Hank, and nodded.

"As your boss," Ted stated, stepping to the bedside, "I'm ordering you to do exactly as Sam says."

"Yes, sir," Jim replied.

"I'll come by and see you tomorrow." He quickly checked his watch. "I mean today," Ted added, patting Jim's arm.

The sheriff and his deputies wished Jim well, then helped the undertaker remove the body. Ted followed them out.

Martha invited Hank to stay for the rest of the night.

"Might as well," Hank replied after thanking her.

"She's thinking they might need you later," Jim said to him. "In case I get violent."

"Well, it's happened before," Sam added, patting Jim's shoulder.

"But that's not why I invited Hank to stay," Martha replied. "I know how Mrs. Harraday hates anyone going in after the door's locked, and I don't want her getting upset with us. I think she's already worried about who will help her with the heavy work after Jim moves out."

"She is," Hank sighed, not sounding very happy. "She asked me if I'd take over."

This made all of them laugh except Jim, who was in too much pain.

While Martha showed Hank where he could sleep, Rose went and got her and Jim's things from the other room. Sam then left them alone, and she lay down beside her husband. When Rose closed her eyes, all she could see was Jim lying on the floor, bleeding. Her body began to shake as she quietly sobbed until sleep finally overpowered her emotions.

Jim had already either fallen asleep or passed out, but the pain woke him a few hours later. He felt disoriented at first and wondered why Rose was next to him. Then he remembered what had happened earlier in the evening. He tried to lie still so as not to wake Rose and managed to doze off again.

Though it was late, the undertaker began to prepare the body. The first thing he did was to strip the clothes and go through the pockets. He was looking for letters or any other information about next of kin. All he discovered was a neatly folded piece of paper tucked into one of the back pockets of the man's pants. He unfolded it and found the contents disturbing enough to make another trip out in the middle of the night. He made his way through the dark streets to the sheriff's house. He was in such a hurry he hadn't grabbed a lantern.

The sheriff, having just gone to bed, answered his door in his nightshirt. He too found the notice disquieting, and first thing in the morning sent a telegram to the US Marshal's office in Bridgetton. Then he took the notice to the freight office and gave it to Ted.

"Are you going to show it to him?" the sheriff asked.

"Not yet," Ted replied.

"Do you want me or my men to keep an eye on him?"

Ted nodded. "I'll have mine help you. But try to be discreet. I don't want Jim to know."

The sheriff nodded.

It was late morning when Martha looked in on Jim. She opened the door with hardly a sound, but as soon as she stepped in the room, Jim sat up in alarm and his hand slid under the pillow.

"Sorry," Martha whispered.

Jim crumpled back to the bed and shut his mouth against a groan. "Where's my gun?" he asked when he'd recovered enough to speak.

"I haven't seen it."

"It was under the pillow in the other room."

"I'll bring it to you," offered Martha, and she left.

Rose stirred and woke up as Martha returned with the weapon.

"I just wanted to see if you needed anything," Martha said, starting to lay the gun on the bureau. Jim reached for it, so she handed it to him. "Hank's already gone, and Sam had an emergency out of town and won't be back for a few hours. Are you hungry?"

Jim shook his head.

"I'll come help you," Rose offered, starting to get up.

"You take care of Jim. That'll be help enough. I have some biscuits for you in the kitchen whenever you want them," Martha said to Rose. Then she left the room.

Rose turned over and kissed Jim's cheek. "Did you sleep?"

"Some."

He lifted his left arm so she could rest her head on his shoulder.

"I'm not hurting you, am I?"

Jim shook his head.

Rose let her hand wander down across his belly and below his waist.

"Not now," he whispered.

"Is it the pain?"

Jim nodded. "Every muscle hurts, too."

"Let me bring you some water," said Rose, getting out of bed.

"Mind if I get dressed first?"

Jim shook his head.

She dressed quickly. Then, after she brought the glass to him and was about to lift his head, she noticed his hand shaking. She took the glass from him, gazing at him worriedly.

"My muscles are still tired, that's all," Jim explained.

"Let's try something. Let me know if it hurts too much." She lifted his head, removed the pillow, and slipped under him, crossing her legs. She laid the pillow on her lap and rested Jim's head on it. Then she grabbed the other pillow and put it behind her back. "How's that?"

"It's fine."

"This way I can help you, and you can relax." She brought the glass to his lips and he drank a little. Then she brushed her hand across his forehead. She could feel the tension in his body as he fought against the pain. "You have nice hair," she commented as she ran her fingers through it. "I don't think I've ever seen any as dark. Does it curl when it gets longer?"

"No. I can't remember the last time I had it cut."

"I'll give you a shave tomorrow," she said, touching his cheek. She used his straight razor on him, and he liked the attention.

"Just let it grow."

"You want a beard?"

"Why not?"

"Why hide your beautiful face under a beard?"

"They must know what I look like now," Jim replied. Then he realized anyone in town could have innocently pointed him out to the man. He also knew that changing his looks would be pointless under those conditions.

Rose felt his muscles tense as he thought about the man who'd tried to kill him and what the implications might be. She caressed his forehead with her fingers. His skin was firm and smooth. Then she slowly ran her fingers lightly across his shut eyes. They were moderately deep-set, and she felt the lashes tickle her skin. She gently drew her fingers under his eyes and slowly across his cheekbones. She let them dance down his handsome nose, over the small hump where it had probably been broken at some point. Then she ran her fingers alongside his nose, feeling the movement of air as he breathed. She traced them above his lips. They were full but not girlish, and his whiskers lightly scratched her. She moved her fingers slowly across his lips and then under them and along his handsomely shaped jaw. It was square at the back but rounded slightly at the firm chin. Then she made a line from his chin to his neck. She brought her fingers gently across his neck and felt the bulge of his Adam's apple.

At some point, she felt him relax and fall asleep. She gazed at his face and thought, not for the first time, how young he looked when he slept. She realized this was because his features, when in repose, appeared almost delicate. She'd seen the same delicacy of appearance in a portrait painter she'd met years ago. She realized that when he slept, her husband had the face of an artist. When awake, the sharp look in his eye and the firm set of his jaw characterized his expression. These changed his aspect completely, and the artist became the freight guard, the warrior. She shook her head. She couldn't contemplate him returning to the stage. Not yet.

She studied each of his features but couldn't find a single one responsible for his striking good looks. She determined it was the combination of all of them, as well as the beauty of his strong, brave, generous soul shining through.

She laid her head back on the pillow behind her and dozed off. When she awoke a little while later, her feet were asleep. She tried moving her toes, but that only made them feel worse. She didn't want to wake Jim so she sat as still as possible, but he woke up a few minutes later. He stirred, then groaned, and all the pain showed on his face for a second before he became fully aware and steeled himself against it. He looked up at her and she smiled down at him.

"I hate to say this, but I have to get up," Rose whispered. "My feet are asleep."

Jim lifted his head with her help, and she managed to roll onto the other side of the bed. Then she began rubbing her legs.

Jim tried to sit up, but he was too weak. "I wish I could help."

"I'll be OK. I'll be back in a minute," she said, hobbling to the door. "You need some food in your stomach."

She returned a few minutes later carrying a tray, which she set on the night table. "Will you eat a little?"

"I'll try," Jim said, again attempting to sit up but failing.

"Lie still." She lifted the pillow with his head still on it.

Then she slipped under the pillow, letting it rest on her lap, and stretched her legs out beside him so her feet wouldn't go numb. She took a piece of toast, dipped it into a bowl of broth, and brought it to his mouth.

Jim nibbled on it.

"I'm glad you let me take care of you," she said, smiling as she fed him. "Some people just want to be left alone when they're hurt and then get mad when you don't do something right."

"I was always left alone before. This is nice for a change."

She leaned over and kissed the top of his head.

"Aren't you going to eat?" Jim asked.

"When you get done. I don't want to get crumbs in your hair." She smiled playfully as she continued feeding him.

"I wish you were naked," Jim whispered between bites, gazing up at her.

"Then you wouldn't want to eat."

He had finished the toast, and she had just gotten him to drink some water when there was a soft knock on the door.

"There's someone here to see you," Martha said to Jim, smiling.

Sarah bounded into the room, followed by Olivia.

"Oh, we're sorry to interrupt your lunch," Olivia apologized.

"Don't be," Jim replied.

"Well, keep eating," Olivia said. "We don't mind."

"I'm done," Jim assured her. "It's Rose who hasn't eaten."

"I had a piece of cheese and some biscuits in the kitchen," Rose replied, smiling. "And how are you?" she asked Sarah.

"I'm fine. Mama didn't want me to come, but I wanted to be sure you were all right," Sarah said, touching Jim's arm. "Does it hurt much?"

"Had worse. Everything OK with you?" Jim asked.

Sarah nodded.

"The other kids being nice to you? Anyone I need to have a talk with?" he asked, letting the child take his hand.

"I had a fight with Billy the other day, but we're friends again now," Sarah said, twisting slightly from side to side. "Is that where you were shot?" she asked, pointing to the bandage on Jim's chest.

"Yep."

"Did you kill him?" Sarah asked.

"Sarah!" Olivia scolded.

"No, one of the deputies did," Jim answered. "I didn't have my gun."

"Why not?" asked the child.

"I was asleep. I don't wear a gun to bed. In fact, I wasn't wearing anything."

"You were naked?" Sarah asked, giggling.

"Yep."

"Are you naked now?"

"Sure am. Rose doesn't let me wear clothes," he teased.

Sarah, Rose, and Martha laughed.

Jim noticed Olivia blush. "Sorry, Olivia," he said. Then he explained to Sarah. "It's because Rose has to take care of me. Your mother took care of me some, and she can tell you, clothes just get in the way."

"Can I help take care of you?" Sarah asked.

"I'm sure I can find something for you to do," Rose answered.

"Really?"

"You can fill that for me," Rose suggested, pointing to the glass on the tray.

Sarah took the glass and walked to the bureau where the pitcher was sitting next to the basin.

"Let me help you," Martha offered, pouring the water into the glass for her.

Sarah carefully carried the glass back and set it on the tray.

"Thank you!" Rose said.

"Why are you sitting there like that?" Sarah asked Rose, who was still sitting with Jim's head and pillow on her lap.

"This was the easiest way to feed him. He didn't feel like sitting up, and this way I can reach him better. See?" Rose took the glass and held it to Jim's mouth so he could drink.

"Mama and I are going to be here tomorrow to help Martha," Sarah announced.

"Help her with what?" Jim asked.

"Get ready for the people coming to your wedding," Sarah answered. Then she looked confused. "But we heard you'd already gotten married."

"We did," Jim replied, noting an odd expression in Olivia's eyes. "But we're still going to have a regular wedding."

"I don't understand," Sarah said.

"After I was stabbed, I thought I was going to die. Your mother can explain it later." Then he turned to Martha. "Who's staying with you?"

"The Petersens, and Mrs. Canady, too. We have the room. I didn't see any reason for them to stay at the hotel. Oh, and the Bowers sent their regrets."

"Let me know what I can do to help," Rose offered.

"Like I said earlier," Martha replied, "you take care of Jim. I can handle the rest."

"I went swimming last week," Sarah announced animatedly to Jim. "And I remembered everything you taught me."

"Good girl."

Sarah leaned close to Jim's ear and whispered, "I even went in the deep part."

"There was an adult there watching you, wasn't there?" Jim asked.

Sarah nodded. "Jenny's mother."

"She knows how to swim?"

Sarah nodded again. "She didn't swim with us, but she knows how."

"Sarah, we should let Jim rest now," Olivia suggested, reaching for her daughter's hand.

"Would you like to help me with something, Sarah?" Rose asked. "That is, if your mother doesn't mind. It'll only take a minute."

Sarah looked expectantly at her mother, and Olivia nodded.

"I need to get up," Rose said. "So if you could just slide your hands under the pillow and help me lift him, I'd appreciate it."

Sarah did as instructed, with Rose's help, and Rose slid out.

Sarah leaned over, whispered in Jim's ear, and he glanced at Rose and nodded.

Rose looked at him questioningly.

"Sarah was just wondering if you'd seen my back," Jim explained.

"Oh, yes, honey. Many times," Rose replied.

"His scars bother Mama," Sarah explained. "Do they bother you?"

"It bothers me that someone hurt him, but I think they give him character," added Rose as she put on her hat.

"Char-act-er?" Sarah asked, slowly repeating the word.

"Your mother can explain it to you," said Rose.

"Going somewhere?" Jim asked her.

"I thought I'd go by our house and make sure the furniture gets put in the right place and tidy up a bit. Since Martha has company coming, we should probably move you there if Sam says it's OK."

"You won't be in our way," Martha assured her. "But we'll see what Sam says when he gets back. I know Jim will be able to rest easier there after they get here. The Petersen children will be all over him otherwise."

"Is there anything you need while I'm out?" Rose asked Martha.

"Yes, thank you."

"I can take Sarah, too," Rose offered to Olivia. "That way you can stay and visit."

Olivia thought for a moment, but before she could reply, Rose walked up to her and took her hand. "I know you don't know me very well, but you're a good friend of Jim's, and we both would be honored if you and Sarah would be in our wedding. You can be my bridesmaid, and Sarah can be a flower girl."

Sarah jumped with excitement at the thought.

Olivia looked surprised. Then she smiled and nodded. "Sarah and I would be glad to, but what will I wear?"

"Any dress you would normally wear to church would be fine. This isn't a formal wedding. Do you have a blue one, maybe?"

"Yes, I do."

"Good!" Rose smiled. "It will bring out your eyes." Then Rose turned to Sarah. "And as for you, little one, I can make you one and have it done in plenty of time."

"You're a seamstress?" Olivia asked.

"Yes. I made this," Rose said, giving a twirl. "Originally it had a lower neckline, but under the circumstances I didn't think that appropriate, so I changed it."

"I liked it before," Jim remarked.

"I bet you did," commented Martha, smiling. Then she turned to Olivia. "Would you mind staying with Jim so I can run out with Rose and Sarah? I just remembered some things I need to take care of."

"I don't mind," Olivia answered.

Rose walked to the bed and gave Jim a kiss on the mouth,

causing Sarah to giggle again.

"I'll be back soon," Rose whispered to him.

After they left, Olivia closed the door and pulled a chair next to the bed. "Is there anything I can get you?"

"I'm fine. So what do you think?"

"About what?"

"Rose. You can't help but like her." He knew that, even though both women had helped care for him, because they'd worked on different nights, they'd rarely met and didn't really know each other.

"She's very sweet, not at all what I expected," Olivia replied, looking down.

"What's wrong?" Jim asked her softly.

Olivia started to shake her head. Then she looked up at him. "It's just that I know Sarah hoped, and me, too, that—" She stopped and looked down again.

Jim thought he knew what she meant, but he wanted her to say it. "That what?"

"That you and I—" She let her voice trail off, still without looking at him.

"I thought about that, too. A lot," Jim replied, and Olivia looked up with tears in her eyes. "But it wouldn't have been good for either of us," he continued.

"I'm sorry," Olivia said, looking away. "I shouldn't be bringing this up now. You should rest."

Olivia was on his right. Jim reached out for her, ignoring the pain. She took his hand and moved closer so he could rest his arm on the bed.

"There were nights when I'd walk by your house, and I'd hear you singing Sarah to sleep." Jim gazed at her hand, rubbing his thumb over it as he held it. "I wanted to walk in and watch you. Then see what happened."

Olivia looked at him in surprise. "I wouldn't have made you leave," she said, barely above a whisper.

"That's what I was afraid of," Jim replied, still not meeting her gaze. "Then I'd think about the next time I had to leave, or the next time I got hurt, and what that would do to you. You'd been through so much. You'd already lost one man, it wouldn't have been right to put you through that again. I even thought about quitting the freight company and just working for the blacksmith. But I knew that the next time someone was hurt or killed on the stage, or a passenger was robbed or raped, I'd wonder if I could have prevented it if I'd been there. Neither of us would have been happy."

"We might have been," Olivia whispered, staring at his hand as it caressed hers. Like the rest of him, it was marred by past injuries, but that just made it stronger and more amazing in its beauty.

"Believe me, I wanted to believe that, too." Jim raised his eyes and gazed at her. "You have a lovely, gentle soul, Olivia, but if I'd acted on my impulses—and they were strong ones—I knew I would destroy you. Not just hurt you, a person can get over that, but I would have crushed you. I didn't want to be responsible for that."

"And what about Rose? You don't think you'll hurt her?"

"Rose is different. She's able to live in the moment. It's not that she doesn't think or worry about the future, I'm sure she does. It's just that she doesn't let that control the present. I'm sure she'll have her moments, but she'll get through them."

"Are you sure she's not just using you?"

"I've thought about that. But when you consider I've been flat on my back for almost four months now, and it'll be at least another couple of weeks before I'm healed, I think if she didn't love me she'd have cut and run by now. Also, she was with me yesterday through the entire surgery. She could have left anytime, but she refused, even after I told her to. That took more than just guts."

"I would have stayed with you," Olivia assured him softly.

"But think what it would have done to you. It bothered you to see me with pneumonia, much less bleeding on an operating table while Sam had his hands and a probe in my chest for God knows how long, and with nothing for the pain."

Olivia looked at him, and he could feel her hand shaking.

"I could have—" she insisted, fighting back tears.

Jim reached up with his left hand and tried to untie the bandage across his chest. The knot was too tight, so he tore the bandage, exposing his wound. "Look at it!"

Olivia looked away, but Jim still had her hand and gave it a pull. "Look at it! That's what you'd have to see, and it looks a hell of a lot better now!"

Olivia gazed at the line of stitches, then turned away.

Jim reached up with both hands and pulled at the wound. "This is what you'd have to deal with!" he growled as he tried to separate the stitches, wincing from the pain.

Olivia turned back, saw what he was doing, and screamed, "Stop!" Then she jumped up and turned away again.

Jim threw the bandage over the wound and let his arms fall to the bed.

Olivia turned back toward him and wiped tears from her face.

"Is that what you want?" Jim asked softly.

Olivia collapsed into the chair and sobbed. Then after a moment she whispered, "You had been so distant, even before your illness. Now I know why."

"I didn't want to hurt you by giving the wrong impression."

"So who proposed to whom?"

"I proposed to her."

"She'd have been a fool not to accept," Olivia said softly.

"Actually, she didn't," Jim replied evenly. "Her first response was 'no.' She thought I was just infatuated. Then she stayed away for a few days but came back when I got worse."

"So that's what happened," Olivia whispered thoughtfully. "I guess she really does care about you."

Jim nodded.

"Do you think it proper for you to stay at your house with her alone?"

"Why not? We're married now."

Olivia looked at him knowingly.

"We've already done that," Jim replied to her look.

Olivia gazed at him in surprise.

"Sam told me to stay quiet, but I had a moment of weakness," Jim explained.

"You? I doubt that."

"Whatever I may be, I'm still a man, with all the needs, for good or bad, of a man."

Olivia started to cry. Jim painfully reached out and took her hand again. She knelt by the bed, laid her head on his belly, and sobbed. Jim reached over with his left hand and stroked her hair.

"You believe deep down that I was right about us?" he asked softly.

Olivia thought for a moment as she cried, then nodded.

"You need a man you can depend on, who'll be there to hold you and comfort you every night, and it's not me." Jim brushed her hair from her forehead. "But you'll find him. You're a beautiful woman and draw every man's attention. I'm sure there's at least a dozen in town who think about you every night as they go to sleep."

She sat up and looked at him. "Is that what you did?"

Jim nodded. "But I didn't indulge myself."

Olivia nodded as well. "It's funny," she said, wiping her eyes. "For months after my husband died, all I could think about was him, until one night I realized I was thinking about you."

Jim wiped a tear from her cheek.

Olivia smiled weakly. "I'm happy for you."

"Really?"

She nodded again. "You were right. Thank you."

Jim lifted her hand to his lips and kissed it.

"You really are amazing, you know," she whispered, gazing at him. "Most any other man would have taken advantage of the situation, regardless of the consequences."

"Don't give me too much credit. I thought about it."

Olivia smiled. "Rose is very sweet, and Sarah has certainly taken to her."

"Like I said, you can't help but like her."

Olivia gave him some water, kissed his forehead, and told him to rest. She sat by the bed as Jim shut his eyes and tried to sleep. After a few minutes, he managed to doze off.

As Jim slept, Olivia thought about their discussion. Her heart ached. She hurt for him because of his current injuries, and she hurt because she longed to find someone to comfort her. She was convinced Jim was right, for he had instinctively communicated in the only manner that can truly convince a woman of anything. He had appealed not only to her intellect but to her heart, her emotions.

She cringed as she recalled him tearing at his stitches, but she had realized in that moment that he was right. His strength of character and noble spirit had saved her from a lifetime of worry and torment. He had freed not only her mind but her heart and left her untethered to search for another. She shook her head. She doubted there was another man alive who could compare to him in either looks or character. She also admitted to herself for the first time that Jim's intensity of thought and feeling frightened her. She realized she needed a man calmed by life, not tortured and untamed by it.

Olivia stayed with Jim until she heard the others return. Then she left the room, shutting the door quietly behind her.

After showing off the material she had purchased for her and Sarah's dresses, Rose went to Jim's room to remove her hat and check on him. The others followed her so Sarah and Olivia could say goodbye. Jim was writhing restlessly in his sleep as Rose entered. She rushed to his bedside and softly said his name. He continued to twist and groan. His eyes fluttered open, unseeing, then shut again. He turned his head toward her, and Rose took his face in her hands.

"Jim," she said again, a little louder.

He threw his eyes open, jerked violently away from her, and raised his left hand in a fist. A second later, he realized who had been touching him and collapsed in pain without striking her. Rose held him close and comforted him. Then she took the glass from the bedside table and gently raised his head so he could drink. As she was setting the glass back down, Jim saw Sarah, Martha, and Olivia looking on from the doorway. In the time it took Rose to blink, his face changed from one of agony to calm acceptance as he steeled himself against the pain.

Sarah ran to him. "Are you all right?"

Jim nodded and took the child's hand in his.

"You should see the material we got!" Sarah said excitedly. "Rose and I are going to match!"

"You'll both be wearing white?" Jim asked.

"No, silly!" laughed Sarah.

"Don't tell him," Rose smiled playfully to the child. "It's supposed to be a surprise, remember?"

Sarah nodded and laughed.

"Tell Jim goodbye," Olivia said to Sarah.

Sarah turned and kissed Jim on the cheek.

"You're scratchy!" she said.

"Yep. That's what men are: hairy, scratchy, sweaty, and we swear."

Sarah laughed and bounded back to her mother. She waved as Olivia led her away.

"You're awfully good with her." Rose smiled as she walked to the other side of the room to take off her hat.

Martha noticed there was something wrong with his bandage and stepped to the bed. "How did you do this?" she asked, lifting it so Rose could see.

"I tore it. Sorry."

"You're bleeding, too," Martha noted.

She left the room and came back with some alcohol.

Jim winced as she cleaned the wound.

"It looks like some of the stitches have come loose," Martha commented as she worked. "Did you fall?"

Jim shook his head. "Just trying to make a point," he replied cryptically.

Martha glanced up. She knew him well enough to read his look and not ask any more questions. "Sam can fix them when he gets back," she said as she retied the bandage. "That should hold you for now. Just be careful. You need to be as well as possible for your wedding." Then she exchanged a look with Rose as she left and shut the door.

Rose walked over to the bed and gazed at Jim, who eventually looked up. Their eyes met.

"Are you OK?" she asked.

Jim nodded.

"Are you hungry?"

He shook his head.

"Sarah and I had a snack when we got back," mentioned Rose as she returned to the other side of the room. "If you don't mind, I thought I'd take a nap."

"Why would I mind? You hardly got any sleep last night."

"If you'd be more comfortable having the bed to yourself, I understand," Rose offered, keeping her back to him as she got undressed and donned her nightgown.

"I don't mind sharing it," Jim replied, watching her.

Rose crawled into the bed beside him. She laid her head on his left shoulder and rested her hand on his chest.

Jim kissed her hair and she looked up at him.

He gazed back at her intently.

"You have the most unusual eyes," she whispered. "It's like there's something burning inside you. It can mean you're happy or angry."

"I can't help it," he said, tightening his arm around her and holding her close.

Rose lowered her eyes and snuggled against him. "Do you still love her?" she asked softly.

"Who?"

"Olivia."

"How?" Jim asked.

"I'm a woman, we can sense these things. If you do, I understand, and I'll—" She started to pull away, but Jim held her firmly.

"No, I don't love her," he replied, looking down at her. She didn't meet his gaze. "I thought I did, but it wouldn't have been good for either of us."

"Did you have sex with her while I was gone?"

"What? No, of course not! What made you ask that?" He looked at her, his eyes flashing.

"A torn bandage and loose stitches," Rose whispered.

"That was to prove a point!" he stated firmly.

Rose looked up at him, noting the same fire in his eyes, but the gaze was hard, not soft as it had been before.

"I love you and only you," Jim assured her, his gaze softening again, even though his eyes still smoldered.

"So you didn't get the least bit interested while you two were alone?"

"No, I still hurt too much to want to."

"If you weren't hurt?"

"I still would want only you. Though a beautiful woman will always get my attention, at least for a moment."

Rose gave him a look.

"Would you prefer I lied?" Jim asked.

She shook her head.

"You worked in the saloon," he continued. "You know you made most of the men stand in their pants every time you walked by. Most of them went home and used it on their wives, and the rest had to make do with one of the other girls."

"So you're still attracted to her," she stated.

"I'm a man. I'll always be attracted to a beautiful woman. That's why I'll always be attracted to you," he said as he brought her face to his and kissed her.

"So you still want me?" she asked.

"Of course. I love you."

"So if you had the chance, you wouldn't have sex with Olivia?"

"I had the chance today and I didn't."

"But you said the pain is still too bad."

"Even if I wasn't in pain, I wouldn't have," Jim replied, gazing at her.

She looked into his eyes and felt the heat from their flame in her heart.

He kissed her again and felt her melt in his arms.

"So you really love me and not her?" Rose asked.

"I love every inch of you."

"What do you like most?"

"That's a hard question. I love your hair."

"Why?"

"Right now it looks brown, but in the sunlight it shines gold and bronze. I love your eyes. They're the bluest, clearest eyes I've ever seen."

"Except yours," she said with a smile.

"Mine don't count. I love your lips."

Rose puckered.

"I wasn't talking about those, but they're nice, too."

She laughed.

"I wish I felt up to it," Jim said softly, stroking her hair. Then he kissed the top of her head as she snuggled against him again.

"This is nice," she whispered.

Jim continued stroking her hair for a few minutes. "So what color's the dress?" he asked softly.

"Green. It's a really pretty shade—" She sat up in surprise and found him grinning at her. "You! I can't believe you!" She swatted him playfully.

Jim raised his left arm to block her blow, so she swatted him some more. "Hey! You're hitting a wounded man here." He smiled good-naturedly.

"Oh, you!" Rose said, pretending to pout as she swatted him again.

Jim caught her arm this time and, careful not to hurt her, pulled her back down against him. "I don't like secrets."

"I don't either. There are a lot of things about me that I haven't told you yet because we haven't had time."

"Same here. Though there's a lot I can't remember."

She looked at him worriedly. "If I knew more about the things you've been through, I might be able to comfort you better," she said as she caressed his cheek.

"What do you mean?"

"I don't know if you realize it or not, but you often have terrible dreams, and you say things."

"Like what?" he asked.

"Usually you say, 'Oh God, make it stop!' Maybe if I knew what you were talking about—" She felt Jim suddenly tense and draw away with a shudder, as though a chill had fallen over him.

He threw himself out of the bed, lunged to the bureau, and opened the top drawer, but all he saw were her things. "Where are my clothes?"

Rose looked at him in surprise without moving. Earlier he hadn't been able to sit up, much less stand.

"I can't breathe in here!" Jim gasped. "I need my clothes!"

Rose saw desperation in his eyes. She hopped out of bed, found a pair of his pants, and helped him put them on. He reached for a shirt after only securing two of the buttons on the pants. She slipped the shirt onto his shoulders, but he turned before she could button it.

Then he dashed out of the room, staggering in his haste. She quickly put on her robe and followed. He tore through the kitchen without even glancing at Martha, who was standing at the stove, and stumbled out the back door.

Rose found him leaning heavily on the railing surrounding the back porch, gasping for air.

"What's wrong?" Martha asked, following Rose outside.

"I don't know," Rose answered. "I just asked him about that nightmare he always has, and he had to come outside."

Suddenly realizing his weakness, Jim fell to his knees and leaned his forehead against the balusters. He still held the railing with his left hand but let his right fall to the ground.

Rose knelt, then reached out and touched his left shoulder. She could feel him shaking. She looked up at Martha with fear in her eyes.

"Jim," Martha said, "you need to come back inside."

He shook his head and continued breathing deeply.

"Jim! You need to be in bed!" Sam said sternly from

behind them.

Martha touched Sam's arm, took him inside, and explained what had happened. Sam stepped back onto the porch and knelt on Jim's other side. He gazed at the young man for a moment, waiting for Jim to acknowledge his presence.

Jim still didn't move or even turn his head.

Sam put his hand on Jim's arm, and he too noticed the young man was shaking. "What's wrong?" he asked softly.

Jim shook his head.

"Tell us," Sam insisted, still speaking quietly.

Jim thought for a moment, then spoke, barely above a whisper. "I thought I'd forgotten it. I had no idea it haunted me in my sleep."

"What?" Rose asked.

Jim shook his head again. "No!" he breathed.

"Jim, what is it?" Rose begged, worry evident in her voice.

Jim shook his head.

"Why don't you come inside," Sam suggested, taking Jim's right arm.

Jim jerked away with a wince. "Not yet. Sorry, but not yet." He pulled himself to his feet with his left hand, walked past Sam and Rose to the steps, and sat. "I can't be inside right now."

Rose and Sam exchanged a glance, and Rose sat beside him. "Why not?" she asked.

"I'm afraid—" He stopped, surprised at his own words. "I'm afraid the walls will fall in."

Rose looked back at Sam, who nodded to her to continue. "Why?" she asked.

Jim shook his head.

"Jim, please," Rose begged. She touched his arm, but he pulled away.

"Does it happen often?" Jim asked, gazing out over the backyard.

"What?" Rose asked in return.

"The dream," Jim replied, still without looking at her.

"Almost every night when you were sick."

Martha caught Rose's eye, and Rose read her lips.

"And when you're in pain," Rose continued. "You said the same thing during the surgery yesterday."

"Damn!" Jim muttered under his breath.

"It's OK," Rose assured him.

"No it's not!" Jim snapped vehemently, and he looked at her for the first time, his eyes flashing.

Rose gaped at him, stunned.

Jim stood, descended the stairs, walked a few steps into the yard, then turned and came back to face her. "You don't understand!" For the first time, Rose saw hurt and fear in his eyes. "I left all this behind! Shut it out of my mind!" He turned his back and dropped his head. He wanted to hit something or start running and not stop until he collapsed from exhaustion. Then realization struck him like the whip that scarred his back. "That's why!" he whispered, raising his head, his eyes riveted on some indefinite point on the horizon. "Damn! All this time and I didn't even know it!" He grabbed up a rock with his right hand. Forgetting about the wound in his chest, he threw it as hard as he could, then doubled over from the pain.

Rose started to run to him, but Sam caught her arm and stopped her.

Jim fell to his knees, still bent from the pain. A moment later, he straightened and gazed out at the openness behind Sam's house. "How could I have been so blind and stupid?" he muttered to himself, not realizing the others could hear him.

He shut his eyes and took a deep breath. "You don't realize how nice it is just to be able to breathe," he continued a little louder, wanting them to hear him. "I was in the mine, deep underground."

The others exchanged a glance as Jim continued.

"There was a dull rumble. Then it got louder. I'd heard it before. I dove toward the wall, but I wasn't quick enough. The ceiling fell on me. It trapped my legs. I tried to move." He paused, took another long breath. "But I couldn't. I tried again and the pain—" He shook his head. "I was used to getting whipped and never screaming, but this—then I heard it again. I covered my head with my hands and more fell on me, pinning me from the chest down. Another rumble. A beam must have fallen. Not directly on me, but on whatever was on my legs. I screamed from the pain. I knew there was no one to hear me, no one to laugh at me. That's when I prayed. With everything in me, from the innermost place in my soul, I prayed, 'Oh God, make it stop!' But it didn't. The next time I was completely buried. All I could move was one finger." Unconsciously, Jim moved his right forefinger.

"When you're in the mine," Jim continued, his voice almost a growl, "you learn to sense the least movement of air on your face. You can feel it, and you know you can breathe. There was nothing. Just dust and dark. Not the dark of night. At least then, you have the moon and stars," he said, raising his eyes to the sunlit sky. "There's no light in a mine. Just hopeless darkness. There was another rumble, and that's when I gave up. I was completely covered, and even more fell. The pain, the pressure—I couldn't breathe, I couldn't move. I couldn't scream, though the pain was the worst I'd ever felt."

He took another long breath. "I knew no one would bother to look for me. One of the miners they'd try to dig out, but not me. I have no idea how long I lay there before I passed out. All I know is that when I woke up, I was in the blacksmith's hut, and it was three days later. The only reason I was found was because they were looking for one of the miners and happened across me. A few days later, when I could travel, the smith left and took me with him. It wasn't until we were four days away from the camp that he told me—" He paused and shook his head slightly, not wanting to continue, not wanting to remember.

"What did he tell you?" asked Sam softly.

"He suspected the man who'd always whipped me had caused the cave-in, intending to kill me. He was the powder man. Unfortunately, five men died and I lived. The smith took me away because he knew the man wouldn't give up until I was dead."

"How old were you?" Rose asked, fighting back tears.

"Around eleven, I guess," Jim replied without turning toward her. "I realize now why I have to run and not stop sometimes, or just be outside. I'm still trying to escape from that damned mine!"

Sam waited a minute. Then he walked up to Jim, helped the young man to his feet, and gave his arm a gentle squeeze.

Jim turned without looking Sam in the eye and walked to the steps. Rose stood, and Jim took her in his arms without meeting her gaze.

"Thank you for telling me," she whispered as he held her tightly.

Jim rested his head on her shoulder, and she felt him shaking. She started to lead him through the door. He balked slightly. Then he took another deep breath and stepped inside. He strode past her in the kitchen, marched straight to the operating room, opened a cabinet, took out a bottle of whiskey, and returned to his room.

Rose started to follow him, but Sam stopped her. "Give him a minute," he suggested.

Then Martha informed him about Jim's stitches. Sam washed his hands, grabbed his bag, spoke to Rose, and hurried to Jim's room. He found the young man sitting on the bed drinking from the bottle.

Jim had taken his shirt off but left the pants on and was sitting on top of the covers with his back against the headboard, holding the bottle in his left hand.

"I need to look at your chest," Sam said.

Jim took another drink, then nodded.

The doctor untied the bandage. "I won't even bother to ask how you managed to do this," Sam remarked as he looked at the wound. He turned toward the door and called for Rose.

She was standing in the hall, just out of sight, but she paused for a moment so it would seem as though she had come from the kitchen.

"I could use some help," Sam said to her as she walked into the room. "Are your hands clean?"

"I just washed them."

"Good," Sam responded as he set to work.

Jim took another drink as Sam tightened the incision, with Rose assisting him. When he was done, Sam put a clean bandage across Jim's chest, then sat in the chair observing the young man.

Rose sat on the edge of the bed near its foot and glanced worriedly from Jim to Sam.

"I need you to give me the bottle," Sam said, reaching for it.

"I'll pay you back," Jim replied, and he took another long drink as he stared straight ahead.

"That won't help you," Sam responded.

Jim ignored him and continued drinking.

"I'd think you'd be happy," Sam continued. "You found out something about yourself today, and now you can deal with it."

"Yeah!" Jim growled, not looking at either of them, his eyes flashing. "I found out I'm a coward!"

"Why?" Sam asked. "Because you were trapped God knows how far underground and you were frightened?"

"Because I thought I'd left all that behind," Jim replied, his voice tense and low. "Instead, it's been on my back the whole time, just like those fucking scars!"

Rose patted his leg.

"Sorry," Jim said to her, apologizing for his language without meeting her gaze.

"Just because something scares or bothers you," Sam explained, "it doesn't mean you're a coward. Don't you get scared when the stage is attacked and you have someone shooting at you?"

"I'm too busy concentrating on what I have to do to be scared."

"But what about after?" Sam asked. "Don't you think about what could have happened? Maybe that night as you go to sleep?"

Jim didn't answer for a moment. Then he replied, "I can't afford to get scared."

"Jim, do you know the difference between a hero and a fool?" Sam asked. When Jim didn't respond, he continued. "A fool does what he does because he has no fear. A hero does what he does in spite of his fear. And I think you're no fool."

Jim looked at him for the first time, and his eyes softened. "Thanks, Sam."

Sam reached for the bottle, and Jim handed it to him.

"Have you eaten today?" Sam asked.

"I had some toast and broth. I'm not really hungry."

"Well, you need to eat anyway in a little while," Sam ordered. "It's the only way you'll get better." Then Sam stepped to the bureau, filled a glass of water from the pitcher, and brought it to Jim. "Drink this."

After Jim drank as much water as he could, Sam helped Rose lay him down, and the doctor left. He strode to his study, unlocked a drawer, and pulled out the journal dedicated to his most frequent patient. After thinking a moment, he began writing. He recorded the pastor's vision and related all Jim had said about his past. He also noted that the bullet should have gone through to Jim's heart but hadn't. This was either because Jim's bones and muscles were unusually dense or the man had skimped on the powder when making the bullet. Then he added that, for whatever reason, it was a miracle Jim was still alive. What Sam couldn't know was that this wouldn't be the last time he would write those words.

Rose sat by the bed and gazed at Jim as he tried to rest.

"It's hard to sleep with you staring at me," he said.

"Sorry. I'm just worried about you."

Jim lifted his hand, and she took it.

"I'll be OK in a few days. At least the wedding isn't this Saturday," he said.

Rose leaned down and kissed his hand.

Later that evening, Jim managed to eat a little. Afterwards, Rose left him to rest while she ate with Sam and Martha. Then she helped clean up and went to bed.

Jim stirred but didn't awaken as she climbed in next to him. Later in the night, he became restless. Rose got a fan, and, as soon as he felt the air on his face, Jim calmed. He remained in great pain over the next few days but stayed quiet, more because of Rose's insistence than due to the discomfort. Each night, Rose was able to quiet him with the fan, and, since he was able to rest, he healed quickly.

After a little over two weeks, Sam was pleasantly surprised to find that Jim was hungry. "What have you eaten today?" Sam asked him.

"Toast and broth," Jim answered. "Just like every other day. No offense, but I'm tired of toast and broth."

"Well, if my nose didn't deceive me when I was in the kitchen," Sam replied, "Martha is making an apple pie, and I think she's baking a chicken. If you get some rest and feel up to it, you can eat at the table."

Jim nodded. "When can I go home?"

"Back to the boarding house?" Sam asked.

Jim shook his head. "My own."

During Jim's time at Sam's, Rose had spent part of each day at their house preparing it for Jim's arrival. The furniture was all in place, and she had purchased sheets, towels, and other necessities. She had even found time to hem and hang lace curtains. She got the sheerest material she could find, because

Jim told her he liked to be able to see outside so he wouldn't feel confined. She also started on Sarah's dress. Martha had been gracious enough to let her use half of the kitchen table for sewing, but Rose spent most of her time there at Jim's side. She noticed he rested easier when she was in the room. He was often restless and tossing and turning when she entered, but he hardly ever did that when she was present.

"You can go to your house tomorrow," Sam said. "If you were wanting to go back to Mrs. Harraday's, I'd have to say to wait."

"What's the difference?" Rose asked.

"If he's with you," Sam replied, "I'll know he's resting. If he's at the boarding house, the blacksmith may send one of his boys to fetch him because he needs some help, and Jim will be back at the forge. I don't think I'll have to worry about that if you're watching him."

"That's true," Rose assured him with a smile.

"But you two will still have to be careful about what you do together," Sam cautioned. "Remember, don't put any weight on him for a while," he said to Rose.

"Does that mean we can—?" Jim asked.

Sam nodded. "If you're careful. Remember, you have to heal on the inside as well as the outside. I know you'll be like a kid with a new toy, but you have to take it easy. Standing up or kneeling is fine, but that will have to do for another week at least."

"We get married again in a week," Jim stated.

Sam nodded again. "And don't lift anything with your right arm, either," he added.

"When will I be able to go back to work? Ted wanted me back after the wedding."

"You won't be able to fire a rifle for another few weeks at least."

"Ted's going to love hearing that," Jim remarked.

"He knows," Sam replied. "I talked to him this morning after he left your room. He just wants you well. Now get some rest before dinner."

Sam left them alone, and Rose sat by the bed. Jim reached out for her hand, and she took it. Then he pulled her to him and kissed her deeply. Rose returned his kiss but stopped his hand as it began to unbutton her dress.

"Sam said we could," Jim whispered in her ear.

Rose gave him a long look, and Jim tossed the covers aside to show her the effect she'd had on him. Rose smiled, walked to the door, and locked it. She stripped and climbed into bed. After carefully pleasing each other, Jim lay back down and dozed off while Rose went into the kitchen to help Martha. When supper was ready, Rose woke Jim gently. She helped him with his underwear bottoms and tied the string for him. Then she helped him with a shirt, which he didn't button. Sam put Jim's right arm in a sling, and Jim followed them into the kitchen.

Along with the chicken, Martha had baked some potatoes and Rose had boiled peas on the stove. Rose cut up Jim's food for him, and while she visited with Sam and Martha Jim managed to start eating with only his left hand. The others were having a lively conversation when suddenly Jim noticed they were quiet and staring at him. He had been trying unsuccessfully to eat his peas and spread them all over his plate.

"I'm sorry," Martha smiled. "We should have prepared something easier for you."

"But that wouldn't have been nearly so amusing," Sam remarked, and he started to laugh. Rose and Martha joined in.

Jim tensed for a second, then sighed good-naturedly.

"Let me help you," said Rose, taking his fork.

She started to mash the peas, but Jim stopped her. "I don't like them like that."

Rose gathered them up and fed them to him.

"You don't look very happy," Martha observed to Jim.

"I hate being fed," Jim replied between bites.

"You hate anything you can't do for yourself," said Rose.

"I can think of at least one thing he doesn't mind," Sam commented, smiling.

Martha nudged him.

"What?" Sam asked. "It's the truth. It's never as good if you do it yourself."

Martha looked at him and shook her head, smiling. Rose couldn't help but laugh.

For dessert, Martha had baked an apple pie, as Sam had guessed, because it was Jim's favorite and she wanted to encourage him to eat. He managed at first, but needed Rose's help with the crust.

Rose smiled as she wiped his mouth after the last bite. "That was fun."

"I'm glad you enjoyed it," Sam said. "Because you'll probably need to help him for a while."

"Sam, you really think I'm going to wear this when I get home?" Jim asked, indicating the sling.

"If you don't," Sam replied, "you'll delay your recovery by at least a week. And I know you want to be well by your wedding. Plus, I'm sure Rose will make sure you keep it on. If nothing else," Sam added with a smile.

Martha nudged him again, but she was smiling too, along with Rose.

Jim stood and took his plate to the sink. Then he turned and headed back to his room, followed by Sam and Rose.

Jim sat on the bed as Sam removed the sling and checked the bandage. Then he and Rose helped Jim prepare for bed, and Sam helped him lie down. Before leaving, the doctor wished him good night.

"I should help Martha," Rose said as she bent over Jim and gave him a kiss. "Will it wake you when I come to bed?"

"I should know it's you," he replied.

Rose kissed him again and left. When she returned later, Jim stirred, opened his eyes for a second, saw who it was, and went right back to sleep. Rose wasn't sure if he actually woke or not. She quietly got ready for bed, whispered to him as she snuggled up next to him, and went to sleep.

Little did she know that another man slept soundly that night as he waited patiently for his chance to rid the world of Jim Morgan.

16

LOVE

The next morning, they all arose early. It was Sunday, and Sam wanted to get Jim home so he could go to church on his way back.

"I can get a wagon," Sam offered.

"I'd rather walk," Jim replied as they readied to leave.

Sam carried the bag Rose had packed that morning, and Rose held Jim's arm while he carried his rifle and slung his shotgun over his shoulder. After the attack, he'd insisted Hank bring them to him. When they arrived at the house, Sam gave Rose some final instructions and left.

"Now, let's get you settled," Rose said as she began unbuttoning Jim's shirt. "I could tell you got tired on the walk, and I want you to rest while I work on Sarah's dress."

"Why don't you get undressed, too?" Jim whispered in her ear as he tried to kiss her.

Rose moved aside and continued to undress him. "Behave yourself. You're in no condition for that right now. I could feel you shaking before we were halfway here."

"You get me home, and then you get mean," Jim said, teasing her.

"I wouldn't have to be mean if you'd cooperate. Now sit down so I can take your boots off."

Jim obediently sat on the bed and let her finish undressing

him. Then he lay down and pretended to be angry.

"I'm sorry if I hurt your feelings," Rose said as she tucked him in. "I just want you well."

Jim didn't look at her, so she leaned down to kiss him. He threw his left arm around her waist and effortlessly pulled her off her feet and over him, rolling toward her onto his left side. She gave a cry and landed on her back on the other side of the bed with him lying almost on top of her. He kissed her neck and started unbuttoning her dress. At first, she was so surprised she melted in his arms, but then she came to her senses and gently pushed him off.

"You're impossible!" she laughed, getting up from the bed.

"You're refusing comfort to a wounded man," Jim replied as he rolled onto his back and threw down the covers.

Still smiling, she looked at him and pulled the covers back up. "You'll just want it all the more later. You need to rest now."

"You've never tried to sleep like this," he said, taking her hand.

"I promise I'll make it worth the wait."

Jim shifted in the bed. "I'm getting harder at the thought."

"Good," she smiled again. "Then you'll make it worth *my* while." She started to walk away but turned back. "If I'm not here when you wake up, it's because I've gone to Mrs. Harraday's to get more of your things. Hank promised to help me carry them."

Jim nodded, closed his eyes, and tried to think of something other than the feel of Rose's body against him.

Rose walked toward her pedal-driven sewing machine. She had placed it next to the table on the side toward the fireplace so she could keep an eye on Jim while she sewed. She finished cutting and pinning the material and then sat down at the machine. Jim stirred at the sound and awoke. He watched her as she drove it with her foot, guiding the material with her hands, her face a beautiful picture of concentration. He dozed back off with the mechanical sound lulling him to sleep. He stirred when it stopped, and again when Rose left, but each time he went right back to sleep.

When Rose returned with Hank, who had carried Jim's extra weapons in their oilskin bag along with a few other bags of his belongings, they found Jim standing in the back doorway. He was gazing out at the field behind the house. Rose was relieved he had on a pair of the pants she'd made and an unbuttoned shirt. She motioned for Hank to set everything down as she approached her husband.

"Are you OK?" she asked, lightly touching his arm.

Jim nodded.

"Was it the dream?"

He nodded again.

Rose kissed his shoulder and then whispered. "Hank's here."

Jim turned and greeted his friend. Then he gazed at all the things around the big man's feet. "Did she make you carry all that?"

"I didn't mind. But I'll need a horse cart to get all of your ammunition here."

"The smith has one," Jim suggested.

Hank nodded, then smiled. "You must be feeling better. It's good to see you out of bed."

Jim nodded too as he walked over to his friend and offered him a chair at the table.

"I need to get back," Hank said. "I promised Sam I'd split some wood for him this afternoon, and after that I think Mrs. Harraday has some things she needs me to do, too."

"So since I'm laid up everyone is going to you?" Jim asked.

"I reckon," Hank replied with a laugh. "I don't mind, though. I offered to help both of them until you're back on your feet. Though I suppose even then you'll be too busy around here to do too much."

"That depends on her," Jim replied with a nod toward Rose, who was lighting the lamp on the bedside table.

"I plan to keep him busy," she remarked as she put the things away. "Won't you stay for a cup of tea at least?"

"No, ma'am," Hank replied. "But thank you, though."

"Some other time, then?" Rose asked him.

Hank nodded.

"The new guards working out OK?" Jim asked, eyeing his friend closely. He always worried about Hank when he couldn't ride with him.

"Yeah, they're OK. But they're no Jim Morgan." Hank smiled. "I'll be glad to get you back, Jimmy." He headed for the door.

"I'll be glad to get back, Captain," Jim replied, following Hank.

"You take care, now," Hank said as he stepped onto the

porch. He patted Jim's left shoulder, then turned, walked down the steps, and headed back the way he'd come.

Jim returned inside and stood the oilskin bag in the back corner by the bureau. Then he turned and stepped behind Rose, who was putting his clothes in the drawers. He kissed the back of her neck and she turned toward him.

"Aren't you hungry?" she asked.

Jim answered by kissing her mouth. He put his left arm around her and began unbuttoning her dress with his right. Then he pulled it off her shoulders, and would have let it fall to the floor if she hadn't caught it.

"Let me hang it up," she whispered.

Jim could hear the urgency in her voice and felt his body react. He followed her as she stepped to the wardrobe and draped her dress over one of the doors. He touched her and kissed her as she undressed. Then she turned to him wearing only her full-length slip. He led her around the foot of the bed toward the kitchen table. She stopped him before they reached it, untying his pants and pushing them down. He stepped out of them, then took her in his arms. She started to remove his shirt, but he took her hand to stop her. He backed her up against one of the four-by-four posts that ran the width of the house after the bedroom wall ended. Then he dropped to his knees and ducked under her garment. Rose groaned, reached over her head, and grabbed the post for support. Her moans soon became wails.

Jim heard something outside, raised her slip, and glanced toward the front window. He saw a man leaning on the porch railing apparently transfixed, watching as he worked to please his woman. Jim didn't see a weapon on the man, so he glared at the observer, turned back to Rose, and continued. He assumed the man would leave now that he had seen him.

Rose wailed even louder, and her hips began to pulse as her pleasure built and started to peak. Jim heard the man cough softly, but he knew Rose was close and would be damned if he'd stop now. Rose's wailing increased in pitch and volume until her body tensed, then shuddered. When she was done, he stood in front of her.

"We have an audience," he whispered in her ear.

"I don't care," she breathed.

"Neither do I," he said softly, touching her breast through

her slip, then taking her hand.

He grabbed his shotgun from under the bed and slung it over his shoulder. Then he tore off the blanket in his haste, threw it over his arm, and led her to the table. Rose had the fabric she was sewing spread over it, so she quickly set it aside. Jim spread the blanket, and helped her up. They were in front of the window now. Rose had her back to it, but Jim faced it, with their onlooker slightly to his left. He glared at the man and set his shotgun in a chair. Though the curtains were sheer, their folds prevented Jim from seeing the man's face distinctly.

There was a gap between the curtains, and from where he stood, the watcher could see Rose clearly. Other than a glance every now and then, he wasn't looking at Jim, and didn't realize the guard had seen him or that he had any weapon ready other than the one he was using to please his wife.

Jim didn't let their onlooker inhibit him. He was in his own house and had nothing of which to be ashamed. He leaned his body against Rose but didn't enter her, and she moaned as he rubbed against her.

"Do you like that?" he asked.

She nodded.

"Answer me, woman!" he said intensely. He knew she liked it when he called her that.

"Yes," she breathed.

"What?" he asked loudly.

"Yes!" she said, raising her voice to match his. "I like it when you're commanding," she whispered.

"Why?" he asked, also speaking softly.

"Because it's so masculine, I guess," she breathed.

"What do you want?" he asked, his voice almost harsh. Though the question seemed directed at Rose, Jim was looking out the window at their watcher.

"I want you!" she answered.

"What?"

"I want *you!*" she cried, and her back lifted off the table as she began to come again, stimulated by his touch.

Jim entered her and she screamed with pleasure. He pounded against her with all his strength as she wailed and her body tensed. He felt her tighten and the muscles inside of her pulse, but still he willed himself not to come. His body slammed into her and caused her to make sounds he'd never imagined a woman could make.

She enjoyed the motion as he strove against her. She could feel the strength of his hands as they held her hips and the tension of her inner muscles as they gripped and released, reacting to his every movement. She knew she was coming again and screamed with euphoric anticipation. She lifted her head, gripped his arms, and hollered with wild pleasure. Her hips pumped and thrust against him as she collided with him in a fierce frenzy of pure ecstasy. Her eyes rolled up. She fell back against the tabletop and lay frozen, her arms and legs spread wide, and came with an intensity she'd never imagined possible. She gasped for air, and her body tensed again.

Jim pushed against her, and his cry tore out of him as he came with a massive explosion deep inside of her. He continued to pulse against her as the sensation ebbed. Then he stood over her, his body dripping with sweat, his breathing hard. He gripped her hips in one last rapturous spasm, then pulled her to him and rested his head against her chest.

She ran her fingers through the hair on the back of his neck and felt his whiskers lightly scratch her skin. She kissed him gently. She was thankful she had such a man, a man who could deliver such pleasure, a man who was a force of nature all his own.

"I told you I'd make it worth the wait," she whispered.

Jim gazed at her. "That was the best so far," he said quietly.

"For me, too," she answered.

Jim moved slightly, left her body, and kissed her cheek.

"I'm going to step outside," he said softly, wanting both to confront their watcher and relieve himself.

Darkness had fallen, but since Rose had lit a light before they started, he knew anyone outside had been privy to all they'd done. He donned his pants again, opened the front door, and stepped out.

What Jim didn't know was that the man had been watching originally because the sheriff had asked someone to keep an eye on the guard. The man quickly walked away when he realized the couple inside had finished and that his watch was almost over. He shook his head because the sheriff had asked his best friend to take this shift, but his friend had a church function so he'd agreed to do it.

When he first heard Rose, he thought she was in pain. He didn't mean to pry, but he'd been unable to tear his eyes away from what he was seeing. He'd never imagined a woman could enjoy a good screw like that. He didn't want to be a gossip, but he had to talk to someone about what he'd witnessed. The sound the guard had made had practically stopped his heart. The next morning, he spoke to his best friend. Much to his alarm, by the afternoon the story was all over town about what Jim and Rose had done and how much she'd liked it.

The news caused most of the women to wonder if they were missing out on something, and the men to congregate wondering if there was something they didn't know. Many of them had never thought about doing what Jim had done initially to please Rose. Some of them even approached Sam with questions, relying on his discretion.

For the man who had seen them, his only relief was that no one had connected his name with the story. Everyone knew someone had watched them, but no one knew whom. The man lived in fear from then on that one day Jim would learn who had seen them and exact revenge, and the man knew Jim wasn't a man he wanted to cross.

"Was someone really out there?" Rose asked, stepping up behind Jim, having first put on her robe.

"I'm glad I kept my shirt on," Jim muttered. He'd just walked back from the far end of the porch and was standing in the doorway gazing out at the street looking for their watcher.

Rose gently touched his shoulders, then moved her hands down and squeezed his butt.

Jim turned to her, smiling, and pulled her close. "I'm glad you had something on, too, or I'd have to hunt the bastard down and kill him."

She laughed and swatted him lightly. Then she looked down and saw a bulge in his pants. "You're hard again!"

"Yeah, I am. You want to do it outside?"

"What?" she asked. "Didn't they already get enough of a show?"

"It's dark now," Jim answered. "No one will be able to see."

He stepped to the table and dropped his pants but kept his shirt on. Then he grabbed the blanket and his shotgun and, after making sure no one was on the street, led her outside. He leaned the shotgun against the house. Then he spread the blanket on the porch swing, sat, and took Rose onto his lap facing him. She slipped her legs under the lowest slat on the back of the swing as she slid onto him.

"This is nice," she said, as Jim began to swing them with his legs.

"You think you can be quiet?" he asked softly.

"I don't know. You afraid I'll draw attention?" she asked, nodding toward the shotgun.

He shook his head. He gazed at her in the soft light from the window and that thrown by the moon as it rose behind him, shining through the clouds. He kissed her, slipped his hand under her robe, and began to touch her. She sighed.

"I don't think I can come again," she said.

"We'll see."

She sighed again, and he felt her getting tighter.

Some people walked by. They could tell someone was on the porch swing, but they couldn't see them clearly. They didn't realize the people swinging weren't fully clothed, much less what they were doing, so they said hello and waved. Jim spoke and nodded, causing a man, his wife, and two children to turn and approach. Rose started to get down, but Jim stopped her. Then he grabbed the sides of the blanket and pulled them up around her. He didn't want anyone to see she was only wearing a robe.

"Now look what you've done," she whispered in Jim's ear as the people walked up.

He grinned in reply.

"You're incorrigible," Rose whispered.

The man introduced himself and his family.

"Pardon me for not getting up," Jim replied. "But I'm a little indisposed at the moment."

Rose had to choke down a laugh.

"Not a problem," said the man. Then he noticed the bandage on Jim's chest. "We heard you'd been hurt. Glad to see you're up and about."

"Thank you. It feels good to be up."

Rose pinched him, but he ignored her.

"I was surprised you folks moved in so fast," said the man's wife.

"I'm in all right." Jim replied with a smile at Rose. "Doctor's orders," he continued. "He thinks I need someone to keep an eye on me. I need a firm hand," he said as Rose gripped his arm in her pleasure.

"There's nothing like a woman for that," said the man with a laugh, and his wife shook her head at him, smiling.

"Can I swing, too?" asked the little boy.

"Not right now, son. I need to check the supports before I'll let children get on it," Jim said, hoping to discourage the child.

"What about me?" asked his younger sister. "I don't weigh much."

"Mr. Morgan said no," replied the mother.

The boy ran off the porch, his attention caught by a cricket chirping nearby. The little girl continued to stand beside her mother.

Jim could tell Rose was getting close so he increased the speed of his right hand, still concealed under the blanket, as he supported her back with his left.

"Are you cold?" the little girl asked Rose as she clutched the blanket.

"I'm fine," Rose said, trying to control her voice as she felt her body react to Jim's touch and the movement of the swing.

"Can you go higher?" the girl asked.

"We don't want to go too high," Jim replied. "We don't want to bump our heads on the roof or break anything off."

The girl laughed.

"That's fast enough isn't it?" Jim asked, looking at Rose, as he began to move his body slightly in rhythm to the swing.

Rose could feel herself beginning to come almost against her will.

Jim could tell, too, and began moving his hand even faster. Rose gasped, but no one noticed as Jim spoke to the man. "So do you have a garden?"

"Sure," the man replied with a smile.

"What did you put in?" Jim asked.

The man listed his crops as Jim pretended to listen.

"So what's coming now?" Jim asked the man, glancing at Rose.

"I'm still waiting on a few things," the man replied. "We haven't had much rain recently. Growing's been hard this year."

"That's not the only thing," Jim replied, looking at Rose.

"I hear you've had it bad here recently," the man remarked.

"It's that obvious?" Jim asked, gazing at the man as he felt Rose's body getting tighter around him.

"Well, yeah," the man replied. "Everybody's heard about you getting attacked." He glanced at the shotgun.

"I'll be better soon," Jim said. "Things are coming along nicely."

Rose gripped his arm with one hand as the other clutched the blanket. Jim felt her suddenly get so tight it caused him to catch his breath.

"Are you OK?" asked the woman.

"I think something just bit me," Jim replied.

"Where?" asked the man.

"On a leg," Jim answered.

"Are you swelling?" asked the woman, noticing for the first time that the man's feet were bare. She thought his legs might be as well but couldn't tell because of the blanket.

"A little, but it should go down soon. Nothing to worry about," Jim said.

Rose pinched his arm, but he just smiled at her.

The boy started a game of tag with his sister, and the children began chasing each other around the yard.

Rose came, clenching her mouth shut to keep from moaning.

"I hope you'll let us have you over for dinner," said the wife. "Then you'll get to try some of the vegetables we've grown in our garden."

"That would be nice," said Rose, taking over the conversation so Jim could enjoy himself. "I hope you'll let me bring something, though," she said as she began rubbing Jim under the blanket, moving her hand over the part of him that wasn't inside of her.

The boy ran behind the swing and gave it a push, causing Rose's hand to hit against Jim.

He grunted softly, but didn't let the blow distract him completely. "Don't stand back there, son," he said softly to the boy. "I can't see you, you might accidentally get hit, and it would hurt."

The boy ran off, racing his sister to the road.

"I'll only come if I can bring something, too," Rose said with a smile as she continued to touch her husband.

A moment later, Jim shut his eyes and came, gripping her hip under the blanket and gritting his teeth. Then he smiled, relieved not to have made a sound.

"That's very gracious of you," the wife replied. "We'll give you a few days to settle in and Mr. Morgan a chance to recover."

"That won't take long," Jim responded, still smiling at Rose. "We appreciate you folks stopping by." He began slowing the swing with his legs as the sensation faded. "Feel free to stop by any time. We'll probably be out here again soon, and I'll try to have it ready for the little ones next time."

"Thank you!" shouted the children as they ran toward home.

"Our pleasure!" Jim called in reply, waving as the family headed to their house on the next street.

The man and his wife bade them goodnight and followed their children, disappearing into the darkness.

"I was right," Rose said, gazing at him when the family had gone. "You *are* incorrigible!"

"But you liked it, didn't you?" he asked as he kissed her.

"Oh, yeah!" she breathed. "But you really are evil, you know."

He smiled.

She laughed as she got up and led him inside.

"What's so funny?" Jim asked as he slipped on his pants.

"I can't believe they didn't realize what you were talking about," she replied.

"Just a matter of context."

"We'll have to eat a cold supper because of you," Rose scolded playfully.

"It's not all my fault," Jim remarked as he followed her into the kitchen.

A few minutes later, they sat down to a simple supper of bread, cheese, and smoked ham. When they finished, Rose insisted Jim get in bed and rest while she did the dishes. Jim sat on the bed and watched her for a few minutes, but he was tired so he lay back and relaxed. He'd never dreamed life could be so good. He heard Rose filling the tub, sat up, and watched her undress and step into the water.

"Need any help?" he asked.

"I just wanted to rinse off a little," she replied as she twisted her hair and secured it with two long combs to the top of her head.

Jim got up, took a chair from the table, and set it beside the tub where he could sit and watch her. When she was done, he handed her a towel. Then he stripped and stepped into the tub, not bothering to change the water. He didn't sit down because he needed to keep the stitches dry. Rose handed him a cloth. He washed as best he could, and Rose helped him rinse.

"We both should get some sleep," she suggested, brushing her hair and wrestling with tangles while Jim dried off.

He nodded, stepping to her, and she looked up in surprise as he took the brush from her hand. She turned away from him and was even more surprised by his care and gentleness as he held the hair close to her head with one hand while he drew the brush through the tangles with the other. Thereby, he spared her the pain of any tugging or pulling. Also, rather than forcing the brush through the hair as she had been doing, he carefully worked it down, loosening tangles with his fingers before pulling the brush through them.

"Where did you learn to do this?" she asked.

"Horses need their tails brushed, and if you hurt them it's a good way to get kicked," he replied, pulling all of her hair back and brushing it to make sure all of the tangles were gone. Then he held the brush out to her.

"Thank you," she said, smiling as she took the brush. "I doubt most men help their wives with their hair."

"I like your hair, so I don't mind helping you take care of it."

She glanced down and expected to see that he needed her again, but he wasn't aroused.

He pretended not to notice the direction of her interest as he turned to empty the tub. He knew his own apparent lack of interest was due to the pain in his right shoulder and didn't want to admit that just brushing his wife's hair, in addition to their earlier activities, had him spent.

Rose helped with the tub, and he didn't argue with her. Then he followed her into the bedroom, lay down, and covered up as she started to put on her nightgown.

"You're not going to wear that, are you?" he asked.

"I'll leave it off if you promise to go right to sleep," she replied with a smile.

Jim nodded, and she climbed into bed next to him.

"Our first night together in our house," she whispered as she laid her head on his left shoulder. Then she thought about earlier. "I hope you only ever shout at me during sex."

"I don't tend to shout in anger," Jim replied softly.

"No, you just get quiet and seethe I bet," she smiled.

Jim kissed her.

"Just promise me that you'll tell me if I ever do anything to displease you," she said.

"I will," he promised. "And I hope you'll do the same."

She nodded.

Jim rubbed her arm with his hand, ignoring the effect her closeness had on his body in spite of the pain, and went to sleep. He slept straight through the night without having any nightmares. When he woke, Rose was already awake and at the stove frying eggs for their breakfast. She put their plates on a tray and carried them to the bed.

"Should I expect this all the time?" he asked.

"Only when you're hurt."

After breakfast, Rose insisted Jim rest while she continued to work on Sarah's dress. She told him Sarah and Olivia would be over that afternoon for Sarah to try it on, so Jim left her alone to do her work. He dozed off and was still asleep when Rose began to fix their lunch. She ate and brought Jim a plate. She said his name softly but he didn't stir, so she said it louder. His eyelids fluttered and opened but shut again immediately as the pain pierced his consciousness.

"I'm sorry to wake you," she said, "but I thought you should eat something and put some clothes on before Sarah and Olivia arrive."

Jim looked at her and nodded.

Rose helped him sit up, and he managed to eat a little. She kissed him, trying to encourage him to eat more, but Jim threw the covers off to reveal his body. She saw he needed her, so she began to touch him. Then she realized she needed him, too. While she stripped, he slipped on a shirt, leaving it open.

"When will they be here?" Jim asked.

"In an hour or so."

They spent the time pleasing each other.

"I better get dressed," she said when they were done. She climbed off him. "You should put something on, too. You'll have to go outside when they get here so Sarah can put the dress on."

Jim nodded. He put on pants and still didn't bother to button the shirt. Then Rose slipped the sling over his head and settled his right arm into it.

"Doctor's orders," she reminded him as Jim scowled. "You want to get better, don't you?"

He nodded. "I just hate wearing this thing."

"I know," she said, kissing him.

Jim walked to the shelf next to the bed on Rose's side, which she also used as a night table. He took a book and tucked it under his right arm. Then he grabbed a kitchen chair and headed toward the back door. Rose held the door for him while he set the chair on the porch.

"I'll get you some water," she said as she disappeared back into the house. "What are you reading?" she asked when she returned with the glass.

"*Moby-Dick*, by Herman Melville."

"Is it good?"

"Yes. I started it over a year ago but never finished it."

"What's it about?" she asked.

"Obsession," he replied.

She looked confused.

"On the surface, it's about whaling," Jim explained. "The captain is determined to kill the whale that maimed him. I have a feeling the whale wins."

Rose laughed. Then she heard a knock on their front door. "I'll leave this open in case you need anything," she said and walked back inside.

Jim heard Olivia's voice and the sound of Sarah laughing. Then he heard running footsteps coming toward him as Sarah popped out the back door. He could hear Olivia calling after her, but Sarah ran up to him.

"How are you feeling?" the child asked, smiling.

"Better now," he replied, gazing at her.

Sarah laughed, then turned as her mother called again. "I have to go try my dress on. Will you come see?"

"If they'll let me."

Sarah laughed again and ran back inside.

A few moments later, Ted came walking around the side of the house.

"There you are," he said as he strolled up to where Jim sat.

"Rose told me you were out here. They're being very conspira-
torial in there," he added with a smile.

"Have a seat," Jim offered, starting to rise.

"No thanks. You need to rest. I hope you're feeling better."

"Some. I could probably work now if you need me."

"We always need you," Ted replied.

"I can shoot with my left hand," Jim offered. Then he noticed
Ted looking at the sling. "I can use my right arm, but Sam has
Rose convinced I need this thing."

"Like I promised, I wouldn't put you on the stage this close
to your wedding, anyway." Then he paused, wanting to tell Jim
about the story going around town but not wanting to upset
him. "I'm not sure how to put this, but—"

"What?"

"It's all over town about what you and Rose did last night."

"What are they saying?" Jim asked, thinking the couple had
figured out what was happening on the porch swing.

"Well, someone saw you two, and well—" Ted shook his head
and cleared his throat. "I'm not married yet, so I hesitate to say
anything, but as your friend, I thought you'd want to know."

"Know what?"

Ted looked at Jim in disbelief. "You don't know what I'm
talking about? Did you two do something else unusual last
night?"

"I pleased my wife," Jim responded with a hint of anger in his
voice, his eyes starting to smolder. "Is that unusual?"

"The way you did it was." Ted thought about mentioning
what people were saying about the cry Jim supposedly made but
decided against it.

Jim shook his head slightly, still not fully understanding.

"From what I've heard, and again, I'm not married so I'm no
judge of this sort of thing, but apparently most men don't put
their mouth where you did," Ted concluded, blushing.

"Well, that's too bad for their wives, then," Jim remarked.
"You said it's all over town?"

Ted nodded.

"I knew someone was watching us," Jim muttered. "I guess
he couldn't find something better to do with his mouth than talk
about us. Any idea who it was?"

"No one knows that part."

"It's not like we wanted it that way," Jim replied.

"Might I suggest you put something heavier over the windows?"

"I like being able to see outside. I don't like heavy curtains."

"Unfortunately, people can see in as well."

"We're at least twenty-five yards from the nearest house," Jim said. "I don't know what that person was doing out there last night. I was in my house with my woman. I don't have anything to be embarrassed about."

"A friend of mine said that often some of the neighbors get together in the evening and take a walk."

"Right by my house, I guess."

Ted nodded.

"Then they'll probably get another show," Jim remarked. "I'm not going to stop enjoying my wife because of the neighbors."

"If I looked like you I wouldn't care either, but sometimes they take their children," commented Ted, looking worried.

"The man watching us didn't have any with him last night, and people can teach their kids not to look in people's windows."

Ted nodded again. "Not meaning to pry, but what about the bed?"

Jim looked at him questioningly.

"It has covers," Ted suggested.

"We have to be careful how we do it right now," Jim replied, motioning to the sling. "It was easier to use the table."

Ted blushed.

"Sorry if I embarrassed you," Jim added.

Ted shook his head. "Anyway, that's not what I wanted to talk to you about. My future in-laws will be traveling to St. Louis, and Sylvia and I plan to meet them there."

"What about Laura?" Jim asked, referring to Sylvia's child.

"She's going to stay with Martha and Sam."

"And you want me to guard the stage."

Ted nodded. Jim was the best man he had, and his entire future family would be in that coach. "But I want you to ride inside."

"Why?" Jim asked.

"You've hardly healed yet, and it'll be safer."

"Ted, my job is guarding the stage, and that's what I'll do," Jim stated. "From the roof," he added.

Ted nodded slowly. He hadn't heard from his superiors yet, and he hoped they were giving serious consideration to his request.

"How long will we be in the city?" Jim asked.

"A little over a week. Maybe longer."

Jim nodded. "There's an errand I need to do while I'm there. I haven't gotten Rose an engagement ring yet."

"What about a wedding ring?"

"She's going to use her mother's."

"Rose could come too if you'd like," Ted offered.

"Thank you. I'll talk to her about it."

"Of course, there's not much privacy in the home stations," Ted reminded him, smiling.

"Don't worry, we won't embarrass you," Jim promised.

"I meant no offense."

"None taken. We'll be discreet. Last night wasn't something I planned."

"Well, I don't think you'll find anyone I've talked to looking in," commented Ted. "I got the impression the wives aren't happy that their husbands don't do whatever it was you did to Rose."

"That's too bad." Then, in answer to Ted's look, Jim added, "Are you wanting me to tell you about it?"

"Well," Ted said hesitantly, "I'd appreciate some pointers, maybe. I've always been so busy with work I haven't had much time for women."

"Don't feel bad. Rose is the first and only woman I've ever been with."

"But you seem to know what you're doing," said Ted. "I admit, I don't."

"But you and Sylvia have been engaged for almost two years," Jim commented.

"I'm a gentleman!"

"I am too, but a man has his limits," Jim stated, remembering taking Rose into the tack room.

Ted looked down in embarrassment.

"I meant no offense," Jim said.

Ted nodded to show he took none.

Jim thought for a moment. "Do you want me to tell you some things now, or wait until it's closer to your wedding?"

Now it was Ted's turn to think. "Sylvia says that there are things we can do before we're married, but I'm afraid to try anything. I don't want her to be disappointed. She seems to be under the impression that I'm a man of the world or something."

Jim put down his book and stood. "Why don't we take a walk?" he suggested.

"I thought you needed to rest."

"I've been resting all day, and we won't go far." Jim stepped off the porch, and Ted followed him.

As they headed out into the field behind his house, Jim explained what he did to please Rose, and Ted listened attentively.

"I don't know if I can do that," Ted said when Jim was through.

"Then you better have strong hands," Jim replied with a grin.

Ted looked worried.

"Trust me," Jim stated, reading the expression on the other man's face. "When you're alone with her and she has her clothes off, you won't think about it."

"I've never seen a woman fully naked," Ted remarked softly.

"Well, from what you've said, it sounds like Sylvia would be happy to remedy that situation."

"I don't want her to think that I don't respect her."

"You're engaged to her. If you do what she wants and make her happy, she'll know that you respect her. Just don't go further than she wants to, and remember to ask her what she wants and give it to her. If she doesn't know, then try something and see how she reacts. What I did last night surprised Rose at first, she wouldn't have dreamed of asking me to do that. Now she enjoys the hell out of it every time."

Ted nodded. "Thank you," he said, shaking Jim's left hand as they returned to the house.

"When do we need to leave for St. Louis?" Jim asked.

"Probably in about four weeks. I want you better before I tell them to leave Pennsylvania."

"Don't let me hold up your plans. I'll be ready as soon as you need me."

Ted thanked him and left without going into the house, and Jim returned to the chair and started reading again.

A little while later, Rose came out onto the porch and asked him if he'd like to see Sarah's dress. Jim followed her inside, and found Sarah standing on a chair in a forest-green dress with off-white trim.

"Do you like it?" Rose asked him.

Jim nodded.

"Do I look like a princess?" Sarah asked.

"Yes," Jim answered. "A beautiful princess."

Sarah laughed.

"Your wife is a good seamstress!" commented Olivia, smiling. She had the dress she planned to wear laid across the table.

"Luckily, the two colors complement each other," said Rose, holding a piece of the green fabric next to Olivia's blue gown. "Do you really like the dress?"

"It's beautiful," Jim answered. "I can't believe you made it so fast."

"I can't either," added Olivia.

"I've been working on it for over two weeks," Rose laughed. "Usually I can make a dress in two days."

"But you've had to take care of Jim," Sarah said.

Rose nodded, still smiling.

"And it fits Sarah perfectly," Olivia commented.

Sarah slowly turned all the way around so Jim could see the back of the dress as well.

"And yours is going to be exactly like it?" he asked.

"Not exactly," Rose answered. "Mine has a lower neckline," she said, glancing at the partially made garment folded and lying in the seat of one of the kitchen chairs. "I'm thinking about doing something a little different with the sleeves, too."

"Like what?" Sarah asked.

"Well, I may make them shorter so I can wear long gloves. But I haven't decided yet."

"Will I really get to toss flowers at the people?" Sarah asked.

"You'll sprinkle flower petals on the aisle, not the people," Olivia informed her.

"Oh," Sarah responded.

"That reminds me," said Olivia. "I talked to the woman about the flowers, and she promises that she'll have some roses still blooming in the hothouse, though they may not all be the same color."

"Good!" Rose said, smiling. "I think different colors will be nice."

"Will I be throwing rose petals?" Sarah asked.

"Sprinkling them," Olivia corrected her. "If there are enough. Otherwise, we may have to gather some wildflowers to mix in."

"I know where some are probably still blooming," Jim offered. He knew the surrounding area well from his rides on Ness.

"We may have to use them," Rose said. "But we'll use roses if we can get them."

"She should have enough," Olivia assured her.

"At least some good is coming from that hothouse," Jim commented. Then he added, when Rose and Olivia each gave him a questioning look, "I don't mind people having money, but some of the pieces were on my stage, along with the man sent to put it together. The glass was sent on a special wagon, thank goodness."

"What was wrong with that?" Rose asked.

"It was heavy, and Hank and I helped unload the glass when it got here, too," Jim continued, "with the little weasel of a man they sent fussing at us the whole time. Then it turned out he didn't know how to read the plans, so I ended up having to tell him how to put it together."

Rose walked up to him and put her arms around his neck with a smile. "And because of that I get to have roses for my wedding."

Jim bent and kissed her. "Like I said, at least some good came out of it."

Then Rose asked Jim to step back outside so Sarah could change clothes. After she was done, Sarah ran out onto the back porch to say goodbye to Jim. Then she bounced back through the house to join her mother, who was waiting by the front door. Jim followed her inside, and he and Rose thanked them as they walked away.

"What did Ted want?" asked Rose after she and Jim were alone. She began adjusting the hem on Sarah's dress.

"He just needed to talk to me about a job. His in-laws will be traveling by train to St. Louis, and he wants me on the stage that'll bring them here. He said you could come, too," Jim mentioned as he came up behind her, put his hands on her shoulders, and leaned over her. He watched her as she sewed and tried to look down her dress. "We'll be in the city for a few days, and it could be a honeymoon for us."

Rose got an odd look on her face, but Jim couldn't see it. "I'll think about it," she replied. "I have a lot to do here."

"This won't be for a few weeks, but you don't have to go if you don't want to. It'll mean a long ride on the stage each way, and that isn't all that pleasant."

"Like I said, I'll think about it," Rose promised. "Oh, Olivia said Martha wanted you to know that your friend will be arriving on the afternoon stage tomorrow."

"Good. I was expecting Sam to tell me when she was due. I figure he'll check on me today to make sure I'm following orders."

Just then, they heard the sound of the doctor's footsteps as he climbed the stairs to the porch.

"Speak of the Devil," Rose said with a smile.

"I'll talk to him outside so we don't disturb you," Jim replied. He walked to the door and opened it before Sam could knock. "I have to stop to fix supper, anyway."

"Don't worry about it. I'll fix it."

"Really?" Rose asked, looking up from her work.

Jim nodded and stepped outside.

"Well, I'm glad to see you're still wearing the sling," commented Sam as Jim closed the door behind him.

"Rose makes me." He motioned for Sam to follow him, and they walked around to the back of the house. Jim removed his shirt with Sam's help. Then he sat in the chair he'd used earlier.

The doctor cut loose the bandage and examined the wounds. He found even the most recent ones almost healed. Sam then removed the stitches he hadn't yet taken out before sending Jim home. The doctor examined the wounds closely before bandaging Jim's chest again and helping him slip his shirt back on.

"I want to keep the bandage on you for another week," Sam said. "You're still oozing, probably because you haven't been as quiet as you should have been. Rose must be taking good care of you, though. They're healing quickly in spite of you. Though I hear you took good care of her last night," remarked Sam with a smile.

"Where'd you hear about that?" Jim asked.

"I expect the whole town's heard about it by now."

Jim shook his head. "That's what Ted said."

"From what I hear, the women are hoping their husbands

will learn a thing or two, and that you won't hang winter curtains up anytime soon."

Jim shook his head again.

"You should be proud, my boy," Sam said, still smiling. "You've started something. I've had at least a dozen men come to my office today asking if what you did is OK and healthy."

"What did you tell them?"

"That there's nothing wrong with it as long as things are clean, and it's fine for their wives to reciprocate. You have no idea how important this could be."

Jim looked at him, confused.

"My father was a physician," Sam explained. "He died while I was still in medical school."

"I'm sorry," Jim said. He started to stand, offering the doctor the chair.

Sam shook his head and leaned on the porch railing as he continued. "He kept a journal. As soon as I expressed an interest in medicine, he told me he wanted me to read it before I started practicing. The day after his funeral, I went into his study and sat in his chair. I guess I wanted to feel close to him. He hadn't been ill long, so his death was a bit of a shock."

Jim nodded. He noticed someone walking in the woods on the far side of the field behind his house.

As he spoke about his father, Sam watched Jim's reaction. He wondered if the young man knew anything about his own. Other than attentive interest, Sam didn't notice any telling emotion on Jim's face.

"I knew where he kept his journal," Sam continued. "I remember lifting it as though it was holy. I'd always wondered what was inside. What observations he'd made. I'd been assisting him since I was twelve, and to this day I feel I learned more from him than I did in medical school."

Jim nodded again to encourage his friend to continue, still glancing behind the doctor at the figure in the woods. No one had ever told him a story before, and he found himself curious about what was going to happen and what had prompted Sam to begin.

"I knew from the date on the first page," Sam said, "that it was written during his first year of practice. As I read, I realized he might have other entries from that time in other journals, because this one dealt solely with one patient. He called her Mrs. H."

"Her initial?" Jim asked.

Sam shook his head. "You have to understand that he'd gone back to his hometown to practice. Mrs. H. was a woman about his age, and, apparently, they had grown up together. He hadn't even met my mother yet and, other than what he'd learned in medical school, knew nothing about women. Also, based on something he said I think he might have been sweet on this girl at one point but never courted her."

Jim nodded to show he understood.

"Mrs. H. was one of my father's first patients. She came to him because she was agitated and having trouble sleeping. After asking her a few questions, my father determined the nature of her problem. She was suffering from female hysteria. Are you familiar with the term?"

"I've heard it mentioned," Jim replied. "But I don't know anything about it."

"It's a problem that's unfortunately all too common. Some physicians use it as a catch-all, but the true condition results when a woman is not satisfied by her husband."

Jim thought for a moment and watched the man in the woods as he considered Sam's words. Then he met the doctor's gaze. "You mean in bed."

Sam nodded. "It's a shame that our society puts so much emphasis on female purity that many women believe they shouldn't enjoy copulation. And their husbands feel no responsibility to ensure their enjoyment."

"So what can a doctor do?" Jim asked. "Talk to their husbands?"

Sam shook his head. "The treatment, according to common practice and the medical books, is for the physician to manually stimulate the woman until she reaches a state of paroxysm."

Jim gazed at him in disbelief. "You're joking."

Sam shook his head.

"So you rub her until she comes," Jim stated, to his credit not smiling.

Sam nodded.

"Women pay you to do that?"

Sam nodded again. "It's the part of the job I like the least. It's very tedious and tiring. If you get too bored it takes longer, and if you get too interested you could get yourself shot."

"Do you have many women who need this?"

"More than you might think."

"No wonder you're exhausted by the end of the day," Jim replied, again without smiling.

The doctor nodded.

"So is that what your father did for Mrs. H?" Jim asked.

"Unfortunately, no," the doctor replied. "Remember, he'd just opened his practice. He didn't feel comfortable performing such a procedure, so he referred her to an older physician in a neighboring town."

"So he took care of her," said Jim, splitting his gaze between the doctor and the man walking slowly just inside the woods. Jim speculated that the man probably didn't realize he could see him.

"From what my father wrote, she went to see the other doctor and discussed the procedure but refused to let him treat her."

"Why?"

"We'll never know. My father didn't see her for a few weeks and assumed she was receiving treatment. It wasn't until she came to see him again that he found out she was still suffering. On this visit, she didn't tell him why she'd refused treatment from the other doctor, but she asked him to help her. He took her into the treatment room and told her to remove any restrictive clothing, as well as her undergarments, and promised to return in a few minutes."

Jim gazed at the doctor, though still aware of the man standing in the woods.

"Apparently, one of his professors in medical school told him the same thing one of mine told me and my fellow students—though not in class," Sam said, settling more comfortably on the porch rail. "Though the term orgasm was never used in reference to the treatment for hysteria, all of us knew that was what the woman needed. So one of my professors told us that unless we were married and had taken care of things with the wife we should take care of ourselves before entering the room. He said that when he was a young and unmarried doctor, he took care of it every morning. He told us it was better to avoid an uncomfortable situation rather than create one."

Jim nodded.

"So while she readied herself," Sam continued, "my father stepped into his private office and took things into his own hands, so to speak. He went back into the treatment room and found her lying on the table wearing only her slip. He reached under and as soon as he touched her, she sighed, and to his surprise, he felt himself becoming aroused. Whether she sensed his discomfort or her modesty felt compromised, he didn't know, but after only a minute or two she asked him to stop."

"Did he?" Jim asked, still eyeing the man in the woods, who had moved closer to just beyond the tree line.

"Of course he did," Sam replied.

"He didn't try to convince her to let him help her?"

"There was a discussion during which she inquired if there was a surgical procedure that would rid her of the source of her agitation," Sam replied, his voice tense.

"Is there such a thing?" Jim asked.

Sam noticed the young man shuddered at the question.

"My father informed her that a part of her body could be removed, but that it wouldn't solve the problem, only make calming it impossible. He mentioned in the journal, though this wasn't part of their conversation, that he'd read about a practice followed in other parts of the world where the women willingly undergo such a procedure, many with seemingly no ill effects. Or none that they will admit. However, in his opinion, and mine as well, it is barbaric, and most likely the result of feminine desperation."

"So she didn't have that done," Jim stated with dread in his voice.

Sam shook his head. "She insisted on leaving, so my father stepped out of the room so she could dress. Before he let her leave, he insisted she make another appointment so they could try again. He explained that her condition wouldn't go away on its own. Which she probably knew, since she'd been married almost seven years."

Jim nodded. The figure in the woods had disappeared. He had a feeling the man was watching him, but convinced himself the man was either taking a walk or hunting and tried to think no more of it.

"The morning of the appointment, she sent my father a note

informing him she had a pressing engagement but was feeling better. When she didn't return, he hoped she'd found her own solution, but didn't feel comfortable visiting her at her residence. He didn't want to cause her any embarrassment, and, since she had young children, treating her at her home would have been awkward at best."

"So was she getting treatment?" Jim asked.

"Well, he notes that he passed her on the street and felt gratified that she seemed more composed, but he didn't question her. Though he wrote in the margin that he wished he had."

"Why?"

"A few weeks later, she was dead."

"What happened?" Jim asked.

"She fell from some nearby cliffs into the river. Her body was never found."

"She fell?" Jim asked, his brow wrinkling in disbelief.

"My father ruled the death accidental. Out of respect for the family he didn't change that ruling, even after he received a letter from her two days later."

"She sent it before she jumped," Jim stated softly.

Sam gave a nod, and drew an envelope from his breast pocket. "Would you like me to read it?"

Jim nodded.

"'My dearest Dr. Thorne,'" Sam began. "'I remember when we used to call you Winnie.' My father's name was Winston," Sam explained. Then he continued. "'I'm writing to tell you that I know you have done your best to help me. Also, I want you to know that I did find help on my own, and I trust that you will keep all details about this subject confidential, as you always have.

"'I am not trying to burden you but, due to our previous association before you became a doctor, an association which made my final visit to your office so painfully uncomfortable for us both, I feel I owe you, and only you, an explanation for my seemingly irrational action.

"'A few months ago, as I was taking a walk long after dark, which was my want after pleasing my husband (or rather after he pleased himself using my person), I found myself strolling through an unfamiliar neighborhood. I always hoped the cool wind on my face would cool the dreadful, heated, longings in other parts of my body, but, as per usual, it did not. I was weary of the constant ache. I tried to feel nothing as my husband ground against me. I longed to be numb to the sensation building and building but never reaching a fruition I knew in my soul must exist. For why building, if only always to end in naught?

"'As I stood in the shadows, I saw a woman exit one of the residences a short distance from where I watched. I could tell from her dress she was older than I, and, as she passed, she glanced in my direction. I don't know what prompted her, whether it was something about my person or something unseen, one tortured soul recognizing another, but she turned and spoke to me. There was not enough light for me to see her face, I could pass her in the bright of day and not know her, and neither her me. She spoke to me. "He's free now. Don't be shy, let him help you. Do you have your card?"

"'When I didn't answer, she gave me hers, assuring me she had another. She then went on her way. I had to cross the street to read the card. There were no lights on this side. The card offered the services of someone named "Mason," who called himself "a help to women" and promised the highest level of discretion, all for less than a visit to the physician. I was hesitant but also curious, so I crossed back to the black side of the street and approached the house from which the woman had exited. The number, as best I could see in the nearly total darkness, matched that printed on the card.

"'A boy answered my knock but didn't raise his eyes farther than to look at the card. The house was dimly lit, and the boy showed me into a room, also dimly lit. The boy assured me his master would be with me shortly and told me to help myself to anything in the room I desired. In the room were a bed, what looked to be a table covered with sheets and a pillow (like a bed but shorter), a fireplace covered by a heavy screen to allow heat but very little light, and a dressing screen in one corner. There was also another table, on which was a tray holding various bottles and a selection of sweets. Upon closer examination of the bottles, I found wine, sherry, whiskey, and even champagne, as well as a pitcher of water. I was about to pour myself a glass of the latter when there was a soft knock on the door and a man entered.

"'As in the hallway outside, the light was too dim to reveal his features clearly enough for later recognition, and I trusted that this assured my anonymity as well. He introduced himself as Mason, but, before I could respond, he told me not to use my real name. I really don't remember what I called myself that first time. Then he poured me a glass of sherry, and, though I protested mildly, he encouraged me to take a little to soothe my nerves. Then he asked me the nature of my complaint. I wasn't sure how to reply, so he asked if I had seen a physician. I replied in the affirmative, and he asked if I had been diagnosed with hysterics. I lowered my eyes. He stepped behind me and gently caressed my shoulders as he assured me he could help me.

"'I asked him what assurance I had that he wouldn't take advantage. He seemed genuinely surprised and asked how I had come by his card, since he supposed I had been referred. I informed him as to what had happened on the street. He nodded and gave me a brief history of himself. He had been a medical doctor. He told me that even in medical school he had noticed most physicians didn't take the complaints of women seriously. When he started practicing, he did his best to special- ize in treating women, though not only for hysterics. He said he found the term often overused by lazy physicians who found it easier to make that diagnosis than search for the true cause of a woman's complaint. Because of this specialization, he was unprepared when there was some sort of accident in the street outside his office. A child was hurt, and he told me with great regret that he had been unable to save her. At the insistence of the parents, who apparently were rather well off, there was an inquiry, and he was found to have been negligent. His license was revoked. He tried to establish himself in a different career but many of his female patients still insisted on seeing him, so he began surreptitiously treating them after dark. When he quit that town and arrived here, it was only natural for him to con- tinue the practice.

"'I asked what had brought him to our town, since ours is one of the smallest in the area. His answer was "detachment." Though cryptic, I heard grief in his voice, and questioned him no further.

"'He suggested I step behind the screen, remove my clothing, and don a gown hanging from a hook. He mentioned that the dim light was not only to protect my identity but my modesty as well, so I obeyed while Mason stepped out of the room. The gown was similar to a sleeping garment, except it buttoned up the front. Also behind the screen were a dressing table and chair, a pitcher, basin, towel, and a chamber pot.

"'I donned the gown and stepped back out. A moment later, Mason knocked again, this time waiting until I answered before entering. On his first appearance, he had been wearing a gentleman's casual coat and scarf. When he returned, these he had removed, and entered in his shirtsleeves, which he had rolled up. He asked if I preferred the bed or the table. Seeing my hesitation, he suggested the table. I lay back, pulling the sheet over me. He suggested I close my eyes. I obeyed, and soon felt his hands on my arms. He told me to concentrate only on his touch.

"'After caressing my arms, he moved to my legs, but only went a little higher than my knees. Then he lightly touched my stomach through the gown and asked if he might move his hands either up or down. I nodded, so he proceeded slowly to move them up my body, though still over the gown. He stopped just below my breasts. Then he moved down, until finally touching me lightly through the gown on the very area in which was the source of my discomfort. He asked if he could touch me directly so as to complete the treatment. I nodded. I felt as though to refuse would have been like a starving person refusing meat. As he began, I tensed, not wanting to experience the dreadful heartache when the sensation stopped. To my surprise, he noticed, and assured me he would not stop until asked. He also assured me he understood the horrible, dreadful longing I had been enduring for so long, and he promised to encourage the sensation to its end.

"'I have no idea how long it took, but with his expert ministrations and encouragement I finally experienced the wonderful conclusion to the building. He wasn't satisfied after the first, insisted on continuing, and I experienced a level of enjoyment I never could have dreamed existed. When he was through, I lay on the table in a state of peaceful satisfaction for the first time in my life, and was thankful you had discouraged me from any sort of surgical procedure. The joy I experienced was so great, it could only be a gift from our Heavenly Father, intended to be shared by husband and wife if only the husband wasn't so selfish as to keep all the pleasure for himself.

"'Mason left the room. I dressed and inquired what I owed when the boy came to show me out. It was much less than I expected, and I was relieved I'd had the presence of mind to bring my purse. I returned home, climbed into bed with my sleeping husband, and slept soundly for the first time in years. I continued to see Mason regularly and found contentment for the first time.

"'Then one night, as my husband again began to please himself, I suggested he try to please me as well. He looked horrified. I asked him to lie on his back, and he reluctantly obeyed, apparently not realizing what I had in mind. When he did, he grabbed my arms before I could position myself over him. I begged him to please me. He reminded me that I was a woman, and therefore it wasn't right for me to enjoy it. I told him it wasn't right for him to never please me. He suggested I see the pastor. I informed him I had and that all the pastor had suggested was that I pray. Prayer helped calm my nerves during the day, but it did nothing to help me as he pleased himself at my expense at night. I told him I had also seen a physician, but he too had been unable to help me. (Forgive me, Dr. Thorne, I know you did your best.) Though I knew it would anger and hurt him, I thought it best to be honest. I told him about my visits to Mason. I tried to explain to him why I had gone, and that it was no different than seeing a physician for the same treatment. My husband called me a whore and sent me from his bed. I hoped he would eventually forgive me.

"'I have endured seven years of heartache and torture, and these last few weeks I have endured my husband's disapproval as well. Tonight, he came to my bed. I took pity on him, but, yet again, he only pleased himself. I begged him to consider my wants as well, but he angrily told me to go to Mason if I wanted satisfaction. I asked him if he released me, and he nodded, then returned to his bed.

"'I have been writing this letter while waiting for him to go to sleep. I hear him snoring now, so I will see Mason yet again. My visits to him have been my only solace. He has always behaved as a gentleman, never taking advantage or asking anything but monetary reimbursement. Though, at times I have sensed more than a clinical interest. We have met on more than one occasion for lunch, and we recently met for dinner one evening when my husband was out of town. He has become more to me than a means for my enjoyment. He has held me when I cried, listened to my complaints, and calmed me with his care.

"'I recently learned he came here because his wife had died and he needed an unfamiliar setting. Tonight I intend to offer that which he would never request. I want finally to experience the act of marriage as it was intended, to the mutual benefit of both parties. If this truly makes me a whore, then so be it. I truly loved my husband when we married, but his selfishness, not just in the bedroom, has killed any affection I once had. I know I may be mistaken, but I feel my betrayal will be judged less harshly than his.

"'I hope that one day my children will be able to forgive me as well. How can I teach them to be honest if I am living a lie? I would continue, try to endure, but the lack of respect my husband has shown me recently has begun to affect their behavior. I prefer to leave them while some of my dignity remains intact rather than have them come to despise me as well. Since he insists they listen and obey him, but cares not if they show me the same respect, their existence will be less confusing in my absence.

"'Again, thank you, Dr. Thorne. I hope you, above all, will not think any the less of me for my action, and I hope God will have pity on this, one of his most imperfect creatures. Lovingly, Your friend....'"

Sam folded the letter and put it back in his pocket.

"Then she killed herself," Jim said softly.

"Her scarf was found at the top of the cliff, but, like I said, her body was never recovered."

Jim thought for a moment, then nodded slowly. "And you said you treat a lot of women for the same thing?"

The doctor nodded. "Mainly widows and spinsters out here. In the city, I even treated nuns. Though, I think the most tragic cases anywhere are the married women. I saw more of them in the city, where the men have more money. It seems the wealthier a man is, the less considerate he is of his wife. Out here, probably because they often have to work together to survive, it has been my impression that most husbands really want to please their wives. They just may not know how."

"That's a shame," Jim said.

"Yes, it is."

"So why not talk to their husbands?"

"My father tried that. From what I read in his journals, he found it effective. That is, until one young husband decided to discuss my father's advice with an extremely zealous preacher."

"What happened?" Jim asked.

"We were given twenty-four hours to get out of town or they'd burn our house down with my father, mother, brother, sister, and I in it."

Jim gazed at him in disbelief.

"My father never went directly to the husbands again," Sam explained. "Instead, he did what Martha and I do now: get to know the couple and thereby offer advice as friends, not professionals."

"Any idea what happened to the woman's children?" Jim asked.

"I was curious, too," Sam replied. "I stayed at home for a few weeks after the funeral, but, still having some time before I needed to be back at school, I went to the town. I figured out Mrs. H's real name from my father's records and found out the family still lived there. I didn't want to just knock on the door and introduce myself, not knowing what kind of reception I would receive, so I stood across the street and tried to discreetly watch the house. I hadn't been there long when the most captivating young woman I'd ever seen walked out the front gate. She paid me no mind, so I followed her at a distance. I did the same thing for the rest of the week."

"Did you ever speak to her?" Jim asked.

"Eventually."

"What happened?"

"I married her," Sam replied with a smile.

"Did you ever tell her why you were there?"

Sam nodded. "I waited until I'd courted her for a while. I wanted her to know before I asked her to marry me."

"What about Martha's father? Did he ever remarry or learn the truth?"

"He married another woman a few years later. But I've never told him the whole story."

"Is his second wife happy?"

"She seems to be," Sam replied. "Obviously, I haven't questioned her directly. She had been widowed, and therefore was more experienced than his first wife. From what I heard one night when Martha and I were staying with them, I'd say he's learned a thing or two since."

"Good," Jim said softly. Then he gazed evenly at the doctor and asked the question that had been bothering him. "Do you really think she jumped, or ran off with Mason?"

Sam looked down with a sigh. "I've often wondered that myself."

"What about Martha? Has she ever considered that?"

Sam nodded. "Yes, and I think truly believes she left."

"She must hate her mother," Jim muttered.

"On the contrary," Sam responded. "She hopes her mother is living happily somewhere."

"That's mighty generous of her."

Sam nodded again. "So you see how important this can be and why Martha and I both have strong feelings on the subject. I firmly believe it is not only unfair but sinful for pastors and theologians to tell women they shouldn't enjoy sexual intercourse. From what I've learned studying the Bible for myself, God wants both parties to enjoy it."

Sam grinned. "So, will there be another show tonight? I thought I might take a walk this way later."

Jim looked at him and shook his head. "I didn't expect anyone to be looking in. Isn't there a law against that or something?"

"I don't know, but you can't expect people not to be curious, especially if you're making so much noise."

"That wasn't me," Jim replied with a grin. "All I was trying to do was obey your instructions. Otherwise, we would've been in the bed and not on the table."

Sam laughed. "Whoever it was heard *you* too, and it apparently scared the hell out of him."

Jim shook his head. "I guess I'll have to find something heavier to cover the windows," he remarked with a sigh.

"And disappoint everyone?"

"Maybe I should sell tickets and invite the whole town," Jim replied sarcastically.

"That would work," Sam laughed again. "And it would be a public service for all the frustrated women of the town. So should I plan my walk for about eight?"

"I'll make sure we're more discreet tonight."

Sam patted him on the shoulder. "Oh, apparently whoever it was got a good look at you," he said, turning back as he was about to step off the porch. "I had to assure some of the men that size really doesn't matter, that it's the motion that counts."

"I'm sure they were glad to hear that, but whoever saw us was exaggerating."

"Don't sell yourself short," replied Sam with another laugh. "I've seen you. Remember? Heard you, too, more than once, and it would've scared me too if I hadn't known what was going on." Then he waved as he walked away.

Jim waved in return, but he was no longer amused as he walked into the house. He prepared a light supper of smoked ham, toast, and fried apple slices sprinkled with sugar.

"You're a good cook!" Rose commented as she ate.

"Thanks," Jim said. "Just please don't expect me to do it often. I really don't like to cook. Plus, I hunt for the restaurants so I can eat for free."

"I won't make you cook again," Rose promised.

"Did you get a lot done?"

Rose nodded as she chewed another bite of the apples.

After supper, Rose washed the dishes and Jim dried them. He'd taken off the sling as soon as Sam left. Rose had just put away the last plate when they heard a knock at the front door. Jim answered it with Rose peeking from behind him.

"I hope we're not bothering you," said a man who appeared to be a few years older than Jim. A woman stood at his elbow holding a basket. "I'm Nick Byron." He offered his hand, which Jim took. "And this is my wife Pat. We live there across the street," he said, pointing to the nearest house on the opposite side of the road.

"We're sorry we didn't get by before," added Pat. "We didn't know you were moving in or we'd have brought something over yesterday."

"Why, thank you," said Rose, smiling graciously. "Won't you come in?"

Jim stepped aside, allowing Nick and Pat to enter. Rose took the basket from Pat, set it on the table, opened it, and smiled.

"You shouldn't have gone to so much trouble," Rose said as she began to remove the dishes from the basket.

"I know you've probably already eaten," replied Pat as she helped set the food on the table, "but I wanted you to have something for tomorrow."

Rose smiled again as she gazed at two pies, a basket full of biscuits, and a jar of homemade jam. "You made all this?" she asked Pat.

"Pat here is known as one of the best cooks in town," replied Nick, smiling proudly.

"Thank you," said Rose, giving Pat's hand a squeeze.

"It was really no trouble," Pat replied.

Rose picked up one of the pies and motioned for Jim to take the other one and follow her to the kitchen cupboard. "Why don't you speak to them?" she asked in a whisper.

"I have my reasons."

"You could at least be polite." Then Rose turned and rejoined their guests.

Jim asked Nick to step outside, nodding toward the back door. Nick obeyed after a quick glance at his wife. Then he followed Jim as he walked down the back steps into the yard. The late-September evening was mild and alive with the sounds of insects. Nick was a naturally garrulous man, but, though Jim's silence made him uncomfortable, he controlled his urge to fill it with idle chatter.

Finally, to Nick's relief, Jim spoke. "So did you see anyone outside my house last night?"

"No. Why?" Nick replied.

Jim turned and gazed at him. The sun had set, but darkness hadn't yet fallen. "You haven't heard?"

Nick thought for a moment. He was sure he knew what Jim meant but hesitated to say in case he was wrong.

Jim noted Nick's hesitation, and his natural reticence left him comfortable even in the presence of the other man's discomfiture. After a moment, Jim took pity on the man and explained, as he started walking again, "I know someone looked in my windows last night. I thought you might have seen him."

"I saw someone walking away but thought he was just going by. I didn't recognize him, sorry. I heard about what happened, and I want you to know that's not how people on this street usually act. Though I almost came over here myself last night—"

Jim stopped walking and turned on him, his eyes smoldering.

Noting the anger in his new neighbor's gaze, Nick explained quickly. "Pat and I thought someone was hurt, but when we realized—we just stayed home." He supposed it was the twilight that made Jim's eyes shine.

"Thank you," Jim said. Then he turned and started walking again.

"Some of the men meet at the men's only saloon on Monday nights to play cards. Why don't you join us?" Nick suggested, changing the subject. He wished he were there with his friends now. "I know when I was first married it helped to talk to older men, though I don't think I'll ever understand women."

"Maybe I can be there the Monday after the wedding," Jim replied, not wanting to make a definite commitment. Then, in response to an inquiry from Nick, Jim explained why they were getting married again as they headed back to the house. The conversation turned somehow from weddings to horses to baseball as they walked.

"So you play?" Nick asked as they stepped through the back door, glad now he'd agreed to accompany Pat to meet their new neighbors instead of joining his friends for cards that Monday evening.

"I did some years ago," Jim answered.

Nick nodded, smiling. "Were you any good?"

"I guess you'll have to wait and see," Jim replied, smiling back at him.

"Well, we won't keep you any longer," said Pat as the men shut the back door behind them.

Jim shook Nick's hand as they parted. Rose thanked Pat again for the food and invited them to the wedding. Then Nick and Pat walked back across the street to their house.

"So what was that all about?" Rose asked after Jim shut the front door.

"I don't want to upset you," Jim replied.

"You embarrassed me by not talking, then you two come back in like you're best friends."

"I needed to ask Nick something."

"What?"

"Remember when I said someone was watching us last night?"

"I didn't think you were serious."

"Well, someone was, and now everyone in town is talking about it."

"What?" she asked in surprise.

Jim nodded.

"So a few people are talking. So what?" Rose responded.

Jim briefly recounted his conversations with Ted and Sam. Then he told her about the men asking the doctor questions because their wives wanted the same treatment.

"Really?" Rose asked with a laugh. "You should be proud."

Jim looked at her in surprise. "You're not upset?"

"I'm proud of you. Like Sam said, you may have started something. Are you embarrassed?"

"No. We were in our own house and we're married. I just don't want every man in town talking about you."

"It sounds to me like they're talking about *you*," she said, smiling again and taking his hand. "Let's see if we can give them something else to talk about."

Jim lit a light. Then, after covering the windows with a blanket, he stripped off his pants, leaving his shirt as Rose undressed. They pleased each other again, and ended up lying on the bed in each other's arms.

"That was amazing," Rose said breathlessly after they finished. She looked down and watched as he softened, only to see him begin to harden again a few moments later. "How do you do that? I'd always heard men had to wait a while before that happened again."

"I don't know. I guess it's because you're so beautiful I can't resist."

She smiled.

They enjoyed each other again. Afterwards, Jim threw himself onto his back, panting, and Rose collapsed beside him. They lay still for a while as their bodies recovered from the glorious sensation.

Then Rose rolled up onto her elbow and kissed him. "I love you."

"I love you, too," Jim replied, gazing into her eyes.

"Why won't you take your shirt off?" She had wanted to ask before but didn't want to upset him.

"I don't want you to have to touch my back," Jim replied, an edge to his voice.

Rose felt his body tense, so she gently caressed his face. "It doesn't bother me."

"It bothers me!" Jim growled, sitting up and turning away from her.

Rose scooted up behind him and lightly touched his shoulders.

Jim slipped on his pants, walked to the back door, opened it, and stood gazing out at the landscape bathed in moonlight. The lamp didn't reach him there, so he could see almost as far as the woods across the field. He drank in the cool air. It smelled of trees, drying leaves, and wood smoke—a pleasant, comforting aroma.

Rose came up behind him wearing her robe and put her arms around him. "I'm sorry. I didn't mean to upset you." She felt his muscles tighten hard as steel beneath his shirt.

"I just can't," Jim said, his voice tense and low. "Not yet."

Rose gave him a squeeze.

He turned, took her in his arms, and gazed at her. "Be patient with me."

She looked up at him. His eyes shone in the moonlight as though lit from within. She stood on tiptoe and kissed him.

Jim held her close. As she wrapped her arms around him, she inadvertently rested her hand on his back. She felt him tense and then shudder as he tried through force of will to relax under her touch.

She moved her hands to his arms and kissed his cheek. "I love you regardless. Never forget that."

Jim nodded and buried his face against her neck.

On the other side of town, Carlos's man, the artist, had just finished with the woman he'd hired for the evening. He smiled and slapped her on the butt as she dressed.

The woman laughed. "How much longer will you be here?"

"'Til it's time for me to leave. Why?"

"I like you. See you tomorrow night?"

The man nodded. Then he set out for a stroll past the house of the man whom he intended to kill. That afternoon, he'd watched him talking to the doctor and wished the guard had been alone so he could take his shot. He'd heard about what had happened the night before and was disappointed the lights were out. He'd been hoping for a show. *Oh well*, he thought, deciding he'd make his move the next day.

17

VISITORS

The next morning, Rose woke early, put on her nightgown, and started working on her dress again. It was the Tuesday before the wedding, and she wanted to finish it as quickly as possible. She was glad she didn't need to use the sewing machine because she didn't want to disturb Jim.

She had worked for a couple of hours when he started to stir. He groaned in his sleep and then settled down, but a few moments later he stirred and groaned again. She turned to check on him and saw his brow wrinkle as he groaned a third time. She wondered how he could hide the pain so well when he was awake since it was apparent how intense it was when he was asleep. Sam had told her it would take the bruising her husband had received while searching for the bullet longer to heal than the stitches.

Jim stirred again, and his eyes fluttered open, only to close immediately. He gritted his teeth against another groan and opened his eyes to find Rose kneeling by the bed.

"Good morning," she said softly. "Is the pain worse today?"

"No. I'm OK. It'll get better after I get up and move around."

She brushed a lock of hair from his forehead and kissed his cheek. "You should let me give you a shave since you'll be going out later."

Jim nodded, sat up stiffly, and rubbed his eyes.

"I'll start heating the water while you wash up," Rose said, standing.

Jim got out of bed, stepped out the back door, then walked to the sink. He cleaned his teeth with a bit of tooth powder and a cloth.

Rose smiled. "You take better care of your teeth than most women."

"Sam taught me," Jim replied. Then he stuck his head under the cold water and washed his face. "He taught me how to shave, too, but I hate doing it. You don't like me with a beard?" he asked as he dried himself with a towel.

"I prefer seeing your face, not fur," she replied, lighting the stove. "It'll take that a while to heat. Are you hungry?"

"Not yet."

Rose turned from the stove, and Jim took her in his arms. "It's so nice not to wake up alone," he whispered.

She kissed his cheek. Jim slipped her nightgown off one shoulder and kissed the bare skin, then worked up to her neck, causing her to sigh. As he kissed her, he slipped the nightgown off her other shoulder and let it fall to the floor, leaving them both naked. She looked down and smiled. Jim led her to the bed. He put a pillow behind him and leaned his back against the headboard. Then he patted his lap and Rose climbed on. She sat facing him, holding onto his shoulders, careful to avoid his wound. After they had satisfied each other, she sat resting her head on his left shoulder.

"That was good," she said softly. "I didn't hurt you, I hope?"

"Not much."

Rose looked up worriedly, but Jim smiled and kissed her.

"And you didn't wear a shirt," she said softly.

"I know," he replied with a smile, and they kissed again.

"Oh! The water," said Rose as she heard the kettle boiling.

She hopped off his lap and walked to the stove, picking up her nightgown on the way and slipping it on. Then she prepared to give Jim a shave. He moved a chair into the kitchen, laid a towel on it, sat down, and relaxed as Rose expertly used the straight razor. She gave him as good a shave as he'd ever had from a barber.

"You're hard again," Rose said as she dried his face.

"I like it when you touch me."

He took her hand and led her toward the bed.

"Again?" she asked.

Jim took her in his arms and kissed her. Then he slipped her nightgown off, kissed the front of her neck, and moved his way down to her breasts. He sat on the bed, turned Rose away from him, sat her on his lap, and they pleased each other again.

"You have such strong legs," Rose said after they finished, running her hands along his thighs.

"I feel like I'm getting fat since all I've been able to do is lie around for the last few months."

"You're not fat!" she said with a laugh. Then she lifted off him and turned around. "You have a perfect body!"

"Thank you. I have no complaints about yours either," he said as he fondled her breasts.

"Careful, or you'll be wanting to do it again, and I have a dress to work on."

Jim lay back on the bed and Rose lay beside him, resting her head on his chest as she stroked his stomach. Her fingers rippled over his muscles. She drew her hand along his arm, then sat up and drew it along his side and down his leg. "You're all muscle. There isn't an inch of you that isn't firm."

"Keep touching me like that and one part of me will be firm again."

"I think twice in one morning is enough," Rose laughed. Then she gazed at him wistfully.

"Something wrong?" he asked.

"I met a portrait painter years ago. He was commissioned by one of my mother's regular customers. My mother was a dress-maker," Rose added, not wanting Jim to get the wrong idea. "When he was young—he was elderly when I met him—the painter had traveled to Greece and Rome and made sketches of statues. They were very old, and they apparently didn't wear a lot of clothes back then. He kept the drawings in a book and showed them to me. I would gaze at the pictures and wonder if any man really looked like them. Every muscle was clearly defined. They were beautiful."

She looked up at Jim. "It wasn't a sexual interest," she explained. "I just thought they were amazingly beautiful works of art. Then, after I began working at the brothel, I realized they depicted an ideal. No man looked like those statues. Even the ones who weren't fat and worked hard all the time didn't come close to looking like them. I'd given up ever finding a man who looked like that until now." She gazed at him and ran her fingers over his stomach again. "Your body is just as beautiful as theirs."

She looked up, and Jim noticed a tear in her eye. "But theirs didn't have scars," he said, his voice low.

"No, they didn't."

"Is that why you're crying? You wish mine didn't either?"

"No! I'm crying because you're so beautiful. The scars just make you look like a man. Of course, I wish you'd never been hurt or had anything bad ever happen to you, but your scars show your strength and courage. I know you might find it hard to believe, but they make you even more beautiful."

Jim touched her face as Rose kissed his mouth.

"Do you want something to eat now, or do you want to wait until before you go?" she asked, wiping her eyes.

"I'll wait."

"You rest now, and I'll have something ready for you when you wake up."

"I'll just eat an apple and cheese later."

"You're easy to please."

"Why don't you get in bed with me?" Jim suggested, touching her cheek.

"No, I have a dress to work on," Rose reminded him, smiling. She kissed him on the forehead as she sat up.

Then she dressed as Jim got under the covers and dozed off.

He awoke a little over an hour later to the sound of Rose's sewing machine. He dressed, served himself a piece of cheese, took two apples, and started to leave.

"Wait a minute," Rose said, getting the sling. She slipped it over his head and placed his right arm in it.

Jim gave her a kiss at the door, then ate the cheese and one of the apples as he walked to the freight office. Martha was already there waiting for Mrs. Canady's stage. Jim greeted her, and she was glad to see he was wearing the sling.

"I'm surprised Mrs. Canady is getting here before the Petersens," Jim commented.

"She said she wanted to have time to visit with you," Martha replied. She smiled when Jim looked almost surprised. "There are people who like you and enjoy spending time with you, you know." Then her brow wrinkled in concern as Jim shook his head and turned away, gazing up the street looking for the stage.

Some of his fellow freight men came out of the office and greeted him, but she noticed they were almost too respectful and kept their distance. *They seem afraid of him,* she thought.

When the stage arrived, Ted came out with a couple of his men.

Jim realized how long he'd been gone when he didn't recognize either the driver or the guard. He nodded to them and then stepped up and opened the stage door. Mrs. Canady poked out her head.

"Well, look at you!" she said to Jim, smiling. "You look like you've grown six inches since I saw you last."

"Ma'am," Jim replied, giving her a hand down.

"Martha, it's so good to see you, too!" The two women hugged. "And Theodore is here to meet me as well."

Ted took her hand and welcomed her after glancing at Jim, wondering why she would make such a comment to a man he believed was at least as old as himself. "I have two men here to help carry your things," Ted said to Mrs. Canady.

"Martha, you go on with them, and Jim and I will follow so we can visit," Mrs. Canady suggested.

Martha and the men walked on ahead, and Ted stepped back into the freight office, trying to decide if Jim seemed any taller than when he'd met him.

Jim and Mrs. Canady strolled slowly toward Sam and Martha's house.

"So when will I get to meet Rose?" Mrs. Canady asked.

"She would have been here to meet you, but she needed to work on her dress. I distracted her this morning," he added with a smile.

"You really shouldn't lie with a girl before the wedding."

"What?" Jim asked. "You must not have heard. We married three weeks ago, after I was hurt the first time. And what made you think I was talking about sex?"

"Why else would you be smiling? So if you're already married, why did I travel all this way?"

"I promised her a real wedding. The other was in case I died, which I did."

"What?" it was Mrs. Canady's turn to ask.

Jim explained what had occurred during his first surgery. Mrs. Canady shook her head.

"Martha wrote and told me about Rose's former place of employment," Mrs. Canady mentioned. "Regardless of what she did or didn't do there, you don't want her to think you don't respect her."

"If a man makes a woman happy, that shows he respects her."

"And do you make her happy?"

"Every time," Jim replied, smiling again.

"Now I'm getting jealous," said Mrs. Canady, also smiling.

"Maybe you should find yourself a man, Mrs. Canady."

"I have."

A woman approached them as they walked down the boardwalk. She greeted Jim with a smile as she passed. Jim acknowledged her, and Mrs. Canady gave the woman an odd look but didn't say anything.

"So you have a suitor?" Jim asked.

"He's a little more than that," she replied. "Our preacher scolded us because my man's wife was still living when we started seeing each other, but he was never unfaithful to her. She'd been an invalid and senile for a long time. He still took care of her. She hadn't been a wife to him for years before we began keeping time with each other, but, as I said, he was never unfaithful."

Another woman walked by, greeting Jim, and he nodded. Again, Mrs. Canady noticed something odd, but continued. "I sat with her sometimes when he had errands to do, and she often smiled when he returned and patted my hand. It was comforting to her to know he wouldn't be alone and unhappy. She and I were close friends. When age begins to rob a person of their faculties, there's a point when they are still lucid enough to realize it. She told me then she hoped he would find someone to comfort him when she no longer could. When you truly love someone, you want their happiness even above your own."

Jim nodded.

"Out of respect for her, we never spent time together at his house, and didn't do certain things," said Mrs. Canady. "She passed from pneumonia." She glanced at the young man beside her, remembering he had just recovered from the same ailment.

"Now that the children are back in school, I give Uma time off a couple of afternoons a week," Mrs. Canady continued. "And now the pastor has even more to scold us for," she added with a smile.

"Does he make you happy?" Jim asked, remembering his conversation with Sam.

"Usually," Mrs. Canady replied.

Another woman passed them. She too spoke to Jim, and he nodded.

"Are you missing a button on your pants, or is something showing?" Mrs. Canady asked after the woman had walked away.

"No," Jim replied after glancing down, and he resettled his gun belt to hide the act of checking the buttons with his hand.

"Well, that's three women now who have been sizing you up, then."

Jim sighed. "Ask Sam about it later. He'll enjoy telling you the whole story."

"I'd rather hear it from you."

Jim dropped behind her as they continued walking. He lowered his head and spoke softly in her ear as he briefly explained what had happened two nights earlier.

When he was done, Mrs. Canady laughed. "I wish I'd been here for that."

Jim looked at her, surprised.

"I may be old but I'm not dead yet."

Jim shook his head.

As they walked, some of the men passing by greeted Jim as well. A couple of them asked him if he'd be at the men's only (or danceless saloon, as they called it). Each time, Jim replied he'd try to get there the next Monday after the wedding.

"I think they have something they want to discuss with you," remarked Mrs. Canady. "Which reminds me of something I'm curious about. Why did you specify no gifts on the invitations? When people come to a wedding they want to give gifts as part of the celebration."

Jim took a deep breath. "I don't like feeling beholden to people. I also want to give you back that five hundred dollars." He was referring to the amount Mrs. Canady had deposited into his bank account shortly after he left Clayter.

"Don't be silly. That was a gift, and you sent me such a nice note thanking me."

"But it was too generous, ma'am," he said softly.

She sensed the true intent behind his words, the deep hurt and, perhaps, suspicion of her motives he was able to hide from everyone except her. "You need to let people do for you when they want to. Sometimes people enjoy helping someone else without expecting anything in return." She glanced up at him, but he was looking down in thought. She considered telling him what she had hoped he would do with the money, but decided that could wait until a later time. "I hope you don't consider it a breach of confidence, but Uma told me about how you had been mistreated as a child." She sensed him tense. "I had supposed as much."

He looked at her in surprise.

"You forget my gift," she explained with a weary smile. "As I said to you the first time I met you, you shouldn't be ashamed of your past. I'd hoped I'd made it clear that whatever happened to you doesn't make any difference to me or anyone else who truly cares about you. What someone does to you is no reflection on you, it's how you react to it that counts." She glanced at him again. When he didn't respond, she continued. "Hatred and bitterness only damage you further. They have no effect on the ones who hurt you. You need to reconcile yourself with your past so you can enjoy your life ahead."

"I wish I could," he muttered.

"You also need to come see me some time," she said, giving his arm a squeeze, wanting to lighten the mood rather than upset him further. She felt him tense at first, then relax, and she sensed it was from force of will.

"I'm sorry I haven't been back."

"I know you've been busy," said Mrs. Canady, giving his arm another squeeze. She noticed he didn't tense that time. Then she grinned. "It can take time to learn how to keep a woman happy."

"I still remember what you told me the night we met," he said seriously, letting the remark pass. "Actions are the only truth." Then he looked at her. "Words *alone* mean nothing."

Mrs. Canady looked up at him and nodded, smiling. "I knew you understood, and your phrasing is better than mine."

"You were right," Jim stated. "Words without actions are meaningless."

Mrs. Canady nodded again.

"I plan to always show Rose how much I love her," Jim added.

"Then she will be a very happy woman, indeed" Mrs. Canady stated, smiling.

When they arrived at Martha's, she showed them in and asked Jim to stay. He replied that he thought it best to let Mrs. Canady settle in first. Martha invited him and Rose to supper that evening, and Jim accepted her invitation so Mrs. Canady could meet Rose. After leaving Sam and Martha's, Jim walked to the stable to check on Ness before heading home. He wished he could go for a ride but settled for feeding Ness an apple instead.

Carlos's man crept on his belly from the woods, through the field, until he was close enough to observe the guard's house. From where he lay, he could clearly see the back door as well as anyone walking up the road from town. He had his rifle slung across his back from a strap. He was glad the grass was tall. He swung the weapon around in front of him and waited. The ground was dry, and twigs and small rocks pricked him through his clothes. A cloud of gnats buzzed around, annoying him with their bites and constant humming, until the breeze picked up and scattered them. His knees and elbows, already raw from having crawled almost a half-mile, began to hurt even more from leaning against the hard ground. His arms started to ache from holding the rifle. He lowered the weapon so he wouldn't start shaking, and still he waited.

He heard the sound of a sewing machine coming from the open window at the back of the guard's house. He wondered what the woman was making and if it was black so she could wear it to her man's funeral.

He saw a wagon pull up loaded with wood and got a glimpse of the guard's woman as she stepped outside to pay. Then he watched as the man tossed the logs by the guard's back door. The man could possibly have seen him if he'd looked up from his work, but he didn't. He left by continuing on around the house rather than turning the mule pulling the wagon.

Almost an hour later, he saw Morgan walking up the road. He raised the rifle, cocked it, and took aim. Just a few more yards and he would have a clean shot. As he watched the guard intently, he noticed the man's gait slow. Then the guard paused, and he could swear looked right at him, though he knew the grass hid him. He adjusted his grip on the rifle and decided he'd go ahead with the shot. His finger touched the trigger. He inhaled, his gaze fixed on his prize. He aimed at the middle of the guard's chest, right where the sling crossed the center of his shirt.

He felt dead calm as he prepared to fire, his mind and body focused on a single point. A point his bullet would forever destroy. Everything around him faded away. He no longer felt the ground, hard and prickly beneath him, or heard the insects buzzing in the grass. His weapon became an extension of himself, reacting to his will as automatically as his finger, as it began to squeeze the trigger. Then, in that last second, the blink of an eye between life and death, a child ran up to the guard. He gasped and withdrew his finger from the trigger. He saw the guard glance in his direction again. Then, as the child led the guard across the street to a neighbor's house, Carlos's man crept away, standing and running the last few yards to the trees after glancing behind him.

Though he was sure Morgan hadn't seen him, he didn't want to take the chance someone would find him, so he headed back to town. He needed to do something soon. The boss had sent him a telegram wanting to know why he hadn't read the guard's obituary in the newspaper. When he got back to his room, he had another telegram from the boss. He'd seen the wedding announcement and wanted him to wait until the night before the ceremony. "I want it to be a tragic end!" the boss had written.

He smiled. That gave him another few days to relax and enjoy the whores and whiskey.

Business before pleasure, he thought, considering what he needed to do. He decided he'd wait until after the guard had been with his woman the night before the wedding. Then, when he stepped out back to piss, he'd shoot him. He smiled at the imagined look of fear and surprise on the guard's face as he shot him dead and left him lying naked on his own porch.

Jim returned home with a loaf of bread from Pat and found Rose hard at work.

"The man delivered wood while you were gone," Rose told

him without looking up. "I hope it's OK that I paid him from the money in the bureau."

"That's fine."

Then he told her about their dinner invitation. He gave her a kiss on the back of her head, grabbed his rifle, and stepped outside. He could swear someone had watched him earlier, and he found the grass crushed where it looked like something had lain. He walked through the field to the trees, gazing around him. He could see where someone or something had walked through the grass but realized it could have been someone simply out for a walk or hunting, like the man he'd seen the day before. Or it could have been deer bedding down for an afternoon nap to enjoy the warm sunshine before returning to the cover of the forest.

He shook his head and decided he was being overly cautious, even for him.

After a while, Rose realized she had been hearing the sound of chopping coming from their backyard. She stepped out the back door and found Jim splitting wood with his left hand.

"What on earth do you think you're doing?" she asked almost harshly, out of concern.

Jim didn't reply, he just lifted the maul and brought it down, expertly splitting the wood. As he was about to pick up another piece, Rose ran to him and stood in front of him to stop him.

"You know you're not supposed to be doing this!" she scolded.

"It needs to be done, and I need the exercise," Jim replied as he reached around her for the next piece.

"James Morgan, you need to put that axe down and rest!"

"Rose, move. I don't want to hit you," Jim replied gently. "And it's not an axe."

"Jim, please!" she begged. "I can get someone else to do this. You'll hurt yourself."

Jim looked at her but didn't drop the maul.

"Don't make me have to tell Sam or Theodore," she threatened.

"Just let me get enough done to last a few days and I'll come inside. I promise."

Rose turned, walked up onto the porch, then turned again to face him, resting her hands on her hips.

Jim split another piece.

"Are you going to stand there and stare at me, woman?" he asked.

"I'm just waiting for you to hurt yourself so I don't have as far to run," Rose replied.

Jim split a few more pieces, and Rose could see he was in pain. Then he piled the split wood beside the steps and walked by her into the house. Rose followed him and insisted on checking his wounds. Jim removed his shirt and sat on one of the kitchen chairs, facing its back so he would have a place to rest his arms. He didn't want to admit both his shoulders were aching.

Rose removed the bandage, and though the wounds looked fine, she was worried, so she stepped outside and asked the Byron boy to go get Sam. The boy returned with the doctor. Pat saw them and met them at Jim's door. Then she left with the child after Rose assured her Jim appeared no worse and that she had just been worried.

When he walked into the house, Sam found the young man still sitting in the chair bare to the waist. He looked at the wounds. There was some redness near the one in Jim's chest. "What have you been doing?"

Rose told the doctor about the wood, and Sam looked at him in disbelief. "I'll split it for you if it's that important," said the doctor.

"I wasn't using my right arm."

"It doesn't make any difference, you have to stay quiet right now," Sam ordered.

Jim looked up at him.

"I'm not joking. I went very deep looking for that bullet, and you're not fully healed yet. For right now, if it hurts, don't do it. Understand?"

Jim nodded.

"Luckily, it doesn't look like you did any damage. Give it a couple more days. Then hopefully you'll be able to start doing more. Now I need to see another patient, and you need to rest. Oh, and if you behave, you'll be out of the sling by the wedding."

Jim nodded again, and his eyes flashed from frustration.

"I'll see you both later," Sam said as he stepped to the front door.

Rose saw him out and Sam turned to her. "I know it's not

easy, but you're taking good care of him." Then he turned and walked away.

Rose shut the door and returned to Jim, who was still sitting in the chair, glowering.

"Why don't you lie down until it's time to leave?" she suggested as she bandaged him.

Jim stood and plodded to the bedroom. He took off his pants and sullenly climbed into bed.

After he settled under the covers, Rose gazed at him.

"If it wasn't for you, I'd be going crazy," he whispered, thinking about how he'd tracked what was most likely a deer through the field.

She smiled, kissed his cheek, then went back to work.

Ever since he'd been sick and wounded, Jim was always surprised at how tired he felt when he lay down. Normally, he would never be able to sleep during the day, but since he'd had pneumonia it seemed he could sleep anytime. He hoped he'd get his energy back after he healed. He soon dozed off and slept until Rose woke him so he could get ready for supper.

Sam met them at the door and let them into the parlor where Mrs. Canady was sitting. Jim and Rose had knocked at the private entrance rather than the door beside it, which led into a waiting room for patients. Jim introduced Mrs. Canady to Rose. Then he sat beside his wife on the small couch across from the older woman.

"It's so good to finally meet you," Mrs. Canady said to Rose. Then she turned to Jim. "She's beautiful, as I knew she would be."

Rose thanked her and smiled.

"Today was the first time I ever saw Jim smile," Mrs. Canady commented, smiling back at them. "From what Martha told me, he never smiled until he met you. You must make him very happy, Rose."

"He's not difficult to please," Rose replied.

Mrs. Canady noticed Jim was holding Rose's hand. She also noticed he appeared happy and at peace, which was quite a contrast to how he had been when she first met him. "Young love is such a beautiful thing," she remarked, gazing at the couple. "I never thought I'd live to see such a change in this young man. I worried about you after you left," she said to Jim. "Not just because you might get hurt, which you have, but because you seemed so alone in the world. It does my heart good to see that you have someone now."

Rose smiled again and squeezed his hand. "Maybe I should see if I can help Martha," she suggested, standing.

Jim stood, then sat back down after Rose left.

"I like her," Mrs. Canady said. "Her smile lights up the whole room."

"Yes, ma'am."

"Your whole demeanor changes when you're with her. I'm glad you're finally happy."

"Thank you."

Mrs. Canady reached out for his hand. Jim gave it to her, and she gave it a squeeze.

Sam came in then and showed them into the kitchen, where Rose was setting the table. Sam and Martha didn't have a dining room. They sat down and Sam said grace. Then Jim let Rose cut up his food, since he knew Sam would fuss if he took off the sling. Mrs. Canady watched, smiling.

"It's his fault," Jim said, nodding toward Sam.

Sam smiled. Then he told them about Jim splitting wood that afternoon, and Mrs. Canady and Martha scolded him gently.

"I don't know what we're going to do after Uma and the children get here," Sam remarked, changing the subject for Jim's sake. "This table is hardly big enough for five the way Martha cooks," he said, gazing at all the dishes.

Martha smiled and explained she'd worry about that when the time came. Then she went on to tell them about the dinner she was planning for Friday evening for the wedding party and out of town guests.

"Ted graciously offered to host the event," Martha explained, "since our house isn't big enough. Uma, Sylvia, Olivia, and I will do the cooking."

"Thank you," replied Rose. "I appreciate all you are doing for the wedding."

"I hear you're going to be Ted's best man," Sam said to Jim.

"Yes, sir."

"I hope he's not offended that you didn't ask him to be yours," Sam commented.

"I explained to him I've known you longer, and he was

actually relieved. He said one wedding was enough for him."

Sam laughed. "He told me he asked you because he credits you with bringing him and Sylvia together, and he appreciates it that you saved her when she was on the stage."

"Just doing my job."

"What happened?" asked Mrs. Canady.

Jim looked to Sam, but he insisted Jim tell her. "I wasn't there," Sam said.

Jim briefly explained about the attempted attack on Sylvia at the home station and how he'd prevented it. Then Sam added some details Hank had given him.

"Lucky you woke up," said Mrs. Canady.

"He's a very light sleeper," explained Rose.

"You should know," added Sam, laughing.

All of them joined in except Jim, who just shook his head tolerantly.

"So have you gotten a lot done on your dress?" Martha asked Rose.

"I should finish it by tomorrow or the next day."

"What about you, young man?" Mrs. Canady asked Jim. "Have you figured out what you're going to wear?"

"Me?" Jim asked.

They all looked at him.

"I hadn't really thought about it," Jim replied.

Rose looked stricken, and the others looked shocked.

Jim gazed at them for a moment as though he was confused. Then he lifted Rose's hand to his lips and kissed it. "I made arrangements over a week ago." The others laughed in relief, and Rose leaned over and kissed Jim on the mouth. He turned to Martha and added, "You should know, you let the tailor in to see me."

"I'd forgotten all about it," Martha replied, still laughing.

"I really believed you," Rose said, smiling.

"I don't know how I'll look," Jim commented. "I've never worn fancy clothes before."

"Oh, you'll look fine," Mrs. Canady assured him. "You'd look good in anything. Or nothing," she added with a grin.

"Did he tell you about that?" asked Sam, laughing again.

Mrs. Canady related what had happened on the street and what Jim had told her, with an apology to Rose, who just smiled.

Then, after getting a nod from Jim, Sam proceeded to give her more details from what others had told him, and he mentioned the men coming to his office.

"So that's what those men want to talk to you about," said Mrs. Canady, and she explained about the men wanting to meet Jim at the saloon.

"Are you going?" Sam asked.

"I suppose," Jim replied. "Though I doubt there's anything I can tell them."

"I'd like to stop by, if you don't mind," said Sam.

"I'd rather you talk to them than me," Jim responded.

"Why don't I invite the wives here?" Martha suggested. "That way we can hopefully help both parties."

Sam nodded. "I'll speak to Nick and you talk to Pat. We'll let them pass the word since Nick's the one who invited you in the first place."

Jim nodded.

"At least it's the saloon without girls," Rose remarked.

"If I was you, young lady," offered Mrs. Canady, "I'd be worried about all those women eyeing my man."

"They can look," Jim replied, gazing at Rose, "but I'll always come home to you." Then he kissed her.

"You know, I almost wouldn't recognize you for the young man who had dinner with me and the Petersens two years ago," commented Mrs. Canady, gazing at Jim. "You've done wonders for him," she said to Rose.

Rose smiled.

After the meal, Mrs. Canady was tired and asked Rose to accompany her to her room. When they were alone, Mrs. Canady sat in a chair and motioned for Rose to sit on the bed.

"So what's troubling you?" asked the older woman. "Having second thoughts?"

"About Jim? No! Never!"

"Then what is it?"

Rose gazed at her. "How did you know?"

"It's a gift. Now tell me."

Rose explained about the trip to St. Louis and the reason she was hesitant to accompany Jim.

"Have you told him about all this?" Mrs. Canady inquired.

"No, ma'am."

"Why not?"

"It's not that I don't want to tell him, it's just that I thought it would be better to wait until after the wedding."

"Tell him tonight when you get home," Mrs. Canady advised. "You should get this out of the way before you two get married. Again."

Rose nodded. "But I'm afraid of what he might do."

"He'll do whatever you want him to do. Women can have a great deal of power over men. Use it, but remember to use it wisely. A man will take only so much."

"Thank you, ma'am," Rose said. Then she walked to the older woman and took her hand. "I must say, I'm a little surprised."

"Why?"

"I really didn't think you'd like me," Rose replied, looking down.

"My dear, we all have found ourselves in impossible situations. It's just that some of us have had more choices than others."

Rose smiled, leaned down, and kissed the older woman's cheek.

"Tell Jim goodnight for me," Mrs. Canady said as she showed Rose to the door.

Rose nodded and walked back to the kitchen. Then she helped Martha with the dishes. Since they refused his help, Jim talked to Sam about a horse the doctor was considering purchasing. When the women finished the dishes, Jim thanked Sam and Martha as he stood. The doctor and his wife showed the young couple to the door. They bade each other goodnight, and Jim and Rose left, walking arm in arm. Rose saw how the women they passed looked at her husband, though he didn't seem to notice. She smiled and gave him a squeeze.

"Mrs. Canady likes you," Jim said to Rose as they walked.

"Did you have any doubts?" Rose asked, smiling.

"No," Jim answered, pulling her closer.

When they arrived at their house, Rose helped Jim remove the sling, and they undressed for bed. She turned out the light, climbed in, and got under the covers.

"Are you tired?" Jim asked as he climbed in too.

"There's something I need to tell you," Rose said as she laid her head on his shoulder.

Jim put his arm around her and felt her shaking. "What's wrong?"

"You haven't asked me about my past," she began.

"You don't have to tell me anything you don't want to."

"There are some things you need to know," she replied, stroking his chest to calm her nerves. "I grew up in St. Louis. After my father died my mother became a seamstress to support us, but she died too when I was thirteen. She didn't leave me much except for the sewing machine, so I went to work as a nanny for Mr. and Mrs. Lucien Oliver. He was one of the wealthiest and most powerful men in town. The children were wonderful, and I was happy, until—" She paused, fighting back tears, and she felt Jim tighten his arm around her.

"Mr. Oliver could be a very cruel man," she continued. "When he met a man of lower status or someone he didn't like, he'd reach out to shake their hand. Then he enjoyed squeezing it so hard that I saw him bring grown men to their knees."

She took a deep breath, then spoke quickly. "I'd been there about a year when, one night when his wife was out, he came to my room, and he—" She felt Jim's muscles tighten, swallowed hard, and continued. "He tried to take advantage of me," she whispered. "He grabbed me hard enough to hurt me and told me to be quiet or else. He started tearing my clothes off, but his wife came home early and found him in my bed. He blamed me. He said I seduced him, and she threw me out that night." Rose swallowed a sob.

"The next day I got a job at a seamstress shop, but that afternoon they fired me. They said they couldn't have someone like me working there. For days, I tried to find another job, all the while sleeping on the street, but no one else would hire me. Even people I'd known all my life wouldn't help me. Like I said, they were a very powerful family."

She wiped her eyes. "Finally, I went to one of the nicer saloons and got a job doing the cooking, cleaning, and eventually making the women's dresses. That's where I met Ruby. It was her who lied about my age, and we left before I would have been old enough to do the work she does. She still works at the saloon here in town, and it was her that kept me from having to do other things at both jobs. She always has a lot of customers and threatened to quit if they made me do things anyway. I want to go to St. Louis with you, but I'm afraid—"

"That you might see him?" Jim asked, his voice low with rage.

"I'm afraid of what you might do," she replied softly. "I don't want you to kill him because then I'd lose you, too," she said, raising herself up on one elbow and looking into his eyes. She could see them burning even in the darkness. "I want you to promise me that you won't hurt him. He's even more powerful now. I think he may be the mayor. I don't want you to do anything that would make me lose you!" The tears began to flow.

Jim brushed some hair from her face. "I won't do anything you don't want me to."

"Promise?"

"I give you my word. Though I'd like to pull the bastard's heart out and show it to him as he died!" Jim added, his eyes flashing.

"Promise me you won't lay a hand on him. If I lost you—" She started to weep again.

"I promise." Jim pulled her to him and kissed her.

"I wouldn't blame you if you hated me," she said, still sobbing.

"Why would I hate you? It wasn't your fault. I love you and always will. I told you before, if you can accept my past, I can accept yours. I'm just sorry that anything like that ever happened to you." He held her close and kissed her again. He remembered living on the street and couldn't imagine what it must have been like for a young girl in a big city alone.

"You really are an amazing man."

"You're the amazing one," he said. "That you can still be so sweet and loving after all that's happened to you."

She smiled weakly, nestling her head against his chest.

Jim held her close and they went to sleep.

The next morning, Jim awoke to the sound of the sewing machine. Rose heard him stir in the bed and rushed to his side. "Good morning," she whispered as she kissed his forehead.

The sight of her face soothed his pain, and he smiled at her. He rose and slowly made his way to the back door.

"Need my help?" Rose asked as he stepped outside.

"Not with this," Jim replied as he relieved himself.

Then he walked to the sink, still moving stiffly. After rinsing his face and cleaning his teeth, he turned to find her watching him, worry evident in her eyes. He pulled her to him and kissed her.

"Now there's something you can help me with," he said. He continued kissing her as his hand found its way under her nightgown and between her legs.

Rose kissed him hard as he began to touch her. She pulled him to the bed and tore off her nightgown.

He lay down. She knelt beside him and began kissing him. She started with his face and worked her way down. She kissed his tip, then took him in her mouth, but lifted off immediately and gagged.

"You OK?" he asked.

Rose nodded. "Sorry," she said, regaining her composure. "It hit the back of my throat."

Then she turned to try again, but he'd softened. She moved up and kissed his mouth. She started to move down again, but he stopped her when she got to his waist.

He pulled her up beside him and gazed at her as he began to touch her. After she was ready, he pleased them both. Then he held her in his arms as their bodies relaxed.

Rose realized she wanted more. After letting him rest a few minutes, she pushed herself up on her elbow and started kissing him, letting her fingers lightly play on him.

He tried to slip a hand between her legs, but she leaned closer. She rested her lips on his tip, and smiled when he sighed.

"Climb on," he ordered softly.

She obeyed. Soon she was wailing with delight and didn't stop until both of them were fully satisfied. She collapsed onto him, his cry still ringing in her ears. They held each other until they heard a knock on the door.

"Just a minute!" Rose called.

Jim put on a pair of pants and a shirt, the latter of which he didn't button. Then he quickly washed his hands, rinsed his face, and stepped outside, shutting the door behind him. He found Pat Byron standing on the porch accompanied by two other women. One was at least ten years older than Pat, and the other appeared to be a few years younger.

"I'm sorry if we came at a bad time," said Pat. They had heard the couple but waited at the street until they finished. "We brought a few things for Rose."

"She'll be ready in a minute," Jim replied.

"Oh, I'm forgetting my manners," said Pat, and she introduced Jim to the ladies.

He took each one's hand in turn and gave a slight bow. "Forgive me for not being properly dressed, I don't like the shirt buttoned. It's uncomfortable over the bandage."

They all enthusiastically accepted his apology as they tried not to stare at his fine physique, finding his damp, tousled hair an attractive compliment to his slight undress.

"I hope you're nearly well," said Pat.

"Getting there," replied Jim. Then, supposing they had heard him and Rose, he added with a smile, "Sam would prefer I stayed quieter, though."

All the ladies laughed, though a bit shyly.

A few moments later, Rose opened the door and asked all of them inside. Jim introduced her to the women by name, impressing them with his memory. Then he excused himself, grabbed his book, and walked back over to where they were standing next to the table.

"We just stopped by to give you an informal pounding," Pat said to Rose.

"I thought I just did that," Jim whispered in Rose's ear, causing her to smile. He inadvertently spoke loud enough for the others to hear. He took a chair, leaving Rose and her guests with one extra, which had fabric lying over it. Then he stepped out the back door, shutting it behind him.

The ladies exchanged glances and looked embarrassed until Rose laughed. Then they all joined in.

"You have to excuse him," Rose apologized after Jim was outside, motioning for her guests to have a seat at the table. "He means no offense."

"None taken," Pat assured her, smiling as she sat.

The ladies were each holding a package, though Pat's was the largest of the three. Rose opened them eagerly to find a pound each of butter, sugar, flour, and salt, the last two from Pat.

"Thank you!" said Rose after she had opened the gifts. "This is so unexpected. Would you like some tea?"

The ladies nodded, so she put some water on to boil.

They went on to discuss Rose's wedding plans, and she graciously invited them and their families to the service. Then they talked about sewing.

"I'll have to stop by after the wedding so you can make me a dress," said the older woman. "My hands just don't work as well as they used to, and it would be nice to have one with an even hem."

"I'd love to make you one," Rose replied, smiling.

"Would you be willing to help me make one?" the younger woman asked. "My mother taught me how to sew, but I just don't feel I'm very good at it yet."

"I wouldn't mind at all," Rose assured her.

"It looks like you'll be keeping busy," Pat said, laughing. "If you're busy sewing, just let me know, and I'll send one of the children over with something for your supper."

"Oh, you don't have to do that," Rose replied.

"It would be my pleasure," said Pat. "I'll need you to make me a couple dresses, too. I really don't like to sew, so we can consider it a trade."

Rose agreed, smiling.

"Do you make men's clothes too?" Pat asked.

"I'm going to try," Rose replied. "After the wedding, I want to make Jim some things. He's been buying his clothes ready-made, and all his shirts are either too tight in the chest or the sleeves are too long. And all his pants are either too big in the waist or too short, and he's still growing."

"How old is he?" asked the older woman.

"Seventeen," Rose answered.

All the women expressed their surprise. They'd all thought him ten years older at least.

"Is he older than you?" the younger woman asked Rose.

"No, I'm nineteen."

The young woman nodded.

"I hope people won't think I took advantage of his age," Rose said worriedly.

"For two years?" responded the older woman. "Heavens, no. Now, if you were my age, that would be a different story."

Rose laughed and the rest joined her.

The ladies finished their tea and stood to leave.

Rose stepped to the back door and called Jim inside so he could tell her new friends goodbye.

She thanked them again for the gifts as she walked them to the door.

"Oh," said Pat, turning, "Martha has invited all of us to her house this Monday evening. Will you be there?" she asked Rose.

"I wouldn't miss it," Rose replied. "Jim will be at the saloon with the men, so it will just be us girls," she laughed, giving him a squeeze.

"We haven't even been married a month, and already you're going to start complaining about me to your friends?" he asked playfully.

The women laughed. Then they said their goodbyes, and Jim and Rose waved to them as they walked away.

When Rose turned around, Jim was buttoning his shirt. Then he put on his gun belt and holstered his weapon.

"Going somewhere?" she asked.

"I have a few errands to do," he said, grabbing two apples from the bowl on the counter.

"When will you be back?"

"I don't know. I might go for a ride."

"Jim Morgan, you know Sam doesn't want you on a horse yet!" she scolded, but not harshly.

"OK," Jim sighed. "Though if I hadn't told you, you'd have never known."

"Yes I would."

He looked at her skeptically.

"You'd come back smelling of horses, and I'd know. Just like I'd know if you were helping the blacksmith, or going out drinking, or anything else you might try to get away with. So you'll just have to behave," she stated, slipping the sling over his head.

He sighed again.

"But I'll reward you if you're good," she said, smiling and stepping close, pressing her body against him.

He kissed her. "I'll expect my reward when I get back," he whispered. Then he walked out the door, rubbing one of the apples on his shirt.

He headed to the gun shop first, where he purchased two items and spoke to the gunsmith. Then he turned toward the tailor's. As he was walking down the street, he had the feeling someone was following him, so he stopped and pretended to look in a shop window. He saw one of the freight men across the street. The man worked in the office with Marcus Livingston, and Jim wondered why he wasn't at work, but supposed one of the man's superiors could have sent him on an errand.

Jim arrived at the tailor's and was relieved both suits fit. Then he asked the tailor to make two minor alterations. The man agreed and assured him both suits would be ready by Friday. He saw the same freight man as he exited. He walked to the barber's, got his hair cut, and when he stepped back outside, saw the freight man again just up the road. Rather than head to his next destination, he turned and strode toward the man. If the man was following him, he wanted to know why.

As soon as the man realized Jim was heading straight for him, he turned and started to walk away. Jim called after him.

The man stopped, turned back, and did his best to seem surprised to see Jim. "Why—Mr. Morgan—it's good to see you're feeling better—I thought you were still recuperating at home."

"I had some things to take care of today," Jim replied, eyeing the man closely. "Didn't I see you near the tailor shop a little while ago?"

"You may have," answered the man, trying to seem nonchalant. "I too had some things to do today—some business, some personal. In fact, I need to get back to the office, but it's good to see you. Take care." Then he hurriedly headed toward the freight office, which was in the opposite direction from the one in which he'd started a moment before.

Jim stood watching him as the man scurried away, wondering if he was being too cautious again. The man glanced behind him a couple times as he made his way up the street, and Jim had the feeling the man intended to keep following him as soon as he turned his back on him. Jim watched the man until he had to turn onto another street to get to the freight company. Jim thought about stepping into a shop to see if the man returned, thereby proving the man indeed was following him, but decided against it and continued on his way. He did stop a few times and look behind him but didn't see the man.

Jim stopped by the stable to check on Ness and give him the apple. The encounter with his fellow freight employee troubled him. Ness sensed his disquiet and nuzzled him. Jim was still wearing the sling and nearly dropped the pocketknife he was using to cut up the apple as he fed it to the horse. He decided to dismiss the incident, supposing he was just being too careful again, and shook his head at his over-caution.

When he returned home, he found Rose hard at work, but she looked up when he entered.

"Sam stopped by," she said. "He told me to have you rest when you got home, but, starting tomorrow, unless you're still hurting or start doing too much, you can stop wearing the sling."

Jim obediently stripped and climbed into bed. He was surprisingly tired and immediately fell asleep. He awoke when Pat knocked at the front door carrying a tray with their supper on it. She handed the tray to Rose but didn't come in.

"What's that?" Jim asked as he dressed.

"Our supper," Rose replied. Then she explained the arrangement Pat had suggested.

"It sounds like you're getting the better part of the deal," Jim commented as he sat and immediately began buttering a piece of cornbread.

"Well, I wouldn't want you to starve," she smiled.

After their meal, Rose washed the dishes, insisting Jim rest. Then she opened the cupboard to store the leftover cornbread. She smiled when she saw a small jug of milk that the dairyman had delivered that morning. She had forgotten about it and was sorry to think it would go to waste. Then she realized Jim must have somehow talked to all the merchants and arranged for deliveries even though confined to bed. She turned to ask him about it and found him standing directly behind her.

"Why don't you take your clothes off?" he suggested, wrapping his arms around her.

"You're supposed to stay quiet."

"I always rest better afterwards, and you promised to reward me for obeying orders."

"Did you?" she asked playfully. "I could smell horse on you as soon as you stepped through the door."

"I took him an apple," Jim replied.

Rose smiled, took off her housedress, and led him to the bed. She noticed he'd already covered the windows with a blanket and lit a light.

After they finished, he opened his eyes and saw Rose gazing at him with an expression of wonder on her face. She lifted off and lay beside him propped on her elbow.

"You looked so peaceful," she said. "You always look like a boy when you sleep, but this was different."

"It's because of you," Jim replied softly.

He stepped outside but heard only the wind as he relieved himself. He snuffed the light after Rose returned to bed from using the chamber pot. Then he walked to the window but barely glanced out as he pulled the blanket down and tossed it on the overstuffed chair as he returned to bed. He stretched out beside Rose and they went to sleep in each other's arms, neither of them aware of the man standing in the shadows a few yards away, watching their house.

The man thought he saw someone moving through the field behind the guard's house and crossed the street, treading as quietly as he could. He'd heard about Jim confronting one of the men watching him earlier that day, and he didn't want the guard to discover him as well. He stood in the shadow of the guard's house, gazing into the field. He wasn't sure if he saw movement or not.

After a few moments, he decided it must have been just the grass blowing in the slight breeze and crept back across the street. It was odd to watch another man's home. He'd felt like an intruder as he listened to Jim and Rose enjoying the privilege of marriage. He was glad their light was out now and that everything was quiet. He hoped his relief would arrive soon. He was tired, too, and after listening to them, wanted to enjoy his own wife before going to sleep. He was able to return home a short while later, leaving the "guarding the guard," as they called it, to another.

In the morning, Rose continued to work on her dress as Jim slept. It was Thursday, and she needed to finish it. When Jim awoke, she noticed he didn't seem to be in as much pain. After serving his breakfast and satisfying his other hunger, she went back to work, insisting he do nothing except sleep or read. He chose the latter and set a chair on the back porch. After lunch, Rose made him lie down and take a nap.

Later that afternoon, there was a knock on the front door, and Rose opened it to find Martha and a woman she didn't know.

"Rose, this is Uma Petersen," Martha said, introducing the woman. "She and her children arrived a little while ago and she insisted on seeing Jim."

Rose shook Uma's hand.

The knock had woken Jim, so the women stepped out onto the front porch so he could dress.

"OK," he called as he finished buttoning his pants. Then he slipped on a shirt as they stepped inside. "Not that it would've mattered if you'd stayed," he commented. "All of you have seen me anyway."

Martha and Rose shook their heads, but Uma looked at him with concern in her eyes.

"I was so sorry to hear that you had been hurt again," Uma said, giving him a hug. "Has he told you what he did for me and my children?" Uma asked Rose.

"Only briefly."

Uma related how Jim had rescued her and her family. She concluded by taking Jim's hands, turning them so she could see his palms and gazing at them. "You can still see the scars from the glass and the burns," she said.

"Just barely," Jim replied. "They've faded."

"I hope you two make many babies together," she said to lighten the mood so she wouldn't cry. "Of course, it's the making of them that's the most fun."

"Oh, he's already found that out," Martha laughed.

"You naughty boy," Uma said, turning to Jim and scolding him.

"It's not like we're not married," Jim replied, pulling out a chair from the table and motioning for her to sit.

"I hear there's more romance in the air," Martha mentioned, smiling and looking at Uma as she too took a seat.

"What have you heard?" Uma asked.

"Uma has a suitor," Martha said softly to Rose, who joined them at the table after putting water on for tea. Then Martha turned to Jim to include him. "Men have been after her for years, but she always turned up her nose, then she found out how young you are, and now—" She laughed, and Uma nudged her.

"Who is it?" Rose asked, smiling.

"The doctor," Uma replied.

"The one who took Sam's place?" Jim asked, and Uma nodded. "I thought he was some young man just out of medical school?"

"He didn't go into medical school until he was thirty-five. He's three years older than me," she explained.

"Did he travel with you?" Jim asked.

"No, he thought it best to stay in town. One of his elderly patients isn't doing well, and there are at least two babies due any time."

"So will there be more babies for you?" Martha asked Uma.

"Oh, I hope not. He has two nearly grown children from his first marriage. His wife passed away almost seven years ago."

"We wish you all the best," Rose said, smiling.

"So how did you two meet?" Uma asked, looking from Jim to Rose.

With Martha's help, Rose told Uma about Jim's illness, as well as her former place of employment.

"So he rescued you, too," Uma remarked.

Rose smiled and nodded.

Then Uma stood and told Martha she knew the way home and wanted to make supper for Jim and Rose. Rose told her it wasn't necessary because they had leftovers from the night before, but Uma insisted.

"Give her some money from the bureau," Jim said to Rose. "She's not a woman to say 'no' to."

Uma smiled, and Rose walked to the chest of drawers and returned with some bills.

"I'll walk with you as far as the store," Martha offered.

Rose made Jim lie back down, and he was asleep again when Uma returned.

"So you fell in love with him, too?" Rose asked Uma, remembering what Martha had said as they worked together in the kitchen.

Uma gave her a long look.

"No offense," Rose added. "It would be only natural."

"I was interested until I found out he was only a year older than my oldest child, Mary."

"Did she help take care of him, too?"

"Oh my, no. That wouldn't have been appropriate at all. She was only fourteen."

Rose looked up questioningly.

"You took care of him and fell in love with him," Uma replied to her look. "Mary would have, too, and she was too young to marry. Good thing for you!" she added with a smile.

Rose smiled in return.

After the food was in the oven, Uma turned to leave.

"Thank you for fixing supper," Rose said to her.

"It was my pleasure. Though after cooking for Mrs. Canady and the children, I'm not used to cooking for just two," she laughed.

Jim had awoken, and he thanked her from the bed, where he was sitting up reading, since he wasn't dressed.

Uma offered him her hand. "It's the least I can do," she said. Then, realizing the couple might want to be alone, she insisted she should get back and help Martha.

Jim and Rose enjoyed each other while their supper cooked and, after they ate, went to bed. Jim got up once in the night because he thought he heard someone walking around behind the house. When he stepped onto the back porch, shotgun in hand, he neither saw nor heard anything and returned inside. As he climbed into bed, Rose snuggled against him but didn't wake.

The next morning, Rose awoke early. She had finished her dress, so she lay in the bed next to Jim and dozed until she heard him stir.

"I need to put some water on to heat," she whispered as she kissed his cheek. "We both need a bath, and you need a shave."

"I'll pump the water for you," Jim offered sleepily.

"You need to rest. Sam still doesn't want you doing too much."

"Just heat it enough to take off the chill," Jim suggested. "Then you won't have to pump the cold."

"You know Sam insists on only boiled water, both inside and out," she reminded him as she stood. "Especially when the weather is warm."

Jim nodded without opening his eyes.

She set a large kettle on the stove and used a smaller pan to fill it with water for their bath. Then, for his shave, she filled the smaller one and set it on to heat as well. When the water in the smaller pan was warm, she called her husband. He laid a towel on a chair in the kitchen and sat down so she could shave his face. They were both still naked, and, as she worked, Rose noticed him get hard.

"Are you always going to want sex after a shave?" she asked as she wiped his face.

"I hope so."

They moved to the bedroom.

"That was wonderful," she whispered after they finished, and she kissed him on the mouth.

"I can't wait until we can do this all day," he whispered.

"All day? I don't think even you can go that long."

"We'll see," he replied and kissed her again.

They bathed, got dressed, and put a change of casual clothes in a bag for after the wedding. While Rose walked to Olivia's to check on a few details, then with her to drop the dresses off at the church, Jim headed to Sam's. When he arrived, he heard the children playing in the backyard, so he walked around the house. They all ran to him as soon as they saw him. Lilly launched herself into his arms and gave him a hug, nearly causing him to drop the bag he was carrying. Mary, the oldest, had been sitting on the back porch, and she stepped inside to let her mother know Jim had arrived.

"Richard?" Jim said to one of the boys.

"No, I'm Paul," replied the boy smiling.

"You've grown!" Jim said, smiling back at the child.

"So have you," remarked Mary as she walked up to him.

"Mary?" Jim asked, and the young woman nodded. "I hardly recognize you. You're not a little girl anymore."

"Since you're getting married, I guess you're not a boy anymore, either."

"He wasn't then," commented Mrs. Canady, who had stepped out onto the porch along with Martha and Uma.

"Do you want to play catch with us?" Paul asked.

"Well, Martha may need me to do something," Jim replied, looking at the stack of wood by the back door.

"James Morgan, if you touch that maul I may just shoot you myself!" Martha said in playful harshness, following his gaze. "Are those your clothes for tomorrow?" she asked, indicating the bag Jim held.

"Yes, ma'am," Jim replied. He offered to carry it inside, but Uma insisted on taking it, so he handed it to her and turned to Paul. "I guess I'm all yours, then."

"Don't hurt yourself," Martha cautioned as Jim and the boys turned to go out into the yard. "Just because you don't need the sling anymore doesn't mean you don't still need to be careful."

"I'll have to use my left hand," Jim said to the boys in acknowledgement of Martha's order.

Jim hadn't played ball for years, but he was a natural athlete and had always practiced throwing his knife with both hands, so before long they had spread out and were tossing the ball overhand to each other. Even with his left hand, Jim was capable of great power and accuracy. The boys, however, in trying to throw the ball as forcefully as Jim, kept overthrowing to each other and spreading farther and farther apart. The ball came to Jim, and he turned to throw it to Bobby, who was now almost fifty yards away from him. Bobby started to move closer, but Jim threw the ball with such force the boy was afraid to catch it and let it hit the ground.

"I'd hate to see what you can do with your right hand!" Bobby shouted to Jim with a smile.

"He's so used to bullets, he thinks the ball's one, too," shouted Richard with a laugh.

They continued tossing the ball, with the boys shouting to Jim and each other.

Rose had taken care of her errands. She was walking up to Sam and Martha's house when she heard a boy's voice calling to Jim, so she too walked around the house instead of knocking on the front door. She stopped and watched as Jim and the boys played.

"Use your right hand," Paul called. "Let's see how far you can throw it."

Jim took the ball in his right hand and started to draw back.

"Jim! If you hurt yourself the day before our wedding—" scolded Rose from where she stood.

Jim lowered his arm, turning and smiling when he saw her. He motioned for the boys to come closer and introduced the children to Rose. Then he took her over to the porch to introduce her to Mary, who was sitting next to Mrs. Canady, and Lilly, who was sitting on the steps. Suddenly shy, Lilly ran and hid behind her sister's chair.

"What a beautiful young woman you are!" Rose exclaimed, taking Mary's hand and smiling. "I should be glad I got to him first, or it might be your wedding he'd be getting ready for." She remembered what Uma had said while they cooked supper.

Mary smiled and blushed. "Thank you, ma'am, but I have

a young man back home."

"Anyone I know?" Jim asked.

"Do you remember Tom, the stable boy who was always chasing after your horse?"

Jim nodded. "Is he your young man?"

"Yes, and he still talks about your horse," Mary added with a smile. "We plan to be married next year."

"Speaking of weddings," said Rose, turning to Jim, "did you go by the tailor's?"

"Not yet." Then he read the look on Rose's face and decided they should leave.

The boys were disappointed but understood Jim had other things to do.

"It was so good to meet you," Rose said to Mary, waving to Lilly, who was peeking from behind the chair. "And to see you again, Mrs. Canady."

"We'll see you tonight," replied the older woman, waving to Jim and Rose as they left.

Rose walked with Jim to the tailor's and they picked up his suits. He had purchased a formal one for the wedding and a less formal one for other occasions. Then they strolled to Mrs. Harraday's to leave the one for the wedding in Hank's room. That was where Jim would change before the ceremony since the boarding house was near the church. The driver wasn't in but had left his door unlocked for them. As Jim and Rose were leaving, Natalie came out from the kitchen to see them.

"Getting nervous?" she asked Jim.

"No, why?"

"Because so many people will be there," Natalie replied, smiling. "I can't wait to see your dress," she added, turning to Rose. "I can't believe you made it so fast."

"I've been sewing since I was a little girl."

"Maybe you could make mine when the time comes," Natalie suggested.

"Anytime soon?" Rose asked, smiling.

"It will be a few months at least."

"I didn't even know you were engaged," said Rose, glancing at Jim. "When did that happen?"

"Right after you bought your house," Natalie answered. "He didn't tell you?"

"I didn't think about it," Jim replied.

"Men," sighed Rose, still smiling. "Well, I wish you all the best. Is he who I think he is?"

"Marcus Livingston," Natalie answered, nodding.

"He hasn't started riding the stage, I hope?" asked Rose, looking concerned.

"Oh, no. He'll stay in the office."

"He's a good man," Jim commented. "I wouldn't be surprised if he got a promotion soon as hard as he works."

"I hope so," replied Natalie.

They heard Mrs. Harraday call her from the kitchen and so bade Natalie goodbye.

"You looked relieved when Natalie said Marcus wouldn't be on the stage," Jim commented to Rose when they were back outside.

"I was. It's only natural."

"It bothers you, doesn't it?" Jim asked as they turned off the main street.

"I don't want to talk about this right now," Rose replied without looking at him.

They walked the rest of the way home in silence. As soon as they were in their own home, Jim hung his suit in the wardrobe, then turned to face her.

"Do you want me to quit the stage?" he asked as Rose turned away from him and took off her bonnet.

Rose kept her back to him and didn't answer.

Jim came up behind her and touched her shoulders. He could feel her shaking.

"I saw you dead on the operating table, then I saw you get shot," Rose whispered, still not facing him. "When you fell to the floor, I just knew you were dead. I don't know what I'd do if—"

Jim gently turned her to face him. "I promise you, you'll always be taken care of, even if I'm not here to do it."

"If you're not here what would be the point?" Rose asked, meeting his gaze. "I'm sorry," she whispered, trying to turn away from him. Jim held her in place.

"We could still have an annulment if you're having second thoughts. But now is the time to say," he said gently.

"Second thoughts about you?" Rose asked, looking up at

him. "Never. It's just that I don't want to lose you."

"Are you going to be able to live with my working on the stage?" he asked.

"If that's what I have to do to have you, then yes. I try not to think about what could happen, but sometimes I can't help it."

Jim held her close as she cried for a few minutes.

"I'm sorry," he whispered. "I can't change who I am."

"You're more than just a guard on the stage," Rose breathed.

"Yes, but the work is important, and right now it's what I have to do."

Rose nodded. "They're lucky to have you," she smiled. "And so am I."

He held her face in his hands and looked deeply into her eyes. He noticed all the variations of their color, from the dark circle at the edge of the iris to the clear blue in the center, made more intriguing by the pattern of lighter lines emanating from the pupil. Her eyes were the color of a warm, sunlit sky.

He held her gaze as he said softly, "I love you and always will."

He took her firmly in his arms and kissed her. He gave her not a light, delicate kiss but a deliberate, deep, passionate one. He allowed the power of his love to pour out of him, through his arms as they wrapped strongly around her, through his mouth as it firmly joined with her, and through his body as it cocooned her within the force of bone and muscle pledged forever to protect her.

He knew intuitively he had to nurture and maintain an emotional connection with his woman. She needed regular reassurance of his commitment and the magnitude of his feelings. He understood on an almost unconscious level that this one act would do more to reassure her than any other. He sensed that this one, single, simple act communicated with her on an instinctual level. This kiss not only showed her his love and passion for her, but it was also a demonstration of his physical strength. By holding her firmly, he assured her not only of his willingness to take care of her and protect her but his ability to do so. He somehow understood that it wasn't enough for his woman to feel his strength during sex, because if he was doing it right she wouldn't be paying attention anyway. She needed to feel his strength fully clothed and without the distraction of bodily friction.

Rose melted against him as he held her. The force of emotion behind the action overwhelmed her. She collapsed into him and let him support her entire weight, which he did effortlessly. She felt his muscles, their incredible power, his body hard as steel against her, enveloping and shielding her. It was as though a force of nature as powerful and unrelenting as a flood engulfed her and swept her away with its will, though not to her destruction. This will, his will, wanted only to protect and preserve her. He wanted to secure her beyond all harm and danger. She instinctively understood his willingness to care for her and trusted in the strength of his body and the determination of his soul. She let him take away her very breath, only to give it back to her filled with his love and passion. As he relinquished his hold, she noticed he wasn't aroused. This was a demonstration of a love beyond the physical, a love that mirrored that of God Himself. For the first time, she understood something she'd heard in church years ago but that had always confused her. She now knew why the Bible referred to the church as the bride of Christ.

They cleaned up, dressed, and headed to Ted's house for dinner. When they arrived, Ted met them at the door. A few moments later, Uma and the children arrived. Since the children only had one set of Sunday clothes, they were wearing clean everyday clothes, but all the adults were wearing a set of their Sunday best.

"Look how handsome you are!" Mrs. Canady commented when she saw Jim in his new suit.

"Just wait until you see him tomorrow," said Rose, smiling.

"You do look good," Ted nodded to Jim. "Maybe I should make you men wear a suit all the time, like the big city stage lines."

"I think I'd have to reconsider my position if you did," Jim muttered.

"Oh, it's not that bad," Ted remarked, patting Jim on the shoulder. "I wear one every day. You get used to it."

"I can't even get used to wearing underwear," Jim replied softly and Ted laughed.

The adults sat at the dining room table, and the children sat at another table off to the side. Laura, Sylvia's daughter, and Sarah were already good friends, and they instantly accepted

Lilly. During the meal, Uma had to get up a couple of times to quiet the children or settle a disagreement, but for the most part the children behaved very well. Jim endured Sam and Ted's stories about him and Ness. He didn't even complain when Hank told everyone about the time two women nearly came to blows vying for his affection.

"Did you lead them on?" Rose asked him, smiling.

"Not at all. I wasn't even interested in them," he replied.

"It's those blue eyes of his," Hank commented. "Women can't get enough of them. I've seen a woman nearly swoon when he offered her a hand down from the stage."

"That was because the motion of the coach had made her ill," Jim explained.

"Trust me," Hank replied. "She was fine. She just wanted you to have to catch her."

They all laughed, even Jim. Some of them had never heard him laugh. His was a rich, deep, warm laugh that comforted the soul as well as the body.

After dinner, Ted led them into his expansive living room. He had made sure there were places for everyone to sit, though most of the children chose the floor. After a few more stories, Ted gave Sam a nod and the doctor stood and addressed them.

"Will everyone here whose life has been saved by Jim please stand?" Sam requested.

Uma and her children stood, along with Hank, Sarah, and Sylvia.

"He saved me twice," piped up Paul.

"That's true," agreed Sam, smiling. "Nine people. That's impressive, and only a fraction of the number he's saved on the stage." The others sat as Sam continued. "I've never met anyone with more courage and dedication to helping others. Jim, I better than most know the high price you've paid, and on behalf of us all, I want to say thank you."

Everyone echoed the sentiment, and Jim nodded to them, hoping his embarrassment wasn't evident.

"I also want to thank Rose," Sam continued, "for teaching him that there is more to life than work and giving him something to smile about."

The adults laughed, and the children looked at each other and shrugged.

Ted stood then and addressed the group. "I want to say that it has been a privilege to have Jim first as an employee and then as a friend. I too have marveled at his dedication, as well as his skills and endurance. I've also learned to trust his judgment, about horses as well as people. From our conversation earlier, I know that all of us are familiar with his horse, but what you may not know is that Jim inspects all of the freight company's horses that serve this area. With his training as a farrier, he has been responsible for preventing many animals from going lame. He has also prevented God only knows how many accidents by recognizing problems with the animals' health, training, or temperament, all on his own time and without extra pay. Jim, I too want to thank you for all your hard work and sacrifice," Ted concluded with a smile.

The others smiled and clapped, and Jim stood and thanked Ted as they shook hands. Ted sat back down, leaving Jim standing unexpectedly before his friends.

"I want to thank you all for being here this evening," Jim said loudly enough for all to hear, even though he felt uncomfortable talking to everyone at once. "I also want to thank Ted and Sylvia for having us, and Sylvia, Martha, Olivia, and Uma for a wonderful meal." The others echoed his thanks. Then Jim paused a moment before he continued. "I never thought a time like this would come for me. If you had asked me a couple years ago what I would be doing now, I know it never would have occurred to me that I would be standing in a beautiful house with my lovely wife at my side." Jim glanced at Rose, who beamed back at him. "It's me who needs to thank all of you. You've shown me that there are good people in the world, who can accept you regardless of your past or troubled present. Thank you, thank you all." Jim concluded with a nod and sat down. He turned to Rose and saw tears in her eyes. Then he looked around the room as his friends applauded his speech, noticing most of the women had tears in their eyes as well.

Ted and Sam stood and shook Jim's hand, and Hank clapped him on the shoulder, fighting back tears himself.

Then the women strolled into the kitchen to do the dishes as the children and men ambled outside to enjoy the warm fall evening. After the women finished, Sylvia called to Ted, who turned and addressed the group.

"I know it's starting to get late, but how about a few songs?"

Every one enthusiastically agreed and followed him inside as Sylvia stepped to the piano. She played and sang a couple songs. Then Ted joined her for a beautiful ballad about love, loss, and eventual reconciliation. After that, Sylvia played a few songs that almost everyone knew, and even Jim joined in for the chorus as best he could. He didn't remember ever singing before or anyone ever singing to him, but he managed to follow the song by listening to Hank, who was sitting behind him, and watching Rose's mouth. After she noticed, Rose tapped the beat on his arm, and he was able to follow along more easily. He and Hank added a rumbling baritone that complimented the higher strains of the other voices. Sarah asked Sylvia if she knew a particular song, and Sylvia nodded. Sarah grabbed her mother's arm and pulled her to the piano. The two of them sang, with Olivia harmonizing in a rich alto to Sarah's soprano.

"Do you sing?" Sylvia asked Rose.

"A little," Rose answered, surprised. Then she mentioned a title, and, since Sylvia knew the tune, Rose stood and hesitantly walked to the piano. She sang a song her mother had taught her when she was a girl. It was an English version of an old Irish folk song. At Rose's insistence, Sylvia joined in, and their soprano voices blended perfectly. Rose didn't look at Jim until the song ended, and she found him gazing at her intently.

"That was beautiful," Jim whispered in her ear as she returned to his side.

Rose smiled.

The last song Sylvia played was a popular hymn. Then Uma took her leave to put her children to bed. Martha left with her to let her into the house. The others realized how late it was getting and took their leave as well. Jim and Rose walked part of the way with Sam and Mrs. Canady. When they reached the turnoff to go home, they said goodnight.

"What a lovely evening," Rose commented after they left the others.

"Yes it was," Jim replied.

"I hope you didn't get too tired?"

"I feel fine, but I'll be glad to get this suit off."

Rose smiled and gave his arm a squeeze.

"I hope you don't expect me to wear underwear all the

time now," Jim said.

"Why not? Would it hurt you to be civilized?"

"I thought you liked me only half broke," he smiled, tickling her waist.

Rose laughed. "I guess I really can't make you."

"That's right," Jim said with a nod. "You never know when I'll throw my head and bolt or scrub you off on a tree."

Rose laughed again.

As they walked, Jim continually had the feeling someone was watching them, but there were too many people on the street for him to know for sure. He glanced around a few times but didn't notice anyone or anything out of the ordinary. He saw someone near Nick's house, but the man was kicking the grass as he walked and appeared deep in thought.

When they arrived home, they immediately readied for bed.

"Is there anything you want to do?" Rose asked as she climbed in and snuggled against Jim.

"Let's wait until tomorrow," he replied as he gave her a gentle squeeze.

Then they kissed and went to sleep.

The bandit crept closer to the house. He had watched as the couple walked up their street arm in arm. He thought about taking his shot then, but there had been another man standing across the street. He wasn't sure if it was one of the neighbors or just someone out for a walk. He stood in the shadows a few yards from the house and thought he saw the man across the street walk away. The light went out inside. He waited, expecting to hear the sounds of coupling. Instead, all remained quiet.

He began to approach the back door, intending to burst in and empty his rifle into Jim, the woman too if necessary. He took two steps, then heard someone approaching from the field behind him. He ducked down to his haunches and waited, listening. He guessed it was a woman from the sound of her dress swishing against the grass. She came toward him and passed within two feet of where he crouched, but she didn't notice him in the tall grass. He took it as a sign. He waited until she disappeared into the darkness heading toward town. Then he crept away. He stopped at the saloon, but someone had already taken his favorite girl. Another girl, Ruby was her name he thought, was just coming down the steps, so he grabbed her arm and started to lead her upstairs.

"Not tonight," Ruby fussed as she tried to pull her arm away. "I have to get up early tomorrow to go to a wedding."

"I won't take long. I promise," he responded without releasing her.

"Well, at least you're honest," Ruby laughed as she let him lead her upstairs.

18

MARRIAGE

The next morning, Rose gave Jim another shave. Then, after eating a light breakfast, they went their separate ways to get ready for the wedding. Rose walked to Olivia's before heading to the church, and Jim strode to Hank's room. Hank answered his knock with a grunt, and Jim opened the door to find his friend struggling with the top button of his shirt.

"I haven't worn this in a while," Hank grumbled.

"Let me help you," Jim offered, and Hank looked up as Jim managed to get the button through the hole. "Can you still breathe?" he asked as Hank lowered his head.

"I can live with it."

After Jim dressed, Hank gave him a long look. "It's hard to believe that you're getting married for real this time."

Jim nodded. "It was real the first time." Then he thought for a second. "I guess I shouldn't wear my gun to the wedding."

"No. Leave it here. I'll bring it to you later."

"Good thing I got these, then," Jim said. He slipped a loaded derringer into a pocket he'd had the tailor add to the back of his pants so he could conceal the gun in the small of his back. Then he put another one in his coat pocket.

Hank just shook his head.

They left the boarding house and turned toward the church. Pastor Brown met them at the door and took Jim into a side room off the sanctuary. He gave him a few brief instructions about the ceremony, and, when he was satisfied Jim understood, he left. A few minutes later, the pastor showed Sam into the room and gave him some instructions as well before leaving them alone. After the pastor shut the door, Jim handed Sam the ring. It was a silver wedding band.

"Where did you get this?" Sam asked.

"It was Rose's mother's," Jim explained.

"So you're not getting her one?"

"I'm going to get her a diamond ring eventually," Jim replied.

"You're supposed to give her an engagement ring *before* you're married," Sam laughed.

"I was also supposed to only marry her once," Jim stated, smiling.

"What about your ring?" Sam asked. "Has she gotten you one? The preacher just said there would be two rings."

"I don't have one yet. I guess I forgot to tell him. I'll let him know when he comes back," Jim answered. Then his brow wrinkled. "She's supposed to get my ring for me?"

"The man buys the ring, or rings, for the woman," Sam replied, "and the woman buys the ring for the man."

Jim shook his head. "I don't want her using her money on me."

Sam put his hand on Jim's shoulder. "You should let her," he advised. "It'll mean more to both of you that way."

Jim nodded.

"Here," offered Sam, removing his wedding ring. "You can use mine. It shouldn't matter for this that one's gold and the other's silver."

"Are you sure?"

Sam nodded. "I'll just need it back after the ceremony." He put the ring into his pocket with Rose's. Then he drew out a pocket watch and handed it to Jim. "My grandfather gave me one on my wedding day, like he did for my father, and I'm giving you one for the same reason."

Jim took the watch and looked at his friend, too surprised to refuse the gift.

"So you won't ever be late for dinner," Sam explained. "Women hate that. I'd give you more advice about women," Sam added, smiling, "but you don't need any."

"I don't claim to be an expert," Jim replied, trying to keep his voice even. Sam's gesture had not only surprised him, it had caused an unfamiliar surge of emotion.

"I'm going to get it engraved for you," Sam added, securing the chain to a button on Jim's suit vest. "I was going to do it before the ceremony, but I barely got it here in time for the wedding."

Jim gazed at the watch before slipping it into the left pocket of his vest.

"If you don't want anyone to know you have it when you're on the road," Sam said, "just have Rose add a button or small loop right above your pocket. That way you can secure the chain in case the watch falls out."

Jim nodded. "Thank you. I—" He paused, truly not knowing how to express his appreciation.

Sam held up a hand and shook his head. Seeing Jim in his suit with the watch chain shining against the dark cloth reminded him of the loss he still felt that his own father hadn't lived to see him married. The stark reminder of the frailty and ephemerality of human existence overwhelmed him, and he prayed in his heart this brave young man before him would live a long and happy life.

A few moments later the pastor returned, escorting them into the sanctuary and showing them where to stand. Jim watched as the guests continued to arrive. He didn't know all the names, but recognized most of the faces. Sam told him the people's names until the church got too crowded and it was too difficult to single people out.

Natalie waved to Jim as she took her seat, accompanied by Marcus and Mrs. Harraday.

Jim nodded in return.

Sam noticed people glancing from Natalie to Jim and whispering. "I think some people are wondering why your sister isn't in your wedding," he remarked with a smile.

Jim shook his head. "I guess they'll figure it out at her wedding when our last names aren't the same."

"What is her last name?" Sam asked.

"Norris," Jim replied.

"People will just think she's your half-sister," Sam commented, smiling again.

Jim shrugged.

As the time of the ceremony neared, Jim began rubbing his hands together and shifting his weight from one foot to the other, causing him to rock slightly from side to side.

"Nervous?" Sam asked him, smiling.

"A little. It feels like everyone's staring at me."

Sam glanced out over the church and replied, "That's because they are."

"Thanks."

Sam laughed quietly. "Just kidding. It looks like most of them are whispering amongst themselves, just like us."

Jim looked out over the people and got a glimpse of Sarah in the vestibule.

Sam had seen her too. "I think things will be getting started here soon. Any second thoughts?"

"Nope," Jim replied, shaking his head. "I've never wanted anything more in my life."

Sam patted him on the shoulder and gave his arm a squeeze. "I'm proud of you, my boy," Sam whispered, feeling tears well up in his eyes.

"For what?" Jim asked, surprised by the doctor's sudden emotion and the strength of his own in reaction to Sam's words.

"For learning to trust. Not just yourself but someone else as well. You're a good man, James Morgan. Never let anyone ever tell you different."

Sam shook Jim's hand as the pianist sat down at the piano and began to play. Jim was glad of the distraction. He felt something stir inside from Sam's statement, and it confused him. Both men gazed toward the back of the church as Olivia appeared, looking lovely in her blue dress. Rose had helped her with her hair, which she always wore up, but Rose had taken a few pieces and let them hang in ringlets around her face. Olivia smiled as she walked down the aisle to take her place. Sarah appeared next. The pastor's wife waited for the proper time in the music and then tapped Sarah on the shoulder. She started down the aisle, daintily sprinkling each side with rose petals. When she got to the front, she turned and smiled at Jim before stepping aside and taking her place beside her mother.

Anyone watching Jim could tell when he caught sight of Rose at the back of the church. He straightened slightly and fixed his eyes on her. The music changed, and everyone stood and turned to look. Rose appeared, with Hank standing next to her. She had never looked more beautiful. Her smile radiated a warm glow all its own. Her dress, like Sarah's, was forest green, with off-white lace to accent it. The bride's, however, was full and flowing, with a neckline low enough to be attractive but still modest. The dress had a fitted bodice, with long sleeves that accentuated the graceful curves of her arms. Though she knew Jim didn't like her to wear a corset, he'd acquiesced just this once, and her naturally thin waist was a graceful compliment to the curve of her hip.

Jim's eyes never left her as she glided down the aisle. Even those at the back of the church could have seen the blue fire dancing in them if they had been able to take their eyes off her to look at him. When she drew close, Jim stepped forward and reached for her hand. He gave it a gentle squeeze as he took it. Then they turned and faced the pastor, who smiled at them as he began to speak.

He began the service in the usual way, but before the vows, he spoke to the congregation. "I want to say that it has been my privilege to get to know these two young people. We have met numerous times over the days leading up to this event, and I have been impressed with their maturity, as well as the depth of the love that they have for each other. I have had the opportunity to talk to each of them alone, and I noticed that each of them, when speaking about the other, always has a sense of pride. Rose is proud of Jim. She admires him as a person, as well as the work he does on the stage. Jim is proud of Rose, of her beauty and grace as well as her inner strength. He knows her strength will help her when he has to be away. We should all have a sense of pride toward those we love. Pride is only a bad thing when we turn it back onto ourselves, not when we take it in someone else." He smiled at the couple.

"I also want to mention love and understanding this morning. As most of you know, these two young people have not had an easy road in this world. If I may," he said, looking at Jim and Rose. They glanced at each other and nodded, so the preacher continued. "Jim has led a difficult life, experiencing things most of us couldn't even imagine. Rose, though she lived amongst immorality, kept herself pure and conducted herself honorably.

Today, as they start their new life together, I want all of you to commit, along with me, to allowing them to forget their pasts. Let them leave their pasts behind in obscurity so they can focus on their future together."

Then he gazed around the room, and the memory of the angel entered his mind as though not of his will. "Keep both of them in your prayers," he said, his voice suddenly strained, tears welling in his eyes. He looked at Jim and felt an almost overwhelming rush of emotion. He knew the young man was not a true believer, but amid the flood of sentiment was a reassurance, a calm beneath the storm. He remembered Christ's words: "With God all things are possible." He raised his eyes to the congregation. "Many of you would not be here today if not for the actions and bravery of Jim Morgan. Remember the words of our Lord when he said, 'This is my commandment, that ye love one another, as I have loved you. Greater love hath no man than this, that a man lay down his life for his friends.'" He looked at Jim and nodded.

Rose looked up at her husband as everyone gathered looked at him as well.

Jim gazed at the pastor, feeling all eyes on him but sensing something else as well, as though someone was standing just behind his right shoulder. Rose squeezed his left arm, and the sensation disappeared.

The pastor then administered the vows. When he was done, he told Jim to kiss the bride. Jim took Rose in his arms and kissed her. It was more than a peck but not long enough to make people uncomfortable. Then, as Jim straightened, the pastor introduced them.

"I now present to you Mr. and Mrs. James Morgan! Again!" The pastor laughed, and those in the audience who knew about the first wedding laughed as well—all except Hank.

The poor man had wanted to cry as soon as he started down the aisle, and, at the pastor's announcement, he broke down and had to cover his face with his handkerchief.

Jim patted Hank's shoulder, then smiled as he strode to the back of the church with Rose beaming at his side. When they reached the door, they waited outside on the step for the pastor, who joined them a moment later. He shook their hands, smiling, and soon others began to file out of the church. Sam came and stood beside the couple and introduced them to the people they didn't know. At Jim and Rose's request, the wedding had been open to the entire congregation and the town as well, so there were many people that they recognized but didn't know by name. They shook everyone's hand as they wished them well.

Then one of the stable boys walked up, leading Ness, who was nicely groomed and saddled for the occasion. Jim mounted, and the stable boy put down a stool for Rose, who stepped up onto it as Jim reached down and easily lifted her sidesaddle onto his lap. Then he turned the horse and headed to Sam and Martha's. When they arrived, Martha, Uma, Olivia, and many of the guests were already there. Tables had been set up outside for the refreshments, and people were milling around. Another stable boy was waiting and helped Rose step down onto a stool. Then, as Jim was about to dismount, Ness stepped to the side and tossed his head.

"I know, boy," Jim said to the horse. "I'll ride you again soon, but right now, I have other things I have to do." Then he shortened up on the reins and dismounted. He told the horse to behave as he handed the reins to the stable boy.

"I have an apple waiting for him when I get him back, as you asked," the boy said to Jim, who nodded and thanked him.

Ness looked back at Jim as he allowed the boy to lead him away.

Sam had even hired a photographer, and he kept Jim and Rose busy for a while taking pictures. Afterwards, the couple was free to visit with the guests.

Hap and Joe walked up and shook Jim's hand, then proceeded to tell Rose how they had met Jim.

"It was unbelievable!" Hap exclaimed. "I saw the bullet go through him and he didn't move an inch, didn't even flinch."

"Hap," Jim said, "I think you're upsetting Rose."

"Oh, sorry," Hap replied, genuinely apologetic.

"It's OK," Rose assured him with a smile.

"Besides, I'm sure she's heard the story before," remarked Joe.

"Not from me," replied Hap.

Then the two men took their leave and strolled toward the tables of food.

Ruby walked up to the couple. She was modestly dressed

and almost looked like one of the regular townswomen, except her red hair was scented and she was wearing a hint of facial makeup.

"I'm so happy for you, Rosie," she said, smiling and giving Rose a hug.

"Thank you," Rose replied, smiling back at her friend.

"I guess you won't have time to make me dresses anymore."

"Of course I will."

"What?" Ruby asked. "Your husband will let you come to the brothel for a fitting?" she asked, glancing at Jim.

"Just come to the house, Ruby," Jim said.

Ruby smiled, then looked back at Rose. "You should be careful. Not every woman in this town is as respectful of the bonds of marriage as I am."

Rose looked worried.

Ruby noticed. "Don't worry, I won't bring anyone with me. The rest of those bitches can get another dressmaker." Then Ruby gave Jim her hand and shook her head slightly. "I don't know which of you is luckier," she commented. Then she smiled slyly and leaned close to Jim. "I heard about the other night. I couldn't have taught you better myself, though I wish you'd given me the chance." She squeezed Jim's hand, smiled again at Rose, and glided away, leaving the respectable people behind her.

Finally, everyone had either congratulated them or wished them well. The boys had been throwing a ball around, and some of the men suggested they have a ballgame. Everyone agreed, so many of the people walked home to change.

"Are you going to play?" Paul asked Jim.

"I can try. It's been a long time."

"You did fine yesterday," Paul commented.

Jim looked at Rose, who smiled and nodded encouragingly. "We have the rest of our lives together," she said. "I suppose I can spare you for one afternoon, as long as you're careful."

Martha showed them into the rooms where she had left the clothes Jim had brought over the day before. They quickly changed, Rose with Martha's help, and met again in the hall.

"Are you sure you don't mind?" Jim asked her as they walked outside.

Rose nodded, and Jim sat on the back steps to slip off his

boots so he could run faster.

"What happened to your running shoes?" Mrs. Canady asked him from her seat on the porch.

"I outgrew them," he replied.

"If you'd written to me, I could have replaced them," she said.

"That's why I didn't," he answered. Then he stood and trotted barefoot to where the other men had gathered.

She laughed as she shook her head.

Nick was captain of one of the teams and chose Jim first. Then Sam walked over to keep an eye on him so he wouldn't get hurt.

"I still want you to be careful with that right arm," Sam said to Jim.

Jim nodded. "I can use it since it's not hurting, can't I?"

"I suppose so."

"You going to play, Doctor?" Nick asked.

"I'll just observe," Sam replied. Then he grinned. "Gotta protect the hands. My most frequent patient might need more stitches," he added, putting a hand on Jim's shoulder and causing the young man to sigh good-naturedly.

Then the blacksmith, who was captain of the other team, bet Sam twenty dollars on the game.

"You're going to bet against Jim's team?" Sam asked him.

"He said himself he hasn't played in a long time," replied the smith. "He's strong, but that doesn't mean he can hit or throw a ball."

Sam accepted the bet, along with a few others.

A coin toss determined Jim's team would be first at bat. Then the two captains agreed to the boundaries and a few other particulars. The first two men got base hits. The third man popped a fly, but the catcher dropped it, so the runner got to first. The bases were loaded, and, on a hunch, Nick had Jim bat fourth.

As Jim was approaching the piece of wood they were using for home plate, Nick spoke to him, pointing out into the field. "See that tree out there?"

Jim nodded.

"If you can hit the ball past that it's a home run."

"Hey, I don't want him hurting himself," Sam reminded them, walking up and overhearing Nick. "Just do your best, Jim," Sam said as Jim took his place beside the plate. "It's only a game."

Jim nodded again as he placed his feet. Then he swung the bat slowly, letting go with his right hand and holding it out straight with his left as he gazed across the field.

The pitcher threw the first ball and the older deputy, who was acting as umpire, called a strike. The next pitch was way outside, and the umpire called a ball. The third pitch came in hard and fast. Jim swung, made contact with the ball, and sent it arcing up toward center field.

"Run!" Sam shouted to Jim, but he was already on the move.

Jim rounded first and looked up to see a man running toward the tree Nick had pointed out, so he headed to second, slowing down so he wouldn't pass the previous runner. He was on his way to third when the man found the ball and held it up. Jim slowed for a second, but Sam, standing by the plate, urged him on. It wasn't until he crossed home plate that Jim found out for sure he had hit the ball past the tree. Sam and the other players on his team congratulated him.

"I thought you said you hadn't played for years," said the tailor, who was on the opposing team.

"I haven't," Jim replied. "But I started swinging a twelve pound sledge before I was ten," he explained humbly. "Swinging a bat is just a change of direction."

The men nodded.

One of the men on Jim's team was elderly and asked if he could pick someone to run for him. Since the opposing team agreed, he picked Jim. Before it was Jim's turn to run, Sam made sure he understood about stealing bases. The next batter hit the ball straight to the first baseman and was out. The batter after that hit the ball toward third base. The ball hit the ground, and the baseman caught it as it rolled toward him. Then the baseman threw the ball to first and that man was out.

The old man was the next hitter. He hit the ball low and straight, right between the shortstop and second base. Jim, who was running for him, made it easily to first. Then, after the ball left the pitcher's hand toward home plate, Jim stole to second. The next time, the pitcher kept an eye on Jim. He made as though he was about to pitch the ball, and Jim took off toward third base since it was unoccupied. The pitcher still had the ball, though, and threw it to the third baseman. In his haste, however, he threw it over the baseman's head. The man chased after the ball, grabbed it as it was rolling away, and ran back to the base as Jim dove toward him. Jim's hand touched the base before the baseman could tag him out, and the third base judge, who was the sheriff, ruled Jim safe.

Jim got up and dusted off. Sam asked if he'd hurt himself, and Jim shook his head with a smile.

The next pitch was a hit, but it was a fly, and Sam told Jim to wait. The fielder missed the ball but caught it on the bounce. Jim took off and made it home by sliding headfirst again. The next batter popped a fly and was out, so Jim's team headed out toward the trees.

At Sam's insistence, Nick put Jim in right field to spare his arm. The first man hit the ball low and made it to first. The second man hit a fly toward center field. Paul Petersen was playing that position, and Jim could tell he wasn't moving fast enough to catch the ball, so Jim ran over and caught it. Paul thanked him, and Jim threw the ball to the pitcher with ease and accuracy. After that, Nick had Jim and Paul switch positions, with Jim promising Sam he'd stop playing if he began hurting.

The first inning ended with Jim's team ahead by one point. By the end of the eighth inning, Jim's team was winning by two points. Jim got up to bat and hit another home run, changing the lead to four. He had batted in all but two innings, and each time he had hit a home run. Now it was the bottom of the ninth, and Jim's team was in the field.

"OK boys, let's hold them!" Nick called to his men as they took their positions.

The first batter hit the ball low and hard, but the second baseman managed to catch it after it bounced, so the man only made it to first. The second batter hit a fly toward right field. Paul missed it, so it ended up being a double. The third batter hit a long fly deep into center field, and Jim took off at a run. He dove toward the ball, rolled, and came to his feet, holding the ball up high so everyone could see he'd caught it. The man on third base took off toward home, but Jim threw the ball all the way to the catcher, who tagged the man out. Then the catcher, who was the blacksmith's apprentice, stood, shaking and rubbing his hand.

"You OK?" Sam asked him.

"He must think that damn ball is a bullet," the apprentice replied. "My hands are calloused, and it still stings."

"That's what I said yesterday," laughed Richard Petersen, who was playing second base. "He doesn't need a gun, just give him a baseball!" he shouted loud enough for Jim to hear.

Jim waved. "I'll keep that in mind!" he replied, causing his team members to laugh.

The fourth batter hit a fly, and the pitcher caught it. The game was over, and Jim's team had won. As he ran off the field, his fellow players patted him on the back and congratulated each other on a good game.

Sam met the blacksmith and the other men who'd bet against him near home plate and collected his winnings.

Ted walked up to Jim and the other men on his team and shook Jim's hand, smiling. "I should put you back on the stage after a game like that," he laughed.

"Anytime, sir," Jim replied.

"Don't worry. I'd have given you a couple weeks anyway to spend with your bride. Plus, I just won five dollars." He held the money up so Jim could see.

"Who'd you bet against?" asked Sam, walking up to them.

"The tailor."

"Why didn't you play?" Jim asked Ted.

"I've never been good at sports. And I've never seen anyone play as well as you, even men who've been playing for years."

"That's hard to believe," Jim commented.

Ted shook his head and smiled. "Maybe you're in the wrong line of work. You can get paid to play, you know."

"That's OK, I don't mind working for a living."

"But the way you throw that ball," Ted said shaking his head. "Maybe I *should* arm you with baseballs."

Jim shook his head tolerantly as the men on both teams laughed.

Rose walked up to them, smiling at her husband. "You were magnificent!"

Jim smiled.

"Wasn't he, though?" Sam commented, also smiling. "He's a natural athlete. I knew he'd be good at this game."

"I doubt we'll be able to make money on the next one, though," added Ted.

Rose understood and laughed.

"Let me make sure you didn't hurt yourself, while you're here," Sam suggested.

Jim nodded goodbye to his fellow players, and they waved and wished him well.

As they neared the porch, Jim unbuttoned his shirt, glad he'd left the watch with his suit clothes. Otherwise, it would probably have been crushed.

Before they got to the steps, the photographer stopped them. He had enjoyed the game, and he'd also taken pictures of the townspeople while the men played. Now he wanted to get another picture of Jim. Rose stood off to the side with Jim gazing at her. The photographer took a picture of the handsome young man with the fine physique, casually displayed by his open shirt, the bandage across his chest adding an element of pathos. No one could have guessed at the time that the photo would make the photographer's career, or the impact it would have on Jim's life.

After the picture, Sam led Jim and Rose into the examining room. Jim removed his shirt, and Rose held it with one finger. "You need another bath," she explained.

Sam examined the wounds. "You didn't tear anything open, at least, but I probably shouldn't have let you play." Then he looked at Rose and held out a roll of bandaging. "Since he's dirty, I won't bother with this. Just make sure to do it after his bath." Rose nodded.

"You let me play because you had money on the game," Jim remarked, smiling.

"That wasn't the only reason," Sam replied with a grin. "Every young man should get to play every now and then. Now go home and play with your wife."

"Only after he's bathed," added Rose with a laugh.

Jim was about to put his shirt on when Rose asked, "Do you really think you should wear this filthy thing?"

"I have to," he replied. As usual, he didn't bother to button it.

They met Martha in the hall. She told them to leave their good clothes there for now, and they thanked her. Jim ran into the room and grabbed his watch. He slipped it into his pocket before rejoining the others in the kitchen.

Martha gave them a basket of food to take home since they'd

hardly eaten anything. Then the four of them walked back outside, with Sam carrying the basket. Jim stopped to say goodbye to Uma, who was standing next to Mrs. Canady.

"How long are you staying?" Jim asked.

"We leave tomorrow," Uma answered. "That way the children will be ready for school on Monday."

"Thank you for coming," Jim said.

Uma put her hands on his shoulders and gazed at him for a moment. "I wouldn't have missed it for the world," she said. Then she hugged him.

When she released him, Jim turned to Mrs. Canady. "Will you be going back with the Petersens?"

"Yes."

"I really appreciate you being here," Jim said, taking the hand she offered him.

"I enjoy a little trip every now and then, and I had to see you get married just so I could believe it," she replied, grinning. Then she turned to Rose. "There will be times he'll need to keep his distance. Let him. Or he'll feel trapped, and then he'll need even more distance," she added with a smile. Then she took Rose's hands and spoke seriously. "Remember, he will be difficult at times, but he'll always love you."

Rose nodded and smiled. "I think I can handle him."

"I know you can," Mrs. Canady stated. Then she turned back to Jim, pulled him to her, and gave him a kiss on the cheek. "Take care of yourself," she said, holding his hands. She gave them a squeeze and released them as Jim nodded to her.

Jim stepped off the porch to where the Petersen children were waiting. Uma had called them, and they gathered around him. He picked Lilly up and she gave him a hug. He set her back down and dropped to one knee to talk to the boys.

"I wish you'd been on our team," said Bobby, who was the only one of them to be on the losing side.

"You had fun, didn't you?" Jim asked.

Bobby nodded. "But it still would have been nice to win."

Jim patted his shoulder, and each of the boys gave him a hug. Then he stood and nodded to Mary. He felt awkward because she was now a young woman and he didn't want to be too forward. Mary gave him her hand, then she pulled him to her and hugged him as well.

"Careful," Rose cautioned. "He's dirty."

"Yes, he is," Mary laughed, dusting off the front of her dress. "That's OK," she added, looking up at him. "I enjoyed watching you play. It was good to see you have fun."

Jim smiled and thanked her for attending the wedding.

"Mine should be in about a year. Can I expect you and Rose to be there?"

"Of course!" Rose replied.

As Jim turned, Sarah ran up to him and jumped into his arms.

"Sarah!" Olivia scolded. "You'll hurt him!"

"She's OK," Jim replied, smiling at the child. "She knows I'd just drop her if she did."

"No you wouldn't," Sarah said, smiling. Then she threw her arms around his neck. "Did you see me at the wedding?"

"Of course I did. I watched you the whole way down the aisle."

"I saw you watching Rose, too," Sarah said with a giggle.

"Of course I watched her. So did everybody else."

"Not the way you did," Sarah replied. "I've never seen your eyes look like that before."

"I have," added Olivia, "but only when he was angry or delirious."

"Well, I was neither," Jim said, gazing at Rose.

"Just in love," Sarah said in a singsong and giggled.

"And what's wrong with that?" Jim asked, tickling her and making her squirm. Then he set her back on her feet and thanked Olivia for being in the wedding.

"It was an honor," she replied.

Rose thanked her too.

Jim took the basket of food from Sam and the two men shook hands.

After various people stopped them a few more times, Jim and Rose managed to get away and head home. When they arrived, Jim put the food in the cupboard and his watch in the top bureau drawer. He was relieved Rose didn't seem to notice it. Since she hadn't been given anything special that day, and he didn't even have an engagement ring for her, he didn't feel comfortable showing her the watch.

Rose was in the kitchen putting water on to heat for Jim's bath. She turned to find him standing behind her.

"What do you want to do while it's getting hot?" he asked.

"Nothing with you, you filthy boy," Rose said, smiling.

Jim stepped toward her, but she stopped him. "Let me get this off."

While she walked into the bedroom to remove her dress and hang it up, Jim stripped and put his clothes in the hamper at the far end of the kitchen next to the screen shielding the chamber pot. He turned and met Rose near the table, but she was still wearing her corset, chemise, and underwear.

"I thought we were—" Jim started to ask.

"Not until you're clean," Rose stated. She laid a towel in a chair, turned it around, and told him to sit.

Jim's brow wrinkled in confusion, but he obeyed, resting his arms on the back of the chair. Then Rose began to rub his back.

"What are you doing?" Jim asked, pulling away, his voice almost harsh.

"I don't want you to be sore tomorrow. Just relax," she said, putting her hands on his shoulders.

"I'll be fine," he replied in the same tone, starting to stand.

"You'll like this, I promise," she insisted, and he let her push him gently back into the chair. "Give me a few minutes, then if you still want me to, I'll stop."

Jim eyed her for a second before turning to face the back of the chair. He rested his head on his hands as her fingers kneaded his muscles. He willed himself to stay still and calm. He felt her hit a knot and pulled away slightly.

"Just take a deep breath and relax," Rose said to him softly as she continued to knead at the knot.

Jim obeyed and felt the knot start to release under her hands. She moved to a different spot, near the base of his shoulder blades, and found more knots, but these she couldn't get to fully release.

"Your muscles are so dense," she said. "This will take more work, but I hope I can help some."

"Where did you learn to do this?"

"From one of the women I used to work with. Do you like it?" she asked, stepping back.

"I guess I can get used to it if you want me to," he replied, standing and turning toward her.

She stepped close and put her hands on his chest. "If you

don't mind me touching you here," she said, gently running her finger over the bullet scar, "you shouldn't mind me touching your back, either."

"Those are different," he muttered.

"Not to me." She stood on tiptoe and was able to kiss his cheek because he lowered his head.

Jim filled the tub so Rose wouldn't have to lift the buckets. Then he slowly sat down. The hot water felt good, but he didn't linger. When he stood, Rose was waiting with a towel for him, and she had undressed completely. Jim dried off. Then he swept her off her feet and carried her to the bed. For the first time, he didn't have to be careful about their position.

After getting her ready, he kissed her deeply as he entered her body. "Finally, I can please you properly," he whispered in her ear as he began to move.

Rose smiled. "You've always pleased me properly."

When Rose was done, he lowered his face next to hers and felt tears on her cheeks.

"Are you OK?" he asked her.

"Yes," Rose breathed.

"Why are you crying?"

"Because I'm happy," she replied.

"Did you come?"

Rose nodded.

Jim moved a few more times and came with a sound that emanated from deep within him. He rested his head on her shoulder and, after a moment, looked up to see Rose smiling at him.

"I like it when you make that sound," she whispered. "It's your roar."

"Roar?"

"Yes. A traveling circus used to come to St. Louis sometimes when I was a girl, and they had two lions. I still remember how they roared, and that's what you sound like. It's nice."

"I'm glad you like it, because it's not something I can help," he responded quietly.

"I embarrassed you!" Rose said, smiling. "I'm sorry, I didn't mean to." She threw her arms around his neck. "I wish you'd do it every time."

"Like I said, it's not something I can control. At least, not easily."

"I'm glad."

"Why?"

"Because it's the real you. You have so much self-control over your emotions, your pain, your body. I want sex to be something you relax and enjoy."

"If I did that you'd never get anything out of it," Jim replied with a smile.

"All right," Rose smiled in return, "I'm glad you have self-control, but you do get to let go sometimes, don't you?"

"Of course, that's why I come." Then he laughed softly.

"What?" she asked.

"Pastor Brown wanted to use my middle name in the ceremony, but I wouldn't let him. Though after what you just said, maybe I should have."

"What is it?"

"I've never liked it," Jim replied, rolling off her and lighting the lamp on his bedside table.

"Tell me."

"Leonidas." Then he looked at her. "It means 'like a lion.'"

Rose laughed, and he looked hurt.

"I like the name," she explained.

"Then why are you laughing?"

"Because it suits you so well." She kissed him as he stretched out on his back beside her. "So you didn't use it in the wedding just because you don't like it?"

"It's also not officially my name. Paul gave it to me."

"Paul Petersen, Uma's son?" she asked, leaning on her elbow.

"Paul Townsend, the teacher I lived with after the mining camp. He had me read about the Spartans and how they whipped the boys to toughen them up. He was trying to help me feel better about having scars on my back."

"Did it help?" Rose asked, gazing at him intently.

"No. Even Paul suspected they'd done more than just physical damage," Jim answered, without looking at her.

"What do you mean?"

"He expected me to turn."

"I don't understand," Rose said, touching his cheek.

"Like a wild animal," Jim replied, still without meeting her gaze.

"Did he say that?" she asked in surprise.

"He didn't have to. He always locked his door at night and blocked it with a chair. Just in case." Jim sat up, facing away from her, but she scooted up behind him.

"Maybe you were mistaken."

Jim shook his head. "I got sick one night and had to knock on his door. I heard him move the chair, and it was sitting beside the door when he opened it. I think he was holding a weapon behind his back, too."

"I'm sorry," she said, kissing his shoulder.

"Why? You didn't do anything."

"I'm sorry because I love you and it hurt your feelings."

"I had no feelings until I met you," he said, turning to her and kissing her cheek. "I'll be back in a minute." He stood and walked out the back door.

He returned and lay beside her.

Rose kissed him.

"I may be too tired to please you again," Jim whispered, gazing at her.

"I wouldn't mind if you pleased yourself first every now and then," Rose replied as she kissed his neck.

"I probably will after I've been away. Six or eight days is a long time."

"I know, and I'll miss you," she said sadly.

Jim kissed her and pulled her on top of him. Rose smiled as she slid onto him.

"I thought you were tired?" she asked.

"Part of me isn't," he sighed.

As she moved, Jim reached up, grabbed the headboard, and found himself biting his lip to keep from coming. He shut his eyes and allowed her to finish through force of will. She came, stopped for a moment, then continued slowly.

"Come for me!" she whispered.

Jim gripped the headboard even more tightly and thrust against her. He roared again, though not as loudly this time. Rose felt him swell as he came, and she looked down and smiled.

"That was wonderful," she said, still moving slightly. "I felt you come."

Jim's body jerked as she moved. "Stop!" he breathed.

"Did I hurt you?" Rose asked, holding still.

Jim shook his head and took a deep breath. Then he gazed

at her. "Too much of a good thing."

Rose smiled, lifted off, and lay down beside him, resting her head on his shoulder. Jim wrapped his arms around her and kissed the top of her head. They lay almost dozing for a while. Then Jim stirred.

"Are you hungry?" he asked.

"A little."

Jim got out of bed. He returned with a plate in one hand, piled high with the food Martha had given them, two glasses in the other, and a bottle of red wine tucked under one arm.

"I didn't know we had wine," Rose smiled.

"I got it as a surprise."

"So you couldn't get me a ring, but you could get wine?" Rose asked, laughing.

"Wine's easier to come by," Jim replied as he uncorked the bottle and poured each of them a glass.

"A toast," Rose said as he was about to drink. "To our life together. May it always be this happy."

They tapped their glasses and drank, then dug into the food. Jim smiled as Rose stuffed a biscuit into her mouth, which caused her to laugh.

"I didn't realize I was so hungry," she explained after a swallow of wine.

When they had eaten their fill, Jim set the plate aside and offered her more to drink.

"I better not," Rose said, putting her hand over the glass. "Otherwise, I'll be asleep in no time."

Jim set their glasses on the bedside table next to the plate and put out the light. He lay on his back and Rose settled beside him, resting her head on his shoulder. She felt a deep warmth, caused by the wine, spread through her, settling between her legs, creating an urgent need for her husband. She rolled further onto him and kissed him deeply, moving her body against him.

Thinking he needed to please her first, he rolled her onto her back and began kissing her belly.

"I want you!" she breathed.

He moved lower.

"Now!" she ordered, cupping a hand under his chin.

Surprised by her urgency, he pushed himself to his knees. She threw herself at him, pawing, licking, and kissing him. In her haste, she was almost too rough. He gently held her arms and moved back until he was standing on the floor. She stood on the bed, grabbed his shoulders, and swung into him, wrapping her legs around him and kissing his face. He lifted her hips with one hand and positioned himself with the other. Then he slipped inside of her.

She groaned with pleasure and leaned back. He held her suspended over the bed as he began to please them both. He gripped her as gently as he could, but her wails spurred him on until he threw all caution aside and thrust against her with all his might. He kept up the pace and force as she screamed and cried out, her arms and legs thrown wide, her body in a frenzy of sexual enjoyment.

To him, it felt as though she came once and then quickly came again more strongly, and then came a third time with even more strength. Finally, she began to relax, and he allowed himself his own pleasure. He came with more force than he had ever experienced before.

His roar burst through her consciousness. She felt its power on her body as it seemed to concuss the air around her and flow over her like a wave. She smiled as the sound lingered, tingling on her skin, and her inner muscles continued to react to his presence. She gently stroked his arms as they held her.

Jim brought her body up to meet his and buried his face in her neck as their bodies trembled together. Then he withdrew, laid her down, and rested gently on top of her.

"That was unbelievable!" she whispered, as she ran her fingers through his hair.

Jim nodded. "I didn't hurt you, did I?"

"Not at all. I hope I didn't hurt you."

"No," he replied. "How many times did you come?"

"I don't know, I wasn't counting," she answered with a soft laugh.

Jim stepped outside while Rose used the chamber pot. When he returned, he pulled the covers over them and they went to sleep in each other's arms.

Carlos's man had been watching from across the street when Jim left the church that afternoon. He had even watched the baseball game. He overheard one of the men mentioning that Jim would be at the danceless saloon Monday night, so he decided that would be when he'd make his move. He had given up trying to kill the guard at his house. There always seemed to be someone around. He wanted the guard dead, but he also wanted to get away clean.

When Jim awoke the next morning, Rose was still asleep. He quietly got out of bed. Then he emptied the tub. He was washing the plate and glasses they had used the night before when Rose awoke. He dried the last glass as she threw her arms around him. Neither of them had bothered to dress. He turned and lifted her as he stepped away from the sink. He held her by her hips and pushed himself inside her. She gasped in surprise, then smiled as he began to please her, holding her against him. A moment later, she was crying out in pleasure.

Neither of them noticed a man, drawn by the sound of Rose's wailing, standing in the road in front of their house. Nick saw him and stepped out his front door, causing the man, who was another of their neighbors, to head for him. The two men talked as they waited for their wives and children to get ready for church.

"Will you be at the saloon tomorrow night?" Nick asked his neighbor.

"The wife seems to think I need to go," replied the man, who was much older than Nick.

"Between the two of us, I'd like to try some things I've heard Jim does and see if they work," said Nick.

"That's what I'm afraid of," the older man sighed. "I might start something I can't finish. At least not without a nap first." He laughed, and Nick joined in.

Then they heard the couple in the house get suddenly louder before growing quiet again.

The men stopped talking as their wives stepped outside and they all set out for church. The older man was glad they didn't hear anything coming from Jim's house right then. He didn't want to have to explain to his thirteen- and fifteen-year-olds what they were hearing.

In the house, Rose and Jim had come at the same time. He carried her to the bed, laid her on it, and settled beside her, resting his head next to her shoulder. They both lay there for a few minutes catching their breath. Then Jim rose, stepped out the back door, and walked to the far end of the porch. He returned to the door and stood on the threshold breathing in the warm morning air. He raised his right arm to stretch his shoulder and casually leaned against the top of the frame. Rose walked up and ducked her head under him.

"Something wrong?" she asked.

Jim looked down at her and smiled. "What do you see?" he asked, gazing out their back door.

"Nothing," she replied as she looked across the field to the trees that bordered a stream, about a half mile away.

"Exactly," Jim said as he turned and walked to their bedroom.

He returned with two blankets, which he handed to Rose. Then he walked toward the fireplace and picked up the over-stuffed chair.

"What are you doing?" she asked.

Jim set the chair on the back porch and motioned for her to hand him one of the blankets. He draped it over the chair, sat, then motioned for Rose to join him. She smiled and spread the second blanket over them as she settled into his lap.

"This way we can enjoy this beautiful day," Jim whispered in her ear.

"And each other," she replied, leaning back against his shoulder.

They sat in the overstuffed chair and both dozed for a while. The sound of their neighbors returning from church awakened them. Nick and Pat's children bounded into the field before they could get inside, so they huddled under the blanket and hoped no one would notice. The children paid them no attention, but then their parents arrived. Nick saw them first and motioned to his wife, who called to the children and sent them home. Realizing Pat and Nick had seen them, Jim waved to them, and Rose pinched him under the blanket.

"Careful," Jim said to her playfully, "or I'll stand up and give them a show."

"You wouldn't dare!"

He smiled at her, and she knew better than to challenge his determination.

"You kids out enjoying the air?" Nick asked as he walked over to them.

"It seemed too nice a day to spend it inside," Jim replied.

It was then that Nick saw two pairs of bare feet under the

blanket and supposed that Jim and Rose had been doing more than just warming themselves in the sunshine.

"Sorry!" Nick said in embarrassment. "I didn't mean to interrupt."

"You're not bothering us," Jim replied. "We fell asleep."

"You should let these two alone," Pat said, walking up and taking her husband's arm. "They're on their honeymoon." Then she too noticed their bare feet and blushed.

Jim explained again that they had just been dozing.

"Do you have food for lunch?" asked Pat.

"Yeah, it seems like you'd have worked up quite an appetite by now," replied Nick, smiling at Jim.

Pat nudged him, but Jim and Rose laughed.

"I think we still have something from yesterday," Jim answered.

"You're welcome to join us if you'd like," offered Pat.

Jim looked at Rose, who nodded, so he accepted Pat's invitation.

"We'll be over in a few minutes," Jim said.

After Nick and Pat disappeared around the house, Jim told Rose to grab the blanket. He stood and carried her inside, with her clutching the blanket to cover herself, just in case.

Jim and Rose had lunch with Nick, Pat, and their children, Faith, Will, and Hope. Then the men gathered in the field behind Jim's house for another baseball game.

"I thought you were going to play behind the church?" asked Sam as he walked up to Nick's team.

"The preacher was afraid we might break a window," Nick answered.

After the two captains picked teams, the coin was tossed and the game began. Jim's team was in the field first this time. Sam was disappointed because he couldn't find anyone willing to make a decent bet on the game. Jim's team won again, and all the men, even the ones on the losing team, enjoyed themselves. The women had gotten together while the men were playing, and, by the end of the game, there was plenty of food for everyone to get their fill. Then, as darkness fell, they all drifted back to their homes. Jim and Rose walked inside and cleaned up. After satisfying each other again, they went to sleep.

The next morning, they awoke and decided to have a picnic.

They purchased a few things at the general store. Then they returned home and strolled through the field behind their house to the stream. Jim spread their blanket and they sat and ate. After their meal, they spent the rest of the afternoon enjoying each other.

Jim started out on top, then rolled onto his back, holding Rose against him. He gazed at her as she rode him. The bright sun enveloped and absorbed her into its light. He shut his eyes and saw a vision of her smiling face surrounded by a red-orange glow burned into his sight. The warmth of the sun blended with the warmth of her body until they became indistinguishable. She was his sun, the light of his soul, and the warmth he would carry with him always.

The animals ignored Rose's wailings, but Jim's roar echoed through the surrounding forest, causing the birds to quiet and the deer to raise their heads and flee.

A man walking nearby heard the cry. He was supposed to be watching Jim but hadn't wanted to intrude on the couple's privacy. Not knowing what had made the sound and fearful for the couple's safety, he thought it best to warn them. He waited until he thought they were through only to find them still entwined in each other's arms. The man was worried that a wild animal of some sort was stalking the couple, so he approached them but stayed at a respectful distance.

"I beg your pardon," said the man, averting his gaze, "but I heard the sound of an animal coming from this direction and wanted to warn you two."

"When did you hear it?" Rose asked, perfectly composed. Jim's body on top of her and the tall grass around them shielded her so completely that all she could see of the man were the tops of his boots and the knees of his pants.

"Just a few minutes ago," the man answered. "Did you hear it?"

"I certainly did," Rose laughed, "but since my husband can't help it, you may hear it again in a few minutes."

Jim didn't look up immediately or stop moving. He too knew the grass concealed them.

"You mean it was your husband who made that sound?" asked the man. He'd heard mention of the rumors but, out of respect, had not listened to the details.

"I do that sometimes," Jim said as he glanced up, giving Rose her first view of the man's face.

"Oh, sorry Mr. Morgan!" said the man, his eyes drawn by the movement of Jim's head. "I was just worried for your safety." He hoped he sounded surprised to see Jim.

"That's fine, Livingston, but we really just want this spot to ourselves," Jim replied. He'd noticed the man while they were eating. Even though Livingston had a rifle, since Jim knew him, he didn't challenge him. He assumed Livingston was hunting.

Livingston apologized again and walked away but stayed within earshot.

"He's such a nice young man," Rose commented. "Polite, too."

"Why do you say that?"

"He tried not to look at us," Rose answered. "I guess it's a good thing you kept your shirt on."

"Do you want to come again?"

"I don't know if I can. I'm kind of tired, but go ahead and please yourself. I'm ahead of you by a few anyway."

Jim hadn't stopped moving, so he let himself come. He held her as his body throbbed within her. Rose kissed his face, and he rested his head on her shoulder.

"You didn't roar," she said. "Embarrassed?"

"No," he answered, "just a little distracted." He knew Livingston was still nearby.

He held her another moment. Then he looked up, smiled, and kissed her before he withdrew and stood. They dressed, but, instead of heading back, Jim carried her across the stream and led her a short distance farther into the trees. He stopped at a small rise someone had cleared. He sat, gently pulled her down in front of him, and wrapped his arms around her. They watched the sunset as it turned the sky into a beautiful display of burning orange changing to glowing salmon as the clouds darkened to an almost royal blue.

"We should probably get back," Rose suggested as the sun fell below the horizon, bathing them in a warm, pink glow.

"I'm getting hungry again," Jim said.

"So am I, but I'm having dinner with Martha and some of our neighbor ladies. I'll fix you something before I go."

"No need," Jim said. "I'll get something at the saloon. They fix a good steak."

They walked slowly back to their house, hand in hand. They were both tired but happy and satisfied.

"I like being married," Rose said as they climbed their steps.

Jim kissed her cheek. "This was the best day I've ever had."

"Me too," Rose replied, looking up at him with a smile.

They washed quickly and changed clothes. Then they walked together into town and kissed as they parted ways.

For years, Jim had been unconsciously observing the people around him during his evening roams. He didn't look in their houses, simply heard their conversations through their open windows or observed them in their yards. From the outside, in the brief moments as he ran or walked by, he soon learned which couples were happy and which were not. Also, unconsciously, he began to understand why. His natural intelligence stored this information, and, just as unconsciously, was able to act on it. It was these observations he drew on in his relationship with Rose, and it was his treatment of her that had led to his invitation to the saloon that night.

He glanced through the large front window of the saloon as he walked by to the entrance. Nick opened the door and beckoned him inside. Jim entered and found Sam and some other men already engaged in a card game. He stepped to the bar, ordered his meal and a beer, then took the drink to a table and sat to wait for his food. The men broke up their game and joined him.

Hank arrived a few moments later, pulled up a chair, and sat down next to Jim.

"So how many times today?" Sam asked Jim.

"For me or her?" Jim replied, smiling, understanding the doctor's meaning.

The saloon owner brought Jim's food to the table, and Jim began to eat.

"You're going to eat all that by yourself?" Hank asked him.

Jim cut some meat off his steak, setting it aside, and separated some of the potatoes as well. Then he called to the bartender to bring another knife and fork so Hank could eat too.

"That's generous of you," commented Nick.

"I have to take care of my driver," Jim explained. "He's worth more to the company than I am."

"I wouldn't say that, now," Hank replied. "You're not just one of the messengers, you know," Hank added, using the official title of the men with Jim's position.

"Then what am I?" Jim asked.

"You're the one who shows the rest of 'em how it's supposed to be done." Hank smiled. Then he raised his voice so all could hear. "Jim here is the only man in the freight company who officially has the title of 'guard.' All the rest are messengers except you, Jimmy."

Jim shook his head and took another bite.

The bartender brought Hank a meal and a beer of his own. "It's on the house," he announced.

"That's mighty generous," Hank said in surprise.

"It's because of Jim," the man explained. "He keeps us in game during the winter."

"So that's where you're always off to," Hank nodded.

"I like to hunt," Jim replied. "I just don't like to clean it," he added with a smile. "Now I'll probably keep some for myself, though," he said to the bartender. "For the wife."

The bartender nodded, also smiling.

"You didn't answer my question," Sam reminded him.

"What?" Jim asked.

"How many times?"

"That's none of your business," Jim replied, hiding a grin by taking another bite and keeping his eyes on his plate.

Sam gazed at him along with the other men.

Jim felt their eyes on him and decided to respond. "Four for me, and at least six for her," he answered, grinning openly.

"No wonder the boy's so hungry," Hank remarked, smiling.

"I saw Livingston too," Jim added.

"Where?" Hank asked.

"In the field behind my house," Jim answered.

"What did he want?" asked Hank.

"To protect us from a wild animal."

"What animal?" Nick asked.

"Me, apparently," Jim stated.

The men looked confused, but Jim just smiled and continued to eat.

After thinking a moment, Sam smiled and nodded, which caused the other men to pester him to let them in on the secret.

"May I?" asked the doctor.

Jim nodded. "If you think you're right, though Nick should know, and the rest of you, too, from what I've heard."

The men looked at Nick, who shrugged, not wanting to guess.

"Well," Sam began by glancing at the men, some of whom had heard their conversation and just gathered round. "I know you never react audibly to pain, but I've heard you react that way to pleasure. Am I right?"

Jim nodded and swallowed. "Sometimes. Rose calls it my roar."

The men laughed but not in a hostile way, and Hank patted Jim on the shoulder. "So poor Livingston heard this?" he asked.

Jim nodded as he chewed.

"What were you doing when he found you?" Nick asked.

"What do you think?" Jim answered with a smile.

"I bet Livingston turned red as a beet." Hank laughed.

"I don't know. Rose spoke to him first."

"You're kidding?" exclaimed Nick.

"I was on top, so he couldn't see her. He didn't even realize it was me at first."

"I bet he nearly wet his pants when he did," replied Hank, laughing again.

Jim laughed and nodded.

"So it must have taken him a while to find you," stated one of the men who had been listening. "I mean, it must've been a while since you did it before," he added when Jim turned to him, his brow wrinkled in confusion.

"A few minutes," Jim replied.

"How could you do that?" asked the man.

"He's young," Sam replied for Jim.

"How old are you?" asked another of the men.

"Seventeen," Jim answered.

"But how do you do it?" Nick asked.

"What? Do you need pictures?" asked the man who'd asked Jim's age, but this question caused everyone to laugh.

"Not that," replied Nick good-naturedly. Then he turned back to Jim. "How do you make Rose happy every time? Can any of the rest of you say that you can do that?"

Sam reluctantly held up his hand.

"Of course *you* can," remarked Nick. "You get to practice on all the widows and frustrated women in town."

"Only as part of my duty as a medical doctor," replied Sam seriously. "Trust me, that's one part of my job I could do without." Then he shook his right arm, feigning fatigue.

The other men weren't sure how to take this action until Jim laughed. Then they joined in.

"Well?" asked one of the other men, looking at Jim for an answer to Nick's question.

Jim looked to Sam, who responded. "Gentlemen, do you talk to your wives during copulation?"

The men looked at each other and shook their heads.

"Why not?" asked the doctor.

"Embarrassed, I guess," responded Nick for the group. "With my wife at least, it seems like a lot of the time she just wants me to get done so she can go to sleep or get back to whatever she was doing."

The other men nodded.

"Trust me," Sam replied, "your wives want more than that in bed. Try pleasing them first and then yourself."

"How?" asked another of the men. "My father told me that I could only use one thing to touch a woman there, and that's my, you know, and often, well—" He shrugged and was relieved to see some nods.

"As a doctor, I can assure you there isn't any reason why a man can't use his hands, or his mouth, or anything else he can find to please his wife, as long as it doesn't hurt her," Sam stated.

"His mouth?" asked one of the men with a look of disgust on his face.

Jim turned to him. "Trust me, if it's clean, you'll enjoy it almost as much as she does."

"And does she reciprocate?" Sam asked. "If I'm not being too forward."

"She tried," Jim answered, smiling. "But I don't mind sticking to the real thing," he added with a grin.

Sam and some of the other men understood the joke and laughed.

Then the doctor turned to the man who had mentioned what his father had told him. "It's OK to touch yourself, isn't it? So why not your wife?"

"My father told me I shouldn't touch myself except to get clean," stated the man.

"And did you listen to him?" Sam inquired.

The man nodded.

"So you never—?" asked Nick.

"Never what?" asked the man in return.

"You never masturbated?" inquired Sam matter-of-factly.

"What's that?" asked the man.

"When you make yourself happy," answered Nick.

"You mean spill your seed?" asked the man, horrified. "No! The Bible forbids it."

"No it doesn't," Sam replied. "From what I've learned, the Bible forbids a man spilling his seed when a woman is available to take it. It recommends marriage over the other, because it can lead to impure thoughts. God doesn't care if a person pleases himself as long as he's not lusting in his heart when he does it. And that goes for women as well."

Sam heard some of the men catch their breath in surprise. "However," he continued, "it's been my experience that, as with most things, all should be done in moderation. Also, the Bible forbids nothing in the marriage bed as long as both the husband and wife agree and treat each other with the same respect they would show their own body, since they are one flesh. Would you agree, Pastor?" Sam asked, looking to Pastor Brown, who was sitting toward the back of the group.

The pastor nodded thoughtfully.

"So it's OK?" asked the man.

"If it wasn't," answered Sam, "God wouldn't have put it where we can reach it."

The men laughed.

"So using other parts of the body is OK, too?" asked another man.

The preacher spoke for the first time. "Sam's right. The Bible makes no mention of anything being forbidden in the bedroom between a husband and wife. Our bodies are given to each other in marriage to pleasure the other, and I think God considers it a sin for a husband not to do everything in his power to please his wife, and vice versa."

"How did you know this?" Nick asked, turning to Jim.

"I didn't," Jim replied. "I just wanted her to enjoy it. And realized it's better for me when she enjoys it, too. In fact, it's amazing."

"Really?" asked the man who had taken his father's advice.

Jim nodded. "A woman's body can do amazing things when she's pleased and happy. There are muscles in there that, well, there's nothing to compare it to."

"So how should I start?" asked the man.

"Just touch her," Sam suggested.

"Any particular place?" asked one of the men.

Sam took a medical book out of his bag and flipped through it. He found the page he was looking for and turned the book so the men could see it. On the page was a drawing of a woman's anatomy with the parts labeled.

"See the clitoris?" Sam asked the men, pointing to the picture. "According to the medical books, young women like to be stimulated there, and more mature women like vaginal stimulation."

"They really tell you that?" Nick asked.

Sam nodded.

"Too bad there's nothing to tell the rest of us," said one of the men, and they all laughed.

"Well," Sam continued, "try one place, or the other, or both to start with, and I say do what she likes regardless of her age. Let her know that you want to please her, and ask her what she likes. Or, if she's used to pleasing herself, watch her."

"They do that?" asked one of the men.

Sam nodded. "There's even a product available called a Widow's Comforter. It's basically a piece of wood or whalebone shaped like a phallus. Women have been using things like it for centuries."

"Really?" asked another of the men.

"Yes," Sam responded. "Apparently, women have felt the need for a toy penis for a long time."

Some of the men laughed.

"But what if she gets one and it's bigger than I am?" asked another man.

"No matter," replied Sam. "As long as it doesn't hurt her, she will enjoy it."

"But won't she like it better?" asked another man.

"I doubt it," Sam answered. "There's really no substitute for the real thing. Just remember, copulation is for both of you. Even if she has a comforter, she still needs your loving attention."

"Besides," Jim added, "even if she does like it better, as long as you get to use yours, what's the difference? You both end up happy, and that's what counts."

The men thought for a moment, then nodded in agreement.

"Rarely can anyone argue with the logic of Jim Morgan," Hank stated with a laugh. "Even if they'd dare," he added, laughing again.

Sam burst out laughing at the remark, showing his hearty agreement, and the other men joined in while Jim shook his head good-naturedly.

Rose met with Martha, Pat, and the wives of the men in the saloon at Martha's house. Most of them had brought food to share with the rest, so they all sat in Martha's kitchen and nibbled as they talked about their husbands. After they finished eating, Martha directed the conversation. She explained to the women that they had just as much right to enjoy copulation as their husbands did. Pastor Brown's wife was present and agreed.

"I know Nick wants to do better," said Pat. "Though I must say, I usually have no complaints, but sometimes—"

"I hope you'll encourage him," replied Martha.

Pat nodded. "I realize now that I should have talked to him a long time ago."

"Would he have listened?" asked one of the older women.

"Who knows?" Pat replied with a shrug.

"Did you have to talk to Jim?" another one of the women asked Rose.

"No," she answered. "He seemed to know how to do things without much direction. Where he grew up, he saw a lot of things a boy his age shouldn't have."

"And apparently he learned a lot, too," added one of the older women with a smile.

"Yes," Rose answered, looking serious and exchanging a glance with Martha. "He doesn't talk about it."

"He seems happy now," said one of the younger ones.

"Yes, and he makes me very happy, too," Rose replied, smiling.

"Every time?" asked the young woman.

Rose nodded.

"How?" asked the older one.

Rose mentioned some of the things Jim did for her. For modesty's sake, she didn't go into every detail.

The women listened intently, sometimes uttering an "Oh my!"

Then Martha proceeded to make more suggestions, urging the women to talk to their husbands and tell them what they wanted.

"I wonder if my husband will have any new tricks after tonight?" asked one of the older women.

"I still think I'd be embarrassed if my husband did those things to me," said the young woman who had visited Rose a few days before.

"Trust me," Rose assured her, "you'll get over the embarrassment real soon when you see how good it feels. I could never have imagined it. And then, like today, it just seems to get better."

"What did he do today?" asked Martha with a smile.

Rose told them about her afternoon, again not going into too much detail. She did include her conversation with Livingston, though not what had attracted the man's attention. This caused most of the women to laugh but shocked the younger one.

"I would have died right there!" breathed the young woman.

"Why?" Rose asked. "Jim was on top, Livingston couldn't see me at all."

Then the young woman laughed quietly.

"Was Jim naked?" Martha asked.

"He had his shirt on," Rose replied.

"And Jim didn't stop?" Martha inquired.

"He didn't even slow down. I think he gets so caught up in the moment he just doesn't care. Though we're not going to strip in the middle of town or anything—"

"Pity," said the older woman, causing all of them to laugh.

"But when we're together," Rose continued, "he knows we have nothing to be ashamed of, which is probably good since he doesn't like heavy curtains."

"Why not?" asked the young woman.

Rose glanced at Martha, not wanting to violate Jim's confidence.

"He's never liked shut curtains," Martha replied for Rose. "I think they make him feel trapped."

"He sounds like a wild animal," said the older woman, meaning no offense.

"In many ways, he is," responded Rose thoughtfully. Then, to explain her comment, she decided to include a more personal detail, since some of the women had heard them together anyway, and those who hadn't had heard about them. "He makes this sound sometimes when he comes that sounds like a lion. I call it his roar. Some of you may have heard him."

Pat and a few of the others nodded slightly.

"That's funny," said Martha, thinking out loud. "He's never reacted to pain like that, and the two sensations are surprisingly similar."

"But he had to learn not to do it because of pain," Rose explained with a hurt look in her eyes at the thought of Jim's torture as a child. She turned to Martha, suddenly overwhelmed with emotion. "Think what strength of will it must have taken for him not to cry out all those times he was hurt, and him just a little boy!"

"What happened to him?" Pat asked softly.

Rose paused. "I'm not supposed to say, but he was horribly mistreated as a child."

"So will you be able to make me a dress?" asked one of the older women, wanting to change the subject.

"Of course!" Rose replied, smiling.

The women then went on talking about lighter subjects until they were interrupted a short while later.

Carlos's man stood in an alley across the street from the saloon. He knew Jim would have to walk toward him to get home, so he readied his rifle and waited. A few feet behind him, there was a hook sticking out of the side of the building. He looped his horse's reins around it and leaned against the wall to his right. He gazed farther to his right at the brightness flowing through the large front window of the saloon and wished he could go in and get a good meal. *I'll be able to get a lot of good meals with the reward,* he thought.

He heard someone moving around in the rooms above him. He was glad there was no light in the window over him. This was his last chance. The boss was tired of waiting and had ordered him back. Though his boss had said nothing in particular about punishment in the telegram, he knew his boss never let failure go "unrewarded," as he put it.

He'd spent the afternoon with his favorite whore. He was sorry to leave her, but he planned to get back every now and then. That is, if he could after killing the guard.

Just a few inches from his feet, under the boardwalk, another drama was unfolding. A mother cat was stalking a mouse. She had kittens that needed to eat, and had to feed herself in order to feed them. She watched the mouse, seeing him as clearly in the darkness as she could in the day. He kept running back and forth, just under the rim joist that hung down from the edge of the boardwalk. Then he'd disappear into the building beside her through a small hole he'd chewed into the wall. The hole, too, was just under the joist.

Since the board nearly touched the ground, there wasn't room for her to sweep her paw under and grab the mouse with her claws. She had no choice but to wait until he strayed out from under it. She watched patiently, crouched, her tail twitching slightly in the darkness. She knew it was only a matter of time before she'd have her prey.

In the saloon, Jim and the other men continued their conversation. The men wanted all the particulars Jim was willing to give, which weren't many. Sam gave more suggestions and answered all of their questions. Most of the men were open to the advice.

"I guess you'll be hanging heavier curtains soon," commented Nick to Jim during a lull in the conversation.

"She insisted on making some," Jim replied. "She'll probably have them done by this weekend at the latest." He shook his head.

"What's wrong?" Nick asked.

"I don't like not being able to see out," Jim answered.

"I thought you wanted privacy?" asked Nick.

"I do. I just don't like curtains," Jim stated. "And although I don't invite people to watch, if I'm in my house with my woman, why should I care who looks?"

"If I looked like you, I wouldn't care either," commented another man.

"That's what Ted said," Jim replied. Then he looked around the room and noticed Ted wasn't present. "I guess he had to work late."

"He's always working," replied Hank. "Though soon he'll be spending more time with Sylvia," he added, smiling.

Jim smiled too, then stood. "Well, I hope you men will excuse me. This conversation has me missing my wife."

The men laughed and parted so he could get to the door of the saloon.

"Next week?" Nick called to Jim.

Jim nodded and stepped outside.

Carlos's man watched as someone left the saloon. The light from the open door shone on the man's face. *It's him!* he shouted in his head. He raised his rifle, intending to shoot the guard as he passed in front of him. It was dark, but there was a light on the other side of the street, and he could take his shot as Morgan passed under it. *Even if Morgan stays on the boardwalk, I'll still be able to see him well enough.* He followed the guard with his rifle. *Now, finally, after all these weeks and all the tries, here's my chance!* he thought. He made a conscious effort to keep his breathing even. He didn't want his excitement to ruin his shot. Again, just like before, the guard seemed to look straight at him. He knew the guard couldn't see him, though. *It's dark,* he told himself to calm his nerves, *and I'm in the shadow of the building.*

He caught a movement from the corner of his eye and looked away from the guard for a second. He saw a woman walking up the other side of the street. Her red hair shone as she passed under a lamp. He smiled. He realized the guard's wife was walking to meet him. Judging from their speed, he figured they'd meet a little to his left under another light. He knew they'd embrace, and decided he'd take his shot then. *Talk about killing two birds with one stone,* he mused.

He kept his rifle leveled at the man as the couple closed the distance between them. The guard waved to the woman, and she called to him. He couldn't understand what she said because she was laughing. He held his breath, his finger resting on the trigger. The guard slowed his pace. *Come on!* he cried in his mind. They were only a few feet apart now. Instinctively, he braced himself for the recoil of his weapon. The woman reached out to the guard. He held his breath as he prepared to end two lives.

At that second, the mouse strayed from under the joist.

The cat pounced. In her excitement, she jumped too high, hitting her head on the underside of the boardwalk and missing her prey.

The mouse darted into the alley.

The cat tore after it.

Running blindly in his fright, the mouse came to something solid and climbed.

It was the horse's leg.

The mouse's nose sensed danger. He turned immediately and ran back down. He leapt to the ground as the horse flung him, tearing away in what he hoped was a safer direction.

Feeling the mouse's claws, the horse shrieked and reared, kicking the cat as his feet left the ground.

The cat screeched, twisted away, and ran off, forgetting about the mouse in her haste to escape the trampling hooves.

The commotion drew not only Jim's attention but that of the person in the rooms above. An old woman stuck her head through the window and held out a lantern.

Jim saw a man aiming a rifle at him and pushed the red-haired woman to the ground.

Realizing Jim had seen him, Carlos's man took his shot.

Jim drew and fired in return.

The old woman dropped the lantern. It extinguished with a crash.

Not knowing if he'd eliminated the threat, Jim ran back toward the saloon to draw fire away from the red-haired woman. He knew the light from the large front window would expose him, so he took the only cover he could. He dove through it. He flew over the unoccupied table under the window, landed on his back, and rolled onto his knees, driving broken glass into his body. Then Jim scrambled back through the glass to the window, still holding his gun.

"Get down!" he called to the other men, gazing intently into the darkness through the hole he'd created and looking for movement.

"Don't shoot!" he heard the sheriff's voice call out.

Jim ran to the door, bent double to keep his head down. Then he crouched low as he stepped outside.

The sheriff had been walking toward the saloon when he heard the shots. He had planned to follow Jim home, hoping to go unnoticed. He hadn't had anyone watching Jim while he was at the saloon because he thought he'd be safe since he wouldn't be alone.

"Sheriff!" Jim called as he cautiously crept toward the street.

"I'm over here," the sheriff replied. "Bring a lantern. I think this man's dead."

Jim called for Hank, who stepped to the door carrying a lantern the saloon owner had lit and handed him.

"Stay here," Jim said to his friend, taking the lantern and then turning and walking to the sheriff.

The sheriff picked up a rifle lying in the dirt. Then he used his foot to turn over the man who had just fired it.

Sam had followed Jim. "He's dead," he announced after checking for a pulse.

"Do you know him?" the sheriff asked.

"He's the man the snake oil salesman had Natalie bring to my room when I was sick," Jim replied. "She can tell you about it. He called himself Colt, but I think that's his gun, not his name."

"Does she know him?" the sheriff asked.

"No," Jim replied. Then he looked down the street. "Where's Ruby?" he asked.

"Who?" the sheriff asked in return.

"She was right in front of me," Jim said.

They both looked to the other side of the street and saw Ruby smoothing her hair as she stepped into the light from the saloon.

"Are you all right?" Jim called to her.

"I'm fine," she replied with a hint of exasperation in her voice but no fear. "I just hope I remember to cross to the other side of the street the next time I see you," she said to Jim. Then she waved and walked off, shaking dust from her skirt.

"What happened?" asked the sheriff.

"I came out of the saloon," Jim answered as Hank walked up and stood beside him. "This man was standing there next to the building aiming his rifle at me," Jim said, pointing. "I fired but wasn't sure in the dark if I'd hit him. I dove through the window in case I missed and he tried again."

Sam stepped back and sent Nick to his house for the stretcher, then returned to Jim. "Let's get you inside so I can assess the damages."

Jim nodded and started to turn. The twisting motion caused

the pain from the cuts to hit full force. He staggered and grabbed Hank's shoulder. Hank reached for him, but Jim stopped him.

"No! You'll get cut!" Jim warned. Now that he'd noticed it, he could feel the glass jabbing and tearing with every move. It felt as though broken glass covered his entire back, and he felt it down his arms as well as the fronts of his legs.

"I don't care," Hank responded.

"Good thing," Jim said, feeling glass in his hands and realizing he'd probably cut his friend when he grabbed him.

"Careful, Hank!" Sam cautioned. "You might drive the glass farther in."

Hank took Jim by the belt and steadied him as he helped him back to the saloon.

As they stepped through the door, the men inside gasped. Blood had already stained Jim's clothes from his knees down, but it was his back that caused Sam to tighten his jaw and Hank to shake his head.

"My God, Jimmy!" breathed the big man. "You better sit down."

"Let's get your clothes off," Sam ordered, grabbing his bag.

"I just want to go home. You can look at me there," Jim insisted, his eyes flashing. He wasn't about to let most of the men in town see his back.

"All right," Sam reluctantly agreed, reading Jim's look. "But let's wait for the stretcher. I don't want you trying to walk."

Jim nodded and continued leaning on Hank. He didn't want to sit down in case he had glass inside his clothes. "I'm surprised I got him. There was a lantern that went out before I fired," he muttered. "I only got a glimpse."

"You always hit what you aim for," Hank replied.

Jim saw a piece of glass sticking out of his left arm and was about to pull it out when Sam stopped him. "Wait until I can do that for you. Otherwise you could bleed to death."

Jim nodded.

The saloon owner was already sweeping up the glass.

Jim turned to him. "Sorry about the window. I'll pay you for it." Then he studied the dimensions of the opening. "But it may take me a while."

The saloon owner nodded.

Jim reached into his pocket, snagging his hip and his

clothes on the glass sticking out of his palm. "Here, at least let me pay for the food."

"No, sir," the owner insisted, gazing at the man's bloody hand staining the money he held out to him. "I already said it was on the house."

"Maybe the undertaker will give you what's left after the man's horse and tack are sold," Jim mentioned.

"That's a good idea," the owner smiled. "I'll ask him."

"I'll talk to him for you," said the sheriff from the door. "Jim here shouldn't have to pay when he barely escaped with his life."

"This must look worse than it is," Jim replied, pushing the money back into his pocket more carefully than he'd removed it. "It's just some broken glass."

Jim's coolness caused some of the other men to whisper amongst themselves.

Hank heard them. "It's not like it's the first time he's been hurt."

The men nodded in understanding.

The big deputy had joined the sheriff. Both men were still standing at the door and jumped back as Nick ran past them carrying the stretcher.

"I'm sorry!" Nick panted. "I tried to stop her!"

Rose ran in right behind him. "Jim!" she screamed when she saw her husband leaning on Hank.

"Stop her, Hank!" Jim commanded his friend.

Hank put himself between Jim and Rose and kept her at arm's length as she struggled against him. "He's covered in broken glass," Hank explained. "No need you getting cut."

Rose stilled and stared at her husband. "At least I was planning to make you some new clothes," she muttered in shock, leaning on Hank's outstretched arm.

Jim noticed and shifted his weight so as not to overburden his friend.

Hank glanced at him and renewed his grip on Jim's belt to assure the young man he could support them both.

"Was Martha coming too?" Sam asked.

"Yes," answered Nick.

Martha arrived and caught her breath at the sight of Jim.

Sam insisted his patient lie face down on the stretcher, which he rested on two chairs so Jim wouldn't have to lower himself to the floor. Then the doctor put two small coffee tins he'd acquired from the bartender under Jim's ankles so the glass wouldn't be driven farther in. He hoped to protect the stretcher as well.

"We're taking you to my house," Sam ordered.

"No!" Jim insisted. "Take me home."

"Jim—" Sam started to argue.

Jim raised his head and looked at Sam, his eyes flashing again. "Take me home, or I'll walk there myself!"

Sam nodded.

Then, with the help of Hank, Nick, the sheriff, and the deputy, Sam carried Jim home. Martha and Rose walked behind them, the older woman trying to comfort the younger one.

When they arrived, the men set the stretcher on two chairs again. Pat came over and helped Martha spread a sheet over the table while Rose caressed her husband's face, fighting back tears.

Jim started to stand. Hank and Sam reached for him, but Jim avoided their grasp.

"You'll both get cut," Jim warned.

"Already am," Hank replied, carefully taking hold of his friend.

Sam reached for Jim again, and again Jim pulled his arm away before the doctor could touch him.

"Not you!" Jim insisted. "I need your hands whole."

Sam stepped back and let Hank help Jim onto the table.

The sheriff, his deputy, and Nick all stepped forward to help, but Hank shook his head. "I got him," insisted the driver.

"Back or front?" Jim asked Sam as he stepped to the table.

"On your stomach," replied the doctor, grabbing the coffee tins so he'd be ready to put them under Jim's ankles again.

Jim stretched out on the table, gritting his teeth to keep from groaning as the glass tore further into him.

Then, since Jim's clothes were a total loss, Sam began cutting Jim's shirt from his body.

Pat had stepped to the stove to put water on to boil. She turned to offer her assistance just as Sam peeled off Jim's shirt. Nick was the only one of them to react audibly to the sight of the scars, which looked worse covered in blood and with pieces of glass sticking out of them.

Jim tensed and glared at Sam.

"I'm so sorry!" Nick said quickly. "I didn't mean—" He shook his head as he looked away.

"Sorry," Sam said to Jim. "I didn't think about it."

"Nick doesn't like the sight of blood," Pat explained to diffuse the situation.

Then Sam made both of them promise to keep everything they saw confidential. Nick stepped back and tried not to look as Sam began treating the wounds. Since Martha was assisting, Pat tended the stove so the water would heat as quickly as possible.

"I'm not trying to torture you, Jim," Sam said as he began to pull glass from the young man's back.

"If you were," Jim replied evenly, "you'd have to try a lot harder."

"I know, son," Sam said softly. "I know."

There was a knock on the door. Hank answered it and Ted ran in.

"I just heard! Are you OK?" Ted asked. Then he stopped and stared, realizing the foolishness of his question.

"He'll be fine," replied Sam for his patient.

"Did you know the man who shot at you?" Ted asked Jim after taking a moment to recover from the shock.

"No, sir," Jim replied. "I already told the sheriff."

Ted glanced at the sheriff and motioned to him to step outside. The sheriff and the deputy followed the freight man through the door, the deputy shutting it behind them.

"How did this happen?" Ted asked as he led the men down the steps, letting his anger show in his voice. "I thought you were going to be watching him tonight!"

"I was," the sheriff replied. "I was on my way to the saloon when this happened."

"Why weren't you there already?" Ted asked, turning on the man.

"I had just finished supper," the sheriff replied, an edge to his voice as well. "I have to eat too, you know. I didn't think he was in any danger while he was with the other men. Have you told him yet?"

Ted shook his head.

"Maybe you should," the sheriff suggested.

Ted nodded. "Sorry, Duncan. I know you and all the other men have been doing your best."

"You know," said the sheriff, "the best man to protect Jim Morgan is Jim himself."

Ted nodded again. Then, after listening to what little information the sheriff had about the incident, he turned back toward the steps.

"Tell Jim we wish him the best," said the sheriff as he and the deputy walked away.

Ted stepped inside just as Sam was removing the last of the glass from Jim's back.

Rose noticed Jim's expression change as Sam poured alcohol over the wounds, but it didn't reflect only physical pain. "Bad memories?" she asked softly.

"How did you know?" Jim replied.

"I know you," she answered as she touched his face. "Look at me."

Jim obeyed.

"Better?" she asked, gazing deeply into his eyes.

"Always."

Sam then treated Jim's arms. Luckily, most of the wounds there weren't deep, but they still required bandaging. Then the doctor had Hank, Ted, and Nick help roll Jim over so he could remove the glass embedded in his legs.

"I can still move," Jim said as the men gathered around him.

"But you'd have to bend your knees, and I don't want that right now," Sam replied. "I also want your back to stay straight."

After getting him rolled over, Sam removed Jim's pants and covered him with a sheet, while all but Rose, Hank, and Martha, who was assisting, turned away.

"All right," Sam said as he finished bandaging Jim's legs. "Let's get you to bed."

"I can walk," Jim insisted.

"OK," Sam said, sweeping the floor with his feet to make sure Jim wouldn't step on any glass that had fallen. Then he and Hank steadied the young man, with Ted and Nick following them in case they needed help.

Ted glanced at Nick and noticed he was staring at Jim's back. He looked ill.

Pat turned away out of respect.

"I want you on your feet as little as possible for the next few days so your legs will heal," Sam said as they walked slowly.

"Why?" Jim asked as he sat on the bed. "You didn't have to put any stitches in them."

"You'll just open the wounds every time you move," Sam explained, motioning for him to lie down. "On your stomach," Sam ordered as Jim started to lie on his back.

"Damn!" Jim muttered as he carefully stretched out on his belly.

"I know you don't like sleeping on your stomach," Sam said "but if you lie on your back, you'll tear out the stitches I did have to put in. I don't want to bandage you there. The wounds are so scattered, you'd be covered from the neck down. Is that what you want?"

Jim shook his head.

Rose propped Jim's feet on a rolled-up blanket so the bandages wouldn't rub against the bed.

Sam turned to her. "As you know by now, keep the stitches dry. Since all of them are in his back, he can bathe to keep the other wounds clean as long as his back doesn't get wet." He looked at his patient. "You need to drink plenty of water, eat, and get as much rest as you can. And don't turn over."

"How long?" Jim asked.

"At least a week," Sam replied.

"Can I—?" Jim asked with a glance toward Rose.

"It would be best not to," Sam cautioned. "Remember, you need to be well as soon as possible for Ted's sake, so I wouldn't do anything for the next three days. Then we'll see. Only get up when you have to, and you know what I mean," he added, remembering when he'd given those orders before.

"We got a couple good days, at least," Jim remarked to Rose, who kissed his forehead.

Ted stepped to the bed.

"Sorry, sir," Jim said. "I'll still be ready whenever you need me."

"Just take care of yourself and get well." Ted replied. Then Jim noticed he got an odd look on his face as he added, "None of this is your fault."

"I'll come back tomorrow to check on you," Sam said to Jim.

Rose showed him and Martha out, along with Pat, Nick,

and Ted.

"Let us know if you need anything," Pat said, taking Rose's hand. "Any time, night or day."

Rose nodded her thanks and shut the door after them.

"Do you need me to stay?" asked Hank from the bedside, eyeing his friend's wounds and shaking his head in concern.

"No," Jim answered.

Hank looked up and saw worry in Rose's eyes, so he motioned to her to follow as he walked to the back door. "I'll take a stroll," he said softly. "If you need me, just step out and holler. If your light's out when I come back by, I'll know you're OK."

"Thank you," she whispered.

Hank stepped out the door, not realizing his life was about to change forever.

SOON!

Part 2
Roaring Crow

If you enjoyed the ride, please leave a review on Amazon or Goodreads.

You can contact the author:
Website: http://klbyles.com/
Twitter: @klbyles
Email: klbylesauthor@gmail.com
Facebook: K. L. Byles and join the Rising Crow Readers Community.

Book Clubs, please feel free to contact the author for discussion via cell phone, Skype, or in person at klbylesauthor@gmail.com.

I look forward to meeting all of you!

Made in the USA
Columbia, SC
10 March 2019